The
Marigold Cottages
MURDER
Collective

For Lynn Nichols

1

MRS. B

Friday morning found Mrs B rummaging for fruit among the leaves that engulfed two sides of her cottage. The passion fruit vine intertwined with bougainvillea and trumpet flowers, like a quilt sewn together by an old lady with a needle in one hand and a margarita in the other.

When a thorn pricked her wrist, Mrs B grumbled about her papery skin. Still, she appreciated the contrast of fragile beauty and piercing barbs. You took the sweet with the sharp, didn't you?

She'd planted the first vines forty years earlier, after her late, reckless, adoring husband had invested an undeserved windfall in the Marigold Cottages, a cluster of units a few blocks from State Street. They'd been built following a long-ago earthquake, and she liked to imagine her fairy circle of cottages sprouting from the rubble. There were six Craftsman-style buildings, with tiny front porches, shingled sides, and multipaned windows.

Mrs B had painted them a matching sage green before she discovered that she was more drawn to diversity than uniformity. Now walls of aubergine and gold, chalk blue and forest green surrounded a drought-friendly, desert-scaped courtyard ornamented by oversized ceramic pots decorated with marigolds.

She enjoyed how eclectic her vines were, too. She'd spent years coaxing them into a bright, raucous balance, more of a mediator than a gardener. And she was attempting the same with the tenants who rented the cottages.

Nicholas lived in the biggest unit, with his secrets and his stilted heart. Then there was overeager, off-kilter Hamilton, because who else would care for a middle-aged man afraid to leave his house? Beside him came the indomitable Lily-Ann, who needed someone to love, and the wounded Sophie, who needed someone to protect.

Ocean and her children rented the cottage beside Mrs B's – Ocean was the daughter Mrs B had dreamed of having, before those dreams dimmed. And last was Anthony, with his criminal past and uncertain future.

People were lovely. If you really talked to them, if you really *listened*, you couldn't help but notice. Of course, sometimes the loveliness was as well-hidden as a passion fruit buried in leaf litter – because people weren't merely lovely, they were also broken.

The world didn't produce unbroken people. Some people despaired of living in a flawed world, but the thought just made Mrs B want to plant flowers and restock her Little Free Library. Maybe she wasn't clever enough to feel the despair. She'd considered that. Only briefly, though; who had time for self-doubt when there were hummingbirds to feed?

When she finally found a ripe passion fruit, she almost laughed at its wrinkled skin. So familiar.

The flawed, broken – if not wrinkled – people of the

a&b

The
Marigold Cottages
MURDER
Collective

Jo Nichols

Allison & Busby Limited
11 Wardour Mews
London W1F 8AN
allisonandbusby.com

First published in Great Britain by Allison and Busby in 2025.

Published by arrangement with Minotaur Books, an imprint of
St. Martin's Publishing Group.

A CIP catalogue record for this book is available from
the British Library.

First Edition

ISBN 978-0-7490-3288-3

By choosing this product, you help take care of the world's forests.
Learn more: www.fsc.org.

FSC
www.fsc.org
MIX
Paper | Supporting
responsible forestry
FSC® C018072

Printed and bound in Great Britain by Clays Ltd. Elcograf S.p.A

EU GPSR Authorised Representative
LOGOS EUROPE, 9 rue Nicolas Poussin, 17000,
LA ROCHELLE, France
E-mail: Contact@logoseurope.eu

Marigold Cottages belonged to her, as surely as she belonged to them. And they needed her help, whether they knew it or not. They were as flawed and foolish as she was – but so young, so absolutely brimming with potential. So she'd ask for their help, and she'd show them how to help each other. That's what you did for the people you loved.

And, of course, you protected them.

2

SOPHIE

The man was at the bus stop again. A big, hulking man sitting alone on the dark street. Long past midnight, even though I knew that MTD bus service ended at 11.40 p.m.

Yeah, I'd checked.

I wouldn't normally care about him sitting on the bench outside the Marigold Cottages. Minding his own business, not bothering anyone. It wasn't like the Upper Eastside was a high-crime neighborhood. Of course, neither was *anywhere* in town, really.

Santa Barbara was safe. Not that I'd come from a rough area. I grew up in the Bay Area, surrounded by every kind of middle-class privilege. A good high school, a great track coach. Summer camps and family vacations and caring – if overbearing – parents. I'd gotten into my top college choice and thrived in the theatre department, and even with my minor in marketing, until my junior year when everything had gone suddenly, terribly wrong.

Safety was a big reason I'd moved here, but every time

I went for a run on the hilly streets of the Lower Riviera, I fell in love all over again.

The coastline faced south, not west, and was sheltered by the long, low Channel Islands. The fog of the marine layer kept the mornings cool, then rolled back and opened a curtain on to the most glorious set ever designed. The sun warmed the red tile roofs, and the Courthouse tower and Grenada building stood sentry over the bustling, almost-European downtown adorned with flowering trees, perennials, and palms.

So the area was gorgeous *and* safe, but the man's appearance at the bus stop still made my stomach knot.

I wasn't indulging in hypervigilance, though. I wasn't. It's just that I'd already caught the man sitting there the previous week, when I'd come home late after drinking with friends downtown.

Well, when I'd *staggered* home.

I'd never seen him before then, but he'd given me a look that had been much more than a casual glance of appraisal. More like he'd recognized me. Or expected me to recognize him.

Which felt worse, somehow.

He'd turned away quickly, almost guiltily. And now he'd returned.

It wasn't my imagination. Not this time. It was the same guy. No doubt about it.

He was impossible to miss: an intimidating slab of muscle with a shaved head and cheap tattoos on his arms, neck, and face. He wore a black T-shirt and jeans and looked like an extra I'd cast to play Serbian Thug or Death Row Inmate.

That is, if my job was casting for a production, instead

of answering phones and organizing fundraisers at the community theatre company.

Anyway, I was right for worrying, because here he was again. And this time he wasn't alone. At least not for long.

Mrs B tottered from her front door toward him, wearing one of her finest kaftans, midnight blue velvet with gold embroidery. If I ever managed to write this as a play, the costume designer would have a field day with Mrs B's outfits.

Mrs B was my gossipy, grandmotherly, strategically doddering landlady who charged a (probably illegal) sliding scale for rent. Dream casting: Judi Dench. When Ocean, the artist who lived across from me with her kids, lost one of her teaching jobs, Mrs B had requested a Protect Trans Kids painting in lieu of rent. Last month, she'd baked Lily-Ann a birthday cake decorated like a sunflower . . . and Lily-Ann was *not* a sunflower. She was more of a magnificent, well-rooted magnolia tree, but Mrs B still saw the sunshine in her. Mrs B escorted Hamilton, the older guy who was terrified of leaving his cottage, to emergency dental appointments. She chatted to crows 'just in case,' and gave dog treats to the UPS driver to distribute on his route.

In short, Mrs B was an eccentric, beneficent fairy. So when I saw her wandering toward the Serbian Thug in the middle of the night, I grabbed my phone and followed.

I stopped at the mailboxes fifteen feet away and pretended to check my mail while Mrs B sat next to the man at the bus stop. Like *directly* beside him, absolutely inside his personal space.

The man frowned at the top of her white pixie cut.

11

Then he frowned toward the Cottages.

'My first lover had a tattoo,' Mrs B told him.

Which was a strong opening line for the play I dreamed of writing, but maybe not the best thing to say to a scary man at a bus stop.

The man didn't give his line. He just watched her.

'He was in the Merchant Marine,' Mrs B prompted.

The man grunted.

'He had two tattoos. A heart and an anchor. That's nothing these days, but back then it was a little shocking.'

I started filming, just in case. When I zoomed in on the man, my phone caught details of the tattoo of an angel's wing on his throat. The feathers became flames behind his ear. As he turned to listen to Mrs B, a sloppier tattoo came into sight on his cheekbone: it said JEWELS, except the w looked a little like breasts.

Which was a bit much, even for my Serbian Thug character.

'I'm Mrs B,' she told him. 'Well, I'm Golda Bakofsky, but everyone calls me Mrs B. And you are?'

'Anthony. Lambert.'

'Not 'Mr L,' then?' she inquired, with a burble of laughter in her voice. 'Well, give it time, you're still young. Do you have a heart, Anthony?'

'Depends who you ask,' he said, his voice a rumble.

'Ha.' Mrs B prodded his thick arm with her finger. 'You know what I mean. A tattoo.'

'I have three hearts, but no anchor,' he said, and frowned toward the Cottages again.

Or maybe toward me, like he knew I was recording. I couldn't tell. My breath came fast and my hands trembled and I had to tell myself that this wasn't anything like What Happened Before.

'My husband once mentioned me in a speech,' Mrs B told the man – Anthony – as if they were chatting at a tea party. 'He said, "After all this time, you still have the eyes of the girl I fell in love with." So *I* said, "Yes, in a jar under the bed."'

Anthony blinked.

'It was at a fundraising event for organ transplant people. Probably not the place for that particular joke.'

Mrs B tended to blurt out whatever was on her mind, but I wasn't sure where *that* had come from. I guess I'd hoped she'd tell the guy to stop loitering at the bus stop and scaring her tenants. Instead she was talking about eyeballs.

'You live in the front house, right?' he asked. 'With all the flowers?'

'For forty years,' she told him.

When he stood from the bench, he loomed. 'Then let's get you home.'

I lowered my phone, my heart clenching. Mrs B would definitely invite the man – Anthony – into her house, which was cluttered with her collection of possibly valuable baubles from around the globe. A set designer's dream, but also a burglar's. I mean, c'mon. A Serbian Thug, at one in the morning?

I needed to do something. I needed to at least call the other tenants. Except I didn't have time to scroll through my contacts. Why didn't the Marigold Cottages have a group chat?

'Is that what you do?' Mrs B asked the man, resting her hand on his tattooed forearm as she stood. 'Find lost women in the night, and shepherd them home?'

He eyed her with a sudden intensity. 'That and dishwashing.'

'Ah.' Mrs B peered up at him in her birdlike way. 'So you're a dishwasher, Anthony?'

'Yeah.'

'That sounds terribly boring, but I suppose one must pay one's bills. I've been having trouble with that myself, lately.'

'Yeah?'

'It's *very* frustrating. So . . .' Mrs B considered as they walked together. 'Were you ever in jail?'

'Prison,' he said.

Well, *that* cut through my hesitation. I took a breath and marched down the stairs toward the bus stop.

'Oh, is there a difference?' Mrs B asked him, with bright curiosity.

'Mrs B!' I called. 'There you are!'

'Good evening, Sophie.' She smiled at me, unsurprised, like she'd known I'd been there all along. 'Any interesting mail?'

'Sorry,' I said, suddenly conscious of my empty hands. 'C-could you come to my place for a minute? I have a question about, um . . . rent.'

The man glowered at me. One of his eyebrows was broken by a scar, and the ligaments in his neck looked like axe handles. I chewed my lip when he watched me for a beat too long, and forced myself not to abandon Mrs B. He turned away suddenly, without speaking. Instead of returning to the bench, he stalked along the sidewalk until the gloom swallowed him.

After that night, I checked constantly but never saw

Anthony Lambert again, almost as if I'd imagined him.

Until two months later, Mrs B rented him the studio apartment attached to Ocean's cottage.

That's when I started jotting down notes. Toying with writing a play about an outsider's arrival disrupting a small community. Trying to recapture my excitement for the endless possibilities of playwriting. And to calm my fears.

3

LILY-ANN

What Lily-Ann enjoyed, after a long day of work, was curling up on her lilac linen sofa in her cream cashmere robe, and getting a little more work done. She didn't care about the specific task. Heck, she didn't care about the specific *job*. What she loved was ticking items off her list, making progress toward a specific, achievable goal.

A therapist had once suggested that perhaps her perfectionism caused her workaholism. Yes. Of *course* her perfectionism caused her workaholism. That was obvious. Lily-Ann didn't mind a little obviousness, but the therapist also wanted to talk about Lily-Ann's weight. She thought the fact that Lily-Ann's weight wasn't a problem for Lily-Ann was a problem.

Lily-Ann loathed leaving things unfinished; still, she only completed three of her eight scheduled sessions with that therapist.

She sipped her Chardonnay, then tapped her laptop as she scanned the purchase order on the screen. She made a few alterations. After a moment, she made a few more.

Better. Done. Finished, like so many things in her life.

Including her marriage and social life.

Not that she'd entirely ended her marriage, not yet. She was merely separated from Piotr, and from their three-bedroom, south-facing house on the Riviera with its spectacular views of downtown Santa Barbara and the harbor. Lily-Ann used to lounge on the flagstone patio, watching the sun fill the clouds with white light in the morning, then paint orange streaks across the sky at dusk. When she'd gazed over the city, from the volleyball beach to the Mission tower, everything had felt orderly and calm – and expansive.

Now look at her. Living in a cottage with one bedroom and no view aside from the neatly trimmed hawthorn hedge out back. Working for mediocre pay as a proposal manager for a transport company. Alone, without even a cat to comfort her.

A humbling fall from grace. Humiliating, except at the moment she was happily enjoying a glass of Au Bon Climat Chardonnay while making her way through a colleague's backlog of work.

If she set aside the bitter, nagging awareness that she *shouldn't* wholeheartedly enjoy her current situation, Lily-Ann whole-heartedly enjoyed her current situation.

She clicked to the next spreadsheet, and her phone dinged.

Sophie Neighbor
Hey Lily-Ann

Sophie Neighbor
This is Sophie from the front house

16

Sophie Neighbor
I saw you through the window and was about to knock
but knocking felt weird so I'm texting

Sophie Neighbor
Now texting feels weird

Lily-Ann stood from the couch, replying to the text as she crossed to the front hall. She hit Send a moment before she opened the door, then found Sophie on the narrow front porch, reading her just-delivered text.

Sophie was a slender young woman of the type that wore their hair in a variety of ponytails. She struck Lily-Ann as jittery and high-strung, uncomfortable in her own skin. She looked Asian, probably East Asian, though her surname was Gilman. Lily-Ann almost asked about her ancestry. She liked to categorize things. She liked knowing how they fit together. Nothing satisfied her more than the snap of a puzzle piece into the greater whole. That soul-affirming *click*.

Sophie jogged most days and left her house with a yoga mat twice a week. Slightly less often, she half-dressed in cropped tops and short skirts and joined her girlfriends downtown. She'd invited Lily-Ann once, which had been sweet. But Lily-Ann had begged off, because the gulf was too wide. The chasm between mid-twenties and mid-thirties, between single and separated, between skinny and fat. Between partying and enjoyment.

Lily-Ann
Do you prefer white or red?

Sophie looked up from her phone with a nervous smile. 'Sorry. Any chance of a gin and tonic?'

'None, I'm afraid.'

'Then whatever you're having. If that's okay. I mean, I'm sorry to bother you.'

'It's not much of a bother,' Lily-Ann said, then spoke over Sophie's blurted apology. 'I'm just finishing up some work.'

'On Friday night?'

'Mmm.' Lily-Ann led her toward the kitchen. 'You're not going out?'

Sophie pushed up the sleeves on her oversized purple hoodie. 'I overdid it last week. I'm taking a break.'

'That's too bad.' Lily-Ann poured a second glass of Chardonnay. 'Breaks are the worst.'

'I guess.' Sophie raised her glass in a toast, then looked flustered. 'Um, so I'm thinking we should have a Marigold Cottages group chat. In case there's a . . . whatever.'

'I'm afraid you're going to have to be more specific.'

'Oh! Sorry. I mean an earthquake or a flood or y'know . . .' She wrinkled her nose. 'Stranger danger. Ocean's kids are wandering around and . . . I sound like my mom, but we're pretty open to the street.'

'Has someone been bothering you?' Lily-Ann asked, because she recalled hearing that Sophie had trouble with a man in the past.

'No, no. Sorry. I heard Mrs B is renting to some random guy, and I'm worried. I guess I'm a bit of a worrier.'

'Random guy?'

'Like a stranger she met at the bus stop at one in the morning.'

'Oh! I see. Yes. That is unusual behavior.' Lily-Ann

sipped her wine. 'So a group chat?'

Sophie nodded. 'Ocean's on board, and so is Mrs B. Nicholas is away, not that we ever see him anyway, but I wondered if you could talk to Hamilton.'

'That's why you came.'

'Yeah. Sorry. I never know what he's going to say and it makes me nervous. But you're not afraid of anything.'

'I'm afraid of inefficiently loaded dishwashers,' Lily-Ann said, then enjoyed Sophie's nervous giggle. 'I'll talk to Hamilton. Though there's no telling what he'll add to the conversation.'

'Yeah.' Sophie bit her lip. 'Should we *not* ask him?'

Hamilton was a wiry, gray-haired man with a penchant for Hawaiian shirts – and for spewing random facts like the poster child for a 'No One Asked' meme. They should probably ignore him, but now that Lily-Ann had agreed to the task, she was determined to complete it. To cross it off her list. Plus, it would eat at her if every tenant were included except one.

'I'm sure it'll be fine,' she said.

4

OCEAN

Listen. Ocean liked how Anthony Lambert looked. She wanted to sculpt him. That big slab of a body reminded her of painting with a palette knife, all hard edges and thick layers. Plus, at first, he'd struck her as tough but when she'd looked closer he mostly seemed sad. So yeah, as an artist? He appealed to her.

19

'But as a mother?' she called to Mrs B, as she settled into the love seat. 'Do I want an ex-con living in the studio apartment attached to my house? Where my kids live? Absolutely not.'

'Oh! That reminds me,' Mrs B said, appearing from her kitchen. 'Should I plant pansies in the courtyard this year, or petunias? Pansies have such sweet faces, like they're always smiling up at you, but petunias—'

'Don't give me your daffy old-lady bullshit,' Ocean said.

Mrs B sniffed as she sat beside Ocean. 'You used to be such a nice girl.'

'And you used to be better at avoiding hard conversations. I don't want him living here.'

'Anthony is a good man, Ocean.'

'How would you know?'

'I looked into his eyes.'

'You have cataracts, Golda.'

'Oh, stop!' Mrs B said, because she didn't like anyone knowing that the Marigold Cottages had been named after her. Her husband had called her Marigold instead of Golda, and only Ocean knew the truth.

'Think of the kids. Riley is teenage-girling like it's her job, and Miles is having some kind of fourth-grade identity crisis.'

'That does sound dire,' Mrs B said, straightening the turquoise bracelets on her wrinkled arm. She'd never avoided the sun and had skin like caramel leather.

'Miles is okay. He just . . . he came out to me the other day.'

Mrs B cocked her head. 'Did he?'

'Yeah, as straight.' Ocean felt herself smile. 'The thing is, he didn't want to disappoint me. Poor kid, I've told him and told him that I don't care. Anyway, he admitted he's got a crush on Ami Dubois.'

'That little French girl across the street?'

'Mmm. He wants to bake her cupcakes. *Cupcakes*.'

'Oh! Should I teach him how to make macarons?' Mrs B pursed her lips thoughtfully. 'Though I don't actually know how to make macarons.'

'I mean, Riley can be a real jerk,' Ocean said, ignoring her. 'She's just like me. We'll fight it out and be fine, but Miles? He's too sweet for this world. I don't know what to do with him.'

'You're a wonderful mother, with wonderful children.' Mrs B took one of Ocean's hands in both of hers. 'You, my dear, are doing a wonderful job.'

Ocean blinked away a sudden well of emotion. 'Stop changing the subject. We're talking about letting this guy move into the studio apartment.'

The kettle whistled before Mrs B could answer. 'Saved by the screech,' she said, and bustled into the kitchen to make tea.

Ocean picked at her paint-encrusted finger as she looked around Mrs B's living room. Family photographs cluttered the top of the piano. A bookshelf was filled with kids' craft projects, gifts presented to Mrs B over the years. Including two from Ocean: an ashtray in the shape of a diseased lung, because Mrs B hadn't yet quit smoking, and a fused glass bird of paradise, because Ocean had been an oh-so-artistic child.

The familiarity warmed Ocean. The blue love seat, the

art deco coffee table, the occasional chairs upholstered in a red silk Napoleonic bee pattern, because Mr B had dreamed of keeping beehives. The three Chinese lamps with their pom-pommed lampshades. Shelves of international keepsakes – netsuke from Japan, muiraquitã from Brazil – and an ironwood iwisa from South Africa. A soapstone carving from Alaska that Mrs B always carefully noted wasn't truly international. The pictures of ornate hands with Hebrew writing that warded off the evil eye. Nothing had changed in thirty years.

Ocean remembered sitting cross-legged on the floor as a child, gazing at the shelves and dreaming of faraway places while her parents chatted with Mrs B.

She'd stolen a wooden shark the size of her pinky, once. A tiny thing, more of a minnow. When her parents discovered the theft, they'd made her return the shark. She'd apologized in tears, braced for an angry, betrayed speech. Instead, Mrs B had wondered why that particular object had caught her eye. Had it been the subject? Did she like fish? The size, the color, the material? The history, the toolmarks made by forgotten hands?

Ocean hadn't been able to answer. She'd wanted it because she'd wanted it. Still, that was the first time she remembered looking that closely at anything in her life. The first time she'd noticed her own attention to details and aesthetics.

She peeled the strip of paint from her finger, then didn't know what to do with it. After a moment, she stuffed it in her pocket and grabbed the sudoku book.

Pretty impressive. Mrs B had finished dozens of puzzles. The old lady was still sharp.

Except when Ocean looked closer, she realized that the

numbers didn't add up. Well, crap. Ocean had moved to the Marigold Cottages as a kid and considered Mrs B a member of the family. A bonus grandmother or less-annoying mother. So flipping through the meaningless jumbles made her heart ache. She'd need to talk to Mrs B – again – about what she wanted to happen when she couldn't look after herself.

Ocean already checked in on her twice a day, and took care of any Mickey Mouse repairs that a tenant needed. And all the residents kept an eye out for her, at least a little. Not that you could *avoid* seeing each other in the Cottages. Still, even Sophie, the new girl, contributed by setting up a group chat that so far consisted of Hamilton raving about some comet that should've been visible, except the night sky was ruined by light pollution, and also he didn't have a telescope.

Everyone except Nicholas pitched in.

'Here you are, my dear,' Mrs B said, returning from the kitchen with the teacups and a bowl of salt-and-pepper potato chips.

'Where did you even find this guy?' Ocean asked, already removing the tea bag from her cup. She liked her tea weak, like her willpower when it came to potato chips. 'I know you didn't advertise.'

'Who, Anthony?' Mrs B squeezed a slice of lemon into her tea. 'Oh, I ran into him here and there.'

'Another one of your lost sheep.'

'Like your parents.' Mrs B gave her a bright-eyed look over her teacup. 'How about this? You show Anthony the studio yourself. If you still object afterwards, I'll tell him that I changed my mind.'

'I thought you already signed a lease.'

'Oh, we did. But he doesn't have a copy.'

Ocean pointed a potato chip at Mrs B. 'You're aware that laws *exist*, yes?'

'Property law is simply ancestor worship,' Mrs B said, with a dismissive jangly wave, 'enforced by state-sponsored violence. Are chips enough? Do you want macarons, too? I'm about to whip up a batch.'

5

LILY-ANN

The key felt sticky in the front door of the studio, and the curtains in the courtyard-facing window sagged noticeably. Good. Lily-Ann enjoyed problems that were easily addressed, which was why Mrs B had asked her to clean up the apartment for the new tenant. The mysterious Anthony Lambert.

She jiggled the key, made a mental note to return with WD-40, and opened the door.

The studio was small, perhaps two hundred and fifty square feet. The air smelled of mildew and dust. Mrs B had converted the space from a storage area when the attached cottage – now Ocean's – had been remodeled. No one had lived here since, so the studio had reverted to storage space. Miscellaneous boxes hugged the wall beside the tiny bathroom, old furniture abandoned by previous tenants crowded the already-cramped space, and the curtains were even worse from the inside.

Lily-Ann smiled.

* * *

Two days later, the key slid easily into the lock. The air smelled fresh, and the curtains were crisp and bright. Lily-Ann had arranged the mismatched furniture into three sections: a sleeping area centered on a single bed with an antique pineapple headboard; a dining area with a flimsy white plastic table and two chairs beside the mini-fridge and cooktop; and a living area comprised of a beanbag chair flanked by a standing lamp and a tiny red bookcase.

The beanbag chair pleased Lily-Ann. She hadn't known they still existed. Also, they gathered dust in folds and crannies that required real scouring. Though something annoyed her about the placement of the now-spotless beanbag.

After a moment's consideration, she shifted it closer to the window. Then she wondered if a grown man would sit in it.

'Lily-Ann?' Ocean asked, from the open door.

'There's always the bed,' she said.

'What?' Ocean asked.

'The beanbag chair. I'm not sure—'

'What're you doing here?'

'Mrs B asked me to give the place a dusting. She's going to rent it.'

'A dusting? You furnished it. You hung art. Is that—' Ocean frowned at the painting on the kitchenette wall. 'I painted that in high school.'

Lily-Ann wasn't sure what to say. She'd found the painting in the corner and liked the crisp lines. So she read the title that was scrawled on the canvas: '*Two Sinks.*'

'Yeah.'

'It's very pretty.'

Ocean made a face. 'Thanks.'

'A little like Mondrian. He's my favorite.'

'You should look at Anne Truitt's work,' Ocean told her, and a shadow fell into the studio.

A knock sounded a moment later, and Lily-Ann turned to see a man filling the doorway. Tall, with a shaved head and broad shoulders. Late thirties or early forties. His tattoos were asymmetrical, as if he'd chosen each one without considering the whole. Which she found distressing and unsightly.

Still, not an entirely valid reason to be impolite.

'You must be the new tenant.' She offered her hand. 'I'm Lily-Ann.'

His hand swallowed hers. 'Anthony.'

She didn't often meet anyone who made her feel physically small. In this case, somewhat to her surprise, she enjoyed the sensation. She imagined he could pick her up and carry her. She might like that, despite the tattoos.

Before she'd married Piotr, she'd met a number of men who'd appreciated a big woman. Then she'd married Piotr. And, she reminded herself, was still married to him. Neatness mattered, and so did oaths, which were a sort of contractual neatness, defining relationships and delimiting behavior.

So she simply said, 'Welcome,' before heading home to rewrite an explanation regarding meeting client requirements via a third-party application.

6

OCEAN

'So that's Lily-Ann,' Ocean told Anthony, when the door closed behind her.

Anthony nodded.

'And I live in the other half, with my kids.' She gestured him inside, away from the doorway. 'Come in, look around. Sorry it's so small.'

When he took two steps inside, he filled the apartment. 'I've lived in smaller.'

She didn't want to think about what that meant. 'Where are you from?'

'Fresno, mostly.' He thought for a second. 'You?'

'Here, mostly,' she said. 'So there's no oven, and only a mini-fridge. And if Mrs B told you that you can use her kitchen, you can't.'

'Okay.'

'The, uh, furniture comes with, unless you're bringing your own, in which case . . .' She doubted that Mrs B had thought that far ahead. 'We'll get rid of this.'

He frowned at the beanbag. 'I don't have any.'

'Then we'll leave it.'

'What is that?' he asked.

'A beanbag chair. Traditionally paired with bell-bottoms and a lava lamp.'

His mouth didn't move, but he smiled at her with his eyes. Like he was afraid of fully committing to the expression.

'Mrs B told me you work as a dishwasher?'

'At the Sidecar.'

'That dive bar downtown?' Ocean almost winced that she'd said 'dive bar,' so she blurted 'do you like the job?' Then she almost winced at that. Who'd like washing dishes? 'I mean, doesn't it get, uh, loud?'

'I don't mind the noise. It's meditative.'

Which surprised her, him using the word 'meditative.' And she knew herself; between that and his shy smile, she was screwed. Unless she managed to find a good reason to tell Mrs B not to rent to him, welcome to the goddamn neighborhood.

'Well, we don't like it too noisy here,' she said.

'I'm quiet.'

'Except I have two kids. You like kids?'

He considered. 'I don't know any.'

'Oh. Uh, my ex-wife grew up in a big family. Three younger siblings. She half raised them herself. But I was an only child.'

Which she'd said in order to see how he reacted to 'my ex-wife.' Except he didn't react. He just kept looking at her. He seemed to have the emotional range of one of those stone heads on Easter Island. And he found dishwashing 'meditative.' He was like a monk who'd spent his life living in a cell. Okay, maybe that was a bad analogy.

She pressed her lips into a smile. 'And that's the grand tour.'

'Just the right size for me.'

'On account of you're so petite.' She exhaled. 'Listen. Mrs Bakofsky's been known to take in strays. If you can imagine.'

He showed her his stony-faced smile again.

'So we look after her. She's getting up there, you know? We pitch in when we can. Help her out.'

'Mmm,' he said.

Apparently the threat of babysitting an old lady wasn't enough to dissuade Anthony, so Ocean told him about trash and recycling, then left him to poke around the studio in private. She closed the front door and sighed. He seemed okay to her. Plus, he needed a place to live. What was she going to do, say no?

As she headed home, she spotted Mrs B, with a watering can at her feet, gazing at the plastic flats of petunias she'd bought. She was strong enough to heft the hanging pots into place herself, but she hated getting her hands dirty. So instead, she left flats of flowers around until someone else planted them.

Which meant she'd been lying in wait for Ocean, to see what she thought about Anthony.

'Satisfied, my dear?' she asked, then nodded before Ocean answered. 'Yes, I knew you would be.'

Ocean flipped her the bird.

Mrs B let out a guffaw of great satisfaction. 'I'll go fetch him the mailbox key.'

7

NICHOLAS

Nicholas spun his chair toward the window. His office in the planning department overlooked De La Guerra Plaza, which was currently a rectangle of dead grass and construction material as the revitalization campaign for the historic square began.

Two pigeons pecking at the ground took sudden flight

and landed on the roof of the now-shuttered *Santa Barbara News-Press* building. The once-excellent local newspaper had faded into a shadow of its former self before vanishing entirely.

Nicholas appreciated the daily reminder that even established local institutions could falter and fail without diligent attention. Sometimes that meant innovating while staying true to core values. Sometimes it meant clearing the deadwood to make room for new growth.

He exhaled and turned back to his desk. Okay. Speaking of diligence . . . he should probably recuse himself from the upcoming discussion, given that he lived at the Marigold Cottages. Well, considering he paid a below-market rate, he should *definitely* step back.

Yet he didn't.

Instead, he went down the hall and took his place in the conference room. In the wake of the latest design and development standards, the office had generated a new zone map. And Nicholas's block – the block of the Marigold Cottages – appeared in orange as 'proposed high-density housing in accordance with the state-based density concession.'

'Which allows what?' his boss asked, wanting clarification on the record.

'Which allows developers to build to sixty-eight feet,' Nicholas told her. 'Multiple-occupant residences. At substantially lower cost, given the new incentives for housing density.'

'So we're allowing . . . no, we're *encouraging* apartment buildings in a neighborhood of mostly single-family homes?'

'Well, that is the goal, after all.'

His boss let out a breath. 'On the Upper Eastside? That is not an easy sell to the community. There are no buildings of special import in that zone?'

They discussed the significance of the historic Bungalow District, and how the state regulations might take into account the city's location: tucked between Los Padres National Forest, with a million acres of hiking trails and campgrounds, and the bustling harbor, pristine beaches, and Channel Islands National Marine Sanctuary. Not to mention the century of meticulous city planning that had made Santa Barbara the jewel of the central coast. Permitting new construction among some of the most charming houses in town would spark more than a little backlash.

The discussion eventually moved on, but Nicholas kept thinking about the Marigold Cottages and his failure to recuse himself. The city needed more housing. Everyone knew that. And if the Cottages changed hands? Well, you couldn't both improve things and keep them exactly the same.

Plus, Mrs B would make a fortune if the property were rezoned. That's what he told himself. Sure, she was attached to the Marigold Cottages, but she'd be fine. Better than fine.

He just needed to make sure that she never learned of his involvement.

8

SOPHIE

Despite everything, I liked working at the New Vic, our local theatre company. I even liked the walk to work. Santa Barbara mornings always felt vibrant, with the crisp ocean air warmed by the sun and the scent of croissants and coffee wafting from the French bakery. A woodpecker knocked on the trunk of a palm tree, and I wondered how to capture that feeling of optimism – like nothing could go wrong on such a beautiful day – onstage.

Then I arrived at the theatre, and remembered that while I liked the job, working there was basically like hurling myself off a cliff into an ocean of jealousy. Because I wanted to write and direct plays. That was my goal, that was my *purpose*.

I'd written a dozen stage plays in college, but they were all meh. Probably because I'd aimed for serious themes. Yet now, after watching the chaos unfolding at the Marigold Cottages, I was less interested in the human *condition*, and more interested in *humans*. That's why I'd started to journal, to use the madness as material. If I couldn't write a halfway-compelling play from all this death and drama, I should just give up.

Giving up was the last thing I wanted to do . . . yet part of me wondered if I already had. At the New Vic, all I did was organize tickets and arrange promotions, and occasionally pretend I was a dramaturge by writing summaries for the program.

Well, I also spent a good chunk of time trying to ignore

the worm of envy in my heart whenever I met actual working writers and directors. At least I was still in the world of theatre. That counted for something, right?

My parents worried about me, and how I felt about the slow decline of my dearest dream.

That was nothing new, though. They'd worried about me since What Happened Before. They worried about me *before* What Happened Before. Then I had the breakdown. And even though I was better now – I was! – they worried more than ever. Which embarrassed me. Nothing even happened, not really. For sure nothing *capital H* Happened. That was the most humiliating part. I'd completely lost my shit over a few rough months that most people would've shrugged off by now.

You suffered from PTSD when you returned from a war zone, not when a stalker scared you in a college library.

My parents didn't want me at the mercy of roommates bringing strange people around, so they helped with the rent. Also, my mother adored Mrs B, even though they were intrusive in completely different ways. My cottage was tiny, though. The smallest one and the closest to the street. I actually liked the location. It let me monitor . . . everything.

Like when Mr Ybarra walked the perimeter of the Cottages, nobody noticed except me.

I'd just returned from a run after work, and I'd paused at the front door to check my distance on my running app. Then I'd caught a glimpse of Mr Ybarra, looking like a skinny Santa Claus, with a white beard and rosy cheeks and his red knit cap. Ybarra Properties owned three apartment buildings in the neighborhood, and Mr

Ybarra lived in one, even though he was rich enough to afford a mansion among the celebrities of Montecito. He was eccentric, like Mrs B. Maybe all the landlords in the neighborhood were eccentric, or maybe I just hadn't noticed the ones who weren't.

Anyway, Mr Ybarra strode onto the property, swishing the golf club he carried because he was scared of dogs. He stroked his beard, then ambled in a circuit around the courtyard. In the old pictures Mrs B had shown me, rosebushes and marigold-themed planters edged a lush lawn, but after the droughts it was more desert-y, with pale gravel paths and glossy succulents.

When Mr Ybarra spotted me, he raised his golf club in greeting. 'So charming!'

'Uh,' I said, too sweaty to handle gallant flirtation from a sixty-year-old.

'Six cottages like pretty little dollhouses,' he continued. 'Left over from a previous age. Have you seen Mrs Bakofsky? We have an appointment, but she doesn't answer the door.'

'Sorry, no. Sorry.'

'A lovely woman, but stubborn.'

'Oh?' I said.

'She refuses to marry me.' His cherubic smile grew. 'She thinks I'm only interested in her money, which is insulting. I'm interested in her *property*.'

I gave a little smile, which was worse than apologizing, and said, 'I'll tell her you stopped by.'

'Twenty more families could live here, on a lot this size. A Spanish-style apartment building. Parking is a problem, but there's a new zoning map, and I . . .' He paused, tugging at his beard. 'I lost my train of thought. Just tell Golda that she's a monster of selfishness and I wept when she stood me up.'

See? Eccentric.

'Will do,' I said, backing into my cottage. 'Err, got to go.'

He saluted me with his golf club and I shut the door.

My phone vibrated as I watched him leave through the peephole. I locked the door, then checked the screen.

'Hi, Dad,' I said.

'Sophie? It's Dad.'

My father considered himself a techie, and yet never quite figured out how his iPhone worked. 'What's up?' I asked.

'Have you heard back about the job yet?'

I frowned as I wandered into the kitchen. 'What job?'

'You told me you were applying for a job.'

'No, *you* told me to apply for a job.'

Dad cleared his throat. 'Don't be difficult, Sophie. Did you apply or not?'

I opened the fridge. 'I have a job.'

'Raising money for a community theatre company is not a career.'

Instead of responding, I peered at the half carton of eggs, the bag of spinach, and the bottles of diet tonic water that had gone flat.

'You can do much better than that,' he said. 'I know what happened in college really, um, shook you up, but you have to—'

'Dad. Enough.'

'You can do so much better, Sophie! There's nothing

35

you can't do. You need to stop hiding your light.'

I closed the fridge and smiled. That was actually pretty sweet.

'Or at least get married,' he said.

'Excuse me, sir, where are you calling from? Nineteen sixty-four?'

'Very funny. What about your neighbor's ex-husband?'

'Piotr? You're joking.'

'Is it a joke that I want to see you settled? Santa Barbara's expensive. He drives a BMW hybrid.'

'How do you know that?'

'I noticed last time we were there. It's a plug-in, so I was interested.'

'Well, did you also notice that he still sleeps with Lily-Ann? They're not even divorced yet.'

'Sophie! Save those conversations for your mother,' he said repressively, before his tone softened. 'You know I love you, right?'

'I can't imagine we'd be having *these* conversations if you didn't.'

My parents did love me, and they also loved pretending they wanted a rich man for me. Yet what they really wanted for me wasn't wealth but security. After What Happened Before, they thought I was brittle and lonely. They'd briefly met Lily-Ann's almost-ex-husband, Piotr, at the Marigold Cottages, and now held him up as some sort of paragon.

And sure, Piotr was rich and hot and charming, but he was *smarmily* charming. Dream casting: Tom Hiddleston.

Also, fortyish was too old for me. My dad thought anyone with a full head of hair couldn't be older than thirty-two. Not that I could attract someone like Piotr anyway. Lily-Ann was so out of my league: an emphatically plus-size, redheaded ice queen. Always immaculately dressed in outfits that cost more than my rent, and OCD enough that she just did her own thing. I was in awe of her. I didn't understand why she was living at the Marigold Cottages, though. Maybe she didn't get any money until the divorce went through? She'd been in her current place for four years already. Slowest divorce ever.

Though my parents weren't entirely wrong about me being lonely.

I messaged college friends. I chatted with people at work. I . . . I kept myself busy. But I didn't engage. I didn't take risks. I was too afraid of losing control.

Well, except for those nights when I lost control completely.

Every now and again, I needed to blow off steam. To open the valve on the pressure cooker of my life. Not my life, my *past*. I needed to prove to myself that I wasn't a timid flinching victim, still living in the shadow of my stalker.

So I'd meet some friends, and I'd dance and sing and match them drink for drink. Until eventually, we'd end up at a seedy bar like the Sidecar.

Well, not 'like' the Sidecar.

Apparently we always ended up at *exactly* the Sidecar; because apparently I always insisted. Which I only knew on account of my friends mocking me about it. Every time drinking switched my brain off, I demanded the Sidecar.

However, not only did I barely remember going there, I never remembered *wanting* to go. Drunk Sophie loved the Sidecar, but *I* found it dingy and depressing.

Which was the second weirdest thing about my nights out. The first weirdest was that I never got a hangover the next day. Instead, I usually woke up early and felt pretty good.

And sure enough, on the Saturday morning that changed everything, I felt fine as I drowsed in bed, watching the sunrise slide across my wall. After a time, I grabbed my phone and scrolled through messages from the previous night. I didn't remember anything about the Sidecar, which meant I'd blanked my entire experience there.

Again.

Luckily, my drinking buddies always texted dozens of snaps to fill me in. How kind. They loved taking pictures of me sloppy drunk and usually added hilarious messages that made no sense the next day.

I winced at the pictures. I looked ruined. Still, at least I didn't look *timid*. Didn't look like I was apologizing for existing.

I drank a liter of water, then peed and started the shower. While I waited for the water to warm up, I watched the street through my window and—

Okay.

Okay, even writing this for my play freaked me out a little.

Okay, deep breath. I watched the street through the window and nothing moved except for the crows. Two of them hopped around the fence, then darted to the ground beneath the bushes, where . . .

Where a man was sleeping.

My throat turned dry and I belatedly felt a hangover

start. A man was sleeping in the bushes ten feet from my bathroom wall. That was fine, I told myself. No problem. Probably just an unhoused guy. I'd never begrudge anyone without a bed a place to sleep.

Except it wasn't an unhoused guy, considering his expensive shoes. So, fine. Someone had gotten drunk and passed out in the bushes.

No judgment. I'd been there myself.

The shower pattered behind me as I watched a crow land on the man's shoulder and peck at his head. His unmoving head.

Then the crow tore off a strip of flesh.

9

LILY-ANN

The coloration of the corpse startled her. The man couldn't have been dead long, but his skin looked almost purple in the dim light beneath the hedge. He stank a little, too, though that didn't alarm Lily-Ann. She'd expected that.

She'd never seen a body outside of a casket. She'd always imagined that death itself was essentially tidy, the equivalent to crossing someone off a list. Yet the corpse struck her as messy. Physically, but also intellectually; the embodiment of unanswered questions. She thought about that as she heard Ocean take a sharp breath behind her.

'Is—is he dead?' Ocean asked.

Lily-Ann peered through the leaves. 'I believe so, yes.'

'Are you sure?'

'His blood is pooling. Beneath his skin.'

'Oh, god. Do you recognize him?'

'No. At least, not with him being so . . . unliving. He looks extremely like a corpse.'

Ocean exhaled. 'He does, doesn't he?'

'I'll call the police.'

'I suppose we shouldn't move him.'

'No.'

'No, of course not. Okay.' Ocean waited for Lily-Ann to call the police, then said, 'Will you go sit with Sophie?'

'Yes.'

'Make sure she's not too upset,' Ocean added, as if Lily-Ann might not have understood the subtext, which was kind of her. 'I'll tell Mrs B.'

They separated, but not for long. Apparently Mrs B had insisted on checking in on Sophie, so she and Ocean soon joined Lily-Ann in Sophie's untidy house.

Then the police and ambulance came. The detective arrived later, along with what Lily-Ann thought were CSI technicians. She watched them with interest. She suspected she would have excelled at either of those jobs – detective or crime scene technician – as both focused on putting puzzles together. Although perhaps she would've been better at the latter, where the human element was, for the most part, dead.

10

VERNON

The last three homicides that Detective Sergeant Vernon Enible had caught: a guy who'd shot his wife, a guy who'd stabbed his girlfriend, and a gang-related shoving match that had gotten out of hand.

What they all had in common? Vernon immediately knew the perpetrator. *Everyone* immediately knew the perpetrator. An investigator's job wasn't a Scooby-Doo episode, putting together clues until you yanked the mask off Old Man Withers. Your job was assembling and documenting evidence for the eventual use of the prosecutor.

You were part of a legal team, not a revealer of hidden truths.

So when Vernon arrived at the Marigold Cottages, his priority was identifying the obvious.

He stood for a moment, watching the red and yellow emergency lights strobe the morning street, flashing against the palm trees on the sidewalk. One of the officers first on scene logged him as present while the other stepped away from the crime tape to greet him.

'Way to start the morning, huh?' the officer said.

'What're we looking at?' Vernon asked.

'Dead guy.'

Vernon gave him a look. 'The tech's not here yet?'

'Due any minute.'

'Get anything from the paramedics?' Vernon asked.

'Victim's in his late twenties or early thirties,' the officer said, leading him onto the property. 'Bashed on the head. They moved him to attempt resuscitation, but he was already cold. Postmortem, uh, what's it called?'

'Lividity.'

Vernon followed the officer between the nearest cottage and the hedge that screened the street. The bushes looked intact, but he'd make one of the younger guys with good knees check for signs of ingress.

He glanced at the corpse lying halfway on a concrete path. Six feet of obvious blood smear pointed to the body like an arrow, which Vernon confirmed was from the paramedics dragging him from under the hedge. A lot of blood. Head wounds did that.

He didn't bother looking more closely at the victim. That was a job for the forensic tech and ME. He'd focus on the bird's-eye view, see if he just happened to notice someone sitting on their porch, conveniently splattered with blood.

Sadly, he didn't. Well, not yet.

'Start the canvass,' he told the officers. 'You take the neighborhood, I've got the property. Eyes out for cameras. Remember cars, doorbells . . .'

'We know,' the officer said.

'And look for the weapon.' Vernon frowned at the cottages facing each other across the courtyard. 'Unless it's hidden in someone's closet.'

'Huh?'

'Chances are this guy didn't just wander off the street.'

'You think someone who lives here killed him?'

'That's the obvious choice,' Vernon said.

He consulted the scene log, then went to talk with the woman who'd found the body. Sophie Gilman of Unit #1, twenty-five years of age, shivery with shock, being comforted by Lily-Ann Novak, thirty-six, of Unit #2 and Golda Bakofsky, eighty-two, of Unit #6.

First impressions:

Sophie Gilman must've weighed a hundred and ten

pounds, would she even have the strength to crack a skull? Maybe, but that didn't matter, because she *hadn't*. A pretty little Chinese girl didn't beat a man to death in the shrubbery.

The big woman tidying Sophie Gilman's cottage had the heft, no doubt about that. Cold as the Arctic, too. She looked at Vernon like she didn't care. Except she also looked wealthy. What had his daughter called it? 'Stealth wealth.' Nothing flashy or obvious about her, but she wasn't some fat lady in the mobile home park with a temper. Plus, she'd still be gasping for breath after that much exercise.

Which left the old lady holding Sophie Gilman's trembling hands. She owned the Marigold Cottages, though she didn't look like she was sitting on ten million dollars in real estate. She looked like she served warm juice after church on Sunday or . . . well, 'Bakofsky,' so maybe after synagogue.

'I'm sorry,' Sophie Gilman told him for the third time. 'I didn't see anything else. Just the crows, and then I-I texted everyone and Lily-Ann came and she found the . . .' She shuddered. 'I don't know why *I'm* so shaken up, I'm sorry, she's the one who—'

'You texted everyone?' he asked, to stop her babbling.

'Sophie made a group chatter for everyone who lives in the Cottages,' Golda Bakofsky told him. 'It doesn't work on my phone, though.'

'It's a group *chat* and it works fine on your phone,' Sophie Gilman said. 'You just don't like texting.'

'Who else lives here?' Vernon asked.

'Sophie lives in number one, which is this unit,' Lily-Ann

43

Novak told him, looking up from straightening a candle on the side table. 'I live in number two. Nicholas lives in number three, at the end, with his own entrance. Hamilton lives in number four. Ocean and her two children, Riley and Miles, live in number five. Anthony lives in five and a half. Mrs B lives in number six.'

When Vernon asked about the other tenants, Golda Bakofsky gave him surnames and approximate ages. Then he chatted for another few minutes. Clues didn't clear murder files, *people* cleared murder files. So you talked. You talked and listened, talked and listened – while gossip spread, while anger simmered – and eventually someone gave you a name.

And if they didn't?

Then you didn't clear the file. That happened about a third of the time, with murders. Well, with reported murders. Nobody knew how many slipped through the cracks.

After Vernon left cottage #1, he started knocking on doors: in numerical order just like Lily-Ann Novak had listed them. Which, in retrospect, was a little odd, how she'd produced that information.

The next two residents were men – Nicholas Perez, thirty-two, and Lawrence Hamilton, sixty-three – and hence two of the most likely suspects. But neither of them answered.

Vernon talked to the single mother in #5. Named Ocean, of all things. Surname: Mist. Well, surname *Mistral*, but you knew what her hippie parents had been thinking. Ocean Mistral. She sounded like a cranberry juice cocktail.

He only exchanged a few words with her before her

daughter started throwing a fit about her phone being at four percent.

Ocean Mistral smiled at him tightly. 'If you're looking to arrest someone, I have a suggestion.'

'I heard that!' her daughter yelled. 'You're just like Mom!'

Vernon frowned. If the girl wasn't her daughter, who was she?

'You didn't plug your phone in,' Ocean Mistral called back over her shoulder, 'that's not my—'

A door slammed. 'I hate you!'

Ocean Mistral ran her hand through her short hair. 'She takes after my ex-wife. If you'll excuse me?'

Oh! Her *very* short hair. Right. Lesbian. Pity. She was a fine-looking woman. And when he gave her his card he noticed the muscles in her forearm. Fine-looking and strong. The landlady had mentioned that Ocean Mistral taught sculpture classes. Hmm. That made her a possibility, except with two kids in the house, who had the time to commit murder?

After he stepped away, his phone buzzed with a document in the secure portal: the forensic tech had already uploaded a file containing the victim's ID. He'd rather talk like a human being, though. She was standing at the crime scene thirty yards away, but he called instead of walking over: her generation paid better attention to a screen.

'Decedent's name is James Dedrick,' the tech told him. 'If you can believe it.'

What the hell was she talking about? 'Consider it believed. Go on.'

'Thirty years old. Huh. His birthday was last week. He

45

lives in Los Angeles. Well, Altadena. Isn't that the place with the Jet Propulsion Lab?'

'Close. What was he doing here?'

'Partying,' she told him, 'is my preliminary wild-ass guess.'

'Based on what?'

'His haircut,' she said. 'Plus, I can almost smell the Negronis.'

'Okay, but what was he doing *here*?'

'Oh, at the Marigold Cottages? That I can't even wild-ass. I just thought you'd want his name and DOB early. Can you access the file I sent to the portal?'

'Sure,' he said. 'Of course.'

'So read it,' she told him, and hung up.

He grumbled for a minute before knocking on unit five and a half. The studio. He hadn't had any luck interviewing the other single men, so he – irrationally – didn't expect anyone to answer.

Then Anthony Lambert opened the door, and Vernon almost laughed.

It didn't get more obvious than that.

11

OCEAN

Ocean didn't want to catch her son Miles's eye across the kitchen. She was afraid she'd make a conspiratorial expression or long-suffering sigh, like it was the two of them against his sister. Or even just like, *Can you believe she's acting like this?*

46

He didn't need that pressure, and Riley didn't need that judgment. So Ocean kept her gaze on the apple she was cutting into wedges for Miles's lunch.

When she felt the Storm Front Riley enter behind her, she said, 'You want apple or tangerine?'

'I'm not a baby,' Riley snapped.

'I didn't ask if you wanted a teething biscuit,' Ocean heard herself say. 'Though considering how you're acting—'

'It's *Saturday*. Why're you making lunches?'

'Oh.' She looked at the sliced apple. 'I guess I'm more shook up than I thought.'

'Plus, you were out all night, Mother.'

'I wasn't out all night.'

'You didn't come home until—' Riley stopped suddenly, and her tone changed. 'What are you *doing*?'

Ocean turned, and found Riley glaring at Miles, who had moved to the side window. He was standing there with his eyes half-closed.

'Eavesdropping!' he told her. 'They're talking in the studio. I've never heard a real detective before.'

So Ocean caught *Riley's* eye and the two of them shared a look: they'd fight later, but first they'd eavesdrop. Ocean was curious about how the detective would react to Anthony. You needed to watch yourself around cops. Qualified immunity meant they could break the law with impunity, and they had the highest rate of domestic abuse of any profession in the country.

That was Ocean's excuse for slipping beside Miles to join his eavesdropping. When a breeze wafted through the open window, the courtyard smelled faintly of cigarettes. One of the cops, no doubt. She almost said something but instead she draped one hand on her son's skinny shoulder. She considered putting her other arm around Riley, but thought better of it. She wasn't sure why Miles had chosen that window until the conversation from the front door of the studio came through perfectly clearly. Well, the monologue.

'You're Anthony Lambert?' the cop asked.

Silence, then a faint rustling.

'No driver's license, huh? This'll do. So tell me where you were last night.'

More silence.

'What're you, a college kid? You watched a YouTube about not talking to the police? You know that's not how this works.'

Still no reply.

'Step out of my way,' the cop said.

'I don't consent to you entering,' Anthony said.

'That's cute,' the cop said. 'You going to stop me?'

Then Ocean heard rustling, footsteps, from the studio. She wondered if she should send the kids away, if they'd overhear something they shouldn't. But she didn't. At Miles's age, she'd been tear-gassed twice, after being dragged to protests by her parents. They'd splashed her face with milk and asked her to analyze the fact that tear gas was banned in international warfare but permitted for domestic cops.

So a little eavesdropping was probably fine.

Paper crinkled, then the cop said, 'There we go. Pay stub from the Sidecar. The landlady says you lived here for three weeks. What else?' More paper rustled. 'Junk mail, junk mail. Utility bills. You should go paperless,

48

Anthony. Better for the environment. Oh, look at this.'

Silence.

'You worked as a bouncer at the Sidecar before switching to dishwashing? That is a curious career path, my friend.'

Silence, except Riley whispered to Ocean, 'Is that allowed? Is he allowed to go through his mail like that?'

'Not legally,' Ocean told her.

'Then we should stop him,' Miles said.

'I'm not sure,' Ocean told him. She didn't want to escalate things.

'And what have we here?' the cop's voice asked. 'Free weights. What're those called, kettleballs?'

'Kettlebells,' Anthony said.

'It speaks! Kettlebells. Fifty pounds, twenty-five pounds. That's all? No little ten pounder? A fellow your size could swing one of those upside a guy's head. What's that for, your biceps? Show me your hands.'

A pause, during which Ocean held Miles tighter.

'C'mon, Anthony. You moved in three weeks ago with prison tats, your apartment's neat as a cell. And look, blood splatter on your sleeve. This is not a story with a happy ending. You want to explain to me what happened?'

No answer.

'Mind if I sit?' The plastic chair scraped. 'Join me, Anthony, I'll tell you what I think, we'll compare notes. What I think – you're not going to sit? Give me a crick in my neck but okay, one of the hazards of the job. Now, I don't know where you met the guy. Downtown somewhere. The question is, why'd he follow you home? Maybe one of you was selling something? Except you'll excuse me if I don't

49

believe that you're in a position to be pushing product at the moment. By product, Anthony, I mean illicit drugs.'

Ocean had heard enough. 'Stay here with Miles,' she told Riley.

'*You* stay here, Mother,' Riley said.

Miles put his hand in his sister's.

'Fine,' she crabbed.

Ocean wiped her palms on her shirt and left the house. She caught another whiff of cigarette smoke, which made her wrinkle her nose. Yeah, one of the cops was a smoker.

She followed the path to the studio, knocked on the open door, and called, 'You okay in there, Anthony?'

'We're good, ma'am,' the cop said, turning toward her. 'Do not enter! Everything's good. Just talking with my old friend Anthony here. Turns out we know each other.'

'You've met before?'

'Not a once,' the cop said, and made a gesture she didn't understand.

Anthony understood, though. He turned his back on the cop, facing Ocean, and put his wrists together for the handcuffs.

'Do you . . .' Ocean took a breath. 'Should I call someone?'

'No,' Anthony said. 'Thank you.'

'So, wait.' She looked at the cop. 'Is he under arrest?'

'Oh, I don't know about that,' the cop said. 'Maybe this is just investigative detention.'

'Lock up when they finish in here?' Anthony asked her.

'They need a warrant for that.'

'Don't you worry,' the cop told her. 'Anthony gave me permission to search.'

'Is that true?' she asked Anthony.

His eyes smiled, a little sadly, and the cop snapped the handcuffs shut.

12

SOPHIE

In my memory, the dead man's legs looked even more motionless than 'completely still.' Like there were degrees of 'unmoving.' In my memory, his shoes and ankles and calves were the shoes, ankles, and calves of a prop, a mannequin.

Which I knew was a defense mechanism, but that was fine. Defenses were good. They defended you.

I'd imagined a dead body plenty of times. My own. I'd thought that envisioning the worst-case scenario would help me, during What Happened Before. But to actually see a body through my window? A corpse being eaten by a crow? It was a scene out of Poe . . . though he would've preferred a raven.

Stage design: unmoving legs, the sound of a crow cawing, the shadow of wings on the back scrim.

For no apparent reason, Lily-Ann stood and went into my bedroom, then my bathroom. Which was abrupt, but not out of character.

Mrs B stayed beside me, though, babbling about a TV show she'd watched, trying to put me at ease. I wasn't that upset anymore, but I didn't want to interrupt her. I was trying to figure out what show she was talking about.

'. . . you think the surprise is that they're all dead,' she was saying. 'But that's not the surprise in the slightest. There's a lovely little town with ice-cream shops and a train. Oh! And a girl robot.'

Robots and ice cream? That didn't ring any bells. 'Is it . . . animated?'

Mrs B shook her head. 'I don't think so. There's a tall beautiful woman, but she's dead, too. They all are, except the robot and her boss, who is played by the bartender.'

'Wait,' I said. 'Which bartender?'

'The handsome one with the . . .' She trailed off, catching sight of something through the window. 'What in the world?'

I looked past her. 'They're arresting the new guy.'

'Why on earth would they do *that*?' Mrs B said, standing abruptly.

'Oh, um . . . I guess—' I gave a helpless little shrug. 'Because of the murder?'

'But why Anthony?'

I rose to my feet, for a better view of them taking him away. 'Because he's the murderer? He killed him?'

'No,' she said.

'Sorry.' I watched the cops fluttering around like yellowjackets at a barbecue. 'Uh. Wow. They move fast.'

'Too fast,' Mrs B said, and bustled through my front door.

A moment later, she appeared in the courtyard, black kaftan fluttering around her like an avenging dark fairy.

I steadied myself on the window frame. 'Too fast' was right. Everything was moving too fast. I couldn't catch my breath. Maybe I *was* still upset. I still saw those mannequin legs and heard the cawing of crows. I was okay, though. It was nothing. I hadn't even left my cottage. Lily-Ann and Ocean had been the ones who'd approached the . . . the body.

I watched the police officer lead the guy – Anthony – away.

Handcuffed, like on TV.

Past the crime scene tape, toward the street.

Mrs B spoke to him, but I couldn't hear her. Despite all the cops and EMS people hanging around, I didn't feel safe. The idea that the guy – the murderer – had been living a few doors down nauseated me a little.

'I organized your medicine cabinet,' Lily-Ann said, entering from the bathroom behind me.

I blinked at her. 'You what?'

'Your medicine cabinet is now organized.'

'I—sorry, you looked in my medicine cabinet?'

'I couldn't have organized it without looking.' She frowned past me. 'They're arresting Anthony?'

I felt flushed and dizzy. 'Yeah. I . . . I don't know why.'

'His tattoos are uneven,' she told me.

'I don't think that's illegal.' I swayed. 'I, uh, I need to lie down.'

Lily-Ann inspected me briefly, then helped me onto the couch. She propped my feet up and tucked a blanket around me. She brought me ice water with a squeeze of lemon, making herself completely at home, which I found comforting.

'I caught him looking at me,' I said.

'You mean Anthony?' she asked.

I nodded and told her about the familiar, expectant look he'd given me the night Mrs B met him at the bus stop.

'She'd met him before then,' Lily-Ann told me. 'Do you still feel faint?'

'She met him before? When?'

'I don't know. I spoke with her about inviting strangers into her home, and she mentioned that she'd met him earlier.' Lily-Ann frowned at my bookcase. 'Though I believe she said that *he* hadn't met *her*.'

'Um, I don't really know what that means.'

Lily-Ann looked perplexed. 'Mmm. Well. Do you still feel faint?'

'No, I'm much better. Thanks. Sorry.'

'You need more toothpaste.'

I resisted the urge to check my breath. 'I-I do?'

'You're running out,' she told me, and gestured to my bathroom.

'Of everything,' I told her.

I shut my eyes to block out my emotions . . . and caught a glimpse of crows flapping in the darkness. The memory made me tremble, so I lay there feeling empty and afraid. After What Happened Before, I'd stopped trusting that my life made sense. My stalker had appeared without warning, he'd left 'gifts' for me every time I'd dared to feel safe. I'd started seeing the world as a minefield, and seeing myself as hollow, blank, a rough copy of a real person.

But while living at the Marigold Cottages, I'd finally started filling myself in again. I'd finally started gaining solidity and heft. Gaining *presence*, I guess. Or regaining it.

And now this. A corpse, a crow, a pool of blood. A killer.

13

LILY-ANN

After Lily-Ann left Sophie's cottage, she crossed the courtyard to the crime scene. One of the police said, 'Can I help you?'

'Yes,' she said, and detailed her questions.

Despite his offer, he hardly helped at all. He either didn't know the answers or he refused to share them.

She wondered if she should bring doughnuts, or if that would be considered an insult. She couldn't imagine who would be insulted by a dozen honey-glazed, but people did seem to have a genius for taking offense.

So she texted Piotr.

Lily-Ann
Will police take offense if I offer them doughnuts?

Piotr
yes

Lily-Ann
What about crullers?

Piotr
WTF? ask one your many friends.

Which was intended as an insult, because she didn't have many friends. She waited for Piotr to say more, to actually answer her question, but he didn't.

So she asked the Marigold Cottages text chat.

Lily-Ann
Will the police take offense if I offer them doughnuts?

Ocean Neighbor
Probably

Lily-Ann
Crullers?

Ocean Neighbor
Don't bother. They won't tell you anything.

Lily-Ann nodded at her phone. She liked that Ocean understood why she was asking.

Hamilton Neighbor
What police?

Hamilton Neighbor
Per Deshaney v. Winnebago, the police have no obligation to protect citizens from harm or to defend you if they witness you being violently assaulted.

Ocean Neighbor
Don't cut and paste into the group chat Hamilton.

Hamilton Neighbor
Wait. The police are here!?

Hamilton Neighbor
What happened?

Lily-Ann
A corpse was found in the hedges.

Lily-Ann
Unidentified, so far. Anthony is under arrest.

Hamilton Neighbor
He can't be.

Hamilton Neighbor
He helped with my hummingbird feeder.

Lily-Ann wasn't interested in that so she turned her attention to the police. After the CSI woman finished, the ambulance guys took the body away. The CSI woman stayed for a while, then she left, too. The uniformed cops remained behind with the police tape. The blood smear remained behind, too.

Lily-Ann made a mental note to clean that, when possible. She didn't think a little gore would upset Mrs B: she was gentle and frivolous, but she had an iron core. Sophie, however, would find the stain distressing. And Lily-Ann felt almost protective of Sophie. Which was new. She didn't often engage with relative strangers like that. Or with anyone. Yet she thought of Sophie coming to her house, asking her to speak with Hamilton, nervously sipping wine. She thought of Sophie almost fainting in her arms, of Sophie looking flustered at the organization of her medicine cabinet.

And she felt protective.

As far as Lily-Ann knew, she didn't have any maternal instincts. She certainly wasn't Ocean, the unofficial den mother of the Marigold Cottages, just like Mrs B was the eccentric granny. Lily-Ann wondered if being a lesbian made Ocean extra maternal. She made a note to ask. You could ask Ocean anything. She would not abide malice, but if you didn't mean any harm, she wouldn't judge you.

So no, Lily-Ann didn't feel motherly about Sophie, but perhaps big-sisterly? There was something delicate and precious about Sophie. Perhaps it was her youth. Or her damaged fragility? Except, no. None of that appealed to Lily-Ann.

It couldn't simply be that she was such a mess, could it? That something about her cried out for tidying? No. Certainly not.

But maybe.

14

OCEAN

After she watched the cop handcuff Anthony, Ocean rushed home to comfort the kids. Except she wasn't sure exactly how, so she defaulted to her usual strategy: staying close and telling them she loved them. Riley ignored her, but Miles chirped, 'Love you, too,' and let Ocean fuss with his hair.

She was about to ask if they wanted Indian food for dinner when she heard Mrs B's raised voice in the courtyard. Her gaze shifted to the door but she didn't move.

'We're *fine*,' Riley told her, not quite rolling her eyes. 'Go see what's wrong with Mrs B.'

'Yeah, it's pretty cool,' Miles said.

Ocean didn't want her son thinking that dead people or cops were cool, so she said, 'Uh . . .'

'He *knows*, Oma,' Riley said, definitely rolling her eyes that time. 'He doesn't think the murder is cool, just the whole situation.'

Ocean knew that, of course, but she still worried about Miles. He was so sensitive. When he was learning the alphabet he burst into tears because it wasn't fair to all the letters at the end. They never got a chance to go first.

Still, hearing Riley call her 'Oma' again – even by accident – made a warm glow spread in her chest. As a little girl, Riley had started calling Ocean's ex-wife Zoe 'Mom' and Ocean 'Momma.' Then she'd started calling her 'O-mom' and then 'Oma,' which had stuck so much that Miles adopted it. Though lately Riley had taken to calling her 'Mother,' which was just mean.

'Yeah, I guess it's pretty interesting,' she said, crossing to the door.

'It's not interesting,' Riley said. 'It's embarrassing.'

'Embarrassing? Why would it be emb— Never mind. You can be on your screens till I get back.'

She found Mrs B in the courtyard, her kaftan fluttering and her silver and amethyst rings flashing in the sunlight as she shook her finger at the detective. Because she was scolding him. Her eyes narrowed beneath her white hair as she snapped, 'I'd like to hear the evidence against him, that's what I'd like.'

'As I said, ma'am—' the detective started.

'There isn't any! That's why you can't tell me. You're just trying to fool an old lady. You should be ashamed of yourself. Trying to pull the wool over my eyes!'

Ocean pursed her lips as she trotted closer. Mrs B always reverted to her defenseless old-lady act when worried she wouldn't get her way.

'The investigation is in the earliest stages, Mrs Bakofsky,' the detective said, 'and I assure you that—'

'Fool me once, shame on you!' she declared. 'Trying to pull the wool like I can't see what you're doing. Where's the evidence? It's a—'

'It's okay,' Anthony told her.

'It's *not* okay, Anthony! You wouldn't know what was okay if I gave you the O and the K! Now, you listen to me, Mister Detective. Anthony isn't a killer, you write *that* down in your little notebook, that's me being a . . . what's the phrase? Not a *bear* witness.'

'A character witness?' the detective suggested.

'A character witness! Write it down! He's a good person.'

'He's so good, ma'am, that he did ninety-two months at Chuckawalla.'

Ocean saw from the flicker of expression on Anthony's stony face that the detective was wrong; he hadn't served ninety-two months at Chuckawalla, whatever that was. Then his gaze shifted to her, and she saw something else. Not shame, exactly, but maybe regret.

'That's easy for you to say!' Mrs B snapped at the detective, getting red-faced. 'You wool-puller! You puller of wool!'

'Mrs B,' Ocean said, touching her arm. 'There's nothing we can do about this right now.'

'They can just take him? With no evidence? No motive? Nothing?'

'They can do whatever they want, they're police. I'll

visit him as soon as possible.' She looked to the detective. 'If you'll, uh, clear me to visit?'

'Yeah, sure, of course,' he said, relieved to get on with his job. 'I'll do that, um, as soon as . . .'

He led Anthony away without finishing the sentence, no longer blocked by the fierce old lady. Who slumped suddenly, in exhaustion and defeat. The combative light dimmed in her eyes, and the grooves on her face seemed to deepen. She was always so strong that seeing her look feeble broke Ocean's heart a little.

'Let's get a cup of tea,' Ocean said.

Mrs B patted her hand and let Ocean lead her into her house and settle her on the love seat. Ocean started the kettle, then pulled the Ferrero Rocher chocolate from above the fridge, which Mrs B considered the height of decadence. She'd been raised poor, back east, and had learned the Great Depression mindset from her parents. She bought laundry detergent with a coupon and reused her tinfoil.

She'd come to California in her twenties, when she'd married her husband, Leonard. After three miscarriages, she'd never had children, which had devastated her as a young woman. She'd worked as a special ed teacher, and one of her prized possessions was a shoebox of letters from students and families whose lives she'd touched. Her husband had started a moving company that went bankrupt. Then he'd started another moving company that also went bankrupt. Then he'd sold life insurance and did well. Apparently he'd been good at expressing the dangers of an uncertain world because he'd been such an irresponsible man himself. A gambler. As a girl, Ocean had always liked him, but he'd been the black sheep of his family, given to sudden impulses. Fortunately, one of his impulses had been buying a run-down complex of properties. He'd fixed them up and given them the pet name of his long-suffering wife: the Marigold Cottages.

Mrs Golda 'Marigold' B ignored the Ferrero Rocher, too worried about Anthony. Which struck Ocean as odd. She knew better than most that Mrs B considered her tenants family, but Anthony was so new. Also, he didn't exactly fit the mold of most of the other residents, who tended toward the eccentric, the needy, or the broken.

Okay, maybe he *did* fit the mold.

After tea, she brought Mrs B to her house while she waited for the police to finish. She didn't want to leave her alone. Except halfway there, she found Miles greeting friends at the street to show off the police tape and try to catch glimpses of the crime scene officer.

She shooed them away and told Mrs B, 'Now I'll have to call their parents to apologize.'

'There's nothing wrong with curiosity, my dear.'

'I don't think blood smears are covered by the spirit of inquiry.'

'How's Riley handling it?' Mrs B asked.

'She's too self-centered to care.'

Though in fact, Riley *did* care. She'd decided that the whole situation was an embarrassment and locked herself in her room.

Which worried Ocean a little. Riley rarely locked her door. What was really bothering her? Something more than a corpse on the property? Ocean should talk to her. Yet at the moment, she was mostly grateful to have Riley out of her hair.

'I told you not to rent to Anthony,' she told Mrs B.

'You gave me your blessing!' She settled on Ocean's sofa. 'And in any case, he didn't do anything wrong.'

'Right? The dead guy bashed his own head in.' Ocean glanced out the window and watched two cops walk past, toward the studio. 'And the cops are searching his apartment for no reason.'

'I shudder to think what your parents would say, to hear you agreeing with the police.'

'They'd say I've internalized my oppression.' She exhaled. 'Maybe they're right. He's probably a great guy. But this is *murder*, Mrs B.'

'Which Anthony didn't commit.'

'Maybe. The timing doesn't look great. Neither does the blood on his sleeve.'

'Maybe shmaybe. I know for a fact that he didn't do it.'

'How do you know that? Ooh, maybe *you're* the killer.'

Mrs B sniffed. 'Who's to say I'm not?'

'You won't even use lethal mousetraps.'

'Well, I'd never kill *anyone* with one of those terrible glue traps.'

Ocean snorted a laugh. 'If they find a chunk of cheddar under the body, I'm going to turn you in.'

'Don't be ridiculous,' Mrs B said. 'I'd use peanut butter.'

Well, at least Mrs B hadn't lost her sense of humor. But why was she so convinced that Anthony hadn't committed the murder? She always liked to think the best of people, and insisted that dumb optimism wasn't naivete – it was a strategic decision calculated to return the best possible life. Though judging from her sudoku book, her ability to calculate was steadily dwindling.

Still, Mrs B's insistence on Anthony's innocence struck Ocean as almost too forceful. Did she have some hidden connection to him? She claimed otherwise. She said that she'd just met him at the bus stop a few times. Ocean didn't quite believe her, though. Like, what had he been doing there, anyway? The busses didn't run late at night, and he wasn't on his way to his previous home.

Perhaps he was merely a stranger who'd tugged at Mrs B's heartstrings. Another lost soul.

15

NICHOLAS

Nicholas heard a fuss on the far side of the property as he left for Santa Ynez that morning. Tenants chattering, doors opening and closing. Even more than usual. Like someone had kicked an anthill.

So he did what he did best: he ignored it.

On a certain level, Nicholas appreciated the Marigold Cottages. He approved of the intimate size and the off-kilter charm. He enjoyed the sense of homey, faded comfort. Everything felt slightly worn, but more like a favorite T-shirt than a leaky roof.

On the other hand, the place was an absolute fishbowl. It was as if the units had been designed to give a bunch of . . . well, he hesitated to say 'weirdos'. A bunch of 'idiosyncratic tenants' an excuse to meddle in each other's lives.

Not that most of them needed an excuse. They'd seized any reason to fuss and chatter. Especially Mrs Bakofsky, who meddled like she was born for it. Which he had his own personal reasons for avoiding, in addition to the normal human aversion to your landlady mucking around in your personal life.

Nicholas preferred to keep his private. So he headed quietly for his car through the back entrance, then drove across town to pick up his date. Her long blue dress swirled when she trotted to meet him in the driveway. She usually wore blue, he suspected to highlight her eyes. She kissed him on the cheek, then settled in for the drive to Santa Ynez.

They'd hung out a handful of times, after he'd made it clear he wanted to keep things casual. He suspected that she resented him a little, because he came across as conventional, the type of guy interested in a serious relationship. He looked okay – at least well-dressed and well-groomed. He had a good job with the city, a nice car, and his own place. So he should be ready to settle down, right?

Except he wasn't. He wanted more. If only he knew exactly what. Maybe just to take a risk. One even edgier than not recusing himself from the zoning committee meeting.

On the drive over San Marcos Pass, his date mentioned that she hadn't visited Santa Ynez in years, and he didn't mention that he came every few months.

His mother had loved Santa Ynez Valley. She'd worked there for years, and she'd brightened every time they'd visited. She'd stood straighter and smiled quicker. Nicholas wasn't much for gravestones, but he liked to wander the hot, sunny village streets, stopping for a snack or a beer, to window-shop and people-watch, as a way to remember her.

He even recalled a few thrilling, effervescent trips to Solvang with *both* his parents. He'd treasured those visits to Danish bakeries and toy stores. Eating fried doughnuts slathered in jam and powdered sugar with his mostly absent father, who'd provided everything they'd needed except for himself. Nicholas had understood, in a childlike way, without ever being told, that his father had another family. He'd daydreamed about them sometimes: in his imagination there had been three kids, all exactly his age, who'd embrace him as their newest brother.

But mostly, Santa Ynez was for his mom.

He didn't mention that to his date, of course, on account of the creep factor. *Hey, want to spend the day poking around my dead mother's favorite town?*

Not a great move.

Still, the valley didn't disappoint. He'd planned on lunch at one of the high-rated local restaurants, but instead they decided on an impromptu wine tasting and gourmet pizzas fresh from a food truck's mobile ovens. They'd sipped and shopped and capped off the afternoon with gelato.

And by the time he returned to the Marigold Cottages, the other tenants had settled down. Which would've been a relief. Except instead of walking in on a silent courtyard, he found a police officer waiting to interview him about a murder.

16

LILY-ANN

The Marigold Cottages group chat buzzed with speculation about the murder. And with Hamilton's endless debunking of various sources of forensic information.

Hamilton Neighbor
The National Academies proved that the science behind so-called bite-mark evidence is completely unreliable.

Lily-Ann silenced the discussion, then returned her attention to her laptop, focusing on the appendix of a new proposal. With a few words, she clarified her company's ability to host virtual training sessions with under-resourced organizations.

Done. Crossed off the list.

She enjoyed her proficiency at her job. Still, she kept thinking how she'd be a good detective or crime scene technician. Which was true, but she imagined she'd also make quite an effective killer.

Perhaps even a contract killer. She was not sentimental or encumbered by a particularly keen sense of morality. She enjoyed problem-solving. And after choosing a course of action, she was meticulous and decisive.

Also, people found her easy to overlook. A fat woman as the contract killer? Impossible. Women didn't do that sort of thing. And if they did, according to every example of film and television, they were striking and size zero, and dressed to attract attention. In the right clothing, Lily-Ann could effectively turn invisible. Though, granted, she would not excel at climbing through windows.

Her phone dinged again. Not from the silenced group chat, of course.

Piotr
there was a murder at your house?!!

Lily-Ann
No.

Piotr
then explain the corpse on the property

Piotr
you know what I mean

Lily-Ann
Yes.

Piotr
are you ok?

Lily-Ann
Yes.

Piotr
working?

Lily-Ann
Yes.

Piotr
doing unpaid overtime as always

Lily-Ann set her laptop aside, trying not to let it bother her that Piotr had turned off his automatic caps lock like a teenager. Always striving to act younger than he was. She stood and stretched, then fixed her hair. The blunt side-parted bob was as straight as she could make it, though she was due for another keratin treatment.

Doing unpaid overtime as always . . .

She knew how Piotr felt about her workaholism, which he blamed for their marriage falling apart. He claimed that she'd never devoted enough time to *him*. Maybe he was right. Still, when she'd forced herself to work less, she'd felt itchy and unhappy. So that hadn't lasted long.

Piotr
i'm coming by to check on you

Piotr
your neighbor is a murderer

Lily-Ann didn't know how he knew so much, but she wasn't surprised. Information often seemed to flow toward Piotr of its own accord.

Lily-Ann
Did they charge him?

Piotr
does it matter? cu soon

'Yes, I'm free right now,' she said aloud. 'Thanks for asking.'

Maybe she'd go for a walk, so he'd miss her. She didn't

enjoy spending time with him anymore. Though she appreciated his concern. So perhaps she'd stay.

She put fresh sheets on the bed, just in case.

Then she emptied her kitchen trash, and as she returned from the bins she caught a glimpse of a man standing in the shadows near Nicholas's house.

On second look, it *was* Nicholas, which made a certain amount of sense. Though he usually left the Marigold Cottages from his private entrance. His was the only unit with private access, which struck her as possibly meaningful.

He was a young man, darkly handsome. She imagined that he counted himself as 'white Hispanic' in the census. He dressed better than most men, and wore more jewelry: usually two rings and a bracelet, though sometimes a necklace, which interested her, though she rarely saw him.

Nicholas kept to himself. Apparently he almost aggressively snubbed any attempt to befriend him, though Lily-Ann had never noticed.

According to Mrs B, he worked for the city.

He seldom smiled.

At the moment, he was scowling at his phone, which dinged repeatedly.

So when Lily-Ann went back inside, she checked her own phone, and found her suspicions confirmed. The group text still filled the screen. She enjoyed knowing she wasn't the only person who it annoyed.

Ocean Neighbor
Mrs B has a request

Ocean Neighbor
She tells me to say it's a demand

Ocean Neighbor
She wants all the tenants to gather at Hamilton's house tomorrow at 7:00

Ocean Neighbor
For what she's calling a Marigold Cottage Murder Collective Meeting

Hamilton Neighbor
MCMCM.

Ocean Neighbor
She will get Levitical on your ass if you don't show up

Ocean Neighbor
(She didn't say that)

Ocean Neighbor
She said: 'That includes you, Nicholas!'

Lily-Ann added an event to her calendar. Five o'clock at Hamilton's house, to help him set up for the meeting. Though he might take offense if she arrived that early to organize the chairs and such. So she changed her note: she'd arrive at five-thirty.

17

VERNON

'My mistake,' Vernon told Anthony Lambert from across the table in the police interview room. 'I apologize.'

Anthony Lambert watched him with impersonal interest.

'You didn't do time at Chuckawalla.' Vernon tapped his file folder. 'No, you caught High Desert. That is not a happy place. Wasn't ninety-two months, either. Well, here's a little insight into my own thinking. I guessed high, hoping you might correct me.'

Anthony Lambert shifted his shoulders.

'See, if you ask a question, a certain kind of person – the sort who decided they're not going to answer you – they *don't* answer you. But if you're incorrect? If you make a mistake, give them a chance to show off a little, prove they know better? Well, it's hard not to correct someone misstating your personal facts.'

Anthony Lambert still didn't speak. Waiting for his court-appointed attorney, who hadn't yet been notified of his detention. No rush. A guy with Lambert's history wouldn't expect the VIP treatment.

Vernon considered trying to unearth the connection between the perpetrator and the victim, a one James Dedrick. On paper, at least, Dedrick looked like a wealthy, shallow, golden boy. Big house, three cars. Social media accounts with pictures of him with smiling 'bitches,' who apparently didn't mind the label. Officially he was a real estate investor.

Unofficially? Well, the Altadena police hadn't reported anything actionable, not yet. One DUI, two domestic disturbance calls that resulted in no charges, and a ten-year-old trespassing charge.

Nothing juicy enough to dangle at Anthony Lambert, so he needed to approach this from another angle.

'What I'm curious about is, why did the old woman rent to you?' Vernon tapped the folder again. 'I mean, she's an eighty-year-old Jewish lady from East New York. You know where that is?'

Anthony Lambert looked at him.

'No, me neither. So I asked, and she told me. Brooklyn. Lived out here most of her life, though. She likes the climate. She also likes, shall we say, idiosyncratic individuals. You know what "idiosyncratic" means?'

Anthony Lambert didn't respond.

'Means fucking strange, my friend. Means abnormal. You've got that Chinese girl strung as tight as a violin, the fat lady who doesn't care, the lesbian soccer mom, the shut-in who didn't answer his goddamn door until my third attempt, and some guy so normal that he raises every kind of red flag.' He paused for a second. 'So why did Mrs Bakofsky rent to *you*?'

Nothing.

'Where'd you meet her?'

Nothing.

'Maybe you helped her across the street, like a Boy Scout. Maybe you found Jesus when you were inside. No? But look at you now, in control of yourself. Yeah, you helped an old lady across the street. That'd impress a soft-headed soul like Mrs Bakofsky. She's got a thing for wounded animals.'

Nothing.

'Then how did you meet? Win some brownie points here, Anthony. You know *she'll* tell me.'

For a second, Vernon thought he caught a flash of humor in the guy's dull eyes. At the very least, a flash of interest. But he continued not talking.

73

18

SOPHIE

I loved the group chat. Partly because I was getting to know my neighbors better, and partly because the chat was my baby. But mostly because I could copy entire chunks of dialogue from the text into my playstorming file.

And when I directed this thing, *someone* would definitely say, *She will get Levitical on your ass.*

I was pretty sure that Leviticus was the most homophobic book of the Bible, so I was glad the gay character said it. I guess I shouldn't call Ocean a character, though. She was just the person I was basing a character on. Hmm. Not sure that made it any better.

I didn't copy the part where Ocean texted That includes you, Nicholas.

I'd lived at the Marigold Cottages for a year and I'd only talked to Nicholas twice. He was like the Loch Ness monster, but less friendly. Well, except to the women he brought around. Never the same one for long. I'd probably only seen him a dozen times, because he used his own entrance.

He was kind of a hipster, kind of hot, kind of a dork, and definitely a little too intense. Dream casting: Adam Driver.

The first time I met him, I said, 'Hi! I'm Sophie. I just moved in.'

Like a normal person.

He said, 'Hello,' and walked away.

Like a weirdo.

Then I said, 'Sorry.'

Also like a weirdo.

And that was that.

The second time I talked to him was even worse. It was five or six months ago. I thought it would be nice for everyone to sign a Rosh Hashanah card for Mrs B. Which, I should note, was a totally normal request. And the thing was, Mrs B had really helped me when I first moved in. She could tell I was nervous or whatever, and she never said anything but for the first few weeks she was just always around. Nearby. In case I needed her.

Well, she and Ocean both. Though I was pretty sure that Mrs B had told Ocean to keep an eye on me, too.

Anyway, I got everyone to sign, to wish her a happy New Year. Even Hamilton. I mean, he gave a little speech about lunar calendars, so I apologized, but he signed the card with a John Hancock flourish.

Then I'd knocked on Nicholas's door and shown him the card.

'No, thank you,' he'd said.

'What?' I'd blurted. 'What do you mean, "no, thank you"? That's not . . . that's not a thing you say when someone asks you to sign a card for an old lady.'

'My mistake,' he'd said, and closed the door on me.

So, yeah. I wasn't a huge fan.

I was just trying to recover, that's all. To catch my balance after getting knocked on my ass by What Happened Before. I just wanted to walk through my own life without feeling like any little bump might send me reeling.

So responding to me like a normal human being would've been appreciated.

I wondered if he'd show up tomorrow night. I also wondered if he'd killed the guy. They looked like the same demographic: cocky, well-dressed young jerks who probably worked in law or finance. Maybe they'd fought over whose dick was bigger. Was it okay to joke about a dead guy's dick? I'd just pretend I was processing.

Speaking of dicks, Lily-Ann's estranged husband came by to see her, so maybe he wasn't that bad. I just hated my father using him as an example of the kind of man I needed. And he spent the night every now and then, so I guess they weren't so estranged.

Anyway, I noticed his car prowling past me as I walked home from buying a bottle of tequila and takeaway bao for lunch, from the Secret Bowl, my favorite restaurant. A burgundy iX M60. I made a note of that, so I could tease my father with the details, but I knew I wouldn't.

When I got home, I reheated the bao and tucked the tequila into the back of a shelf, to hide it from myself. I'd already finished the gin. Sometimes I tried not keeping alcohol in the house, to spare myself the temptation. Which was great for my health, but terrible for my wallet on the nights I slipped out to Capriccio, the hole-in-the-wall Italian place a few blocks away, to drown my anxieties in Bellinis.

After a minute, I returned to the shelf and grabbed the tequila and poured myself four fingers. I took a slug and winced. I rarely drank tequila, but nothing got me drunk faster.

I took another slug and—

And finally recognized Anthony.

His face. I knew his face. Not just from the bus stop.

From somewhere else. Somewhere I'd slammed shots of tequila. Somewhere blurred and noisy and overheated. Somewhere sweaty and spinning. I could taste the burn of liquor in my throat. I could feel the place, but I couldn't picture it.

At least not until I was halfway through my bao. Then I remembered. He was from the Sidecar. From that dive bar where I indulged in too much Jose Cuervo. Anthony was one of the bouncers from the Sidecar.

I didn't know how to feel about that, except frightened. I let my dinner go cold and just . . . shut down a little. Is that why he'd looked at me like that, the first time we met?

Had he recognized me? Is that why he moved in, to stalk me?

I'd seen him moving bags of sculpture clay for Ocean. I'd seen him sitting on Mrs B's porch, drinking tea from a cup that seemed tiny in his hand. But he hadn't looked at me once in all the time he'd lived here.

I wasn't sure what that meant, though. Just like I wasn't sure why he'd kill some stranger outside my house.

I wasn't sure I wanted to know. But I was still going to write my notes, I was still going to brainstorm scene ideas for a stage play set at the Marigold Cottages. I'd been handed this golden opportunity to write a play based on the events around me, and I wasn't going to blow it.

And it was better not to know too much about the murder. One of the quotes taped to my wall was by the director Anne Bogart: '*The most remarkable experiences in theatre fill me with uncertainty and disorientation.*'

So I'd just keep adding to this file, and embrace the uncertainty.

19

OCEAN

When the doorbell rang, Ocean was sitting cross-legged on the living room floor with Miles, trying to convince Riley to play cards with them before dinner. Which meant shouting down the hallway at her closed door.

'Deal three hands,' she told Miles, as she unfolded her legs.

'Still not playing!' Riley called from her room.

'Just one game?' she begged. 'Pleeeease?'

Riley didn't answer. Yeah, something was definitely off with her. Probably. Definitely probably. You just couldn't tell with kids. In some ways you knew everything about them, and in other ways they were complete mysteries.

Ocean opened the front door and found Sophie standing there with a plate wrapped in tinfoil.

'Am I early?' Sophie said.

'Uh,' Ocean said.

Sophie looked past her into the living room. 'Oh, god, I'm sorry! Mrs B told me to come for pizza. Oh, no. She just didn't want me left alone tonight and now I bust in unannounced and—'

Riley poked her head into the hallway. 'Did someone say pizza?'

'Mrs B told me she ordered from Capriccio,' Sophie said, chewing her lower lip. 'I'm sorry. I don't know what I was thinking. They don't even deliver.'

'They do for Mrs B,' Ocean told her. 'She used to babysit the owner.'

Sophie shifted nervously, and maybe a little tipsily. 'Well, I, um . . .'

'Come on in,' Ocean said, stepping aside.

Her cottage had a small living room beside an open kitchen, with three tiny bedrooms along a stubby hall. Ocean liked to think that the place read 'casual family chic,' with her unsold paintings on the walls, the sagging gray velvet couch, and the blue-and-white vases – plus, the Legos, nail polishes, and abandoned homework littering every possible surface. These days everyone wanted homes that looked like a cream and terracotta Instagram post instead of a place where kids actually lived.

'What'd you bring?' Ocean asked, deciding against apologizing for the mess.

'Oh, sorry. I stress-baked shortbread cookies this afternoon.'

'Sounds like the tasty kind of stress. Miles, put the cards away and set the table, please.'

Ocean threw a salad together until the pizzas arrived. Mrs B followed with a loaf of garlic bread, then told a long complicated story about her nemesis in her senior strength class at the Y. Their enmity seemed to revolve around stacking chairs; the other woman acted like Mrs B wasn't as strong as she was, though in fact she was stronger. Then Riley monopolized Sophie, talking about *her* nemesis in high school. A real woman-to-woman chat. Sophie, bless her, listened without a hint of dismissal. Then Miles explained the rules of his favorite online game to the happily uncomprehending Mrs B. who insisted on playing her favorite *offline* game, Egyptian Rat Screw, which she'd introduced a few years earlier, to the great titillation of the kids.

Normalcy strikes again.

Sophie visibly relaxed. So did Miles and Riley, but that didn't take much. After dessert, the kids retreated to their rooms and Mrs B said, 'I wanted to talk to you two about Anthony, before the meeting tomorrow.'

'What *is* the meeting tomorrow?' Sophie asked.

'A concentrated dose of batty old lady,' Ocean told her.

Mrs B ignored her. 'Anthony is innocent.'

'Listen,' Ocean said. 'He's my kind of guy. Quiet and capable, that's what I like in a man. But one thing Anthony is not, is innocent.'

'Of *this*,' Mrs B said. 'He did not kill that man.'

'We don't even know who that man is,' Sophie reminded her. 'He could be a – I don't know – a criminal . . . person, who Anthony knows from, uh . . .' Her face scrunched. 'Somewhere.'

'They didn't even arrest him properly,' Mrs B said. 'He's simply being detained. Is that legal?'

'Did you call the police station?' Ocean asked.

'Of course! The young woman on the phone was very helpful. Or very pleasant, I should say. She wasn't *helpful* at all.'

'What'd she tell you?' Ocean asked.

'She went on and on about his record, and how the police take care to honor every citizen's rights, like she's never even watched TV.'

'What exactly is Anthony's record?' Sophie asked.

Mrs B sniffed. 'Well, that's Anthony's business, isn't it?'

For a moment, Ocean thought Mrs B was being circumspect, then she realized: 'They wouldn't tell you, huh?'

'No matter how many times I asked,' Mrs B admitted.

Sophie giggled, which was adorable.

'However,' Mrs B continued, 'Hamilton promised that he'd ask his friend.'

'Hamilton has friends?' Ocean said.

'Don't be unkind, dear,' Mrs B told her. 'I once wondered what kind of adult people play his computer games, and he mentioned that one of his friends is a local policeman.'

'He's asking his friend for information about Anthony?'

'Then we'll compare notes,' Mrs B said, with a brisk nod. 'I'm sure if we put our heads together, we can straighten this out.'

'That's why we're meeting tomorrow?' Sophie said, her eyes shining with excitement.

Which surprised Ocean. Maybe Sophie was addicted to true crime podcasts or something, but she would've thought that this particular crime had hit too close to home.

'Exactly,' Mrs B said.

'Well, there's act two!'

'Huh?'

'Nothing, sorry,' Sophie said. 'I mean, um, nothing.'

Ocean shook her head and turned to Mrs B. 'So you think a bunch of random people are going to what, crack the case?'

'Another one of Hamilton's game friends lives in Vietnam, isn't that interesting? Oh, and one is a wedding photographer!'

Ocean was still smarting from '*don't be unkind*,' so she said, 'Thinking about getting remarried? Second time's a charm.'

Because while Mrs B had loved her late husband, he'd been a bit of a gambler. Though his bet on the Marigold Cottages had paid off big.

Mrs B merely pressed her lips together and said, 'I'm not interested in cracking the case, dear. I don't care about punishing the guilty. I care about protecting the innocent.'

20

NICHOLAS

As a rule, Nicholas stayed away from the courtyard between the cottages. The last thing he wanted was to get involved with Mrs Bakofsky – or any of the residents who were intent on interfering with each other's lives. Which meant all of them. He wouldn't have lived here at all if he weren't paying far below market rate for his cottage. It wasn't that Nicholas wasn't grateful to Mrs B, as everyone else called her. It was that he figured the best way to thank her was to stay out of her life.

He even kept a low profile while getting his mail. Still, after he considered the police investigation, he made a point of visiting the crime scene. Because he felt an uncomfortable connection to the murder.

The police had asked if Nicholas knew the victim. James Dedrick. They'd shown him a picture, and yeah, Nicholas recognized him, though he wasn't about to admit it.

One of his jobs at the planning department was providing zoning information to the public – mostly developers. It was a thankless job, but *someone* had to preserve the city's unique beauty, character, heritage, and architectural traditions. Aesthetics mattered to Nicholas. Which felt trivial, given all the crises in the world. Still, he'd grown up in Santa Barbara and truly cared about protecting the city, in his small, bureaucratic way. That was as close as he ever got to feeling like he was making a mark on the world.

'I can't tell,' he'd told the cops, squinting at the picture of Dedrick. 'I'm not sure. He's kind of a type.'

'What type is that, sir?' the woman asked.

'The bad kind of bro-y. His name's familiar, though. Dedrick. Is he an architect?' Nicholas knew he wasn't an architect. 'I might've met him through work.'

The cops had said that they couldn't say, then asked a few more questions before leaving the Marigold Cottages. And now, Nicholas found himself worried about how he'd come across. Based on TV shows, he figured that lingering at the crime scene was an indication of guilt, but surely showing no interest at all was even more suspicious?

So he headed outside. As he stepped into the courtyard, he checked the group text on his phone. Mostly as an excuse to keep his head down. To his surprise, he was starting to enjoy the back-and-forth. Half of the comments read like an earnest Reddit thread, r/oddlysupportive or something. Then Hamilton would drop a partially relevant fact and Lily-Ann would ask for clarification, and the girl in the front cottage would respond with a string of emojis that Ocean would claim made her feel ancient.

Mrs Bakofsky never contributed, and neither did Nicholas. He'd only joined because Lily-Ann had stood at his door until he'd agreed. Not aggressively or anything.

Just like she was waiting for closure.

He crossed the courtyard, head bowed, and discovered that the crime scene didn't look like much. James Dedrick's life had ended in a scruffy corner between a hawthorn hedge and a wall.

As Nicholas stood there, he heard the girl in the front cottage – okay, *Sophie*, he knew her name – talking through an open window. She was right there, an arm's length from the police tape. Chatting with her friends. Sounding a little tipsy.

Except nobody else spoke. She was talking to herself. Or . . . was she reciting lines from a play?

Yeah, that's exactly what she was doing. The realization made him cringe with secondhand embarrassment. Still, he found himself wanting to eavesdrop . . . so he didn't. He'd seen her at the theatre once, looking too young for him, though apparently she wasn't. He'd taken her for a college girl until Mrs Bakofsky had mentioned, with an interfering light in her eyes, that she was only a few younger than he was.

That was another reason he needed to avoid Mrs Bakofsky. She was a matchmaker, and she'd noticed him noticing the girl in the front cottage. Which made him dig in his heels. So because she'd tried to nudge him toward the girl, he refused to even eavesdrop. Hell, he'd never acknowledged to anyone that he even knew her name.

However, he did have to acknowledge that a dead body had shown up on the property. He didn't want anyone to report him to the police as callous or weirdly uninterested. He pondered how much time he should waste looking solemn at the crime scene, decided it had been enough, and started back toward his house.

He caught a glimpse of Mrs Bakofsky emerging from Ocean's front door, so he veered from the courtyard, cutting behind Lily-Ann's unit. He walked silently in the shadow of the hedge and heard a man murmuring to her, his voice low and persuasive and too-intimate.

C'mon! All he wanted was to avoid interacting with the other tenants. First he heard some tipsy girl reciting a play, and now this prelude to lovemaking? Was it any wonder he wanted nothing to do with them?

He slipped quickly away, then turned the corner to his unit before he heard anything else. Phew. He might've been tied to the Marigold Cottages with cords of emotion, of family and history and even money, but he still hated getting tangled in the knots.

21

LILY-ANN

The next morning, sunlight shone through the window across from Lily-Ann's bed, making a nice crisp square on the wall. On the rug between the bathroom and hallway, she watched the light as she held her stretch – eighteen, nineteen, twenty – then pivoted to her other side.

'Damn, girl,' Piotr said, watching drowsily from her bed. 'Looking good. Did you lose weight?'

'No,' she said. *Fourteen, fifteen, sixteen . . .*

'What happened to that gym membership I gave you?'

'Nothing,' she told him, straightening and rolling her neck. 'It's still there.'

He laughed like she'd been joking. His teeth were extremely white and Lily-Ann wondered why he'd said, 'Damn, girl.' That was a new affectation. She expected that he'd seen it somewhere. Piotr tended to parrot phrases – and opinions, for that matter – that he saw gaining popularity online.

'Up, up,' she told him. 'I need to change the bedding.'

After he stood, she stripped the Frette sheets. They came exclusively in classic white, possibly because they were so nondescript and wrinkle-free that only obsessives like herself ordered them. As she remade the bed with a starched set of the exact same sheets, she watched Piotr go into the bathroom. He looked good, as though he'd ordered his perfect body from a catalog, the way Lily-Ann ordered linens.

As per their long-standing tradition, Piotr took her to Régina's for breakfast. The shabby chicness of the restaurant always appealed to her. She couldn't abide overstuffed furniture and mismatched patterns at home, but she appreciated the vibe nonetheless. Who could live with wallpaper, for fuck's sake? Still, she loved staring at the green William Morris design with the partridges and cabbage roses. She forced herself not to notice the seams in the wallpaper, and vowed in her next life she would be a carefree bohemian.

Piotr ordered her the avocado salmon toast without asking, then told her about his recent triumphs in cryptocurrency and related technologies.

'You should invest,' he told her. 'Blockchain's basically just an online database. You love databases.'

'True,' she said. 'But blockchains are distributed across

peer-to-peer networks, and you know how I feel about peers.'

When he laughed, she felt a glimmer of pride. She'd always enjoyed making him laugh.

'I'm worried about you,' he said.

'My blood pressure is 110 over 70.'

'Not your health, Lily-Ann. Living in that ridiculous hut, surrounded by whackjobs.'

'They're not whackjobs.'

'A *murderer* moved in.'

'An alleged murderer.'

'You said he's covered in shitty tattoos, and the cop arrested him on sight. What if he did something to—' Piotr reached across the table and took her hand. 'I just don't want anything to happen to you.'

'Oh,' she said.

'Are you still working too much?'

'No,' she said.

'Are you working weekends and evenings, for no pay?'

She hesitated. Just because she worked ten or fifteen extra hours a week didn't mean she was working too much – but Piotr would think it did.

'Jesus, Lily-Ann. You're letting them take advantage of you. You need to come home. You need someone to look after you.'

'I like the work.'

He frowned. 'At least that dirtbag is locked up.'

'If I understand correctly, this is a temporary investigative detention.'

'So he'll be released soon?'

'If I understand correctly.'

Piotr gazed through the restaurant window, watching the traffic outside. 'If he shows up at the Marigold Cottages again—'

'He lives there, Piotr. He will show up again.'

'Just call me. Tell me when he gets back. I need to know. Will you promise me that?'

'Yes,' she said.

She found his concern touching, if unexpected. And perhaps not unwelcome? She didn't know about that, though. Maybe she'd talk to Ocean and Mrs B; they enjoyed giving advice, and she enjoyed hearing it, even if she rarely let it affect her behavior.

22

SOPHIE

I hadn't told my parents about finding the body, not yet. I would, but only after I'd braced myself. They were going to freak out. Still, I considered retreating home for a few days, to get away from the memory. My parents made me crazy, but no more than the normal amount, and I found the prospect of rehashing our old arguments and annoyances pretty comforting.

I couldn't leave the Cottages, though. Not with Mrs B determined to 'sort out' the accusation against Anthony. Not with her calling a meeting at Hamilton's house to . . . what? To crack the case?

It was so perfect.

An elderly landlady, an artistic single mom, an eccentric shut-in, and a grumpy city planner were going to solve a mystery. I loved Mrs B, of course. Who wouldn't love a woman who wore elaborate kaftans year-round, layering turtlenecks under them in the winter? She was sweet and protective, wore too much gold eye shadow, and maintained a Little Free Library of Banned Books on the street – despite having trouble paying her bills. But this was seriously one of her more loopy ideas.

Loopy and *theatrical*.

So I stayed home. Well, and worked. I spent most of Sunday planning the upcoming fundraiser as I hate-listened to the *Arch Theatre* podcast about a twenty-four-year-old nepo baby. She'd written and directed her first play off-off-Broadway. Some nakedly award-hungry thing about generational abuse at a prep school that reviewers called 'slyly satirical' and 'by turns raw and beguiling.'

Sounded awful. Though maybe that was just my envy talking.

Should I replace the dorkily dysfunctional characters of the Marigold Cottages with slicker, sicker people? Pathology sold, and what did *I* have? Mere eccentrics.

Well, and a meeting at Hamilton's house. Hamilton was a lot, not even including being called Hamilton, which was his last name. He was about sixty years old, with a mop of gray hair and a love of Hawaiian shirts. Also, he refused to leave his cottage except in case of an emergency. I'd only met him because Mrs B introduced me when I moved in.

Now he wouldn't stop talking on the group chat, droning on about how Anthony helped with his hummingbird feeders. Well, interspersed with boring bird facts.

* * *

Hamilton
Chickens use forty-four unique vocalizations to communicate.

To be fair, that one was kind of interesting.

Sophie
That's more than the number of emojis Ocean knows

Ocean replied with a chicken emoji.

Hamilton
We're still on for seven tonight? Because I'm planning on seven tonight. If we're still on.

Ocean
Yes. We are. Mrs B says be there or be square. No, she just says BE THERE.

Hamilton
Be there or be square is a saying because if you're not there you'll be 'a round.'

I replied with an exploding-brain emoji, then thought about naming the chat The Marigold Cottages Murder Collective.

I went for a jog after work. I'd been on the track team in high school and college and was starting to find running meditative again. Finally. Years after a fairly horrific experience with Track-Trackr, the exercise app that led me straight into What Happened Before. I'd set my phone to share my location and that . . . hadn't worked for me.

Anyway, the run cleared my head.

I still didn't know what Mrs B was going to do other than declare Anthony innocent, but I was looking forward to finding out. Frankly, the idea that Hamilton was getting inside information from a cop friend struck me as beyond dubious. But that was okay. I didn't need the *investigation* to move forward; I just needed the *drama* to move forward.

I needed to feel like I could actually write this play. I needed to feel like a *person* again. I needed to feel like anything other than a victim.

23

VERNON

Considering Anthony Lambert's record, the murder investigation was as good as over. Well, barring any sudden stumbling blocks. That's why Vernon kept working to keep the path clear – like now, putting a pin in the reason that James Dedrick had come to town, by visiting the last person in Dedrick's call history before his death.

Gregory Ybarra's apartment covered the entire top floor of a three-story building a few blocks away from the Marigold Cottages. Neatly trimmed juniper bushes lined the walkway, but the stucco building was painted a calamine-lotion pink. Ybarra's neighbors must've considered it an eyesore.

The interior told a different story. The apartment

featured one wall of shaded windows overlooking the treetops and the rest was wood-paneled, like a rich guy's study on TV. Vernon took a seat on the leather couch and looked at the bronze sculpture of a bucking bronco on the glass coffee table.

'On the phone you told me that you'd called James Dedrick about a real estate investment,' Vernon said, accepting a glass of water. 'Have you worked with him before?'

Gregory Ybarra tugged at his bushy white beard. He looked good, wearing an expensive beige tracksuit like some kind of aging mogul.

'We never brought a project to completion,' Gregory Ybarra said, patting the bucking bronco sculpture before sitting. 'But we tried a few times. I met James during a spec project in Altadena. This is, oh, five years ago?'

'And you contacted him when?'

'The specific day? I don't know. My phone will tell us if it matters. Four, five weeks ago. I asked him to come up for a day and we'd look over some possibilities.'

'And Friday was that day?'

'Well, we were going to meet on Saturday, but he must've swung by for an early look and . . .' Ybarra let out a sigh. 'Shall we cut to why he was at the Marigold Cottages? I suspect that's the important part.'

'I suspect you're right,' Vernon said, putting his water glass on the table.

'You've probably met the property owner, Golda Bakofsky? She's full of life, she's always been that way, as long as I've known her. But, well, she's not getting any younger.'

Vernon raised an eyebrow. Ybarra was no spring chicken himself.

'And you know, there are two types of property owners in town. The ones who only care about the bottom line, and the ones who also care about the locals. Well, you've met her. You can guess which type Golda is. I'm the same. Locals matter. So we agree about the important things. And we've known each other a long time.'

'But now she wants to sell?'

'No. Not as far as she knows, no.' Gregory Ybarra smiled ruefully. 'But we've talked about it over the years. See, where we differ is, Golda thinks cutting rent helps people. But that's just a Band-Aid. What we really need is more units. Which is encouraged by the new zoning initiative. So I thought I'd make an offer she couldn't refuse.'

An unfortunate choice of words. Vernon knew Gregory Ybarra hadn't meant it in *The Godfather* way, but he still said, 'What kind of offer?'

'An eight-figure one. I wanted to bring James in to capitalize the deal. I suggested he combine business and pleasure, and spend the night. You know that new hotel in the Funk Zone? Wine-tasting rooms, rooftop terraces, Moroccan tiles? Yeah, that is exactly his type of place.'

'*Was* his type of place,' Vernon said. 'So he liked expensive things?'

Ybarra grunted agreement. 'Fast cars and faster women, that was his motto.'

They'd found Dedrick's car parked half a block from the Marigold Cottages. A late model Porsche that cost as much as Vernon made in a year.

'So James Dedrick liked the ladies?' he said, to prompt Ybarra to keep talking.

'I think he mostly liked the chase. He told me he once moved on a girl at her own bachelorette party.'

'And you told him to come look at the property whenever? Middle of the night?'

'No, no! I just gave him the address, that's all. I didn't expect he'd come for a moonlight inspection. That must've been spur of the moment.'

'An odd impulse on a Friday night, for a guy who liked nightlife.'

'Well, he probably wanted to get one over on me. That would've been like him. If he checked out the place before we met, he'd know more than I knew he knew.'

Vernon jotted down a meaningless note and thought about how the prosecutor would tell the story to the jury:

Poor James Dedrick, boyishly enthusiastic about his big real estate deal, came to Santa Barbara for a late-night glimpse of the Marigold Cottages. After a few drinks downtown. That checked out, according to his credit card receipts.

And there, on that fateful day, his path crossed with that of Anthony Lambert. A violent ex-con. We may never know exactly what happened that terrible night, but we knew two things for certain.

One, James Dedrick's life was brutally ended when an attacker crushed his skull.

And two, an attacker with a history of brutality lived fifty feet from the murder scene.

'Thank you very much, Mr Ybarra,' Vernon said, standing from the couch. 'I won't be needing anything else.'

At least, nothing other than a quick conviction. Which felt almost inevitable at this point. He'd done a damn fine job, if he said so himself. Identify the perpetrator on day one. Arrest him. Done.

24

OCEAN

'Even if you're right about Anthony,' Ocean told Mrs B, 'there's nothing we can do.'

She watched Mrs B fiddle with her necklace in her bedroom, getting ready for the meeting at Hamilton's. She was wearing what Ocean considered her 'business kaftan,' a navy-blue-collared dress that buttoned all the way to the floor. 'Shirtdress' might've been a better description, but it still billowed.

'First, dear, I *am* right,' Mrs B said, adding silver bracelets to both wrists, which reminded Ocean of handcuffs.

'Based on what, exactly?'

'On my long history of impeccable correctness.'

Ocean made a face at her. 'You think *The Little White Horse* is the greatest book ever written.'

'See? Impeccable!' Mrs B frowned at herself in the mirror, then attempted to fix her smudged silver eye shadow with spit on her index finger. 'Well, or nearly.'

Ocean met her eyes in the reflection. 'You can't *know* that Anthony is innocent.'

'However, I do. And second, what do you mean there's nothing we can do? I shudder to think what your parents would say. You know they loathed nothing more than a . . .' She paused. 'I've forgotten the word. Not "abomination" of responsibility.'

'Abdication.'

'Abdication! An abdication of one's civic duty.'

'One's civic duty is to advance the rights of disempowered communities, not protest the innocence of a possibly guilty ex-con.' Ocean gestured toward the door. 'Now, are we going or not?'

'Give me your elbow, you rude child. You, of all people, should know how to escort a lady.'

Ocean smiled as she linked arms with Mrs B and they followed the path toward the courtyard. A cool evening breeze brought the scent of the sea and rustled the leaves of the sycamore tree that edged the property. A car puttered past on the street, with music blaring from the window. To Ocean's amusement, it sounded like opera.

'You don't hear that every day,' Ocean said.

'And the world is sadder for it,' Mrs B said.

'Since when do you like opera?'

'Only Sondheim.' Mrs B took a breath then sang 'Send In the Clowns,' before pausing halfway to Hamilton's cottage. 'Err, let's make a slight detour.'

'What?' Ocean asked, before she realized. 'Oh. Nicholas isn't coming.'

'We can but ask.'

'We already but asked,' Ocean said. 'He got the text.'

'Yes, well. Technology.'

Ocean inspected Mrs B's lined face. She didn't

understand why she cared so much about Nicholas, when he so thoroughly resisted her efforts to get to know him. Perhaps because he was the only lost soul Mrs B couldn't find a place for. Ocean used to tease her about that. Then she'd stopped. She and Mrs B teased each other about many things, but somehow jokes about Nicholas fell flat.

So she just said, 'Fine.'

'Thank you, dear,' Mrs B said, and continued toward Hamilton's.

Hah. The old bat. She wanted *Ocean* to beg Nicholas to join them while she just joined the others. Ocean shot Her Majesty a sour look, then crossed the courtyard to Nicholas's door.

He didn't answer when she knocked. The prick. She knew he was home.

Soon after Nicholas had moved in, Ocean ran into him downtown at La Arcada, a shaded walkway of boutiques, art galleries, and restaurants. She'd been indulging in a spicy mango doughnut while trying to keep Riley from feeding hers to the turtles in the fountain. Nicholas had gracefully helped Ocean extract herself from one of those minor catastrophes of parenthood – a cranky toddler, a crying baby Miles, a broken stroller, and general panic. She'd been grateful and impressed. So when she'd discovered that his behavior at the Marigold Cottages skewed toward the unfriendly, she'd confronted him. He'd apologized politely, then continued to treat them all just as icily.

She hadn't wasted any time on him after that.

She knocked again.

The third time, he opened the door.

'She wants you to come,' Ocean said.

'I'm afraid I have other plans,' he told her.

'Of course you do,' she said.

He watched her for a moment, then told her to have a good night and went back inside.

Prick. Ocean showed the closed door both of her middle fingers, then turned to the courtyard. Well, it was probably for the best. God only knew what Mrs B had planned for this meeting.

When she reached Hamilton's cottage, the door opened a moment before she knocked.

'Good evening and welcome,' Hamilton intoned.

'You look snappy,' she told him, because he was wearing a white button-down shirt for once, with a red tie, over his usual shorts and Birkenstocks.

'Oh! Um . . .' He gestured her inside. 'Would you like a glass of milk?'

She didn't laugh. 'No, thank you.'

'Is Nicholas coming?' he asked, in an undertone.

She shook her head as she stepped into his living room. She was impressed at how open and uncluttered the place was. Two white slip-covered couches sat against pale gray walls with intricate crown molding, and the oak floor was polished to a sheen.

Well, he didn't have kids, that was clear.

She raised a hand in greeting to Mrs B, who was chatting with Lily-Ann, then sat beside Sophie. Who was awkwardly holding a glass of milk.

'Good for your bones,' Ocean said.

Sophie grimaced. 'I didn't know how to say no.'

Without a word, Ocean took the glass and put it on

an end table. Which was probably a little too pushy, but she couldn't help herself. She wondered if Sophie had told her parents about the body. She was from the Bay Area, if Ocean remembered correctly, but one of the non-sexy cities like Alameda. She also wondered if she should tell Sophie to call her parents about the body, but that was definitely too pushy.

Sophie was an adult; she could take care of herself. Probably.

Sophie twitched a grateful smile at Ocean, then opened a note-taking app on her phone. She typed faster with her thumbs than Ocean did with all ten fingers.

'Thank you all for coming,' Mrs B said, her voice wavering. 'Thank you. I know this is an imposition and a . . . Well, I won't even *tell* you what Ocean called me, simply for asking for a quick meeting.'

'An abomination,' Ocean muttered.

'Still, I'm afraid I need to ask for your help with Anthony.'

Sophie took a sharp breath. 'What did he do?'

'Nothing! Nothing at all, that's the problem. I need you to clear his name. He's innocent.'

Mrs B really expected them to solve a murder. Send in the clowns, indeed.

25

SOPHIE

The inside of the cottage wasn't as impressive I'd hoped, in terms of visual impact. I wanted towering piles of newspapers, a neon sign that flashed HAMILTON'S PUB, and a huddle of beach chairs for our meeting. It would've made a far more striking stage set.

Instead, Hamilton's living room was polished and almost elegant. Completely unlike Hamilton himself. I'd never fault him for his costuming though. The dress shirt and tie with shorts? Chef's kiss.

'I need you to clear his name,' Mrs B said. 'He's innocent.'

Hamilton said, 'I hereby call this meeting of the Marigold Neighborhood Watch to order.'

Ocean asked, 'Neighborhood Watch?'

'The Marigold Cottages Murder Collective,' I said, then offered to take notes.

Hamilton said: 'Are we a collective or a co-op?'

'Uh, you want me to jot that down?'

'No,' Lily-Ann said.

Y'know, what if I just wrote my notes in stage-play format? That was easier and quicker, and would help me envision the production. Well, the *possible* production. First, I had to actually write the script.

I used to dream about the art of playwriting, about the theatricality. Now I dreamed about the control: characters standing where I wanted and saying what I chose. Nobody lurked in the shadows, nobody loomed from the dark. As a playwright, I wouldn't need to apologize for existing; I'd need to command the goddamn stage.

Plus, the Marigold Cottages drama was perfect for a play, with the central courtyard already a theatre-in-the-round. If I closed my eyes, I could see the set design. But I didn't close my eyes. Instead, I started jotting down scene breaks and dialogue . . .

Act I

SCENE . . . NO IDEA

HAMILTON's living room. Possibly polished,
possibly beach chairs. We'll see . . .

MRS. B sets her glass down loudly, for attention.

MRS. B
Thank you, Hamilton. For hosting this, and for all the work you've done. Before we start, are there any questions?

SOPHIE
I have one. What exactly is happening right now?

MRS. B
We're pooling our resources.

LILY-ANN
To prove Anthony's innocence.

SOPHIE
Do we really think he's innocent?

Shit, I don't want to be in my own play. Maybe later I'll give my lines to Ocean and Lily-Ann. Or I'll create a whole new character. I'll just be S for now.

OCEAN

What <u>we</u> think doesn't matter. Mrs B has consulted the stars, and she is convinced. At least, enough to bully us into helping.

MRS. B

I'm not bullying you, Ocean, and if you say that again I will steal your lunch money. Now, Lily-Ann, will you begin?

LILY-ANN

The name of the dead man is, or was, James Dedrick.

S

No way. Really?

LILY-ANN

Yes. According to the police who conducted the second round of interviews, that was, in fact, his name.

S

So the dead man is Dead Rick?

HAMILTON

Dead Richard if you're formal.

>   (MRS B clears her throat, chastising S and
>   HAMILTON.)

LILY-ANN

In any case, ~~Sophie~~ S found him at approximately 6:30 a.m. on Saturday morning. When I checked for a pulse, the corpse was already cold. Alarmingly so. None of the residents admit to recognizing Dedrick, or to arranging to meet him. Unless that has changed?

(LILY-ANN waits for a response. There is none.)

Every resident, save Nicholas and Anthony, has reported that the victim is unknown to them. I haven't heard from either of them. Anthony, because police took him into temporary custody while searching for evidence of his guilt.

S
Nicholas, because he's an eel.

LILY-ANN
Hamilton?

HAMILTON
I have no opinion of Nicholas's eelish-ness. However, I do know that we have no idea how eels reproduce, which is an odd blank spot—

LILY-ANN
I meant, why don't you share what you learned?

HAMILTON
Oh! Right. My turn. Okay, um, first I should thank Lily-Ann for helping declutter the living room. Err, well then . . .

(This is HAMILTON'S time to shine, so he emphasizes his presentation with images printed on flimsy paper. The first one is a picture of what looks like Robin Hood.)

HAMILTON
I am friendly with a local police officer. We play <u>Realm of
Rangers</u> together. That's the online multiplayer game I
told you about, Mrs B. I'm the leader of our guild. Well,
the co-leader, along with—

OCEAN
That's how you know a cop?

HAMILTON
Yes. Correct. I've known him for several years. He's in
the guild, of which I'm the co-leader, as I said. And I paid
him for information about the case.

(Everyone ad-libs various levels of surprise, other
than MRS B, who smiles proudly.)

S
You bribed a cop?

LILY-ANN
How much did that cost?

(HAMILTON shows a picture of a fantasy bow.)

HAMILTON
Gold coins, mithril ingots, and this – a Banshee's
Crossbow.

S
Wait. You bribed a cop with in-game currency?

HAMILTON
And a Banshee's Crossbow is worth more than gold. Err,

have you heard of online crime clubs? They research cold cases and mysteries. I told my friend that I'm starting one, so he slipped me a little, as he says, tea.

OCEAN
That means gossip, Mrs B.

MRS. B
Oh! Because one gossips over tea? Well, I like that very much! Is there such a thing as 'crumpets'? Because one can gossip over them, as well. Though I'm not entirely sure what they are. Muffins? Biscuits? I think we're drifting from the point. What were you saying, Hamilton? Oh! An online crime club. Can you imagine?

OCEAN
Yeah, what kind of delusional idiots would think they could solve a crime?

HAMILTON
Well, in any case . . . er, so to speak. Any *case*? Ha! No? Um, so the victim, James Dedrick, was struck once on the head by a blunt instrument. He staggered into the bushes after the blow, where he died almost immediately. He lives – lived – in Altadena, which means 'high money' in Italian but 'high fever' in Maltese.

OCEAN
It means 'upper 'Dena,' as in upper Pasadena.

HAMILTON
I didn't know you spoke Maltese.

MRS. B
Ocean is a woman of many talents. What else did
your officer friend pass along for your online detective
club?

HAMILTON
Dedrick is a real estate investor. He came to town
looking for real estate investments. There is dashboard
footage that shows him entering the Marigold Cottages.
The clip is blurry, and he's mostly out of frame, but he's
alone, and, um, intentional. That is, I mean, he's not
lost or anything. And so . . .

  (HAMILTON reveals three sheets of paper, one at a
     time, each with a single sentence.)

HAMILTON
He came alone. / Nobody followed him. / The murderer
was already at the Cottages.

S
Holy fuck! Sorry, Mrs B. The murderer was already here?
Why? Who was already here except, y'know, us?

LILY-ANN
Anthony fits.

MRS. B
Except Anthony is innocent.

LILY-ANN
Did the cop tell you anything about his history?

HAMILTON
Only that he was in prison for about five years for a violent
crime. Um, assault I guess. Some kind of bar fight.

OCEAN
Charming.

MRS. B
People change.

LILY-ANN
Do they?

MRS. B
All the time. We can't help it. That's not merely the human
condition, it's the greatest delight of getting old – watching
people discover themselves, over and over again.

HAMILTON
And that's about all, so far. Um, James Dedrick lived
alone. Spent the evening downtown, at various bars or,
um, hot spots. There was nothing of note on his phone.
Given the cash in his wallet, they don't think this was a
mugging gone wrong.

S
There's no link to Anthony?

HAMILTON
Not that I know of. So where does that leave us?

OCEAN
Sitting around drinking milk.

LILY-ANN
There's no <u>acknowledged</u> link to any resident, but we haven't asked Anthony or Nicholas yet. Talking to them is the next step.

MRS. B
Oh, that police detective did promise I could visit. I've never been to a jail. Do you think they'll . . . What's the phrase? Pat me down?

OCEAN
I'll handle that.

LILY-ANN
Can you also talk to Nicholas? I have a different item to check off the list.

MRS. B
S can do it. S is definitely the right person for Nicholas.

Why me? I was definitely not '*definitely* the right person.' Obviously Lily-Ann would be better at getting information from Nicholas. Though Lily-Ann had her mysterious 'different item,' and for once I guess I didn't mind being put on the spot. Because I couldn't believe Nicholas hadn't shown up, if only to be polite to Mrs B. She really seemed to like him, and he acted like a jerk.

So yeah, I'd talk to him. If I got lucky, I might even discover the clue that proved he was the murderer.

Not that I cared much about the crime. *Nobody* cared much about the crime.

I cared about the inspiration for a play.

Lily-Ann cared about tidying a messy problem.

Mrs B cared about Anthony.

Ocean cared about Mrs B.

Hamilton cared about having visitors.

Maybe the cops cared about the crime? That made sense. It was their job, after all.

26

VERNON

Most states granted police the power to detain citizens for seventy-two hours before the prosecutors needed to charge or release them. However, California, in all its hippie glory, chopped that down to a scant forty-eight hours.

Fortunately, even in California, the police weren't held responsible for 'reasonable misjudgments of the law.' So if a detective sergeant detained a suspect for forty-eight hours and then 'accidentally' detained him for *another* forty-eight hours?

No harm, no foul.

And a guy like Anthony Lambert understood that. He didn't waste everyone's time yapping about his legal rights.

Vernon cared about rights. Of course he did. He cared as much as a dentist or a plumber did – and just like them, he still didn't want that shit interfering with his personal workday. You filled cavities, you fixed toilets, you arrested criminals. What kept you engaged was working alongside people who supported you, who shared your values.

Other than that? You did the job, then you went home.

So that's what Vernon did.

27

LILY-ANN

Lily-Ann didn't consider herself a facile liar – in fact, she had trouble *not* telling the truth – but she knew that sometimes lies came quickly to people's lips. And a bloody corpse was enough to make even an innocent person shade the truth. So perhaps no one living in the Marigold Cottages did know the dead guy, James Dedrick.

Yet perhaps they did. That remained a possibility, but not the only one.

Fortunately, while Lily-Ann struggled with lying, omissions came more easily. For example, at the meeting at Hamilton's place, she hadn't mentioned the third man who needed speaking with. Sophie would take care of Nicholas, while Ocean would visit Anthony.

And Lily-Ann?

She'd investigate the other suspect . . . the man who had stalked Sophie.

She'd never heard his name, but Mrs B would know. She'd mentioned that he was living in town. Lily-Ann suspected that discussing him in the group meeting would distress Sophie, so she'd handle it quietly.

As she returned toward her cottage, she put pieces together in her mind. What if the stalker had discovered that Sophie lived nearby? What if he'd started stalking her again? Then James Dedrick caught him peeping in her window. They fought, and the stalker killed Dedrick.

Lily-Ann liked how well that fit together. Now she just needed to establish if it was possible. Which was a good, straightforward task. However, despite the satisfying neatness of that scenario, she gave a shiver when she thought about a stalker in the bushes. Anyone could slip onto the property from the street.

The shadows around her cottage suddenly looked thicker, and more ominous.

Her heart started pounding. She walked faster to her door. Her key slid smoothly into the lock, and turned just as smoothly.

Then she was inside, with the door closed behind her.

'Well,' she said aloud.

She didn't consider herself highly imaginative, but apparently the murder had affected her more than she'd expected.

After a glass of water, she started her calming nightly routine as she let the discussions at the meeting sift through her mind. She took a moment to gaze with pleasure at the luxe beauty products on her bathroom counter. She knew drugstore products were equally effective, but the expensive packaging and scents gave her joy. That's what Piotr had never understood about her. She wasn't being 'taken advantage of' by working on weekends; she was doing what she enjoyed.

Extra work, tidying Sophie's bathroom, solving a crime . . .

As she used Caudalie Vinoclean Micellar Cleansing Water to remove her makeup, she acknowledged that her prime suspect – quite tediously – was Anthony. The police did this professionally, and logic often required deferring to the expertise of professionals. Also, the circumstantial evidence pointed to Anthony: he lived in the Cottages, and had a history of violence and asymmetrical tattoos.

The only puzzle was, why did Mrs B refuse to believe his guilt? Simply because she preferred to see the best in everyone? Or was there something more?

On the other hand, Anthony wasn't the only person who lived in the Cottages.

What about Hamilton? He had the perfect alibi, as someone who never left his house. But was it *too* perfect? She knew he ventured out once or twice per year, for things like emergency medical treatment or termite tenting. So he *could* leave.

Lily-Ann applied her antiaging serum and switched her thoughts to Ocean. She was short, but she was strong. She taught clay sculpture and stone carving. She probably had carving tools that could cave in a man's head.

She wasn't the type to lose her temper, but she'd kill for her kids. No question. Maybe even for Mrs B. Of course, if Ocean had killed Dedrick, she would've admitted she'd done it. Hmm. Though *would* she have? Not if it meant breaking up her family.

And she'd been gone part of that night, ostensibly on a date.

What about the kids themselves? Riley was tall enough, but Lily-Ann put her into the category with Miles and Mrs B as 'highly unlikely.'

Though Ocean had mentioned that Riley had been acting up even more than usual. Probably just teen drama.

Nicholas, on the other hand, was a strong possibility. Lily-Ann opened her Tata Harper night cream and inhaled the dreamy scent. Delicious. Okay, Nicholas. She didn't know anything about him, except that he didn't interact with the other residents, worked for the city, and had a private entrance. Which meant his whereabouts – and his entire life, really – were far less discernable than those of any other tenant.

Which left Sophie. That nervous, wounded girl. High-strung enough to kill? Perhaps, if combined with her drinking. Plus, she'd found the body. Still, Lily-Ann didn't think she'd faked her shocky reaction to the corpse. Though what if she'd been shocky because of what she'd done?

No. Cross Sophie off the list. If she'd killed a man, the first thing she would've done was apologize. That would've been the second and third thing, too. In fact, she wouldn't have stopped apologizing yet.

Which meant that Lily-Ann still needed to address the question of Sophie's stalker. She'd get his name from Mrs B.

She climbed into bed, making lists in her head. Something nagged at her. Something she'd overlooked. For a moment, she wondered if it was just an echo of that sudden fear she'd felt while returning home.

Then she thought perhaps she'd subconsciously discovered a clue.

But finally she realized what she'd missed. If she was considering all the residents' motives for murder, she needed to include herself. Of course, she hadn't killed the man, but ignoring the possibility would render the data unfinished.

So: Lily-Ann Novak. What if she'd killed Dedrick in a fugue state? She was cold enough to murder. She was strong enough, and wouldn't panic. God knew she'd remove any evidence with utmost efficiency. She hadn't killed him, of course. But what if she had?

28

HAMILTON

Even after the guests left, Hamilton's house smelled of other people. The scent of strange soaps swirled in the air. Perfume and shampoo, conditioner and lotion.

He crossed to the window and gazed through the blinds at the quiet courtyard. Sleepy now, after the hubbub of the day. When he caught a glimpse of his face in the window, he smiled. That wasn't his usual reaction to his reflection, but he couldn't help feeling a certain lightness when he remembered the gasps of incredulity and admiration about him 'bribing' a cop.

He liked his neighbors. He liked hosting them, and texting them. He liked watching them in the courtyard. Not in a creepy way! Just in a normal, neighborly way.

Sophie worried him, though. He regretted that she'd been the one to find the body. Of all of them, she seemed the least able to cope with that sort of ugliness.

He wished things had turned out differently. Though at least Ocean's kids hadn't seen the corpse. That would've been worse.

He turned from the window, no longer smiling. If they got lucky, Lily-Ann would discover the next body. Not that Hamilton expected another homicide. Of course not. Still, if the killer did strike again, he didn't think Lily-Ann would mind. And in truth, he wouldn't, either. One murder was a tragedy, but two were a pattern.

29

OCEAN

Ocean still felt a pang every time Miles headed off in the morning, walking to school without her. She'd watch his little wave goodbye before he tilted forward to balance his backpack like a mime fighting a headwind.

She'd walked with him for years, talking about little kid nonsense: Pokémon and Batman and video games. Until, precisely on schedule for his psychological development, Miles had announced that he'd start walking himself.

Sometimes Ocean hated that development schedule. She missed wearing a baby sling, sitting at the edge of sandboxes, admiring his LEGO figurines, holding his tiny hand.

At least she was spending her morning travel time with Riley now. A month into her freshman year, Riley had declared that only losers rode the city bus to high school. The cool kids had friends old enough to drive them. However, having failed to secure a junior or senior friend, Riley had tragically resorted to asking Ocean to bring her.

Ocean treasured those ten minutes together every school day. Just the two of them. She adored her sullen child, this upgraded reflection of her own childhood self. They mostly rode in silence, but at least Riley mumbled, 'You, too,' before she walked away.

Except this morning, as Ocean paused for construction on Garden Street, a thought struck her. Riley spent a lot of time in her room, checking TikTok and gazing out her window. So maybe she'd seen something important without realizing it.

'Did you ever see Anthony before he moved in?' she asked.

'Huh?'

'On the street or—anywhere? Like, I know Mrs B saw him at the bus stop.'

Riley flipped her hair in the way Ocean had noticed her practicing in the bathroom mirror. 'Nah. I'd remember. He's kind of hot.'

Ocean shot her daughter a look. 'He is?'

'Audrey says he looks like if you put Post Malone and Vin Diesel in a blender.'

'You sent your friends pictures of him?'

'No, snaps.'

'Right, snapshots.'

A long-suffering sigh. 'No, Mother. I sent my friends Snapchats of him. Why do you care about him, anyway?'

'I like him. Even if he would make a disgusting celebrity smoothie. And . . .' Ocean paused before telling the truth. 'I keep wondering if he's got some connection to Mrs B.'

'Oooh!' Riley almost smiled at her. 'What if he's her long-lost son? Like she put him up for adoption back in the day.'

'Mrs B could never carry pregnancy to term.'

'Yeah, because she had a teen birth that went bad.'

Ocean carefully didn't laugh at her. 'You think Anthony is like sixteen years younger than Mrs B?'

'You old people all look alike,' Riley said.

'Which means *I'm* kind of hot, too!'

Riley made a retching sound as Ocean pulled to the curb outside the high school.

'I like you thinking out of the box, though. Long-lost

son is good. Don't forget to ask about your swim dues.'

'I won't.'

When Riley opened the door to leave, Ocean almost asked what was wrong. Because Riley had been on edge for days now. Distracted and prickly and maybe even a little guilty. And she *should've* asked. But they were getting along for once, and she didn't want to ruin the mood.

So she took the coward's way out and just said, 'Love you.'

'You, too,' Riley said, and swaggered away.

Ocean watched until a horn honked behind her, then she waved an apology and drove off.

She'd talk to Riley later.

Next stop, City College. Her supplier had delivered two tons of stone to the wrong department. Mostly alabaster, for the beginning stone sculpture class, but also some of the travertine and marble. Which meant she needed to ask the physical plant guys to help her move it. Fortunately, they all liked her and her crappy Spanish. She always got along with workmen. It was the butchest thing about her. Together, she and the guys lugged the stone onto the cart, then unloaded it at the sculpture yard, a fenced area with a few half-enclosed stalls.

After she finished, she collapsed on a bench that overlooked the harbor and Leadbetter Beach, the bike path, and the maritime museum. City College had the most spectacular views. Great school, too. Instead of worrying about the kids' eventual college, Ocean watched kite surfers sailing across the waves, and wondered what colors she'd use for the sails. Magenta and cadmium green? She thought about that . . . until she found herself thinking about the murder.

She managed not to wonder what colors she'd mix to match the exact shade of the victim's blood, and called Mrs B.

'Where did you meet Anthony?'

'And hello to you, my dear,' Mrs B said.

'I'm waiting.'

'As I mentioned, Ocean. I first met him at the bus stop.'

'What aren't you telling me?'

'He was kind.'

Ocean frowned as sea urchin divers unloaded their haul on the dock far below. 'Have I ever told you you're like a sea urchin?'

'I presume you mean prickly and difficult, my dear, but sea urchins aren't even kosher.'

'Difficult yes, but you're not *dumb*,' Ocean continued. 'Which means there's a reason you're so sure Anthony's innocent. Which means what? That you saw something? Yeah, you saw something.'

'I did?'

'At least . . .' Ocean stood from the bench as the realization struck her. 'Oh! Listen. At least you *think* you saw something, but with your cataracts, you're not sure. Right? Right. You're not sure what you saw, but you're protecting someone, anyway.' She started to pace. 'Yeah, that sounds exactly like you.'

'In that case, I must say that I sound quite wonderful.'

Ocean huffed. 'Wonderful, but annoying. What are you keeping from me?'

'I do like your little story, dear, but there really is

nothing to tell. Except I find myself thinking . . .'

'What?'

'Well, what if the assailant didn't intend to kill him? People are essentially good, don't you think?'

Ocean stopped pacing. 'Didn't mean to kill *him*.'

'I'm just a blind old bat, but yes, that's most likely, I think. Oh, that's Hamilton's milk delivery, I'd better go.'

'No, wait—' Ocean said, before the connection dropped.

Mrs B prided herself on being terrible with technology, but she was pretty quick to hang up her cell phone when she didn't want to talk.

Ocean watched the sunlight on the velatura waves beyond the harbor, and thought about the attacker. Had they meant to kill someone else? Either that's what Mrs B had seen, or what she'd concluded. That in the dark, late at night, the attacker had whacked some random guy on the head, instead of their intended target.

So the target must've been someone who lived in the Marigold Cottages, but who? And would the killer try again?

30

SOPHIE

'Yes, Mom, I'm sure,' I groused into my phone, hunched over my table in the Public Market.

I was treating myself to twenty-dollar Bangkok street noodles for lunch. What could I say? I still hadn't gotten over finding a corpse outside my window and I needed the solace of the bougie food market. Except now I was

119

talking to my mother within eavesdropping distance of the lines for the falafel place, which wasn't exactly relaxing.

'If we leave now,' she said, 'we'll be there by seven. Your father is packing the car.'

'I'm fine! I promise. Tell Dad to stop. They already arrested the guy.'

'The ex-con who lives across the courtyard from you?'

I never should've told her about Anthony. She just had a way of pulling information out of me so she could make me feel bad about it later.

'Mrs B—' I started, then almost said, *Is sure he's innocent.* '— is taking care of everything, don't worry.'

'I'm going to call that . . . what's her name? Ocean.'

'Don't you dare, Mom,' I snapped, before smiling apologetically at the people in line who'd overheard. 'I'm fine, I promise.'

'A dead body!'

'I didn't even see him,' I lied. 'Lily-Ann found him.'

'Still, you know how you get in a . . . crisis.'

'I know how I *used* to get. That was years ago. I'm different now.' I tried to infuse my voice with conviction. 'I'm so much better.'

My mother sniffed her disbelief. 'Still no boyfriend? All those actors you work with. You'd feel so much safer with a man around.'

'Or I could get a Rottweiler,' I muttered.

'Hmm?'

'Nothing.'

'And this man, he's already arrested?'

'I watched them lead him away in handcuffs. If anything, the Marigold Cottages are safer than ever. What're the chances that something like this would happen twice in the same place?'

'Sophie,' my mother tsked.

'I've got to go, Mom. *Do not drive down.*'

Five minutes later, when I finally managed to end the call, I actually felt a little better. I often felt better after I scolded Mom for being too worried about my safety. There was probably an obvious psychoanalytical lesson there, but I wasn't about to delve into my neuroses.

Still, maybe I'd give the 'S' character in my play anxious parents. Never seen, only heard via telephone calls broadcast as the Voice of God from above.

As I finished my noodles, I worried about the play's structure. With the perpetrator arrested so soon, there was no tension. On the other hand, I wasn't writing a thriller. So maybe the dramatic momentum continued as long as the amateur investigation continued?

Yeah, that could work. Even if – or maybe *especially* if – the tenants had no chance of solving anything. Which obviously we didn't. I mean, the police already had Anthony in custody, just like I'd told Mom.

Except I didn't really trust the police. They hadn't listened to me when I'd gone to them about What Happened Before. Not the first time. Or the second time. Or they'd listened, but they hadn't helped. They hadn't done a thing.

Of course, this was different. This was an actual murder. That had to be their highest priority, right? I thought about that as I wrapped up my leftovers, then my phone dinged.

A blur of messages on the Marigold Cottages Murder Collective chat.

* * *

Ocean
I think Mrs B saw something

Ocean
But she's not sure what

Hamilton
What?

Hamilton
Oh, she's not sure

Ocean
Enough to convince her that Anthony is innocent

Hamilton
Crime witnesses over the age of seventy tend to be more susceptible to memory distortion caused by ambiguous post-event information.

Lily-Ann
Let Ocean finish.

Ocean
Her vision isn't great. Especially at night. She won't say more.

Ocean
She's afraid of pointing the finger at the wrong person

Ocean
I think. She told me two things

Ocean
One. Anthony isn't guilty

Ocean
Two. James Dedrick wasn't the target

Ocean
Which means someone else was

Ocean
Ok I'm done

Hamilton
So you think the killer meant to kill one of US?

Ocean
Not you. You don't leave the house.

Lily-Ann
Has anyone followed up on our tasks since the meeting,
as agreed?

Sophie
Not me not yet

Lily-Ann
I haven't either.

Ocean
I'm meeting Anthony tomorrow in jail

Hamilton
I'm collecting public information online. About the crime
and victim. There isn't much. Still looking.

Sophie
If this were a play, there'd be a secret in Mrs B's past

Ocean
Her secrets are all victimless

Hamilton
Who'd kill one of us?

Lily-Ann
Friends, family, spouses, exes. Business partners. I have a spouse, Ocean has an ex. We all have co-workers.

Ocean
Maybe your game guild has it out for you Hamilton.

Sophie
So our theory is that someone killed Dedrick while thinking he was someone else?

Sophie
Would Piotr confuse James Dedrick for you?

Lily-Ann
On a dark night, after a few drinks?

Lily-Ann
Never. I presume the same is true of Ocean's ex.

Ocean
My ex is too lazy to kill me, and she lives in Prague. And if she killed me, she'd have to raise our children

Ocean
We can rule her out

Hamilton
Prague is home to the largest castle in the world. Eighteen acres.

Sophie
The actual target must look a little like Dedrick. So Hamilton or Nicholas. Or a visitor

Ocean
Piotr visits

Lily-Ann
We need to follow through on the original suspects.

Ocean
What if Anthony was the target? An old inmate with a grudge? I'll ask him tomorrow

Hamilton
I'll keep researching

Sophie
I'll talk to Nicholas. He's just so damn slippery

Sophie
Like an eel with a pretty face

Nicholas
. . .

'Well,' I said aloud at my table. 'Shit.'

31

LILY-ANN

Lily-Ann baked the spanakopita for five minutes longer and at twenty-five degrees hotter than the package instructed. She enjoyed shopping at Trader Joe's, even though Piotr mocked her for her 'basic bitch' taste. He thought she didn't appreciate the better things in life, but she'd never quite understood his distinction between 'better things' and 'things you enjoyed.'

He'd rather pay more and enjoy less than do the opposite.

She took the spanakopita from the oven. Golden perfection. Molten hot, too. She texted Hamilton, then slid the spanakopita onto a ceramic tray and left her house.

Halfway across the courtyard, she noticed the flowers. Splashes of violet and magenta carefully placed on the ground beneath the eaves, waiting to be planted. Velvety petals trembled in the breeze. She paused for a moment, admiring how balanced the composition was: the same number of plants waited on each side of the yard.

When she approached Hamilton's cottage, he opened the door before she knocked.

'Is that . . . ?' he asked.

'Spanakopita.'

'I love Greek food.' He stepped backward to let her in. 'Tzatziki!'

'It's too big to not share,' she told him. 'I hope you haven't had dinner yet.'

'No. No, I'm a grazer. I graze. But I'd love, I'd like, I'm

happy to—' He smiled, flustered. 'Here, won't you join me in the kitchen?'

He moved a stack of books off the kitchen table, then set two places and poured two glasses of milk.

'Wait, I should've asked.' His eyebrows drew together. 'Do you prefer buttermilk?'

'No.'

'Yeah, it's more of a morning drink.'

She served the spanakopita, then took her seat. 'Have you heard the name Neal Hesse?'

'Not that I recall, no.'

'He's the man who stalked Sophie in college. I got his name from Mrs B.'

Hamilton frowned as he forked a wedge of spanakopita. 'I'd heard that something happened, but not what, exactly.'

'He terrorized her for two months. He followed her. He'd appear at random, beside her on a sidewalk, at the next table in a restaurant. He liked to stand outside her window at night. Any time she let her guard down, he was there. He built . . . well, he called them "fairy houses". Little constructions of twigs and coins and bullet casings, paper clips and flowers, and condom wrappers. He left them where she'd stumble across them.'

'Like a . . . a menacing bowerbird,' Hamilton said.

'Items went missing from her bedroom,' Lily-Ann said. 'Then her cat disappeared.'

'Fucking hell,' he said.

'Yes.'

He took a slug of milk. 'So you think this Neal Hesse guy . . . what?'

'I don't know, but he's linked to the Marigold Cottages.

Maybe he was stalking Sophie again. Then Dedrick spotted him in the bushes and confronted him. We need to rule him out along with Anthony. They're the only two suspects with a criminal history.'

Hamilton blinked at her. 'Anthony's not a killer. He helped with my hummingbird feeders.'

'I'm not sure those are mutually exclusive.'

'No, I mean . . . I looked into Anthony, a little. He's been in and out of trouble since his teens. First arrest was because he bumped into a guy in a bar and spilled his beer. The guy swung at him and Anthony, um, took offense.'

'I see.'

'That was simple assault. With the aggravated charge, these two guys didn't like his hat.'

'Let me guess. He took offense?'

'Yeah, but nothing happened until they catcalled some girls, which apparently was the excuse Anthony needed.'

'That is almost incomprehensibly stupid.' Lily-Ann considered Anthony's tattoos. 'Though also, believable.'

'Yeah, but he was a kid back then, is my point. He's not a kid anymore.'

'So he's matured? Perhaps. However, the reason I'm here is that apparently Neal Hesse lives in town.'

'He lives *here*? Sophie's stalker?'

'Apparently. I need you to find his address and whatever else is available.'

'Okay, will do.' He pronged another wedge of spanakopita. 'I mean, do you really think we can find out who killed Dedrick?'

'I'm not sure. I have trouble letting things go, though.

And if it eases Mrs B's mind, that gives me an excuse to keep digging.'

32

OCEAN

There is no expectation of privacy in a jail facility.
Social visits may be monitored or recorded.
Visitors may bring in one car key and if with infant –
one diaper, a reasonable amount of wipes and one
pre-mixed formula/white milk bottle per infant.
Any device capable of audio, video, or photography
recording and/or cell phone communications
WILL NOT BE PERMITTED.
If a visitor is late, disruptive, or dressed inappropriately,
the visit will be canceled. Missing or canceling a
scheduled visit counts as having a visit.

Well, good thing Ocean hadn't let Mrs B send her with the fresh-baked chocolate chip cookies. Or dressed inappropriately. She usually wore Carhartt pants and button-downs, though she'd recently unearthed her little black dress. Trying to get out there again, finding women on the apps, then meeting them downtown for low-stakes dates.

That's where she'd been the night of the murder. She'd told Riley she was in charge that evening, then she'd returned home depressingly early. The whole thing made her feel old. A different generation. She didn't even know if the same jokes applied: What do lesbians do on a second date? Move in together.

Not anymore, apparently. Or maybe it was just her.

Anyway, for visiting the county jail, she'd added a black blazer. She had no metal and no infants. She stood in the line with the other women and watched the mean cops treat them like dirt and the nice ones treat them like children.

Ocean kept a leash on her temper, because she wasn't her parents. She smiled tightly, then sat in the chair until Anthony arrived. To her surprise, there wasn't a divider or a little telephone thing. He just took a seat across from her in the crowded, echoing room.

She halfway expected him to remain silent, but to her surprise he spoke first.

'You dressed up,' he said.

'Only the best for you.'

He showed her his unsmiling smile.

'So this guy I barely know convinced one of my favorite people in the world that he didn't commit a murder.' Ocean took a breath. 'Mrs B is . . . upset.'

'I'm sorry,' he said.

'Are you innocent?'

He started to speak, then didn't, and she remembered that warning to visitors about not expecting privacy here. She remembered, and didn't care. 'Did you kill James Dedrick?'

'No,' he said.

'Did you know him?'

'No.'

'You never met him before?'

'Not that I remember.'

'You have one friend, Anthony, and she's a batty old woman. Help her help you.'

'Only one, huh?'

'Can you think of a second?' she asked, making it clear that he couldn't count on her, that she was only here for Mrs B.

'I knew this guy upstate,' Anthony told her. 'He used to say, every Friday, he'd say, "TGIF!", like, y'know, the day of the week made a difference inside. He'd moan about Mondays, he called Wednesday "hump day," like we just needed to get through to the weekend. So we called him "TG." He's a friend. He taught me how to mark time.'

Ocean couldn't help herself; she was interested. 'So he was a good influence?'

'Not really.' Anthony's gaze turned fond and distant. 'TG never met a lesson he couldn't refuse to learn. But he was a friend. We got our tats together and . . . well, he's out now. Having a long weekend down on the Ventura Pier. At least I hope so. That's all he ever talked about, fishing off that pier.'

'You don't keep in touch?'

'Condition of his parole. I'm what's called a known associate.'

'So you're back down to one friend. Are you sure you don't know Dedrick?'

'Not unless he came to the Sidecar when I was working the door.'

'Oh, right. You were a bouncer.'

'Yeah, that's where . . .'

'That's where what?'

He looked at the table instead of answering.

'Fuck you, Anthony. You want to break that old lady's heart? She sees something in you, god knows why. Talk to me. Have you talked to anyone in the past two days?'

Anthony's smile turned unfriendly. 'Guy in my cell won't shut up. He's just a kid but damn. For hours on end. So scared he can't stop babbling. And his name, I shit you not, is Talking.'

'"Talking"?'

'Talken, ends with *E-N*, but still.'

'Funny, but you're avoiding telling me what happened at the Sidecar.'

'I'm trying to. You're such a . . .' He groped for the right word, and Ocean braced herself. '. . . mother. You've got that glare.'

Ocean didn't speak.

'Okay. So. I worked the door at the Sidecar for almost a year. Every couple weeks, Sophie shows up with those friends of hers. If you want to call them that. Most of the time – every time – she ended up blackout drunk. And she, uh, she's got that appeal, you know?'

'Young and pretty and drunk.'

'More than that. There are men who, when they see something fragile and beautiful, they want to protect it.' He shrugged one of his meaty shoulders. 'And there are men who want to break it.'

That sounded perilously close to victim-blaming, but this wasn't the time.

'One night after my shift,' he continued, 'I found Sophie, three blocks away. Passed out in the bushes.'

'Oh, shit,' Ocean said.

'No, no. Nobody'd touched her. Nobody'd even *saw*

132

her yet, but . . .' He shrugged again. 'I tried to wake her up. I didn't know what to do. Can you see me pulling Sophie out of a bush and carrying her off like a . . . a snack I'm going to enjoy later?'

'Not a good look,' Ocean agreed.

'But I couldn't just leave her there. So I found her address in her wallet and brought her home.'

'Mrs B saw you?'

'I didn't realize at first, but yeah.'

'That's why she trusts you.'

'Yeah.'

'She saw you carry the young, drunk girl home to keep her safe. And for her, that was enough.'

He grunted. 'Like bad people never do good things.'

'Which one are you, Anthony?'

'I'm trying. God as my witness, I'm trying.' He fell silent, frowning at the wall. 'When she's drunk, she's not just fragile and beautiful. She's . . . fearless.'

'Sophie?' Ocean asked. 'Fearless?'

'Yeah. I know, but yeah.'

'And that's why you helped her?'

'No. I don't know. I guess I wasn't thinking who *she* was. I was thinking, 'Who do *I* want to be?''

Ocean exhaled. 'Okay, that answers that. Why she trusts you. What about the blood on your shirt?'

'I broke a glass washing dishes at work. They've got witnesses to that.'

'Then why did they charge you?' she asked. 'They've got nothing.'

'I'm not charged. Just detained.'

'For three days? That's not even legal.'

Humor glimmered in his eyes. 'Legal maybe isn't as cut-and-dried as you think.'

'Are you mocking me?'

'Yeah, but nicely.'

She grunted, ignoring the urge to flare up against injustice like her parents would've. Wouldn't do any good, other than to attract attention to herself. She used to accuse her folks of loving attention more than they hated injustice. If they were still in town, they'd be picketing the jail by now.

'You have any enemies?' she asked.

'No.'

'C'mon, you don't have any . . . I don't know, prison grudges? Criminal, uh, vendettas?'

'No.'

'No gang stuff? No drug stuff? Nothing?'

'Nothing at all. That's my goal: nothing. That's why I started working in the kitchen. There was too much *something* at the door.'

'Fine. Then do you know anything about the murder?'

'No.'

'Okay. So why'd you come back? To the Cottages? After you dropped Sophie off that first time?'

'You mean sitting at the bus stop? I thought I should tell Sophie what happened. And, I don't know, tell her to stop drinking. And get better friends. Some kind of scared-straight bullshit? I don't know. But I couldn't find the words.'

'Instead Mrs B found you.'

'Yeah.'

'She never told Sophie, either?'

'Nah. She said Sophie is fragile. She said that hearing

that some guy – me – that I carried her home might send Sophie spiraling.'

Ocean rolled her eyes. 'She's such an interfering, infantilizing old woman.'

'She just didn't want to hurt her.'

'Yet she still pisses me off. Meddlesome old bat.' She took a breath. 'If you hurt her, I swear I'll . . . be very upset.'

He didn't speak, but his eyes understood.

'And if you don't?' she said. 'You might end up with one and a half friends.'

33

NICHOLAS

Nicholas was sitting at the breakfast table browsing murder statistics when he heard a thump at his front door. An hour earlier he'd decided, given the recent events, that he should know more about local crime. So he'd been scrolling through stories of previous murders in Santa Barbara. Most were gang- or family-related, and they struck him as sadder, somehow, than the death of James Dedrick.

Maybe because he didn't care that Dedrick was dead.

At the thump, Nicholas looked toward the front door but he didn't stand – not until he heard a scratching. Like fingernails scraping against the wood.

Then he scrambled into the foyer and threw the door open and found Mrs Bakofsky standing outside. She looked feeble and wilted. Her shoulders were slumped and her head bobbled, and he felt a spike of alarm when she blinked at him with watery, uncertain eyes.

'A . . . a glass of water?' she asked.

'Oh, god, of course.' He took her elbow and bundled her inside. 'Are you okay? What happened?'

'Just need to sit and . . .' She exhaled unsteadily. 'Have some water.'

He brought her into the kitchen and settled her on a chair. 'Should I call someone?' He grabbed at his phone. 'I'll call Ocean. Hold on one second, let me just—'

'Or coffee,' Mrs Bakofsky said, her voice suddenly strong. 'Since you already have some brewing. Three sugars, if you don't mind, and a little too much milk.'

He turned to find her sitting upright at the table, gazing at him with steady bemusement. Looking absolutely the opposite of feeble and wilted.

'What are you doing?' he demanded.

'Asking for a cup of coffee, Nicholas. Obviously.'

'What were you, pretending to have a stroke?'

'Of *course* I was pretending. How else could I convince you to let me in?'

He slumped into the chair opposite her. 'You almost gave me a heart attack.'

'That's so sweet of you to say.' She gave him an expectant look. 'Now, then . . . that coffee you offered?'

He shot her a look, but stood and fixed her a coffee with too much sugar and too much milk. 'You want me to warm it in the microwave?'

'Yes, please. I prefer my coffee fiery . . . like my men.'

'Uh-huh,' he said, instead of giving her the gratification of a real reaction. 'So what can I do for you?'

'I need a little favor.'

136

'Why?'

She tutted. 'No, my dear. The question you mean to ask is, "What?" And the answer is, "For Sophie."'

'That . . .' He shook his head and ignored the spark of curiosity. 'That's not an answer to "what?"'

'Well, I'm glad we agree!' Her expression turned somber. 'Have you heard what happened to Sophie in college?'

'She was stalked?'

'Mmm. Quite terrifyingly. He . . . the man's name is Neal Hesse. He tormented her, and I don't think that's putting it too strongly. Psychologically. And the favor is for her.'

The microwave dinged in the silence. Nicholas brought Mrs Bakofsky her coffee and sat down again and took a sip of his own, which tasted suddenly bitter.

'That's awful,' he said. 'But, uh, I don't know how to say this . . . I imagine the last thing Sophie wants is male attention.'

'I'm not asking you to date her, Nicholas. Sophie deserves better than to be one of the women you won't commit to.'

'Well, at least you're minding your own business.'

'I'm asking you to go on a very brief field trip. To the Mesa.'

'What?' he said. 'Why the Mesa?'

'That's where he lives. Neal Hesse. Hamilton found his address. And I'd like you to . . . have a look at him.'

'You want me to *look* at him?'

'I don't think it's too much to ask.'

'But . . . why?'

'I'm an old-fashioned woman, Nicholas. There's only so much one can learn secondhand. If you really want to know someone, you have to look them in the eye. However,

I'm not the best person to do that with Neal Hesse. A man closer to his own age is better.'

Nicholas pinched the bridge of his nose. 'So you want me to knock on his door, look him in the eye . . . and then what?'

'Get a sense of him.'

'You realize that this is . . .' He trailed off, not wanting to say *insane*. '. . . bizarre?'

'I realize that Sophie is in pain. And checking if this man is a threat to her may be important.'

Nicholas set his coffee aside. He was almost certain that this was another of Mrs Bakofsky's attempts to bring him and Sophie closer. She was a yenta; she couldn't help herself. But also, the idea that Sophie was in pain . . . bothered him. Like, he didn't care if she was flighty or anxious or whatever. But if she was in pain? No.

'Have you told her you're asking me?'

'Did I rub salt in her wound? Of course not.'

'How am I supposed to—'

'You work at the city planner's office. Knock on his door with your business card and talk to him about zoning or whatever it is you talk about.'

He thought for a second, then shook his head. 'No. This is insane. You expect me to go peek into his soul?'

Mrs B's gnarled hand grasped his across the table. 'Please.'

The Neighborhood on the Mesa was mostly tract homes and Teslas. Nicholas couldn't quite believe that contractors had once built cookie-cutter houses just blocks from the beach. This was a *literal* mesa, with the Thousand Steps stairway leading down to the ocean, and only fifty years ago the construction had still skewed middle-class.

A lost era.

Of course, given the real estate booms and busts over the last few decades, the houses had been upgraded one sale at a time. Now they boasted glossy stone walkways and new extensions, each one loudly individual yet with the same bones. He enjoyed the variety as he rolled along, looking for Neal Hesse's address.

'What the hell am I doing here?' he muttered when he found it.

He knew, though. He was paying Mrs Bakofsky back for a debt she didn't even know he owed. He knew that when she said 'please,' he'd do almost anything. That was one more reason to avoid her.

Though, yeah, he also wanted to look at this scumbag who'd tormented Sophie. Though in general he was a pretty chill guy, part of him wanted to do more than just look.

And what if Hesse was still stalking Sophie? What if that had put him on the property at the time of the murder? Mrs B had told him that Lily-Ann wondered if that made Hesse the murderer, but Nicholas wondered if it made him a witness.

He thought about that as he pulled to the curb.

'Okay, here goes,' he said to himself.

He grabbed a business card and clipboard, stepped out of his car, and looked at the sidewalk. The sidewalk looked okay. He rehearsed a stupid spiel about asking for homeowner feedback regarding zoning changes, then rang the bell.

A skinny blonde woman opened the door. She looked

surprised and defensive, so Nicholas quickly said, 'I'm from the planning office, doing an informal survey about lot size.'

A guy pushed past her to the door. 'Can I help you?'

The woman receded into the house and Nicholas considered the man. Lots of freckles. Tall, wearing bicycle shorts and one of those ugly nylon shirts with logos, like he'd just come back from a sponsored ride.

Still, the guy seemed pretty normal as Nicholas nattered on for a minute, talking absolute nonsense. 'Most of the lots on the Mesa are zoned R-1 or E-1, single family residential, though there's some DR and D-2, and I'm just, uh, taking a little stroll to get a . . . to get a sense of the neighborhood, and I didn't want to alarm anyone.'

The guy said, 'Walking on the sidewalk isn't that alarming.'

'True! True, but, um . . . so are you Neal Hesse?'

'I am.'

'Ah, good.' Nicholas had absolutely no idea what to say. He fluttered the pages on his clipboard. 'I guess my map is telling me the truth. So . . .'

'What, you want permission to come onto my yard?'

'Oh! Yes, exactly. Yes. Thank you!'

'Be my guest,' Neal Hesse said.

'Won't take long,' Nicholas assured him, then edged toward the side of the house, trying to look inquisitive.

What the hell was he doing? Playing *Mission: Impossible*? He felt ridiculous as he peered here and there, trying to crease his brow as if weighing serious zoning considerations. He was supposed to be evaluating Hesse, but he'd dropped that ball completely. Too nervous for critical thinking. So he just squinted at an orange tree, then the property line, then the side of the garage.

He wandered closer and peeked inside the window. Room for two cars and what must've been an unpermitted washer and dryer.

Then he caught a glimpse of an array of objects arranged in rows on a workbench. Hair scrunchies and blue-and-yellow pennants, those little college flags. A charm necklace dangled from a peg on the wall, with letter charms: an *X*, an *A*, and a *T*. Looked like a shrine to Mrs Hesse's college career.

Welp, it took all kinds. There was no sign of anything wrong, though. At least not that Nicholas could discern from his insane snooping.

So he'd just frown at the neighbor's yard and then take off.

Except when he took two steps, he heard a noise inside the garage. He backpedaled and caught sight of Hesse moving things around on the workbench. Tugging a tarp over the pennants and scrunchies.

He was hiding the college shrine. Why would he do that?

34

LILY-ANN

Some people thought that secrets gave you power, gave you tools to wield against other people. Some thought that secrets were shameful; if you were truly healthy, you wouldn't hide any part of yourself.

Lily-Ann didn't keep many secrets, but she found them tidy. Like pigeonhole compartments for things only she knew. And fortunately, one of those compartments held the key to Anthony's studio, which she'd kept after she'd finished cleaning.

The impulse to keep his key had surprised her. Was she truly finished with the job if she hadn't returned it? Yet another part of her, a less articulate part, had felt on some unthinking level that returning the key would've left larger issues unresolved.

She'd wondered what he was doing here. Who was he, and why had Mrs B rented to him?

So she'd kept the key. Entering his apartment without permission didn't bother her. True, she liked rules and parameters, but she'd never really cared about morality. That was Ocean's purview.

Morality struck her as too vague a concept to measure.

As Lily-Ann closed the studio door behind herself, she braced for the scent of microwaved meals and dirty laundry. Possibly cigarette smoke or a candy-smelling vape. There was no telling what horrors lurked in the home of a man with asymmetrical tattoos.

Yet the studio apartment was both impeccably clean and distressingly untidy.

The kitchen counters were spotless. The silverware drawer was well-organized, if sparse. The same with the food in the cabinets and fridge. Nothing from Trader Joe's, which was a pity. A bowl of bananas ornamented the white plastic dining area table, and the air smelled faintly of Pine-Sol.

In the bathroom, the toothpaste tube was capped. Lily-Ann noted the dental floss with approval. The medicine cabinet contained Band-Aids and ibuprofen.

Anthony's shaving gear was lined neatly on a shelf dedicated to shaving gear. No smudges or water deposits on the mirror.

She hadn't expected neatness from someone who'd tattooed absolute chaos on their skin. Perhaps he'd learned organization in prison. She'd have to ask, if she ever spoke with him again.

The untidiness, on the other hand, had clearly been caused by the police search. There was scattered mail. Open drawers. Cushions askew and clean laundry tossed on the floor. She looked for anything of interest. Such as bloodstains. Murder weapons. Signed confessions. Ciphers, secret doors, drug stashes.

Right. As if she was going to find a single clue. Well, no reason not to straighten along behind herself as she searched. She inspected the meager contents of the fridge again. Butter, eggs, bread. Cold cuts, carrots. Mustard and mayo. Nothing green, but she appreciated the organization.

Unlike the clutter on the fridge door beneath the recycling schedule magnet. Lily-Ann couldn't stand that kind of randomness. There was an out-of-focus picture of a woman holding a wine bottle aloft, a handful of postcards, and a faded photo of a young man with a pierced septum and a fishing rod.

She was folding Anthony's scattered shirts into the drawer when she heard a footfall behind her.

'What are you doing?' Ocean's daughter, Riley, asked from the door.

'Putting away laundry,' she said.

'But . . . *why*?'

Lily-Ann turned from the drawer. 'That's a big question. I suppose I'm trying to impose order on a chaotic universe.'

'You came here looking for clues, didn't you?'

'Nonsense! Whatever gave you that idea?'

Riley gave her a mischievous look. 'Because *I* came looking for clues.'

'Well, don't let me stop you. Just don't make a mess.'

'I won't,' Riley promised, then didn't move. 'I actually thought you were him. When I heard you moving around in here. But my mom is visiting him in jail.'

Lily-Ann nodded toward the picture hanging in the kitchen. 'Your mom painted that. *Two Sinks*.'

Riley squinted at it. 'She's so embarrassing.'

'I like it.'

'I like it, too, but she doesn't act like an adult. She acts like an artist. She's always *looking* at things.' Riley wrinkled her nose. 'I like your nails. What do you do?'

'Visit various manicurists, hoping to find one who is as neat as I'd like.' Lily-Ann examined her metallic taupe nails. 'No luck yet. I bring my own polish, of course.'

'No,' Riley said. 'I mean for a living.'

'Oh. I'm a proposal coordinator.'

'See? That's a career, not like 'artist.'' Riley shifted. 'I feel bad for him.'

'For Anthony?'

'Yeah. He's nice. Quiet, but nice.' She hunched her shoulders. 'I made fun of his tattoos to a friend of mine, which was mean.'

'That's not mean,' Lily-Ann said. 'It's the truth. His tattoos are horrible.'

'They are not!'

'The one on his face?'

Riley scowled. 'You shouldn't judge people on how they look! You know they only arrested him because he looks like that. It's not fair.'

'I'm not sure fairness matters,' Lily-Ann said, folding the last shirt and nestling it into the drawer.

'Fairness matters more than anything. Without fairness, nothing else even matters.'

'You take after your mother,' Lily-Ann said, and braced herself for a blast of denunciation.

But Riley just said, 'God, I *know*! It's so embarrassing.'

'Your mother cares about people – and doesn't give a shit what they think about her. That's pretty badass, Riley.'

'Ugh,' Riley said.

Lily-Ann began sorting the socks in silence, as Riley wandered around the room. Then Riley started replacing mail on the table, in not-quite-neat-enough stacks that Lily-Ann would fix later.

'Do you think he killed him?' Riley asked.

'I don't know.'

'I hope not.'

'Me, too.'

Riley tossed Lily-Ann a wayward white tube sock. 'I want to tell him that, y'know, someone's on his side? Because I guess, I think, probably no one's ever really been on his side before?' She flushed. 'Don't tell Mom I said that.'

'Of course not,' Lily-Ann said.

'Can you keep a secret?'

'Yes.'

'I wasn't inside that night,' Riley said. 'The night of the murder. Not all night.'

Once the dam broke, Riley admitted everything. Which surprised Lily-Ann, as she didn't consider herself a natural confidante. Still, she listened while Riley spoke and sniffled and wiped her eyes. Then Lily-Ann vowed she wouldn't repeat anything she'd heard.

Another secret for her pigeonhole compartment.

35

SOPHIE

So the first thing I did after Nicholas caught me calling him 'a slippery eel with a pretty face' was die. Then I went home, died a little more, and didn't contact him for two days.

I filled my time doing the last bits of organizing for Martini Night at the theatre. After months of work, it was finally happening this weekend. I was pretty proud of myself. It had been my idea to have a fundraising event for our production of *Martini with a Twist*, five one-act plays by the same playwright. One was about a college girl whose ability to smell lies kept her from making friends, which touched a nerve for some reason. Of course, another was about a severed head in a suitcase and I related to that one, too.

I was good at organizing fundraising events. It took a special skill to create a party that donors actually wanted to attend. I only wished that writing and directing came so easily. I'd love to direct people's interactions, give them dialogue, and approve their costumes. Instead, I chose cocktail napkins and finalized the liquor order.

And forced myself to text Nicholas.

Sophie
Can I ask you some questions?

Sophie
This is Sophie

Nicholas
Yes

Sophie
Did you know James Dedrick? Like, was he coming to visit you or something?

He didn't answer for forty minutes.

Nicholas
Meet for coffee?

Sophie
Oh! Sure. Okay. How about Capriccio? In an hour?

Nicholas
Sorry. Meant to send that to someone else.

'Prick,' I said.

Nicholas
OK. Capriccio in 1 hour

Sophie
Still me. Sophie!

Nicholas
I know

Sophie
Oh. Ok. See you there

And I did. I did see him there.

What happened was this. I hustled four blocks across State Street and reached the restaurant a little early. I felt out of breath and frazzled, so I checked my reflection in the window to see how bad I looked. I looked out of breath and frazzled, which didn't exactly surprise me. What surprised me was spotting Mrs B at a table just inside the restaurant.

Having lunch with a gentleman.

A gentleman with a bushy white beard. Mr Ybarra. Huh. Looked like he'd finally got the chance to romance her. He gestured with a breadstick like a baton, his cheeks even rosier than usual.

So I took a picture and sent it to the Marigold Cottages Murder Collective chat.

Sophie
Saucy lunch with Mrs B

Because they were having Italian. Saucy. Not my best, but not too bad off the cuff.

Ocean
We all need a little romance. Well, mostly me

Sophie
I might have you beat

Ocean
She looks unhappy, though

Ocean
Mrs B does

I peered through the window, checking Mrs B's expression. Ocean was right. She didn't look comfortable. Ybarra was doing all the talking, so maybe it really was a date, and he was monopolizing the conversation. Almost like he was a . . . man.

On the other hand, Mrs B could hold her own in any conversation. She wasn't exactly shy and retiring. But she looked genuinely ill at ease.

Sophie
Should I go in?

Ocean
Don't meddle

'Sheesh,' I grumbled. 'I was just asking.' And if Ocean were here, she definitely would've meddled.

When I looked away from my phone, I caught sight of Nicholas on the sidewalk, strolling toward me from the corner. He was kind of gorgeous in an army green dress shirt and black chinos, which counted as SoCal formal. He must've felt my gaze, because he suddenly raised his head from his phone and looked toward me.

He smiled in greeting, like a normal person, and then stopped short.

He stood there for a few seconds. No longer smiling.

Then he turned and walked away.

I texted the group chat.

Sophie
BTW Nicholas is a prick. A slippery eel prick

Nicholas
. . .

36

OCEAN

Ocean only got five steps past the mailboxes before she heard Mrs B's kitchen window opening.

'Nu?' Mrs B called. 'How is Anthony? Is he okay?'

'Come over for a coffee and I'll tell you.'

'I already made you one,' Mrs B said, lifting a glass to the window. 'Wait right there.'

Ocean didn't bother to wait. She opened Mrs B's front door and went to her kitchen doorway and watched her add ice to the instant coffee before pouring in too much condensed milk. Repulsive, but Ocean had liked it as a teenager, so Mrs B still made it for her.

'Oh!' Mrs B said, noticing her. 'You're here. We're going to Hamilton's.'

'I thought you wanted to know about Anthony.'

'You'll tell me on the way.'

'How was lunch?' Ocean asked.

Mrs B tilted her head. 'What does that mean?'

'At Capriccio with Ybarra.'

'Is nothing secret? Well, he asked me to lunch, is that so strange? So we had lunch. Yes, at Capriccio.'

'You didn't look happy.'

Mrs B drew a breath. 'You were *there*?'

'No, but nothing is secret. What's going on?'

'He's a little overbearing, that's all. You know how he talks.'

'Is he still pressuring you to sell?'

'Well, of course,' Mrs B said, with an uncharacteristically brittle smile. 'He's like a little boy with wooden blocks; he just wants to build build build.'

'Is he bothering you?'

'Of course not, dear.'

Ocean sipped her horrible coffee and followed Mrs B from her cottage toward Hamilton's. 'I'll talk to him if he's bothering you.'

'Don't be silly. It's just some new zoning thing.'

Ocean smiled a little hungrily. 'I'd *love* to talk to him.'

She didn't like Ybarra, his fake bonhomie and his stupid beard. She wasn't an aggressive person but she didn't shy away from confrontations when she felt they needed to happen.

'Don't bully poor Mr Ybarra,' Mrs B told her, with false cheer. 'How's Anthony?'

'He's fine. He's . . . used to it.'

'That might be the saddest thing I've ever heard.' Mrs B nodded to the front of Hamilton's cottage. 'Get the door, won't you? He left it open.'

The living room still looked surprisingly airy, but Hamilton was waiting for them in the more cluttered second bedroom that he'd turned into an office.

A computer with three monitors faced the doorway. Some kind of economic data scrolled on the two outer screens. Stock or rates or something. Ocean was barely financially savvy enough to have a money market account in addition to checking. She didn't know exactly what Hamilton did, other than consulting for financial advisors. Remotely, obviously.

He wasn't a hacker, despite the setup, but he knew his way around the internet.

'The key to productive searching is phrasing effective queries,' he told them when they entered, instead of a more traditional greeting such as Hello. 'Well, and having access to the paid databases. And, of course, playing a level thirty-two Meadowstrider.'

'That's a sort of ranger,' Mrs B explained to Ocean. 'From the *Ranger Realms*.'

'Okay,' she said.

'*Realm of Rangers*,' Hamilton corrected. 'The multiplayer game online.'

Mrs B peered over her coffee at Ocean. 'Hamilton is looking into Piotr for us.'

'Lily-Ann's ex?'

'They're still married,' Mrs B said, 'though I don't quite understand why.'

'What're you looking for?' Ocean asked Hamilton.

'Financial troubles,' he told her, making new incomprehensible windows pop up on his computer screen. 'Piotr's all over the place.'

'So he's out of money?'

'Hard to tell.' Another window flashed. 'These look

152

like infusions of investment cash.'

Ocean took another slug of syrupy coffee. 'So you think Piotr . . . what? That the dead guy—'

'Dedrick.'

'Yeah, Dead Rick. You think that he was involved with Piotr somehow?'

'We have no idea,' Mrs B said. 'But Hamilton is sending you the address.'

'Sent,' Hamilton said.

'Whose address?' Ocean asked, feeling her phone buzz in her blazer pocket. 'What?'

'Piotr's office, of course, dear,' Mrs B said, as if explaining a simple fact to a slow child. 'You're taking me to visit him tomorrow.'

37

VERNON

Civilians thought that the biggest hurdle in murder investigations was identifying the perpetrator.

Not so. Identifying the perpetrator was usually about as tough as finding an address. No, the biggest hurdle was building a prosecutable case. You didn't struggle to find the killer; you struggled to find actionable evidence.

That's how the system worked.

And despite the promising start, Vernon didn't have enough evidence to keep the murderous Anthony Lambert behind bars. If he didn't find something soon, he'd need to release him.

That was the system, too. Yet there was still time to find

the evidence, if he looked in the right place.

So he opened the door to the interview room and sat opposite Mr Ian Talken. Twenty-one years old. He'd slept with a sixteen-year-old who'd said she was eighteen. Looking at possible felony charges and sex offender registration, even though she claimed she'd consented.

'Mr Talken,' Vernon said. 'I'm Detective Sergeant Enible. Looks like you've gotten yourself in a bit of a fix.'

'I— yeah. Yeah.'

'As it happens, I'm in a bit of a fix myself.'

'Are— you are?' Talken gave him a nervous look. 'I don't understand how, um . . . Why I'm here?'

'I asked you to join me because I hope we can help each other,' he said. 'With our respective fixes.'

'Oh! That would be good. Great. Yes, please.'

Vernon consulted his folder. 'You spent the last several days sharing accommodations with Anthony Lambert?'

The boy nodded. 'Uh-huh.'

'Well, I would be obliged if you'll share any conversations you might've had, about his involvement in the homicide at the Marigold Cottages.'

'Uh, he doesn't talk much.'

'That's fine. If he didn't say anything, I can't help you.' Vernon waited a moment. 'Though it would be a pity, for your sake.'

'So you want information about . . . the Marigold Cottages?'

'That's right. Where a man, roughly ten years older than yourself, was bludgeoned to death from behind. One blow to the head.'

'In the street.'

'Near the street, yes. Beside the bushes.' Vernon shook his head sadly, then described the events before standing to leave. 'Well, wrack your brain, Mr Talken, see if you recall anything that Anthony Lambert might've mentioned, and we'll meet again tomorrow.'

The seed was planted; that's all Vernon could do. Make the offer, see if the kid was willing to help himself out. In the worst case, he'd release Anthony Lambert, then bring him back in when new facts came to light.

38

OCEAN

Most of the buildings on the beach-facing blocks of Cabrillo Boulevard were for tourists. Boutique hotels, upscale cafés, and bike rental shops. Ocean slowed to a stop at a crosswalk for dog walkers and a tourist family in one of those six-person, bicycle, surrey things.

'We should rent one of those with the kids,' Ocean said.

'No, we shouldn't,' Mrs B said. 'That's exactly the sort of activity that looks more fun than it is. And stop changing the subject. I'm going to call the mayor's office. I knew her father.'

Ocean pressed on the gas. 'I'm not sure the mayor can help with jail.'

'Forty-eight hours is forty-eight hours! It's been almost a week. His rights are being violated.'

'I already called legal aid,' Ocean admitted. 'Plus, the jail. Plus, the police oversight board.'

'What a lovely squeaky wheel you are.'

'Unlike you, always keeping your mouth shut.' She glanced at Mrs B. 'Why didn't you tell me about Anthony bringing Sophie home drunk? That's why you're so sure he's not guilty.'

'To protect Sophie's privacy, Ocean.'

'Like you care about privacy.'

'She's just so fragile.'

'I had no idea she was such a big drinker.' Sure, Ocean knew Sophie liked to party, but it had seemed a normal amount for a twentysomething woman. 'Passing out on the street?'

'It doesn't happen often.'

'You black out once, that's too often.' Ocean turned into the parking lot. 'And you saw him carrying her home?'

'Like Beauty and the Beast.'

Ocean snorted a laugh. 'Don't tell me you're setting them up.'

'Not at all. I just . . .' Mrs B smiled fondly. 'He was so gentle with her.'

'Huh. You ever hear why he was in prison?'

Mrs B looked toward the beach. 'I've decided I'd rather not know.'

'Yeah.' Ocean rolled down her window to accept a parking ticket from the kiosk. 'He thinks you're a fool for trusting him.'

'And that, my dear, is reason to trust him all the more.'

Ocean parked, then said, 'What's the game plan here?'

'We're talking to Piotr, that's all. I've never approved of how he looks at Lily-Ann. There is no plan.'

'I can't believe you're doing this.'

'At my age, it's important to keep active.'

'By investigating a murder?'

'It beats bingo,' Mrs B said, and opened the car door.

They crossed the street to Piotr's office building, a faux Spanish-style construction with a red tile roof. They climbed the outside stairwell to the second floor and found the office of CREATIVA WEALTH, DIGITAL ASSET PORTFOLIO STRATEGIES. There was a classy plaque on the classy front door, along with the view over the street toward the sea, which sparkled in the afternoon sunlight.

'How rich is he?' Ocean asked.

'Lily-Ann pays full market price for rent.'

Ocean touched the bell and heard a buzz inside. '*I* pay full price.'

'Of course, dear,' Mrs B said.

'What? You mean I *don't*? Jesus. You promised that I did. You said you were charging me market rate.'

'Well, what you failed to take in account was that I was lying.'

'We're going to have a long talk about that.'

'Oh, good. You know I always enjoy talking with you.'

Ocean gave up in the face of Mrs B's expression of impenetrable smugness. 'Fine, you old bat. Who else pays full price?'

'Lily-Ann and Hamilton.'

'Not Sophie with the help of her parents?'

'She pays *old* market price.'

'What does that even mean? What kind of funhouse sliding scale have you concocted?' She pressed the buzzer again. 'How about Nicholas?'

That was what she really wanted to know. She'd never

quite understood Mrs B's relationship with him. He'd moved in when Ocean was living in Calabasas with his ex-wife, Zoe. In the early, enraptured days.

'He pays almost old market price.' Mrs B peered toward the boulevard. 'I knew his father.'

'Your tattooed lover?'

'Don't be silly. His father didn't have tattoos.'

The door opened and Piotr greeted them with a well-constructed smile. 'Mrs Bakofsky, welcome.'

'And this is my dear friend and neighbor, Ocean,' Mrs B told him. 'So you're not the only one with an ocean view.'

Ocean cringed, but Piotr laughed obligingly and invited them into an office that looked more like a living room than a workplace. He led them across the Spanish tile floor to a caramel leather couch that faced the picture window. He sat in a matching chair with a small side table that held his open laptop. Ocean didn't understand why Piotr even had an office – or a business name. As far as she knew, he only invested his own money. Probably for some kind of tax deduction. Or for self-importance. That seemed more likely, considering his perfect hair and that gray button-down, opened to hint at his toned chest. He looked like he paid for self-tanning.

'Espresso?' he asked, gesturing to the well-appointed kitchenette.

'My espresso days are long over, I'm afraid,' Mrs B said, leaning into her eccentric old-woman act. 'I had a shocking experience in Montenegro once, with Turkish coffee.'

'Ah,' Piotr said, momentarily baffled before he turned to Ocean. 'How about you?'

'She takes hers with sweetened condensed milk,' Mrs B said.

'Oh.' Piotr blinked. 'That's, um—'

'I'm fine.' Ocean would've loved an espresso, but asking for one would only prolong this meeting and she already regretted coming.

'Well!' Piotr arched his eyebrow at Mrs B in a practiced motion. 'When you called and said you were Lily-Ann's landlady, I wasn't sure why you wanted an appointment.'

'She's so wonderful, isn't she? Such a clever mind, and so beautiful!'

'I worry about her health,' Piotr said.

'If you're so worried,' Mrs B said, 'how could you let her go?'

To Ocean's surprise, Piotr didn't take offense. 'Believe me, I didn't want to. But I'm hardly a match for Lily-Ann when she makes up her mind.'

'She is quite strong-minded,' Mrs B agreed, with a too-dramatic sigh. 'Though the poor thing is all alone now. In her cottage, I mean. Did you hear what happened? With the body and the—' She mouthed the last word. '—murder?'

'Uh, yeah. I stopped by.'

'Well, that's *something*, I suppose.' Mrs B tilted her head. 'Do you know they arrested the wrong man?'

Piotr leaned forward. 'No. No, I didn't know that. He's being released?'

'That's what we've been told. Apparently there's no evidence. Of course, he doesn't have an alibi, but alibis are foolish, don't you think? I barely remember as far back as twenty minutes ago.' She sighed. 'Poor Ocean! She's so angry that I'm asking everyone about alibis.

159

What was it you told me, my dear?'

Ocean had no fucking clue. 'Uh, that I'm angry you're asking everyone about alibis?'

'Well, I'll admit that demanding one from the mailman was rude. But he could've done it!' She leaned toward Piotr, her eyes twinkling. 'You'll never guess where he was.'

'At home?'

'At a strip club! Or what do they call them now?'

'Gentlemen's club?' Piotr offered.

'I'm surprised you'd know such a thing,' Mrs B said, suddenly prim. 'In any case, Ocean thought that interrogating him, as she called it, was too much.'

'Only when you kept asking if he'd paid for a lap dance,' Ocean said, getting into the spirit of things.

'I would never!' Mrs B said loftily, before turning toward Piotr. 'Where were *you* last Friday night?'

Piotr looked alarmed. Probably because he wasn't sure how crazy Mrs B was going to get. 'Uh, Vegas. I flew back late that night.'

Mrs B narrowed her eyes. 'Is that true?'

'Yes?'

'I told you!' Mrs B beamed at Ocean. 'I told you I'd worm an alibi out of him without him suspecting anything.'

Ocean shook her head in defeat. 'Yeah, he's none the wiser.'

'Can you prove it?' Mrs B asked Piotr.

'If I had to, sure. I was networking with investors.'

'In Las Vegas?'

'At the high-roller tables. That's where you meet guys who thrive on risk. I took a few of them to dinner. Used my Amex Black, so that's proof. And Vegas is wall-to-wall surveillance cameras.'

'Mmm. How do you know James Dedrick?'

'I don't.'

'You don't sound so sure,' Mrs B said.

He'd sounded pretty confident to Ocean, though.

'And if god forbid Lily-Ann was the one who'd died,' Mrs B continued, 'you wouldn't have to pay alimony anymore.'

'Uh, nobody touched Lily-Ann.' Piotr raised a hand to stop Mrs B from speaking. 'So this is why you came? To see if *I* killed him?'

'Yes,' Mrs B said.

'No!' Ocean said, frantically trying to save the situation. 'You're the emergency contact on Lily-Ann's rental form. So I wanted to make sure you knew what happened. I was going to call, but Mrs B . . .' Ocean gave him a look, like *pardon this delusional old lady.* 'Decided to visit in person.'

Mrs B stood suddenly and told Piotr, 'I wanted to look into everyone's eyes. They're the windows to the soul.'

'Okay,' Piotr said.

'I'm so sorry,' Ocean mouthed, as Mrs B moved to leave.

Piotr gave her a sympathetic look, with an edge of impatience.

'One last thing, Piotr.' Mrs B turned at the door, like Columbo. 'Money talks, but bullshit runs a marathon.'

Then she swept away. Ocean caught the door and followed her to the parking lot. The *bee-tweep* on Ocean's car fob was lost in the lapping of the tide and the clatter of skateboards in the park.

Ocean drove Mrs B in silence along the shoreline for five minutes before saying, 'A shocking experience in Montenegro?'

Mrs B made a snorking noise.

Ocean cracked a smile. 'The strip club?'

Mrs B hooted with laughter.

'You're a mad old bat,' Ocean said.

Mrs B kept laughing. 'That's how investigations work, my dear.'

'Okay, Miss Marple.'

'I know he's not guilty, but I've been looking for an excuse to see how he feels about Lily-Ann.'

Ocean turned at the light. 'Then what the hell is "bullshit runs a marathon"? Have you been watching *The Sopranos* again?'

'No, dear,' Mrs B told her. 'That's Wesley Snipes in *New Jack City*.'

Ocean didn't often do portraits, but she suddenly wanted to paint Mrs B looking fully regal and title it *Bullshit Runs a Marathon*.

39

SOPHIE

So I was banging on his door a little. So what? I wasn't drunk, just a little tipsy. And angry, even though I've never been great at anger.

Hours earlier, I'd finally gotten over the humiliation enough to tell my boss about Nicholas. About how he'd taken one look at me outside Capriccio the other day, then turned and walked away. Nicholas 'the Eel' Perez.

She'd said, 'Nicholas Perez?'

'The Eel,' I'd added.

'He's a member of the New Vic.'

'No! Really? I *knew* I recognized him.'

I'd checked his donation history, hoping for another reason to resent him. Instead, I'd found way more generosity than I'd expected. In fact, he'd even donated to *Martini with a Twist*. So I swiveled in my chair and riffled through the file cabinet. Sure enough, I found a thank-you note addressed to him, along with two tickets to the show. I upgraded them, to prove that I could – mad with power – then tucked them into my bag.

Home again after work, I took a shot of tequila and banged on his door.

And when he opened it, instead of looking mortified – considering he hadn't merely stood me up but had literally fled at the sight of me – he said, 'Thanks, but I'm fully stocked on Thin Mints.'

'Do I look like I'm a Girl Scout?'

'Uh, no. No, you don't.' Finally, he looked slightly embarrassed. 'I'm sorry about earlier. I— something came up. Suddenly. Urgently.'

I found him stupidly attractive with his shirt untucked and his wavy hair tousled. It made it harder to remember what an eel he was, but I persevered.

'What came up?' I demanded.

'Uh,' he said.

'You can't even think of a lie!'

'I can! I mean, not a lie.' He exhaled. 'It was IBS.'

'Really? Good. I hope so!'

'Okay,' he said.

I shoved the envelope against his chest. 'This is for you.'

'Ow.'

'I work at the New Vic Theatre. It's for your donation. There's tickets in there. For the play. I upgraded your seats.'

'Thank you?'

'You're welcome,' I snapped. 'Are you coming to the meeting?'

'Of the Marigold Potluck and Murder Club? No, thank you.' He scratched his arm with the envelope. 'I can't believe you're involved with that nonsense.'

'Why not? It makes Mrs B happy. As if you care.'

'Do they even know who the dead guy is?'

'Yes. Of course. Do you? Wait, did you *know* him?'

'No.'

'Are you lying?'

'Yeah, it wasn't really IBS.'

'Shut up. You know what I mean.'

He met my gaze offensively steadily. 'I didn't know him personally. He's an investor from L.A. The kind who boasts about the special character of an unspoiled coastal town, then throws a tantrum when zoning restrictions preserve the special character of the unspoiled coastal town. Well, I guess he doesn't throw tantrums anymore. That's kind of a relief.'

'So you're happy he's dead?'

'Well, I'm not sad.'

I eyed him narrowly. 'Did you kill him?'

'No, Sophie. I didn't kill him.'

'What do you do?'

164

'I work in the city planning office.'

'Oh.' For some reason that took the wind out my sails. It just seemed so normal. 'Why won't you come to the meeting?'

'Because it's ridiculous. And the ex-con is guilty. A guy with a felony assault charge moves in. Three weeks later a stranger is felony-assaulted to death – it's not a big mystery.'

'That'd be the worst plot twist ever, that the obvious suspect is guilty. Why would—' I stopped as realization struck. 'Oooh! That's kind of neat, actually. Nobody would suspect the obvious suspect! Maybe that's the end of act two.'

'The end of act two?' he asked, and eyes sparked with interest.

I did not notice how green they looked in the fading light. 'That's the low point, when the audience feels that all hope is—'

'It's not a play, Sophie,' he said.

'Not yet. Err . . . I'm maybe taking notes. In the hopes of dramatizing it. Partially. Maybe.'

For a moment, that seemed to stop him. 'Huh. Okay. But you're attending the meetings to make the landlady happy? Not to gather material?'

'Yes! Mostly. Both. I hope you enjoy the show!'

And on that parting jibe, I started to storm away. So maybe I'd had *two* shots of tequila.

'I'd be interested in seeing them,' he said, behind me.

'What?' I turned back. 'My Peanut Butter Patties?'

'Those, too,' he said, then immediately added, 'Your notes! I mean your notes.'

'Why?' I demanded.

'Because I, uh, I like theatre. I majored in classics, then fell into urban planning later.' He looked a little uncertain, which frankly was an improvement. 'I love a Greek comedy. And it's impressive that you can write a play. Putting yourself out there like that. It's . . . impressive. I want to hear more.'

'Ha!' I said, and marched off to Hamilton's cottage.

Hamilton opened the door, wearing a blue Hawaiian shirt. 'Oh, good! You're the last one.'

'Sorry. I, uh—sorry.'

'Unless . . . is Nicholas coming?'

'I don't even know why he's invited.'

'Was he rude again?' Mrs B asked me, from her place near the front. 'That poor man.'

'Poor me,' I said, taking a seat.

'We're all here!' Hamilton announced. 'And as the bard said, "Every house where love abides and friendship is a guest, is surely home, for there the heart can rest."'

'That's Shakespeare?' I asked.

'No, Henry van Dyke. A friend of Helen Keller.'

'*The* bard?' I said, because I was in a petty enough mood to pick a fight with Hamilton.

'Well, *a* bard,' he said.

I nodded as if that made sense, then started taking notes.

MRS. B
So what is on the vendetta tonight?

LILY-ANN
The agenda, Mrs B.

166

MRS. B
Yes, that, too.

HAMILTON
I looked into James Dedrick. In summary, he made a lot
of money and he spent a lot of money, but he still had a
lot of money. Also, he died intestate.

OCEAN
He died where?

HAMLITON
Intestate. Er, without a will.

Of course Ocean already knew that. She'd only asked in
case someone else didn't know, but was too embarrassed
to admit it. She was such a den mother.

HAMILTON
So his estate goes to his cousins. Public records, of
course, don't reveal if there's a hidden reason to kill him,
but nothing looks strange.

S
What about mistaken identity? Like if the killer wanted
to kill someone else?

LILY-ANN
That's the element we are best positioned to resolve. Mrs
B, you suggested that the perpetrator accidentally killed
Dedrick?

MRS. B
Well, I can't imagine anyone doing such a thing on purpose.

OCEAN
No, no. She means accidentally killed <u>Dedrick.</u> That's what you said, that the killer didn't mean to kill <u>him.</u>

MRS. B
Oh, no, dear. I said the killer probably didn't <u>mean</u> to kill him. What kind of person would—

(At a knock at the door, Hamilton leaps to his feet.)

HAMILTON
I didn't order any Swedish Fish.

(He opens the door and is flustered.)

Well, hello! You're out of jail! The big house. The pen, the clink . . .

ANTHONY
I got a note from Mrs B telling me to meet her here.

MRS. B
Anthony! Oh, please, come in. Let me look at you! Did you lose weight?

HAMILTON
The hoosegow.

S
Durance vile.

(Anthony remains at the door, reluctant to intrude.)

OCEAN
Close the door behind you. That seat's yours.

HAMILTON
Would you like a glass of milk?

ANTHONY
Yes.

(Hamilton is pleased and rushes to the kitchen.)

LILY-ANN
We're discussing the possibility that James Dedrick was either killed accidentally, or accidentally killed.

ANTHONY
I might need something stronger than milk.

HAMILTON

(offstage)

I'm fresh out of buttermilk!

OCEAN
We're proving your innocence.

ANTHONY
Why?

OCEAN
Because Mrs B.

LILY-ANN
And because, despite appearances, you keep a tidy house. Your silverware drawer is impeccable.

OCEAN
How do you know about his silverware drawer?

LILY-ANN
I searched his apartment.

(General surprise and hubbub. The only person unaffected is Anthony.)

Don't worry, I didn't find anything. A well-organized medicine cabinet. Clean sink. You should consider eating more greens. I tidied up after the police.

ANTHONY
I noticed. Thank you.

LILY-ANN
Three questions. First, you claim you didn't kill Dedrick, and don't know him. Is that correct? Second, did you see anything that night? Third, what is that tattoo on your face?

ANTHONY
That's correct. I didn't. A mistake.

OCEAN
So the big question, other than the whodunit, is what was Dedrick doing here? Right?

S

There's no way to know that yet. Character motivation comes later.

OCEAN

What are you talking about, character motivation?

S

Er, well, just motivation. Like, we need the basic facts first.

HAMILTON

(reentering)

And he's a character, right? Dead Rick! What a quirky guy.

OCEAN

He's not quirky, Hamilton; he's dead.

HAMILTON

Maybe he's both?

LILY-ANN

In any case. Anything else to report?

MRS. B

Your husband has an alibi, dear. And such a pretty office! Overlooking the beach. He was in Las Vegas.

OCEAN

Mrs B and I spoke to him. Well, she spoke to him. Well,

she babbled at him like a deranged crone, but he *did* say he was in Vegas Friday night.

LILY-ANN

I can't imagine Piotr is the murderer, but I will check his alibi. He pays for travel through the business. I have access to those records.

S

Well, I, uh, spoke with Nicholas. I forgot to ask where he was the night of the murder. Sorry. He knew the victim, though, at least a little.

HAMILTON

So is he our number-one suspect? We need one of those. Also, a whiteboard.

MRS. B

You can't possibly imagine that Nicholas is the killer. He's such a sweet young man.

(Everyone disagrees, talking over each other.)

MRS. B

Well, that's easy for you to say – and very wrong and shortsighted. Nicholas is a bit shy and perhaps a trifle abrupt, that's all. He wouldn't hurt a fly if you gave him a swatter.

OCEAN

We can't keep ruling out people because you're silly enough to like them. No offense, Anthony.

ANTHONY

None taken.

S

What if someone followed Dedrick from Altadena? Maybe he owed money or . . . people get killed over drugs all the time, don't they?

(Everyone looks at Anthony.)

ANTHONY

People get killed for wearing the wrong hat.

OCEAN

Who'd follow someone to a different town to kill them? Maybe they ran into each other downtown, but the question is still, what was he doing <u>here</u>? At the Cottages.

LILY-ANN

That's a good point. Anything else?

MRS. B

Nicholas is sweet! He's so sweet that he investigated Hesse for me. And in fact he found something rather—

S

Hesse? *Neal* Hesse? You sent him to—

Okay, enough with the quasi-playwriting format.

After Mrs B's inadvertent admission, she confessed to me that yes, she'd sent Nicholas to speak with Hesse. What she didn't say was, *in case he'd been hiding in your bushes.*

Then she told us that Nicholas had spotted what looked like a shrine to his wife's college career in Hesse's garage, but otherwise seemed normal.

Anyway, I lost my composure a little.

Ocean held me and Mrs B apologized. Hamilton offered

everyone sweet-corn-flavored soda, which I had not seen coming. Anthony vanished and Lily-Ann . . . well, she mostly just stood there.

But as my tears cleared, I realized that she mostly just stood there like a plus-size Valkyrie. Guarding me. Taking care of me, in her own way. That was their first instinct, their strongest instinct: to work together to protect one of their own.

So yeah, I may have lost my shit, but I don't want to talk about that. I don't want to talk about my weakness. I want to move toward my strength.

40

HAMILTON

Each planter was roughly a foot in diameter, and almost that deep. Hamilton didn't know much about flowers, so he'd instructed Anthony to use all-purpose potting mix and to tuck three petunias in each pot. In neat triangles, equally spaced to give them room to grow.

Then Anthony hung the planters on the eaves and watered them while Hamilton supervised from his window.

The courtyard looked good. Bright and comfortable. Hamilton took pleasure in the outdoors as long as he himself remained in the protective embrace of his home. It was a hot morning for March. So early that Hamilton and Anthony were the only two stirring. Yet soon everyone in the Cottages would want to sit in the yard. Well, everyone but him and Nicholas, each for their own reasons.

Hamilton eyed the once-elegant, now-rusting iron

174

chairs and considered speaking with Mrs B about purchasing new furniture. Perhaps he might ask Lily-Ann to do the shopping? She would happily oblige, and she was a woman of impeccable taste. He nodded to himself, pleased with the decision . . . then his gaze drifted toward the crime scene behind Sophie's cottage.

A man had died there. His corpse had gone rigid and cold. Murdered. Blood sticky on the ground. Poor Sophie, falling apart like she had during the meeting of the Marigold Collective.

Hamilton believed that witnessing violence was more difficult on women, or more personal, somehow. Anthony, on the other hand, struck him as entirely unmoved by the murder. He watched him wipe his hands on a rag, then Mrs B came toddling out of her cottage in her morning muumuu.

She admired the hanging petunias, her face alight with pleasure. 'I do love our succulents, and drought-resistant landscaping is so wonderful, don't you think? Such an *arid* beauty.'

'Exactly what I was thinking,' Anthony said, completely deadpan.

'Though there's nothing like flowers.' She spun almost girlishly, taking in the blossoms hanging in a U around the courtyard. 'Such brightness and life.'

'Yeah,' Anthony said.

'Will they take too much water?' Mrs B wrinkled her nose at the newly potted petunias. 'I don't want to be ecologically irresponsible, even if I do want flowers.'

'You don't have to worry,' Hamilton called from his window. 'Our water usage is well below average.'

Mrs B peered at him through the screen, then laughed.

'I didn't see you there, Hamilton! Well, that's good to hear. And you must tell me if I should hire a gardener instead of imposing on the two of you.'

'We're happy to do it,' Hamilton said, then realized that he hadn't actually done anything. 'Well, uh . . .'

Anthony nodded. 'Yeah.'

Hamilton appreciated the agreement, and he gave a little wave as Mrs B led Anthony into her cottage for pancakes, like she was rewarding a child.

Which would've been sweet, except he caught a glimpse of an odd expression on her face as she departed. Like she was nervous, or uncomfortable. Or perhaps . . . pained? Yeah, pained. Well, a man had been killed on her property, naturally she felt less-than-happy.

Hamilton hated seeing her like that. Usually Mrs B was the most comfortable, relaxed, carefree person. She needed a distraction. She needed to get away from the Marigold Cottages for a day. Or just to feel productive, somehow, to feel useful.

With that in mind, he sent a quick text to Ocean, with a suggestion. Then he pressed his palm against the window and looked toward the crime scene again. So far beyond his comfort zone. And yet still so close.

41

LILY-ANN

To Lily-Ann's dismay, Mrs B nattered at her during the entire drive south.

She enjoyed Mrs B, of course, but she also enjoyed

silence. Or at least wordlessness. On the other hand, Mrs B hadn't even wanted to come. Though neither had Lily-Ann.

In fact, she still wasn't entirely sure how it had happened. Ocean had somehow twisted both their arms. Lily-Ann figured that Ocean had suggested the trip to investigate James Dedrick because she wanted to distract Mrs B, who still seemed unsettled about the murder, even after Anthony was released.

Except Ocean taught classes today, so she couldn't drive. Which left Lily-Ann, a day of personal time, and her hybrid Volvo.

And enduring Mrs B's chattering. She asked if she wanted to listen to music, and Mrs B said yes, then kept talking. Should she turn up the Mozart? She wondered what Anthony listened to. If you spent years in prison, did your tastes become more or less narrow and strongly held?

She'd ask him. The question was probably rude, but he wouldn't care. If he didn't want to answer, he'd remain silent. A sensible system. She approved. She often attempted the same, but people tended to experience her silence as an affront.

Lily-Ann took the Altadena exit and drove into the hills, where trees overshadowed the winding road. The neighborhood looked comfortably middle-class at first, then a few gates appeared, guarding increasingly elaborate properties.

James Dedrick's house was not blocked by a gate. It was contemporary and bland, and so low to the ground that she couldn't see much except the three-car garage that faced the street.

She parked outside it. 'What now?'

'The poor man,' Mrs B said, her voice thin.

After a shaky moment, she stepped from the car and didn't seem to notice the heat. Lily-Ann noticed. Maybe she should invest in some cotton kaftans, like Mrs B. Valentino made some nice ones. She followed her down the stairs leading from the driveway onto a shaded path that ended at a recessed front door.

Mrs B knocked, then peered in the window, then knocked again. 'I don't think anyone's going to answer.'

'Well, he is dead.'

Mrs B fiddled with the silver rings on her fingers. 'I-I wondered if there were mourners.'

'Oh,' Lily-Ann said.

Mrs B took a breath, then went around the side of the house, peering into a window. Lily-Ann pointed out the alarm system decal, but Mrs B didn't seem to care. So Lily-Ann looked as well, and saw a room with the generic charm of an upscale barber-shop. There was a billiard table and a bar. Bottles of liquor lined slate shelves and as Lily-Ann wondered how they were organized she heard a sniffle.

Mrs B was crying.

Just standing there beside Lily-Ann, looking into the room and crying. Not loudly. Not much more than breathing deeply, but a few tears trickled down her grooved face. She pressed both her hands to her heart and said a few words in Hebrew.

Lily-Ann didn't know what to say. She knew what people said when they comforted her, and she knew that words never helped.

So she touched Mrs B's elbow.

Mrs B smiled at her with teary eyes. 'He was so young. A pool table. Still a boy.'

'We should go home.'

'A life cut short. I can't say that I . . .' She dabbed at her eyes with a handkerchief. 'It's hard when things are so terribly irreversible.'

Lily-Ann wasn't sure what that meant, so she said, 'If you're not feeling well, we should go.'

'Only a little *verklempt*,' Mrs B said, then fell silent for a full minute.

'Are you sure you're all right?'

'Just being a silly old woman. Don't mind me.'

'What would you have said if there were mourners?' Lily-Ann asked.

'I suppose I'm sorry, the way one does. The way one *is*.'

'Oh,' Lily-Ann said, though she never said that herself.

With a sigh, Mrs B turned to the stairs to return to the street – and Lily-Ann heard footsteps approaching from across the driveway.

Private security, no doubt. Well, or the local police, if they kept an eye on murder victims' homes, which struck her as a strong possibility.

So she took Mrs B's elbow and hustled her back toward the front door.

The footsteps paused.

Lily-Ann raised her finger to her mouth to hush Mrs B.

The footsteps started again, coming closer down the stairs, then along the walkway. There was no way to avoid a confrontation, so she'd let Mrs B handle this. They hadn't done anything illegal, after all. Maybe a little minor trespassing. Nothing that a sweet old lady couldn't talk her way out of.

Then a young woman in a sleek black suit stepped around the corner. Straightened hair, big sunglasses, and a pretty face. Lily-Ann thought she was a realtor until she saw the bouquet of pink roses in her hand.

'Oh!' the woman said when she spotted them.

'Hello, dear.' Mrs B stepped forward. 'You must be a friend of James's.'

The woman gave a brittle smile. 'Oh. Yes.'

'We never met him,' Mrs B confided. 'We, ah, found him. Afterward. And thought we should pay our respects.'

'Oh! That must've been horrible. I'm, uh, his ex-girlfriend, actually. I heard what happened, and thought . . .' The woman showed them the bouquet in her hand. 'Well, I thought I should do *something*.'

'He was fond of roses?'

'He loathed them,' the woman admitted. 'Even on Valentine's Day, he refused to buy a single long-stemmed rose. He was an awful boyfriend. I, uh, was hoping to drop these off and sneak away.'

'What was he like?'

'Controlling,' the woman immediately said, before considering. 'But generous, if he wanted something.'

Mrs B smiled gently. 'I'm not sure that is generosity, dear.'

'No.' The woman laid the roses at the door. 'All he really cared about was power moves. Dominating the opposition. He'd show up late for meetings, to make the other guy wait. That's common, right? But James took it one step farther. He'd do recon first.'

Mrs B tilted her head. 'Recon?'

'He'd get to appointments hours early, before anyone else, to set the stage. He once unplugged a power strip so when a meeting started none of the tech worked. He saved the day by plugging things back in.'

'Clever,' Lily-Ann said.

'And manipulative.' The woman smoothed her hair. 'But I sometimes thought that if he ever grew up, he might turn out okay.'

'And now he never will,' Mrs B said, a forlorn note in her voice.

Lily-Ann wasn't interested in that, so she said, 'What did he do for work?'

'He made bank up and down the coast, leveraging other people's money into even more for himself.' The woman gave them a wry look. 'That's how he described it.'

'It sounds terribly nerve-wracking,' Mrs B said.

'Not for James,' the woman told her. 'Say what you will about him, he had balls of steel.'

And with that lovely epitaph ringing in her ears, Lily-Ann led Mrs B back to the car and the blessed air-conditioning.

42

OCEAN

Ocean spent the day subbing at a private middle school. She taught art classes and reveled in the resources: the wealth of supplies that were nowhere in her own children's public schools.

Even worse, she liked the private school kids. Though

most of them were a little too well-behaved, a little too eager to do everything right. They were the kind of people who, as adults, would want to make great art without making mistakes, which just wasn't how anything worked.

Still, she loved the small classes; the creamy, expensive pastels; and the multiple sets of luxuriant graphite pencils. Hell, the weight of the paper in the sketchbooks almost made her moan. She even managed to stash a used charcoal drawing set in her bag, for Miles and Riley. In – she told herself – a Robin Hood way, not an office-supply-theft way.

Maybe she should've become a lawyer like her mother wanted, and tuck the kids in at night in beds made of sable paint-brushes. Well, except her mother wanted her to work pro bono for the Innocence Project.

'Should I go to law school?' she asked Miles that evening, as he unloaded the dishwasher while she threw dinner together.

'Yes!' he said. 'That way you can defend Anthony.'

'He's home anyway.'

'She-Hulk's a lawyer,' he told her. 'You're a little like her.'

'She's the one with huge knockers?'

Miles made a face. 'O-ma!'

'They're superheroes,' Riley said, from the dining room table where she was painting her nails. 'They've all got huge knockers.'

'She defends people caught in the system,' Miles told Ocean, standing on his toes to slide a mug into place. 'And civil rights and stuff.'

'And kicks butt, too?' Ocean started chopping carrots. 'That does sound like me. Except it takes years to get a law degree. Then you have to study for a horrible test before they let you practice law.'

'They make you take the test before you even start *practicing*?'

'Ha.' She told him what practicing law meant, then sent him off while she finished making dinner.

'Do you really want to be a lawyer?' Riley asked, inspecting her freshly painted nails.

'If I was, I could send you to private school.'

'Oh, god no. Carly goes to one and she told me on their over-night biking trip a seventh grader gave a blow job to a ninth grader.'

'Ew.'

'That's what I said.'

'I bet it's what she said, too,' Ocean told her, instead of responding like an adult.

She figured that had been one of Riley's *Is Your Mom Too Controlling?* tests. Like, was she going to call the school in a huff? Also, she didn't have to pretend to be shocked that Riley knew what a blow job was. They'd had plenty of discussions about consent and waiting and birth control, during which Riley really enjoyed questioning her lack of personal expertise.

Riley laughed, and Ocean chopped the carrot with a little extra flair. It'd been a while since she'd made her daughter laugh.

'You *should* defend Anthony,' Riley told her, somewhat to her surprise.

'Why's that?'

Riley lifted her gaze from her nails. 'Do you think he did it?'

'I don't know.'

Ocean thought about Anthony gently carrying a drunk Sophie home; she thought about him talking to her in the jail. But she also thought about him as a younger man, beating some guy into the hospital. He was no stranger to violence. He hadn't been framed back then, or falsely accused. He'd been guilty. And maybe *she* didn't trust the prison-industrial complex, but *he* thought he'd deserved to do time. Still, she liked to believe that Mrs B was right, that people changed – and she'd never felt a hint of violence from Anthony.

'No,' she continued. 'Not really.'

'That's why you should defend him,' Riley said.

'Can I just befriend him? Is that enough?'

Riley shot her an amused look. 'As if there's any difference.'

'Why do *you* think he's innocent?'

'Because I do, okay?'

'Yeah, but why? Did you see something or—'

Riley stood from the table. 'Jesus, Mom, what the hell? Can't I ever just *say* something?'

Then she stormed off . . . which was a little hair-trigger even for Riley. And made Ocean wonder again if she really had seen something that night. Or some*one*. Would Riley have mentioned that? Yeah. Yes. Definitely.

Unless she found it too embarrassing. Or she just didn't want to. Hmm. Ocean thought about that as the pasta water overboiled on the stove.

43

HAMILTON

On Hamilton's computer screen, a flying drone spun in a lazy circle, filming a herd of wild horses. The operator talked about range and battery life and literally expanding your horizons.

Which wouldn't be so hard. At the moment, Hamilton's horizons were the walls of his cottage.

His cursor hovered over the Purchase button, but he didn't click. He loved the idea of a streaming camera darting across the Cottages, poking around the corners of the property. Popping in to watch Ocean paint, maybe, or to talk with Mrs B, who he knew with absolute certainty would happily chat with a drone.

But they'd think he was even stranger, and they already thought he was odd enough.

They figured something terrible must've happened to keep him inside: some traumatic event in his past. But nothing had triggered him. His preference for staying home had simply grown over years. What had once been an inclination now felt more like an imperative.

Though of course he did leave. Sometimes. If absolutely necessary.

Still, he wasn't like Sophie. She had a *reason* to fear. She'd survived an actual ordeal.

And he wanted to help her. Largely because he still felt terrible about her finding the body, and how that must've retraumatized her. Other people could focus on helping her grow past her fears, but that wasn't realistic for Hamilton.

However, he was in the best position to show her how you could build a life despite them.

He considered texting her, but wasn't sure what to say. So he leaned back in his chair as the light slanted through the blinds and gazed at the hummingbird feeder, hoping for inspiration.

Instead, he saw Nicholas leaving his house, all dressed up. He watched him for a moment. Nicholas had his own peculiarities. He wasn't afraid of leaving the house, but he *was* afraid of Mrs B. Hamilton had noticed that he slunk away every time he spotted her.

He leaned forward and called through the open window. 'Evening, Nicholas! You're all dressed up!'

Nicholas startled. 'Oh. Hamilton. Yes.'

'Out for a hot date?'

'Dinner, actually. At, uh, that new oyster bar place.'

Well, Hamilton didn't care for seafood, but he did have an interesting fact to share. 'A single oyster can filter up to sixty gallons of seawater every day.'

'Okay,' Nicholas said, and headed for his car.

Hamilton leaned back in his chair and texted Nicholas that the most expensive bottle of champagne cost over two million dollars. He knew which restaurant Nicholas was going to. He kept up on all the new restaurants in Santa Barbara that offered DoorDash. However, the oyster-and-champagne bar only used Uber Eats, which Hamilton had no truck with. He quickly perused their menu, then texted Nicholas to order the Duval-Leroy. 'Best value,' he told him.

That sorted, he focused on helping Sophie. Though, after seeing Nicholas startle at his voice, perhaps surprising her wasn't the best idea.

Instead, he called Mrs B. 'I'm thinking of buying Sophie a quadcopter drone with camera stabilization and a forty-minute flying time?'

'What a lovely thought, Hamilton!' she said, warmly. 'I'm sure she'd have absolutely no interest in that.'

'Oh, great. Wait. What?'

'If you want to do something for her, search the web for anything about Neal Hesse. Her stalker. Can you do that? Check his comments and his Facebooks and his hobbies. Find out why he tried hiding those college flags from Nicholas, and what that little charm necklace meant. The *X*, an *A*, and a *T*.'

Hamilton idly tapped the characters on his keyboard, then wrinkled his nose at them. '*X*, *A*, *T*? That's chi, alpha, tau. Possibly the name of a fraternity?'

'Perfect! You dig into that, my dear, and let me worry about quadrangle drones.'

He explained that the word was 'quadcopter,' and why, but oddly Mrs B didn't seem very interested.

44

SOPHIE

Dressing up for work that evening wasn't a silly job requirement. No, it was a role. A performance. Opening night, even. At least that was what I told myself as I snaked through the crowd, my tray of martinis held high.

Most of the donors were old, of course. The average theatergoer in town was sixty-something, and the members were even older. They were cool, though. They supported the arts in practice, not just in theory. Like, they'd show up happily for Tennessee Williams, whom they found comforting and nostalgic, but they'll also represent for a Czech musical they found baffling and alarming. They didn't expect the arts to cater to them; instead, they felt the obligation to cater to the arts. Heroes, in my mind.

Then there was Nicholas, who wore a beige blazer and black jeans. Talking with an old woman in a hot pink pantsuit about the American playwright Martyna Majok, which I found alarmingly sexy. How many straight men our age knew about Martyna Majok? So far, in my experience: one.

If only he weren't a jerk. Running away from me outside Capriccio like that.

Though I now realized that his sudden retreat hadn't been about me. Well, I now *suspected* it wasn't. He hadn't been avoiding me; he'd been avoiding Mrs B. When I'd caught him looking at his phone, he must've seen the picture I'd snapped of her having lunch with Mr Ybarra.

That's why he'd fled.

Which made me curious. What did he have against Mrs B?

So when his conversation ended, I sidled next to him and said, 'Care for a martini, sir?'

'Yes, thank you. I—' He jerked slightly when he recognized me. 'Oh!'

'I wasn't sure you'd come. I didn't think you actually went to things you're invited to.'

'Mmm.' He eyed me. 'I like your waiter outfit.'

I was wearing a black button-up suit vest with no top and black wide-legged pants. I hadn't tried to dress like a waiter; it was fashion inspo from Instagram – and perfect for the role of young playwright forced to organize successful theatre fundraisers for a living.

'This is very in right now,' I told him. 'It's like you've never heard of social influencers.'

'No, I just didn't know they influenced caterers.' ·

I huffed. 'I'm the caterer who came up with and organized this entire event!'

He smiled, as I walked away, which surprised me.

I wasn't sure that I'd really come to grips with his character. For my play. So I kept an eye out for him, as a source of material. I only caught glimpses of him until the fundraiser ended, though, and the bell sounded for everyone to take their seats.

Five minutes before the curtain rose, I spotted Nicholas in the audience. I'd given him good seats, but not great ones. Didn't want him to get a bigger head. He was only using one of his free tickets: the seat beside him was empty.

At least until I slipped into it.

To my surprise, he smiled again and said, 'I'm starting to feel like you're stalking me.'

I froze.

'Oh, god, I'm sorry!' he said, clearly alarmed. 'I'm sorry, Sophie, I wasn't thinking. I'm happy – always happy to see you. I didn't mean, uh—'

'Does *everyone* know?' I asked.

'Uh . . . I overheard Mrs Bakofsky talking.'

'How'd you even get that close? You're afraid of her.'

He looked confused. 'Of Mrs Bakofsky?'

'She terrifies you!' And I was still flustered, so I said,

'Where were you the night of the murder?'

'Sophie, this isn't, um—excuse me, but that seat is taken.'

'Shut up and answer the question.'

'I can't do both.'

'You know what I mean. Where were you?'

'At home.'

'So *you* claim.'

'Well, yeah.'

'But you admit you knew Dead Rick. And you didn't like him. And you're the only one who knew him. You don't even care that he's dead. Rick.'

'Neither do you.'

'I didn't know him! Also, you're the creepiest person in the Marigold Cottages.'

'I am not!' He had the audacity to look offended. 'I'm at worst the third creepiest. No, fourth.'

'You're number-one creepiest,' I told him. 'How can you be afraid of Mrs B?'

'*She's* number one. Always up in everyone's business.'

'That poor woman! She looks after everyone and – and can't even pay her bills.'

'What are you talking about? Of course she can. And what does that have to do with anything? I just want to be left alone.'

'Liar. I saw you chatting earlier with hot pink suit about Martyna Majok.'

'Fine. Sometimes I don't mind company.' He gestured vaguely. 'Speaking of which . . .'

I squinted at him. 'What?'

'The seat?'

'I'm not moving until you answer all my questions.'

'Okay, but right now I really need you to let my date in.'

And that's when I noticed the pretty woman in a bodycon blue dress at the end of the aisle smiling confusedly at Nicholas.

'Well, isn't that convenient,' I told Nicholas in what I hoped was a threatening tone.

He looked amused, so probably not. Then I had to say, 'Excuse me, sorry, pardon me, I'm so sorry,' as I squeezed down the row, which wasn't the most dramatic exit.

I really needed to work on my blocking.

Anyway, I slunk away and replayed our conversation in my mind, making it more embarrassing each time, because that was how I rolled. But also, I thought back to him calling her Mrs Bakofsky like he couldn't even say her nickname. He really was afraid of her. Which meant they shared some connection.

I vowed to find out what it was.

45

LILY-ANN

Lily-Ann's husband had named his company Creativa Wealth in order to 'evoke the concept of creating wealth with technology.' She remained unconvinced that swapping the last letter of 'creative' with an *a* was as evocative as he'd intended, but no doubt she simply hadn't understood the target demographic.

That was one of their most fundamental disconnects: Piotr invested serious effort into performing for an audience that Lily-Ann suspected was entirely imaginary. He strove to impress nonexistent spectators. She, on the other hand, didn't care about the prestige of the whiskey he bought; she simply wanted him to mix their cocktails in the correct proportions.

Once she'd asked why he didn't work in his home office, and he'd reacted like she'd suggested that he didn't actually prefer his steaks rare. Thank god they no longer spent enough time together for him to explain how many reps would strengthen his hip flexors.

On Saturday morning, while trying to confirm Piotr's alibi, she discovered that her remote access to Creativa didn't work any longer. Not that she truly suspected him of the murder; he wasn't that good at keeping quiet about his achievements. Still, she'd told the others that she'd check his alibi, so she would. An unkept promise was an intolerable loose thread.

So she left her house and stood there for a moment, gazing across the courtyard toward Ocean's cottage. Then toward Anthony's studio. Remembering his expression when he'd thanked her for recommending that he eat more greens. She didn't think he'd been teasing her. She was almost certain he hadn't been. But she wasn't sure he'd been thanking her for the specific recommendation, either.

It seemed to her that he'd been genuinely thankful for *any* expression of interest in his health or situation. He was just grateful that she cared.

Upon reflection, Lily-Ann realized that he himself was a loose end of sorts, someone who hadn't been the subject of much concern. So instead of going directly to her car, she went to his studio.

The door was propped open, and before she knocked she heard a piping voice saying, 'Thanks, Tony!'

Then Miles ran toward her from inside the studio, a white T-shirt in his hand and a smile on his face. He dodged Lily-Ann and said, 'Oopsie!' and scurried away.

Lily-Ann knocked on the open door and Anthony appeared in front of her.

'Do you prefer Tony?' she asked.

'No,' he said.

She nodded, appreciating the information. 'I'm going to Corazón for lunch.'

He watched her.

'The one on the east side.' She tried to keep her gaze locked on his eyes instead of that cheek tattoo. 'It's the best Mexican restaurant in town. Some people prefer La Picosita. They are wrong.'

'I'll keep that in mind,' he said.

'I'm stopping there on the way to Piotr's office.'

'Your ex?'

'We're separated.'

He nodded.

'I'd like you to come along.'

He watched her.

'Are you familiar with Korean dramas?' she asked.

'No.'

'There is a trope in Korean dramas in which a person who exits jail eats fresh tofu. For luck, perhaps, or simply as a tradition.'

'A trope?' he said.

'Yes. However, you do not seem like the tofu type. I think a homemade tamale is the perfect substitute in California.'

'I need all the luck I can get,' he said, and moved to join her outside.

'I'll drive,' she told him.

'I don't have a car.'

'Then it's settled.'

'Yes,' he said.

When he walked beside her to the car, she found herself thinking about his size again. Not libidinally. Just aesthetically. The two of them were built along the same scale. She rested a hand on his arm when she stepped down from the curb. Maybe he wasn't symmetrical, but he *was* solid.

She adjusted the passenger seat for him. He sat and asked what 'trope' meant, so she told him. Then she said, 'After years in prison, did your tastes become more or less particular? For instance, are you only comfortable now in smaller places? Or do you find that you don't care at all, as long as you're not in prison?'

He thought for a minute, then said, 'I'm not sure. I think I'm more relaxed now.'

'More relaxed?'

'I care less. Especially about the little things.'

'Intentionally?' she asked. 'Because being less relaxed got you into trouble?'

'Yeah. Although also, I'm older now.'

She nodded in satisfaction. 'I didn't think you'd mind if I asked.'

'No. I like simple. If you want to ask, ask. If you don't, don't. What I like is – I like people who are unapologetically themselves.'

Lily-Ann thought about that as she parked near the

restaurant. *She* was unapologetically herself. She didn't know how else to be. Sophie, on the other hand, was apologetically herself. Piotr, she sometimes suspected, was unapologetically someone else. She couldn't think of anyone who was *apologetically* someone else, but she imagined it wasn't too uncommon. Faking your way through life, then apologizing for the pretense.

The restaurant looked like nothing special, just the usual Spanish tile floors and basic seating. However, the food deserved a setting as grand as Régina's, where she usually ate with Piotr. She told the server to seat them in the least busy corner, then ordered for them both. Pozole with radish and hominy, chicken with Oaxacan black beans, a plate of tacos, and two kinds of tamale. When the chips came, with a little tray of various salsas, Anthony lit up. He was not an expressive man, but his delight at sampling the salsas gave her pleasure to witness. Fresca, habanero, peanut, pineapple, and avocado.

He ate almost delicately, which surprised her. Dipping a corner of a chip. Tasting. Considering. Then the main courses came.

Before he ate his tamale, Anthony said, 'To tropes.'

'To tropes,' she said.

They ate in silence, for a time, then she said, 'I'd like to stop at my husband's office after this.'

'Okay.'

'To check his alibi. He claims he was in Las Vegas. I can access his computer from his office to see if he purchased a ticket and used his credit card in Nevada.'

He took the last bite of his tamale. 'Okay.'

'He's probably not there on the weekend. But possibly.'

'You think he's going to make trouble?'

'No. Why? Oh! You think that's why I invited you along, in case he made trouble?'

He nodded.

'No. I just thought we both might enjoy the company.'

He almost smiled at her, before wiping his mouth with a napkin.

'That's a horrible tattoo,' she told him.

His smile finally appeared. Just for a moment, before it vanished. 'It's not my worst,' he said.

'I can't imagine,' she said.

But then, on the drive to Piotr's office, she imagined.

'Look at that,' Anthony said, while climbing the stairs to Piotr's office.

'The ocean?' she asked.

'Yeah.'

So she stood outside the Creativa door and looked with him toward the beach and the sea, the moored boats and the distant islands. A couple of kids bodysurfed in the waves and a formation of pelicans glided past.

'You haven't been to the beach?' she asked.

'Not for a while,' he said.

'You've been out for years.'

'I came a few times but then I . . . forgot.'

'Easy to overlook,' she said. 'It's only the Pacific.'

He made a noise like a laugh. 'A friend of mine fishes off the Ventura Pier every day. Well, I hope he does.'

'He's not the kind to forget the largest ocean in the world?'

'Mind like a steel trap, that's TG.'

She liked feeling Anthony relax around her. So she stood there another minute, looking out over the water.

'You ever heard of gray whales?' he asked.

'I'm familiar with the concept.'

'They can weigh forty tons. That's like five school buses, and all they eat is crabs the size of your fingernail.'

'You're interested in whales?'

'I watched a show inside,' he explained, and his voice turned wistful. 'There's something about them. They swim ten, fifteen thousand miles a year. Imagine that. Five miles an hour and you cross a whole-ass planet.'

'They swim through here.' She nodded at the ocean. 'Just offshore.'

He turned to her. 'No.'

'They do. This time of year, actually. Through April, maybe early May.'

'You . . . can you *see* them?'

'There are whale-watching trips; you go out on a boat.'

'And they . . .' He swallowed. 'They just let you do that?'

She didn't know who he meant by 'they,' but she said, 'Yes.'

He gazed at the water for another minute before Lily-Ann grew bored. So she stepped to the Creativa door and pressed the code into the keypad.

'2-0-5-8-4,' she told him. 'That's Piotr's favorite number. The total unique words in *Infinite Jest*.'

'I've never seen it,' he said.

When she led him inside, Anthony gave an impressed whistle. Probably at the office, though maybe he was still dreaming of gray whales. She crossed to the computer and he walked around, his hands in his pants pockets, looking without touching like he was in a museum.

She told him that *Infinite Jest* was a novel, then grunted when her login worked. Piotr had disabled remote access. Probably paranoid of hackers. She checked if he'd bought a ticket to Vegas. He had. She checked the dates. They fit, too. She checked his credit cart and bank activity. Yeah, he'd definitely been in Vegas. Which made sense, if he was trying to raise money. He'd always claimed that gamblers made the best investors. He admired men who enjoyed taking risks and – more vitally – who enjoyed being *seen* taking risks.

'Blue clubs?' Anthony said behind her.

Lily-Ann turned to see him eyeing a golf bag propped against the humidor in the corner.

'Those are Mizuno,' she told him. 'High-end. Only the best for Piotr.'

'You play golf?' he asked.

'No,' she said. 'Listen to this. The airport is approximately fifteen minutes from the Cottages. Piotr's flight landed a little after eleven. I don't know why he'd visit in the middle of the night, or why he'd meet Dedrick there, but it's possible.'

She dug around a little more, then switched to the customer portal of his cell carrier.

'I don't know how to check if he made any calls at that time, or from where.' She closed the portal and turned to look at Anthony. 'Still, I just can't see it. He's not a killer.'

'Most killers aren't,' Anthony told her.

'No?'

'No. They're scared or desperate. Or embarrassed. That's a real killer, embarrassment.'

'You mean like pride or—'

The door opened and Piotr stepped inside. He stopped

short when he saw Lily-Ann, then said, 'What the fuck?'

'Hello, Piotr,' she said.

'What are you doing here?'

'Checking your computer.'

'I can see that. Why?'

'To confirm the information that you gave—'

'Shit!' Piotr spotted Anthony in the corner and scrambled backward. 'Jesus fucking what the hell?'

'That's my friend Anthony,' Lily-Ann said. 'Anthony, my husband, Piotr.'

'Hello,' Anthony said.

'What the—' Piotr took a ragged breath. 'What are you *doing* here?'

'I told you,' Lily-Ann said. 'I'm checking the—'

'Shut up! *That's* Anthony? As in Anthony who murdered that guy?'

'He is that Anthony, but he didn't murder the guy.'

Piotr's jaw clenched. 'Are you sure about that?'

'No,' Lily-Ann said.

'Don't admit that in front of him! Are you—' He shifted closer to the door, as if preparing to flee. 'Did he force you here?'

'No. As I said, Anthony is my friend.'

'You don't have friends,' Piotr said.

Anthony grunted.

Piotr glanced at him nervously, then looked back to Lily-Ann. 'So you, you're hanging around with a murderer for fun?'

'He wasn't convicted of murder. He was convicted of aggravated assault.'

'Oh, good. So he's only a violent felon.'

'Why are you here?' Lily-Ann asked.

Piotr exhaled in exasperation or disgust. 'It's *my* office. I—I came to get my tie.'

'The gecko tie?'

'Why are we talking about me?' Piotr demanded, maybe a little defensively 'You're sitting here with . . . Look at him! You need to stay away from this guy, Lily-Ann. He only – You know he's only after one thing.'

Lily-Ann felt almost flattered. 'Is that right? We could ask—'

'Does he *know* how much you're worth?'

'Oh.' Not so flattering. Piotr assumed Anthony was after her money. 'I don't know.'

'He does, doesn't he? You watch yourself. This is going to end in fucking disaster.'

'Speaking of which, why do you want your tie?'

He grabbed his tie from a drawer in the credenza. 'Why do you think? I had a run of bad luck in Vegas. I need a reset. And no, I didn't lose much. A couple grand. I'm just nipping any problem in the bud.'

'It's his lucky tie,' she told Anthony.

'I've got a trope like that,' Anthony said.

Lily-Ann smiled. 'Apparently Michael Douglas wore it in a really old movie.'

'Not fucking *apparently*,' Piotr snapped. 'He *did* wear it. You came to check my alibi?'

'Yes. And from what I saw, you could have reached the Marigold Cottages in time to kill James Dedrick.'

'That's the murdered guy? Why would I want to?' Piotr put his hand on the doorknob. 'Look around you, Lily-Ann. You're fucked up but you're not stupid. *I'm* not the one with a history of violence.'

Then he stepped outside and slammed the door behind him, leaving a well of silence in the room.

'A lucky tie?' Anthony asked.

'He thinks it's from a movie where a stockbroker gets away with insider trading.'

Lily-Ann logged out of the computer and locked the door behind them. Back in the Volvo, she thought about Piotr saying, *Does he know what you're worth?* She wondered what Anthony had made of that, but didn't ask.

46

OCEAN

Most of the models Ocean hired for her adult education class were skinny college girls. Which wasn't bad in terms of understanding musculature and skeletal structure, but she always kept an eye out for larger or older women – or for any men, because they were rarely willing to model.

So as she left her house, she glanced toward Anthony's door. She was dying for him to model. She'd been thinking about it since they'd met. The pay was good for three hours of sitting still. Though she figured she should wait until after the whole murder thing was resolved. Adult ed would fire her if she paraded a naked killer around her art students.

So she kept walking. She needed to remind Mrs B to check with the kids while she taught her weekend class. Miles had a California Mission report due on Monday, and Riley was monitoring mold growth for her science report. Hell, maybe she could ask Mrs B to talk to Riley about her recent mood, too; god knew that Ocean hadn't, despite all her resolutions.

She opened Mrs B's door without knocking, as she always did.

'—at your age,' she heard a man say in the living room. 'Getting your estate together.'

Ocean paused inside the door, trying to place the voice. Only took a second. It was Gregory Ybarra, who'd been having lunch with Mrs B. Who was always hassling her to sell the Cottages.

'My estate, as you call it,' Mrs B said, 'is together.'

'For now, yes. But unforeseen events tend to happen without . . . Well, the clue is in the name – they're not foreseen.' Ybarra chuckled. 'And if something should happen to you, where would that leave your tenants? Where would that leave your *property*?'

'I appreciate your concern for my health, Gregory,' she said.

'Oh, there's more than health to worry about, Golda. I'm not sure they have the best care at the—'

Ocean slammed the door. 'Hey, Mrs B!'

'Oh, there you are, dear,' Mrs B said, relief evident in her voice.

Ocean stalked into the living room to find Ybarra sitting in the love seat, a fedora propped on his knee, while Mrs B eyed him from her own chair, the cheetah-print pillow clutched in her arms.

'Good afternoon, Ocean,' Ybarra said. 'We were just speaking of you.'

'Were you?' she said.

'Well, no, not specifically,' he admitted. 'But you as a tenant in this impossible rental market? Yes. And I was encouraging Golda to plan ahead for care. Or for— for any eventuality.'

'She doesn't need to plan ahead,' Ocean told him, even though she wasn't sure she believed it. 'She's already surrounded by people who care.'

'Oh, true. Very true. We've known each other for such a long time, after all.' Ybarra glanced sharply toward Mrs B. 'You poor woman, serving a *life sentence* of me down the block.'

'It hasn't been easy,' Mrs B said, showing a little spark.

'I need to speak with Mrs B alone,' Ocean told him.

Ybarra stood from his chair. 'Well! Promise me that you'll at least think about it, Golda. There are worse things in the world than estate planning.'

He popped his fedora on his head and grabbed his golf club – which for a moment Ocean mistook for a walking stick.

After he left, Ocean said, 'What was that about?'

Mrs B waved the question away. 'You know Gregory and his little obsessions.'

'Yeah, getting his claws on the Marigold Cottages. What's he after? First lunch, now this.'

Mrs B didn't answer for a moment, smoothing the cheetah-print pillow. 'He wants the name of my heir. Well, for me to confirm. He thinks he knows. He knew my husband and . . .'

'And the big secret is that the property's going to your husband's family?'

'Well, I set aside a little something for you, but yes. The

property . . . yes. That's going elsewhere.'

'Listen. I don't *want* the property. I don't want any of that weird shit coming between us.'

'Nothing ever could – except your terrible language. You don't need to swear.'

Ocean huffed a laugh. 'As if I don't remember you shouting at that rat trapped in your bedroom. Uh, but we do need to talk about what happens if you break a hip or something. So if you're in the hospital, they'll notify me. Maybe tell them I'm your daughter?'

'Nothing would make me prouder,' Mrs B said.

'Well, you raised me more than my parents did.'

'In all modesty, I must say that I did a wonderful job.'

'I don't know. You could've pressured me to go to law school.'

'You've the soul of an artist, my dear.' Mrs B took a breath. 'However, speaking of lawyers, I'd like to give you my power of attorney.'

Ocean eyed her.

'Nothing's wrong! Nothing's wrong. Gregory spooked me a little, is all.'

'Well, sure. Um. We can talk about that tonight. I've got to get to class. Can you help Riley with her mold project? And Miles has to draw his mission. La Purisima. It's not as pretty as it sounds.'

'Of course. Err, but before you go . . . I didn't want to mention this in front of Sophie. I'm afraid that bringing up *that man* upsets her.'

'You mean the stalker? Neal Hesse?'

Mrs B nodded. 'Hamilton looked on his computer, and he thinks Hesse is stalking some other girl.'

A chill touched Ocean's skin. 'So he wasn't in the bushes spying on Sophie because he's victimizing someone else now?'

'Unless he was *also* in the bushes, yes. Hamilton found his . . . I don't know, exercise tracker?'

'Yeah, that was one way he used to find Sophie.'

'Well, it shows that Hesse bicycles past this girl's sorority most nights. And he also goes to a coffee shop near the New Vic theatre. Where Sophie works.'

'So he might've seen her. Followed her home.'

'That's what Hamilton says.'

'Shit.' Ocean rubbed her face, feeling a clench of anger in her chest. 'This guy gets away with everything, doesn't he? Thinks nobody sees him. Maybe he needs to know that somebody's watching.'

47

SOPHIE

This isn't for the play. This isn't notes or brainstorming. I don't know what this is.

This is for me.

After a late breakfast, I wandered out to the mailboxes. I was shuffling through junk mail when Nicholas appeared next to me. Even though it was Sunday, he looked like he'd come from work, wearing slate blue chinos and a navy button-down. A few tasteful silver rings on his fingers, a matching bracelet on his wrist.

He said, 'It's rough.'

'Huh?'

'Your play. It's rough.'

It's possible that he'd texted me after Martini Night and I might've accidentally forwarded him the current draft of my play. Still, there was no reason to ambush me like this.

'It's not a play!' I told him. 'It's notes. It's just notes and ideas and snippets. It's not a play.'

'It's rough,' he repeated, 'and—'

'I know it's rough! Did you hear what I just said?'

'And I wonder if you need a few set pieces. Big moments. Opportunities for the characters – or the actors – to dig deeper into things.'

'It's just notes,' I said.

When he smiled, his eyes looked green in the late morning light. 'I love it, Sophie.'

I frowned at him in suspicion. 'You do not.'

'I love it.'

He sounded so earnest that I looked away, toward the sun setting in the distance, turning the sky a pale pink.

'You're on to something here. The humor, the relationships. Comedy without slapstick or cynicism. I'm just . . .' He let out a laugh. 'I think I'm jealous. That you're putting your work out there, and it's so fucking good.'

I didn't know how to respond to that.

'I only have two specific suggestions,' he continued. 'Other than, I don't know if I mentioned that it's rough?'

I shuffled my mail, jittery with excitement – and with relief that we were back to our normal interaction of him criticizing me. I'd have to unpack the rest later.

'Do you want to hear them?' he asked.

'No,' I said. 'Yes. No.'

'Uh,' he said.

'Shut up. Yes! Tell me. Quick.'

'First, I think there's a real problem with the way you're portraying the character of this guy Nicholas.'

When I'd forwarded the file, I might've included notes and ideas about him. 'Well, he's the villain. Possibly the murderer.'

'Maybe he's just misunderstood.'

'He's mean to the old lady.'

'He's not mean to her! He just avoids her. And maybe he has a reason for that.'

'Good point, yeah. The most compelling villains always have secret backstories that involve pain inflicted by sweet old women.'

'He's not a villain!' he said. 'He's a red herring at best.'

'A red *eel*.'

'And my second comment is about this other character. S?'

I squinted at him. 'What about her?'

'Let people see Sophie,' he told me. 'We need more Sophie.'

That's what he said. *Let people see Sophie. We need more Sophie.*

48

OCEAN

When Anthony opened his door, Ocean just stared at him.

'Hi,' he said, after a pause.

'Why the hell,' she said, 'are you wearing a homemade *My Little Pony* T-shirt?'

'Miles gave it to me.'

'That's why he wanted my fabric paint?'

'I guess.'

'Okay. But why are you wearing it?'

'It was a gift,' he said.

Ocean eyed him. 'He took one of your undershirts and painted it and gave it back as a gift?'

Anthony nodded.

'I'm not sure he understands the spirit of giving.'

'I never got anything like this before. That a kid made. I, uh . . .' He shrugged one pony-clad shoulder. 'Nobody ever, y'know, drew me a finger painting for the fridge or, uh . . .'

'Okay,' she said. 'Don't start crying about it.'

He snorted a laugh.

'Now change into something a human might wear before we go.'

'We going somewhere?'

'Sophie's stalker's house.'

He lost the smile and she followed him inside. He took off the shirt, and yeah, he'd make a fine model for clay sculpture class. Muscular, but not with bulging gym muscles. Chest hair, which on a visceral level: ew. But on an aesthetic level: nice. More tattoos, a bit of a belly.

Yeah, she'd invite him to class one day.

He folded the *My Little Pony* shirt away with Lily-Ann level precision, then grabbed a blue button-down from his closet. Which meant they looked like twins, except he was wearing flip-flops.

In the car, she told him about Riley and Miles. Mostly to keep a lid on her anger at Neal Hesse, who sounded like the kind of banal monster who ruined lives without ever making a headline. Leaving wreckage in his wake, but not enough to call attention to himself. So she bragged about her kids a little, which she tried not to do, but Anthony was a good listener.

When she reached the neighborhood, she drove past Neal Hesse's house, frowned at the car in the drive, then said, 'Shit.'

Anthony didn't respond.

'He's married. Looks like his wife is home alone.' That made things trickier. 'You stay in the car.'

'Okay,' he said, instead of asking why she'd invited him along in the first place.

'Nicholas saw stuff in the garage,' she told him. 'Blue and gold pennants, and a sorority necklace.'

'Yeah?'

'Hamilton figured it came from Chi Alpha Tau. He searched online and found social media posts from a college girl in Isla Vista. She started finding "fairy houses" around.'

'I don't know what that means.'

'It's one of the ways Neal Hesse stalked Sophie. He'd leave fairy houses like . . . offerings. Or warnings, I don't know. Shrines. They started with flowers, ended up with doll heads and rusty blades. This girl, the new one? She dropped out of college.'

Anthony listened.

'She came home one night and found a construction on her bed. Her toothbrush and tampons arranged in a little house.' Ocean exhaled to calm herself. 'I hope that's all that happened. Hamilton couldn't find anything else.'

'You're warning him off Sophie?'

'I'm not mentioning Sophie. The last thing I'm going to do is draw his attention to her. I'm just going to let him know that he's drawn some attention of his own.'

'Except he's not here. You'll talk to his wife?'

She thought for a moment. 'Yeah.'

'And you don't want me to come with?'

'Not with his wife at home. I don't . . . We can't make things worse for her.'

He nodded and stepped out of the car when she did. She thought she'd have to tell him to stay there, but he didn't move. He just watched as she walked to the door.

Ocean wondered how to approach this. Her main goal was to ensure Sophie's safety: check that this guy wasn't stalking her again, that he hadn't been lurking outside her house before being caught by Dead Rick. But she also worried about the new girl. And the wife, too.

The woman who opened the door was carrying a baby in a sling. She looked exhausted, wearing pregnancy pants and a gray shirt stained by baby spit. Her hair was drawn back in a claw clip and the circles under her eyes were highlighted by yesterday's mascara.

Ocean couldn't decide if Hesse was abusing her or she'd just had a rough night with the kid. But first step, see if she'd give her husband an alibi without knowing that's what she was doing.

'Kelly Hesse?' Ocean asked.

'Yes?'

Ocean still hadn't decided on an approach until she heard herself say, 'I'm a reporter with the *Independent*. I'm here about the woman who saved a kid from drowning,

210

around the corner?' She paused for a reaction, then said: 'You didn't hear about that?'

'Oh! No. What happened?'

'This was late at night. The Friday before last? Apparently she heard a toddler crying and splashing. She climbed a fence and saved this girl from drowning in the pool. The parents rushed to the hospital and forgot to ask the woman's name. So I'm knocking on doors, trying to find the Good Samaritan.'

Kelly Hesse shook her head. 'It wasn't me, I'm sorry.'

'You didn't happen to see anyone outside late Friday night? Maybe walking a little white dog?'

The baby began to fuss and Kelly bounced in place, one hand on the door. 'I don't think so.'

'Do you think your husband might've?'

She shook her head. 'I know he didn't. I—we have a strict schedule.'

'Do you?'

'We watch his shows on Friday. We don't like to miss them.'

'Of course.'

Kelly smiled shakily. 'Sometimes he bikes at night. Or cycles. I'm supposed to call it cycling.'

Ocean just looked at her, waiting for more.

'So that night he was home. Friday night. For his shows.'

'Well, thanks anyway. I'll let you go.' Ocean didn't move though; she just looked closer. 'Listen. Your husband isn't Neal Hesse, by any chance?'

The woman shushed her baby. 'You know him?'

'By reputation,' Ocean said.

The woman lowered her head over the baby.

'Leaving is scary,' Ocean told her. 'Especially with a newborn. I have two kids myself. And leaving can feel impossible. Especially if we think we're at fault. Or that we're responsible. But y'know, nobody deserves to feel afraid or alone. You don't deserve that.'

The woman closed the door in her face.

'Welp.' Ocean slipped a women's shelter brochure under the jamb and called, 'Check under your door!'

She walked back to the car and Anthony said, 'She slammed the door?'

'Yup.'

He waited for more.

'She says her husband was home the night of the murder,' Ocean said. 'I don't think she's lying.'

Anthony climbed into the passenger seat.

'One thing though.' Ocean buckled her seat belt. 'She's scared of him. She's terrified.'

'Like Sophie,' he said.

'And this college girl,' Ocean said, starting the car. 'And who knows how many others.'

49

SOPHIE

An hour before work on Monday, I stood in the center of my living room, surrounded by index cards on the floor. Each one contained a potential scene from my play, tentatively entitled *Close-Knit Strangers*. The idea being that the arrival of a disruptive force – i.e. Anthony – revealed that the members of this 'close-knit community' were actually strangers to each other.

I knew that, in fact, we'd grown closer since he came, but that wasn't going to sell tickets. I needed secrets, betrayals, trauma. Also, I planned to have the Mrs B character knitting all the time, to double-justify 'close-knit.'

I turned in slow circles, letting the scenes blur together below me. Anthony, Ocean, Kids, Sophie, Lily-Ann, Hamilton, Nicholas . . .

Where did *he* fit?

Everyone else I easily built a character around, but Nicholas didn't really work. Except as the villain. He wasn't an integral part of the community. He stood apart. Even his cottage was different. I frowned at his index card. Everyone else meshed pretty well, but I was still looking for a way to get him into bed with us.

My phone buzzed before I could think too closely about how I'd expressed that.

Nicholas
Small town

Sophie
Very well, thank you. And how are you this morning?

Nicholas
Isn't this Lily-Ann's ex?

He attached a photo of the interior of a restaurant, but I didn't look. I was too busy thinking about the play.

Sophie
What do you think of the title Close-Knit Strangers?

Nicholas
Cable-Knit Sweaters.

Sophie
You are dumb.

Sophie
Are you only texting me because you think you saw Piotr?

Nicholas
At the bathhouse

Sophie
You saw him at a bathhouse???

Nicholas
It's an oyster bar.

Sophie
Wait. Are you trying to prove that you're . . . investigating?

Nicholas
No.

Sophie
Okay, Sherlock.

Nicholas
Good morning. How are you today?

So I texted 'small town' to bring us full circle.

Then I twisted my wet hair into the sloppy bun I'd been trying lately and put on tinted lip balm and mascara and left for work. With a spring in my step for no particular reason.

I mean, I also checked the windows and the peephole, but that was *not* hypervigilance anymore. Not since I'd found a goddamn corpse on my front step.

I went down the stone steps of the Marigold Cottages onto the sidewalk and found myself half a block behind Anthony and Miles. Walking together. Which was weird.

Not that Miles seemed to think so. He was gesturing and chatting, and every now and then Anthony would gaze at him and nod. It looked like a butterfly having a conversation with a tree stump.

I fell back, because . . . I didn't know why. I was still a little shy of Anthony, I guess. He and Miles paused at the corner with the riot of purple Mexican sage. The flowers swayed in the breeze of a Subaru topped with surfboards, and I paused, too, farther back.

As I stood there, I glanced across the street to where a bunch of kids were waiting for the school bus heading south. A few of the older ones were picking on a littler one. Making fun of his cartoon backpack and calling him names.

I felt my skin prickle. I hated confrontation, and middle-school kids were the absolute worst. But I was trying to be an adult here and I couldn't just walk past some kid being bullied.

So I waited for a break in traffic, then saw Miles and Anthony already on the other side of the street. Miles greeted the kid getting bullied, and I expected Anthony to say something, or do something, but he just stood there, his back to me, facing the bullies.

They stared at him in what looked like nervous awe. Exactly how I'd felt when I first saw him.

After a moment, Anthony seemed to pat his chest. Like *Look at me*, I guess.

It worked. They stopped messing with the kid with the *My Little Pony* backpack.

I scuttled past without Miles or Anthony seeing me. Invisible, as usual. Which I'd wanted, but it also bothered me. I'd learned to make myself small. To shrink away from the fear of my stalker even when he wasn't there. I'd thinned myself into two-dimensionality, like if I turned my face I could disappear.

We need more Sophie.

And that's what I wanted to become: more. I wanted to take more space, to seize more attention. To walk onto the stage and claim the spotlight.

50

VERNON

Two black-and-whites parked on the street near the bus stop, but the officers stayed back as Vernon entered the Marigold Cottages. He ignored the old lady's house to his left and the Chinese girl's house to his right; though if the girl was home, she probably wasn't ignoring *him*. Spying through her peephole.

Pink and purple flowers fluttered in the hanging pots that lined the courtyard, making the place look festive. Fit his celebratory mood.

He heard a scratching noise and turned to see the lesbian's daughter scraping a tray of what looked like mold into the bushes. Probably some kind of online challenge.

'The flowers are nice,' he said, when she scowled at him. He was familiar with the expression. His own daughter addressed him with a degree of scorn only umpires deserved.

'What do *you* want?' she demanded.

'Oh, same as anyone,' he told her. 'Justice for the dead.'

'Bullshit,' she said.

Jesus. 'How old are you?'

'Old enough that my mother told me to never talk to the police.'

'Doing a good job with that, sport.'

She slammed into her cottage and Vernon went and thumped on Anthony Lambert's door until he answered.

'You're under arrest for the murder of James Dedrick,' Vernon said. 'You know the Miranda, let's take it as told.'

Give ex-cons credit, Anthony Lambert just grunted and turned around for the cuffs. Fast and easy. The lesbian's daughter didn't even have time to come complain.

Vernon took him in personally. No muss, no fuss. Polite, professional, cool. Yeah, he still had the touch. He left the booking to the clerk, reviewed the file, then reunited with the perpetrator in the interview room.

He took the seat opposite Anthony Lambert and said, 'There are things I know and things I don't know. First, I know you killed Dedrick. I've got your own admission about that.'

Anthony Lambert did not respond to that news bulletin.

Vernon tsked in mock disappointment. 'Telling an upstanding kid without a criminal record that you committed the deed? Bad decision. And second, I know why. Finally. We've got motive, and between you and me that's what kept the prosecutor vacillating.'

Anthony Lambert looked at him.

'That means dithering, hesitating. DA doesn't like prosecuting without a motive, even if we have a confession.'

Anthony Lambert looked at him.

'I know!' Vernon said, with a warm chuckle. 'I feel exactly the same. You and me, we understand. You don't need motive to kill someone. How many of the killers that you did time with had a reason that made any sense?'

Anthony Lambert looked at the wall behind him.

'Yeah, but try telling that to the DA. What they are, fundamentally, is civilians. They won't let me proceed without a water-tight case. You know what that means, yeah? Yeah, you know. The new evidence is duck-ass tight.'

Anthony Lambert looked back at him.

'That's why you're here. You know how this goes. You wouldn't be here if we weren't certain. Now, you're too fucking silent to actually tell me that you're innocent, which, I'll admit, is annoying. But between you and me, let's say you *did* claim that?'

Anthony Lambert said nothing.

'Then I'd tell you: So what? Say what you want, I've got the evidence. Your confession. Videotape. Yeah, you heard me. Video. No murder weapon, though. That's the only thing I *don't* know.' He paused. 'So why don't you help with that? It'll make your life smoother.'

Anthony Lambert didn't make his life smoother.

'Fair enough,' Vernon said. 'I pride myself on my conversational skills, but I know when I'm beat. I'll just say, keep this in mind. You wouldn't be here if we weren't certain. You *are* going to serve time.'

Anthony Lambert exhaled.

'Yeah. Sixteen years if you confess. That's a long stretch, I won't lie. But you can still build a life on the other end of it. If you *don't* confess? Then DA's pushing for thirty-five years. No parole. That's game over. You'll come out an old, old man.'

Anthony Lambert looked at the table.

'You know what I want,' Vernon told him. 'If you sign a confession, that'd make my job easy. Makes me look good. But it also saves you two decades of your life. Either you spend twenty extra years behind bars or you sign a piece of paper. That's a win-win. Your decision, though. Sleep on it.'

51

LILY-ANN

The Quality Assurance Project Plan ran to twenty-three pages, but Lily-Ann focused on section 'C: Validation Procedures.'

Polishing the QAPP wasn't, strictly speaking, her job. That was perhaps one reason why her manager was more than happy to let her work from home. Though, in fact, she was so happy that Lily-Ann sometimes wondered if her willingness contained some sort of implicit criticism.

Still, Lily-Ann enjoyed working at the desk tucked in the corner of her bedroom. She could play classical music to block out the street noise and didn't need to bother with shoes.

She was double-checking a paragraph when her phone buzzed.

Hamilton Neighbor
Eggplants are members of the nightshade family.

Lily-Ann already knew that, but saying so would be rude. So after a moment, she texted:

Lily-Ann
Where did they originate?

Hamilton Neighbor
Unknown, though they have been cultivated in southern Asia since prehistory.

Hamilton Neighbor
I made too much moussaka.

Hamilton Neighbor
If you would like to join me for lunch, we can discuss Anthony.

Lily-Ann
You need more hummingbird feeders?

Hamilton Neighbor
He was arrested for the murder.

She put her shoes on and went to his house.

He greeted her at the door with a glass of celery-flavored soda, then apologized for suggesting that they eat at his computers.

'I am trying to unearth more information,' he explained.

So she tidied the kitchen, replated the moussaka, then joined him in front of his three screens. To her surprise, the middle screen showed a fantasy-themed game; even more surprising, Hamilton was actively playing.

'What are you doing?' she asked, after taking a bite.

'Trying to solve the archlich's riddle.'

'Why?'

'That's the only way to get the last Shard of Ry'na. Which is one of the broken pieces of the arcanum, forged into a dagger that possesses the power to—'

'*Hamilton*,' she said.

'Hmm?'

'First, this is delicious. Nothing beats grilled eggplant in enough olive oil. And the potatoes are cooked perfectly. Is that nutmeg?'

'Just a hint. Fresh ground.'

'Second, what does this have to do with Anthony?'

'Oh! Oh, yes. Well, my friend in the police will give me more information – such as regarding the arrest – but he wants more than in-game currency.'

'He wants the last Shard of Ry'na?'

Hamilton nodded. 'Which is the only Shard I have trouble getting.'

'Show me,' she said.

The archlich's riddle was a shifting sequence of pattern-matching mini-games you needed to complete while under attack by snake-people.

Hamilton did the fighting while Lily-Ann handled the puzzles. And to her surprise, she found the game quite satisfying, though she disliked the sound effects.

Winning the Shard was a triumph. She may have whooped in celebration. And Hamilton may have told her about his high score on an arcade version of *Centipede* in celebration.

When Hamilton contacted his friend via an in-game messaging system, the friend responded immediately, despite being at the police department. Which was handy, because after he sent them a summation of the evidence against Anthony, he promised he'd get his hands on a copy of the video, too.

52

SOPHIE

Act II, maybe

SCENE 2, PERHAPS

Curtains open on HAMILTON'S living room. LILY-ANN, SOPHIE and HAMILTON are present. There is, for no apparent reason, unremarked, a hand-drawn poster of a curved fantasy dagger on his whiteboard. OCEAN and her kids enter and are greeted at the door by HAMILTON.

HAMILTON
Clamato juice?

RILEY
What is that? Clam tomato?

HAMILTON
Hence the portmanteau.

RILEY
Uh. No, thanks.

HAMILTON
Then shall we convene this emergency session of the
Marigold Cottages Murder Collective?

LILY-ANN
Let us begin. Anthony was arrested for the murder of
James Dedrick.

RILEY

(snickering)

That's his real name? I thought Oma was just calling him
Dead Rick.

OCEAN
Of course, that's his real name. Dead Rick.

MILES
Be serious! How're we going to help Anthony? We need to
get him out. All he wants is to watch the whales.

SOPHIE
To what?

MILES
He just learned about whale watching and he— there's

only three weeks before they're gone! We need to help him. He needs to see them.

HAMILTON
There are two pieces of evidence. New evidence. Which are the basis for the arrest warrant. Or the bases? Lily-Ann?

LILY-ANN
Bases.

HAMILTON
No, I mean, uh . . . why don't you explain them?

LILY-ANN
First, the police claim that Anthony implicated himself in the murder while in conversation with his cellmate. That he confessed. The cellmate says Anthony admitted he argued with Dedrick downtown. Dedrick followed him home, where Anthony said – according to the cellmate – that Dedrick attacked him, so he defended himself.

OCEAN
In conversation with a cellmate? Sure, we all know what a chatterbox Anthony is.

SOPHIE
Right? When I say hi to him, he barely nods. I watched him drop that new birdbath on his foot and he just stood there quietly until it stopped hurting.

HAMILTON
I wondered where the birdbath came from. It's right outside my bedroom, in the perfect spot for—

OCEAN
Anyway, Anthony doesn't talk. Do we really think he admitted a murder to some guy in jail?

MILES
He talks to me.

RILEY
Dude, he listens to you. Talk about chatterbox. If you were the one in jail, we'd believe it.

LILY-ANN
The cellmate has no record; he has no reason to lie. A young kid. Uh . . .

(checks notes)

Ian Talken. First time he's ever been in trouble. Why would he lie?

SOPHIE
I believe him lying before I believe Anthony talking.

HAMILTON
That's hearsay anyway, isn't it? Inadmissible in court.

OCEAN
Anything's admissible if the judge admits it. And prosecutors are worse than cops. You know what happens to a prosecutor who puts the wrong person in prison for decades? A promotion.

RILEY

Step away from the megaphone, Mother.

LILY-ANN

And the second piece of evidence is videotape. We haven't gotten a copy yet, but apparently it shows Anthony breaking into Dedrick's house in Altadena, the night before last.

MILES

He wouldn't do that! He wouldn't. He just wouldn't, I know he wouldn't.

(As the others continue, OCEAN and RILEY engage in a furious pantomime in which OCEAN tells RILEY to take MILES home.)

HAMILTON

If there's video, that's breaking and entering, but it doesn't mean he killed anybody.

LILY-ANN

It's one more data point. He was in prison for a violent crime. He lives here. He broke into the man's house. He confessed in jail. None of those things alone means anything. But added together, that's enough for a jury to convict.

(Having lost the pantomime, RILEY grudgingly leads MILES away.)

MILES

(on the way out)

Thanks for the Clamato juice.

HAMILTON
It was invented by a chemist who was trying to create a
cocktail that tasted like Manhattan clam chowder.

SOPHIE
I, uh, saw him. The night before last. When the video was
taken. I saw Anthony.

LILY-ANN
Doing what?

SOPHIE
Leaving. Here. Dressed in dark clothes. I'm sorry. I saw
him. He looked . . . furtive.

LILY-ANN
When we visit him, we'll ask.

OCEAN
Breaking into the guy's house? I don't know. I can't see
it. What's he going to do, pawn stuff to buy more leafy
greens? What was stolen?

HAMILTON
Jewelry, sneakers, two TVs. Power tools.

SOPHIE
Power tools?

HAMILTON
Yeah, and kitchen appliances.

SOPHIE
Lily-Ann should break into his studio again.

OCEAN
The cops already searched. If they'd found something, it'd be on the list.

SOPHIE
I'm sorry, but is it possible that he's . . . guilty? I mean, that does seem most likely. As much as Mrs B doesn't want it to be true, at some point we're going to have to face the facts. I didn't do it. None of you did it. Who else here would even be capable of killing someone?

(MRS B appears on the balcony, or rising from a trap door, in a puff of smoke.)

I'm not sure about the specific staging, but I wanted something that emphasized her complete certainty. She is speaking with almost-authorial authority here. Like a one-woman Greek chorus who simply *knows* things.

MRS. B
Anthony is not guilty of this crime.

SOPHIE
Sorry! Sorry!

OCEAN
Good people do bad things all the time, Mrs B.

MRS. B
Anthony did not kill James Dedrick. And if you don't prove his innocence, I will.

End of scene.

53

OCEAN

The cheaper the boxed macaroni and cheese, the better the kids felt after eating it. Neon orange, full of preservatives? Miles's tears stopped, and Riley's recriminations slowed.

Ocean didn't know when they'd become so fond of Anthony. She didn't know if they were just picking up on her fondness. Hell, she didn't even know why *she* liked him. You met people like that, sometimes. Didn't matter if you had nothing in common; for some reason they were just your people.

After homemade chocolate chip cookies – more comfort per ounce than even Oreos – she said, 'Who's in the mood for a re-watch of some *Last Airbender* episodes?'

'Not me,' Miles said, for the first time ever. 'We should talk about how we're going to help Anthony.'

'I'm not sure there's anything we can do.'

'The whales won't be here for long!' Miles said, suddenly on the verge of tears again. 'He's going to miss them!'

'I'm going to tell Grandma you said there's nothing we can do,' Riley told Ocean, saving the day with her salty tone.

'Please, no! She'll send instructions for making a giant protest puppet again.'

A few years earlier, Ocean's mother had bullied them into making a huge paper-mâché cucumber for a march against pesticides. Ocean had added a dress and crown of ferns . . . and built the entire thing upside down.

Miles sniffed. 'I liked Pickles.'

'His name wasn't Pickles,' Riley said.

'*Her* name,' Ocean said.

'He had a dong, Mother,' Riley said.

'He didn't!' Ocean said. 'I mean, *she* didn't. It was a cucumber stem. It just ended up . . . on the bottom, and escaping her dress. She was the Green Goddess; she protected planet Earth.'

'With her mighty dong,' Riley said.

Miles started giggling, mostly as a release from his frustration about Anthony. No doubt that's why Ocean and Riley giggled along. Well, that and the combination of fake cheese sauce and chocolate chunks.

'We'll talk to his lawyer, the public defender,' Ocean promised the kids. 'We'll make sure she knows there are people who care about him, who are in his corner. Okay?'

'*And* we'll write letters,' Miles said.

'Deal.'

'And I'll bake her cupcakes,' he added. He always thought cupcakes were the key to anyone's heart, romantic or platonic.

'I thought you might say that,' Ocean told him. 'I've already bought the ingredients.'

54

LILY-ANN

Hamilton opened his silverware drawer and grabbed two forks, saying, 'Okay, but Mrs B absolutely *insists* she's not wrong.'

Behind him, Lily-Ann pulled the hot roasting pan from the oven. 'That is a universal belief among those who are incorrect.'

'It's also a pretty universal belief of those who are right, though.'

'True,' Lily-Ann said. 'Which is why we'll ignore her opinion entirely.'

He squinted at her. 'You don't think Anthony is guilty either.'

'We're also going to ignore *my* opinion entirely. We're looking for facts, Hamilton.' Lily-Ann shooed him from his kitchen. 'Now go set the table.'

'How can I set the table when we're investigating a murder?'

'Did you know that the first tablecloths functioned as communal napkins?' she asked, pulling a carving knife from the wooden block.

'Of course I did! What does that have to do with anything?'

'It doesn't, but it's all I'll talk about until the table is set.'

He harrumphed at her, then Birkenstocked his way into the dining room.

Lily-Ann had made roast chicken with fennel and tangerine for lunch. A new recipe. She carved while Hamilton set the table. The chicken smelled good. The scent of anise and citrus combined with the almost-caramelized tang of the crisp skin.

She took her seat and said, 'Nicholas is hiding something.'

'You mean the way he avoids Mrs B?'

'Mmm.'

Hamilton pronged a forkful of chicken. 'So maybe Nicholas killed Dead Rick in order to . . . I can't think of a reason.'

'Yes, his motive is obscure. But that's true of us all. At least Nicholas has actually met the man.'

Hamilton started to reply, then looked at his plate. 'This is delicious. The oranges really add something. I'm usually against fruit with meat.'

'They're tangerines.'

'Oh! Tangerine means 'from Tangiers,' the Moroccan city.'

'A tree down the block is fruiting early, so they gave Mrs B a bag. She left some on your doorstep, so I took them.'

He nodded in understanding. 'I . . . don't open the door unless someone rings. And I still don't step outside and . . .' He set his fork down. 'Everyone's right about me being homebound. I am.'

'I know.'

'You do?'

'We all do, Hamilton. You never leave.'

'Oh, well, yes. True. I never leave. My whole life, I spend here. Inside.'

'Does that make you unhappy?'

'Well, not so much now that I have guests.' He gave a faltering smile. 'I mean, the truth is that *leaving* makes me unhappy. Staying in makes me happy.'

'That's how I feel about working. Piotr says I work too much and the company's taking advantage of me. But I *like* working all the time. He makes me feel like I'm wrong to like what I like.'

Hamilton considered her. 'I don't see what's wrong with working all the time if it makes you happy.'

'And I don't see what's wrong with staying in all the time if *that* makes you happy.'

'I suspect this means that we're bad influences on each other.'

She raised her milk in a toast. 'Then here's to the bad influences that make us happy.'

'To bad influences,' he said and clinked her glass.

55

OCEAN

The kitchen was messier than usual, even though Ocean was fixing half as many lunches these days. She still made Miles three snacks tucked into a bento box, but Riley had declared that bringing a lunch box from home was embarrassing.

So the food prep wasn't the reason for the mess: Miles's letter-writing campaign was. He used the kitchen bar as his command center to draft the notes he was sending to their congresswoman and state rep and both senators, to the mayor and the chief of police and, for reasons that escaped her, to Paul Rudd on Twitter.

Riley's show of support was more visual. She'd drawn on her face and neck in permanent marker, in the style of Anthony's tattoos. Although – to Ocean's gratification – substantially more artistically. Still, she'd half expected a call from school after dropping Riley off.

She wiped down the kitchen, then emailed a gallery

owner about her newest piece and heard the front door open.

'I need a hand!' Mrs B called.

Ocean trotted to the front hall and found Mrs B holding two cups of coffee and a brown paper bag that smelled of bagels. She took the cups and started for the kitchen, but Mrs B went into the dining room, which meant she wanted a serious discussion.

So Ocean grabbed a cutting board and plates, and they chatted about the kids as Mrs B laid out the fixings tucked in the bottom of the bag. She'd been treating Ocean to bagels since she was six. In horror, at first, when she'd discovered that Ocean liked cinnamon raisin. She'd converted her to poppy seed, then introduced a faint smear of cream cheese. That had been the gateway drug to adding fresh tomato, and a few years later red onion.

By high school, Ocean was adding capers, and after art school, to Mrs B's beaming delight, she'd finally developed a taste for lox. Though she drew the line at whitefish, and pickled herring was an abomination.

'Don't freak out,' Mrs B said, setting her coffee down.

'What? Where'd you learn that expression?'

'I hear things. Anyway, I'm hoping – well, expecting, though it's very wrong of me – that you'll look after everyone at the Cottages when I'm gone.'

'*What*? What's wrong? What is it? Is it cancer? Please tell me it's not melanoma. I told you to wear more sunscreen! How many times did I tell you? When did you get the diagnosis? I can't believe you didn't take me to the appointments. What were you—'

'I said *don't* freak out! I'm not dying, Ocean. I don't

have cancer, knock on wood.' She rapped on the dining room table. 'I don't have anything. Really, I promise I'm not dying.'

'Well, *I* am, now that you've scared me half to death.'

'And of course I'd take you to my medical appointments.' Mrs B put her jeweled hand on Ocean's forearm. 'You might meet a nice lady doctor.'

'They're just called doctors, Mrs B.'

'Well, I didn't want to say a nice lesbian doctor,' Mrs B explained. 'Anyway, this is about estate planning. For when I'm gone.'

'Ybarra really got into your head.'

Mrs B nodded serenely. Her white pixie cut glowed in the sunshine streaming through the window. She looked angelic in a sky blue silk kaftan that hid her YMCA-toned arms and made her eyes appear almost turquoise.

'He's right that sometimes shocking changes happen without any notice. And one must be prepared, and I need—' Mrs B's smile faltered. 'I need you to look after the people I care for. Just in case.'

'Look after how?' Ocean asked.

'I wrote a list, but first you must tell me that you understand that you and the children are at the top of my list.'

'Sure.'

'No, Ocean. You need to say the whole thing.'

'I understand that the kids and I are at the top of your list.'

'Good! Now, then . . .' Mrs B patted the skirt of her kaftan, as if hoping to find a pocket. 'I forgot the list at home. You'll find details there. First, cover anyone's rent who needs it. If they get in trouble, I mean.'

'How'm I supposed to do that if the place is willed to someone else?'

'If I'm gone but not dead, dear, that's how. If I'm . . . what's the word? Incompetent or absent.'

'This isn't making me feel any better,' Ocean said.

'You'll live,' Mrs B said. 'Next is a secret. You know the man who delivers Hamilton's milk?'

'No. What? Like DoorDash?'

'He's a local farmer. But he refuses to sell to Hamilton; they had a falling-out. So he thinks he's delivering it to me.'

Ocean laughed. 'Okay.'

'Lily-Ann's hedges must be trimmed every three weeks, without fail. She doesn't mind the noise.'

'I do.'

'Yes, but not as much as she dislikes unevenness.' Mrs B pulled a tissue from her bosom and wiped her nose. 'I'm sure you're aware that Sophie struggles with drinking?'

'I'm aware Anthony carried her home after she passed out.'

'Almost every week she stumbles home from an evening out, considerably worse for wear. She's been better lately, but if it happens again, check that she gets inside and locks her door.'

'Got it.'

'And finally,' Mrs B said, 'give Nicholas another chance.'

'At what?' Ocean asked, playing dumb. 'He's rude to you.'

'He has his reasons. Nicholas . . . he needs us. Will you do that for me?'

'Fine. If it's what you want.'

'Oh, what else? The UPS deliveryman is allergic to walnuts.'

'So?'

'His favorite cookies are ginger snaps. I give him some every few weeks, because he's here so often for Hamilton. The bus driver has three children, and his daughter's quinceañera is coming up, and she loves skateboarding, so I thought—'

'Whoa, whoa, whoa. Are you going to go through every single person you know?'

'Don't be silly. Just the ones I care about.'

'Yeah, so every single person you know. I'll read the list later, Mrs B.' Ocean stood from her chair. 'I've got to get ready for class.'

Mrs B began collecting the breakfast mess. 'Stone carving?'

'Contemporary art. Today I'm springing Julie Mehretu on them. She's the greatest living contemporary artist.'

'Nonsense, dear!' Mrs B said, kissing her on the cheek. 'At best, she's the *second* greatest.'

'Uh-huh,' Ocean said.

'After you, I mean.'

'I know what you mean, you daffy old lady.'

Mrs B paused at the door. 'Take care of them, my dear. And yourself. You're precious to me.'

Ocean was in the classroom, double-checking that she and the projector understood each other, when Sophie called, incoherent with news.

'Slow down,' Ocean said. 'Take a breath.'

'Sorry. Sorry.' Sophie fell silent for a fraction of a

second. 'She confessed. She confessed. To the murder, she confessed.'

'Who?'

'She— I saw her with a shopping bag. I thought she was going to the grocery store.' Sophie took a hurried breath. 'She got into a Lyft, and I-I didn't know. I didn't know where she was going. She confessed!'

'Sophie, what are you talking about? Who confessed?'

'Mrs B,' Sophie told her. 'She says she killed James Derick.'

56

VERNON

Walk-in false confessions didn't happen. People didn't just wander in with self-incriminating lies, not on low-profile cases. Maybe if you had a cultural touchstone murder – a little blonde beauty queen – then okay, that was catnip for crazies.

Something like this, though? A thirty-year-old wealthy white guy? Who cared? Throw a gluten-free muffin in a pretentious coffee shop and you'd hit three more James Dedricks.

Except *someone* cared, because Vernon was sitting at his desk listening to Golda Bakofsky fuck up his day.

'I certainly *did* kill the poor man,' she repeated, after he scoffed.

'Look at your wrists, ma'am. You couldn't arm-wrestle a jellyfish.'

'I'll have you know that I am the strongest woman

in my senior strength class at the Y, and I killed James Dedrick.'

'What you're doing is, you're trying to muddle my case against Anthony Lambert.'

Her lips narrowed. 'Nonsense.'

'Okay, then,' he said. 'Why did you kill him?'

'I am not prepared to say.'

He pinched the bridge of his nose. 'Well, now, you've convinced me.'

'Shouldn't you be arresting me?' she demanded.

'For knowingly making a false report of a crime? I will if you insist, but that's just paperwork for me and a fine for you.'

'I am not making a false report,' she said.

'So, you killed James Dedrick, did you?' He grabbed his notepad. 'Why was he at the Marigold Cottages?'

'I'm not prepared to say.'

'Did you know him before you brutally cut him down in the prime of his life?'

'I did not.'

'So it wasn't a grudge.' Vernon tapped his pen on the blank page. 'Let's chalk this up to a sudden murderous impulse, shall we? Except I've been a detective for a few years now, ma'am, and in all modesty I've been getting better every year. I like to think I've learned to read people a little, so can I ask you a question?'

'Of course,' she said.

'Do you eat veal?'

'No.'

'Because of the poor calves.' He tapped his pen once more. 'Yet you killed a man in cold blood.'

That flustered her. 'No, I–I'm not saying in cold blood, I was angry and afraid and – and veal is not kosher, due to – I can't remember the phrase – the suffering of animals – so of course you're right that's why I won't eat it. I won't eat foie gras either.'

He stood politely. 'Well, thank you for coming in, ma'am. Do you need a ride home?'

'I don't – I'm not *going* home!'

'You didn't know the victim and you won't say why you killed him. You're not physically capable of killing him. There's no motivation, no evidence, no capability, yet—'

'Oh, I have evidence!'

Vernon paused. 'You do?'

'Indeed, I have. It slipped my mind.' She gave him a sharp look. 'Because I wasn't expecting you to accuse me of *lying*.'

'I'm sorry if I crossed a line,' he said. 'I should've just accused you of homicide.'

She rustled around in her reusable shopping bag. 'Well, I'm sure you meant no offense.'

'Mmm. So what's your evidence?'

'The murder weapon,' she told him, and pulled a club from the bag.

Three feet long. A straight shaft with a heavy wooden ball the size of a grapefruit on the end. Golda Bakofsky called the club a 'knobkerrie.' She said it was a gift to her husband from a lovely gentleman they'd met in Africa.

She apologized for her absent-mindedness and said, 'It was quite late at night. I was doing the crossword puzzle when I noticed a stranger on the property. James Dedrick, though of course I didn't know his name. I went outside to ask

240

him if I could help him. I took the knobkerrie with me and—'

'Do you often grab a club before asking people if you can help them?'

'I sometimes use it as a walking stick, so it was right by the door.'

Vernon scratched his temple with the capped end of his pen. He needed a cup of coffee. He needed someone to drag this little old lady out of the building.

'Okay,' he said. 'Go on.'

'Then he threatened . . .' She gave a little shudder. 'Me. He threatened me. So I tried to scare him off with a swing of the stick.'

'And you accidentally killed him.'

'Exactly.'

'So your evidence is a walking stick that you've had in the house for years?'

'Also known as the murder weapon. Surely, your CIA people can match the weapon to the injury.'

'My CIA people?'

'Like the TV shows. *CIA: Miami* and *CIA: Vegas*.'

'You mean *CSI*, ma'am.'

'So you admit it!'

'What? No, I'm just saying that's the name of—'

'Not to mention the blood.'

He took a breath. 'What blood?'

'James Dedrick's blood,' she said, turning the club to reveal a sticky patch on the otherwise shiny wood. 'On the knobkerrie. See, you can see it, right there.'

He pinched the bridge of his nose. 'You've got to be shitting me.'

'I am most certainly,' she said, 'not shitting you.'

57

SOPHIE

The tequila bottle on the windowsill glowed golden in the sunlight. Only five or six shots left. I'd been cutting back, but after reading Mrs B's note . . .

I wasn't due at work for another hour. I didn't start until the afternoon some days, when I stayed late to staff the box office. I didn't mind the schedule. I liked the chatter of the audience during intermission. Anyway, that's why I'd still been home when Mrs B slipped a letter under my door. Hell, I'd still been in *bed*, catching up on social media, wallowing in the comfortable cocoon of self-doubt.

Why was I even pretending to draft a play? I'd never get anything produced. I'd never direct. Dad was right; I should take a grant writing class and become a director of development.

Hearing someone at my door had dragged me from my unhappy daze. By the time I peeked outside, I only caught a single glimpse of Mrs B getting into the Lyft.

Then I read the note.

Her confession.

Holy shit.

The note said she'd been afraid to tell Ocean herself. Yeah, I bet. She'd written Ocean's phone number for me to call, like I didn't have it in my phone.

I waited until Ocean picked up before totally losing my shit.

Then after I passed along the news, I looked at the tequila bottle and decided that I'd never run across a better excuse for morning drinking.

Mrs B confessed to murder. She turned herself in. The sweetest, kindest, gentlest person I'd ever met was sitting in jail. She was innocent, of course, just trying to get Anthony released, like the icon she was.

Imagining her in a concrete box, wearing an orange jumpsuit, being bullied by guards, made my stomach ache. Still, I only took one shot of the tequila. Then I just . . . sat there, my mind spinning in circles: murder, jail, cops. Peeing in a metal toilet with no privacy. Bars slamming, inmates mocking her.

After too long, I grabbed a yogurt from the fridge and made myself focus on the only thing that seemed to settle my nerves these days: my play notes.

What a plot twist.

What if, in the play, Mrs B is the actual killer? Some kind of evil landlady, maybe?

Or a desperate one. I'd overheard her tell Anthony, that first night they met, that she was having trouble paying her bills. And I hadn't told anyone. So maybe this was all my fault. Well, I'd told Nicholas, but he'd just dismissed me.

No. I couldn't write Mrs B as the killer. It was more believable if she was murdered and we had a Raskolnikov situation. Too hard to suspend disbelief when I knew the real Mrs B.

Of course, reality was stranger. She'd turned herself in for murder? *Really?* Just how far was one old lady willing to go to help a tenant she barely knew? There had to be some other link between them.

As I thought about that, Ocean updated the group chat.

* * *

Ocean

I just got off the with the detective

Hamilton

Off the what? You dropped a word.

Ocean

Mrs B says she killed Dead Rick

Ocean

Turned herself in

Sophie

She didn't do it

Ocean

She says she saw an intruder. And hit him with her walking stick

Hamilton

Zulu iwisa or Ndebele ibisa?

Hamilton

Induku?

Ocean

Hamilton. Shut the fuck up

Ocean

Dead Rick's blood is on the stick

Ocean

She's in jail. I'm losing my fucking mind

Sophie

What are we going to do?

Lily-Ann

Where are you now, Ocean?

Ocean

On the way home. From the county jail

A private text popped onto my screen.

Lily-Ann

Sit with her so she's not alone.

Sophie

Ok. Um, Mrs B was having trouble paying her bills

I'd call in late for work, not a problem. I even . . . a part of me liked that maybe I could help Ocean, instead of the other way around. Maybe I could be the strong person, for once.

Instead of responding to my private text, Lily-Ann switched back to the group chat.

Lily-Ann

I enjoyed trying to solve the puzzle. And I like Anthony.

Lily-Ann

But this isn't a game anymore.

Lily-Ann

We need to bring Mrs B home.

58

LILY-ANN

The database blurred on Lily-Ann's laptop screen, the rows and columns braiding together. She looked away, out the window to the squared-off hedge where bees clumsily crawled into the little pink flowers.

She felt clumsy, herself. Putting the pieces together, but not as quickly or clearly as she'd like. Possibly because she was trying *not* to connect a number of obvious dots.

1. Mrs B had the murder weapon.
2. Mrs B never doubted that Anthony wasn't guilty.
3. Mrs B protected the people she loved.

Numbers 2 and 3 implied that Mrs B knew the identity of the murderer. Lily-Ann had assumed that for a week. However, what about number 1?

Number 1 implied that Mrs B *was* the murderer. No doubt by accident, of course. And she would've gotten away with it if an ex-con hadn't been living at the Marigold Cottages. An ex-con who she wanted to protect. That's all that made sense. How else would she have the blood-smeared weapon?

Well, she could've found it. Except she would've said something immediately.

She could've been given it, except by whom?

She could've faked it. How?

By adding the blood later.

Oh. Hmm. That was possible – and comforting. Lily-Ann thought it through for a moment, then reached for her phone.

Lily-Ann

The scene was bloody. Even after the police left. The blood remained.

Lily-Ann

It would've been easy to smear blood on a walking stick long after the murder.

Lily-Ann

If she wanted to implicate herself.

Ocean Neighbor

Of course! OMG of course!!!

Ocean Neighbor

That's exactly what the old bat would do

Ocean Neighbor

You queen

Ocean Neighbor

You absolute empress

Sophie Neighbor

Can't they match the weapon to the wound?

Lily-Ann

I don't know.

Hamilton Neighbor

Blunt trauma? Not with precision.

Sophie Neighbor

Still, she confessed. She has the blood, the weapon. How do we get her out?

Hamilton Neighbor

If we clear Anthony, Mrs B won't have any reason to confess.

Hamilton Neighbor

That's probably why she did all this in the first place.

As the texts continued, Lily-Ann looked away from her phone. She picked up a yellow notepad and began to write. What other dots needed connecting?

1. Mrs B's true link to Anthony.
2. Anthony's furtive departure on the night of the Dedrick burglary.
3. The video of Anthony at the scene of the burglary.
4. The cellmate's statement/Anthony's confession.
5. Nicholas's connection to Dedrick; Sophie said he was happy to hear of his death. For that matter, Nicholas's connection to Mrs B.
6. Mr Ybarra had invited Dedrick to town; he's the only one with a proven relationship to him.
7. Why was Sophie taking copious notes? Some kind of Munchausen's?
8. Ocean? No. There were no dots to connect there. Unless extremely well hidden.
9. The only thing suspicious about Hamilton was the water-tightness of his alibi. On the other hand, if he *did* leave his cottage, he wouldn't get farther than

the edge of the property. So luring the victim close made sense.

Lily-Ann eyed the list. A few possible avenues of investigation appealed to her, but none of them mattered at the moment. All that mattered was bringing Mrs B. home.

59

HAMILTON

The concept of imprisonment didn't bother Hamilton. At least not the idea of being locked in a cell, unable to leave, though he knew that choosing to remain confined and being *forced* to remain confined were very different things. His lack of fear might've been naïve, but still the thought of imprisonment itself didn't frighten him.

On the other hand, actual existing prisons terrified him. The prospect of sharing a cramped cell made him sick. The endless noise and waves of odor would be hellish. The lack of access to the internet would feel as if he'd lost a lobe of his own brain. And eating slop in a mess hall, crammed together with strangers . . .

So the reality of imprisonment terrified him. He'd do anything to avoid it.

Yet when Lily-Ann explained her plan, he agreed. He complained and vacillated – then agreed. Partly because Lily-Ann had asked, and she understood him. She respected him. Partly because he'd done so little for Mrs B, and she'd done so much for him. And partly because – well, it was a rare thing, being able to take a stand without leaving your house.

So he agreed, then spent the rest of the day in bed.

60

NICHOLAS

Watching kids crack *cascarones* – confetti eggs – on each other's heads during street festivals brought back fond memories for Nicholas. He still wasn't too old to enjoy the satisfying crunch of eggshell and billowing confetti on his own head. It was his favorite thing about Fiesta and Solstice, more than the parades or the mariachi bands or the churros.

However, when he was a kid, the confetti had been made of paper. Now it was mostly mylar, which posed a risk to sea turtles and dolphins. So he'd implemented the seasonal placement of filters over storm drains to keep the debris from the creeks and ocean.

Every year, he needed to fight for budget and labor – and against accusations of being a killjoy.

Speaking of killjoys: the door of his office slammed open, and Sophie stormed in. Since they'd spoken at the theatre, she'd scolded him twice for mistreating Mrs Bakofsky. As if staying the hell away from her was the same as mistreating her.

It was the opposite, actually. It was the kindest way to treat her.

Given the expression on Sophie's face, he braced himself for another blast of the same accusation. Coming to his workplace was pretty shitty, though. And surprising. Didn't seem like Sophie. She tended toward the nervous and twitchy. Though there was a deep vein of passion there, too.

She slapped her hands on his desk. 'Do you not care at all?'

'And hello to you,' he said.

'It's not funny!'

'It's a *little* funny,' he said. 'That I don't even know why you're yelling at me.'

'We've been talking about it for hours!'

'This is the first time I saw you today.'

Her nostrils actually flared. 'On the group chat!'

'Oh. I muted that.'

'You— what?'

'For a meeting,' he lied. He'd actually muted it days ago.

'So you haven't seen . . .' She blinked at him. 'You don't know . . . anything?'

'I know the chemical composition of mylar. It's polyester. Now I sound like Hamilton.'

She collapsed into his guest chair and told him about Mrs Bakofsky's false confession. The weapon she'd doctored, the note she'd left. She told him that Ocean was devastated, that Lily-Ann seemed even more remote than usual – and she started to cry.

So he sat in the chair beside her. He didn't touch her. He didn't know if she wanted to be touched. But he sat with her and he listened when she said that she'd started to feel comfortable at the Cottages. Despite the body and the murder, despite everything she'd started to feel at home. Surrounded by people who cared for her, people she cared for. She felt . . . not protected, but secure. Or not even secure, but like she belonged.

And without Mrs B, that would all come to an end.

'Can you do anything?' she asked. 'You work for the city. Can you do *anything*?'

He told her he couldn't, but what he thought was: He'd kept his secret this whole time, and it hadn't been enough to protect her. He'd done his best to stay out of her life. Now, maybe it was finally time to get involved.

61

SOPHIE

End of Act II / Beginning of III?

HAMILTON'S living room. OCEAN, LILY-ANN, and
SOPHIE sit in glum silence until HAMILTON steps
in with an array of spoons on a plate.

HAMILTON
Peanut butter? Anyone? There's creamy and crunchy and extra-crunchy, but no extra-creamy.

SOPHIE
What? Why?

HAMILTON
I'm out of milk.

(The spoons each have a scoop of peanut butter.
And everyone takes one, too depressed to refuse.)

LILY-ANN
So what exactly happened, Ocean? You spoke to the detective?

OCEAN
About how Mrs B rigged the club? Yeah, he said he'd take the information 'under advisement.' He doesn't think she's guilty either, but she showed up with a bloodstained murder weapon.

LILY-ANN
So it fits the wound.

OCEAN
It's 'consistent,' he said, which means maybe, maybe not.

SOPHIE
So once we clear Anthony, she'll retract her confession and then they'll both be safe. Or . . . or do we just need to clear her?

HAMILTON
Better if we clear them both. Without doing anything tremendously stupid.

(NICHOLAS knocks and enters, sits beside
SOPHIE.)

NICHOLAS
I heard about Mrs Bakofsky. I wanted to come.

HAMILTON
Peanut butter?

NICHOLAS
I wouldn't say no to a cup of tea.

HAMILTON
What? Tea? No, I don't have anything like that.

LILY-ANN

(pointing an accusatory spoon at NICHOLAS)

What is your connection to James Dedrick?

NICHOLAS
He annoyed me at work a few times.

LILY-ANN
That's all it takes for you to be happy he's dead?

NICHOLAS
Did Sophie tell you that? Yeah, I'd be happy if every rich out-of-town asshole investor dropped dead. They don't add value. They just raise rents and make it impossible for normal people to live here.

OCEAN
You want to explain your history with Mrs B?

NICHOLAS
Not really.

SOPHIE
He means yes.

NICHOLAS
She knew my father. She thinks she owes him, but she doesn't. She definitely doesn't owe me. And if I pretend

she does, that's just taking advantage of her. So I stay away from her. That's all. She doesn't need one more person to take care of.

LILY-ANN

(to SOPHIE)

Have you done self-defense training? With a baton or similar?

SOPHIE
What? No. Should I?

LILY-ANN
I just don't think it's an accident that we found Dedrick outside your unit. You need to protect yourself, Sophie.

(to HAMILTON)

How often do you leave your cottage?

HAMILTON
Never.

SOPHIE
You do, though.

HAMILTON
Only for medical emergencies and only then when Mrs B makes me. When she comes with me. She helps. She never says anything but she helps. Maybe she understands? Or maybe she doesn't. She makes it okay, though. She makes me okay. I don't, I don't like . . .

(He starts to lose his composure, and OCEAN,
despite being raw with fear, comforts him.)

I don't know what I'm going to do without her. I don't
know what any of us will do.

(The lights dim, and are replaced by spots. One
on each character. They're still illuminated, but
now separately. Each person is frozen in a solitary
beam. Because MRS B is the connection between
them. Without her, they are alone.

Maybe hold that silent, alienated beat for so
long that the stillness makes the audience
uncomfortable . . .

Until eventually OCEAN ends the moment.)

OCEAN
When my wife divorced me, I fell apart. Nothing made
sense anymore. I cried to Mrs B for three months.
Nothing worked, nothing helped. Until one day she
told me, she said: 'Everything's broken, Ocean. Our
politics, our media, our bridges. Our bodies, our jobs,
our garbage disposals. Our marriages. Everything is
broken. And think about all those jagged edges and
imperfections. All that pain. It's a terrible thing, Ocean.
Think about all those people, too. Everyone, everyone,
is in need of repair. All of us. But here's the thing. We
can't be fixed. No, I'm sorry. That's the truth. We can't
be fixed. All we can be is together.'

LILY-ANN

(after a pause, businesslike)

256

So! Shall we continue? Gregory Ybarra owns a few buildings in the area. He's the only person with an ongoing relationship to James Dedrick. He's the one who invited him to visit.

NICHOLAS
That's the guy with the beard? Walks around with a golf club?

SOPHIE
He's afraid of dogs. Though I'm not sure how a golf club would help.

NICHOLAS
Drive them away.

SOPHIE

(dead-eyed)

Ha ha.

OCEAN

(to LILY-ANN)

You know he's always pressuring Mrs B to sell the Cottages. Ybarra is.

HAMILTON
You think <u>he</u> killed James Dedrick?

LILY-ANN
No. He's not sloppy enough to kill a murder victim on

the property he's trying to buy. And he wanted Dedrick's money, not his death. I'm simply saying, he is perhaps a way to divert attention away from Mrs B or Anthony. Away from anyone here.

NICHOLAS
Wait. You want to frame him?

LILY-ANN
Of course not. I don't want to frame anyone. Though if we did, he'd be my first choice.

HAMILTON
I like that better than your current plan.

SOPHIE
What plan?

HAMILTON
The one where Lily-Ann asked me to—

LILY-ANN
Not now, Hamilton.

OCEAN
We're not framing anyone. So what's the first step? Proving that Mrs B doctored that so-called murder weapon herself?

Lily-Ann asked for any photos of the crime scene after the police left, to prove there was enough blood for Mrs B to smear on her knobkerrie. And as the conversation continued, I realized that she didn't really care if Anthony or Mrs B had killed Dedrick; she just wanted to untangle the mystery.

On the other hand, Ocean *did* care – but she'd do anything to protect Mrs B.

Nicholas was quiet. Even Hamilton was quiet. In the end, everyone was quiet, and it wasn't just the peanut butter sticking to the roofs of our mouths.

62

OCEAN

This visiting room at the jail was worse than the first one, even though it was just down the hall. Uglier, harsher. More oppressive and depressing. Ocean felt the weight of the state on her neck just from sitting there. She felt herself begin to sweat.

Anthony looked unruffled, though, as he considered her question.

'Just tell me where you were that night,' she repeated. 'If you weren't breaking into Dead Rick's house.'

'I can't say. Not here.'

She frowned at him. 'Not even for Mrs B?'

'It won't help her.'

'I don't know about that, Anthony. It'd be a pretty big goddamn help if you were breaking into his house after you killed him.'

He thought about that, then nodded.

'What does that mean?'

'Comes to that,' he said, 'I'll confess.'

'Comes to what?'

'Mrs B serving time.'

'You'll confess in order to save her from prison, but you didn't do it?'

'Right,' he said.

'Right,' she echoed, and for a second she felt her heart unclench. 'Good. Good.'

'We'll get Mrs B back home.'

She nodded agreement, but her heart clenched again. 'No. Fuck. I can't – I can't ask you to do that.'

'Why not?'

She exhaled and wanted to cry. God, it had been a week. 'Because I can't.'

'There are other benefits.'

'To confessing?'

'Yeah.'

'To a crime you didn't commit?'

'I only wish I had one more month outside.'

'Just one?'

His eyes seemed to focus past the prison walls. 'This year, they're expecting twenty-eight thousand gray whales. Mothers and calves, right off the coast. Swimming from Mexico to Alaska. Borders mean nothing to them.'

'Are we talking about whales right now?'

'Barnacles grow on their skin in these big rough patches.' He shrugged one shoulder. 'Like tattoos. They weigh them down, but also show how far they've come.'

Ocean scrubbed her scalp with her fingers. 'You're a metaphorical whale, I get it. You know Miles wants to see them with you? He's writing letters to get you out. To the mayor and Paul Rudd.'

'Who's that?'

'The highest-ranking official in a local government.'

He looked at her, not smiling again.

'He's an actor. He played Ant-Man. Never ages. I don't know what Miles thinks he can do. Bring you a tiny chisel? And Riley's drawing tattoos on her face.'

'Oh, no,' he said.

'In solidarity, she says.'

'Shit.'

'It's okay, hers looks better than yours.' She eyed him – fondly to her dismay. He really was a whale of a man. 'Who's your third friend, then? Lily-Ann?'

'Maybe.' His eyes looked brighter than usual. 'Yeah. Maybe.'

'You want me to ask her to visit?'

'Please,' he said.

'Oh, my god, you've got a thing for Lily-Ann. You do!' She felt herself smile. 'She's a married woman, Anthony. Shame on you.'

'I know. But damn, she's all woman. C'mon, tell me you haven't noticed.'

'Not my type,' Ocean said.

'Yeah?'

'Too straight. Now, what were we talking about again? Oh, yeah: the reason you snuck out the same night *someone* burgled Dead Rick's house.'

'I didn't.'

'Sophie saw you,' Ocean told him.

'I left, but I didn't do any B&E.'

Ocean nodded. 'Okay. Then explain the prisoner who says you confessed to the crime to him.'

'The prisoner,' he repeated, making fun of her use of

words for some reason.

'Sorry, I'm not up on the lingo,' Ocean said. 'God, this is worse than Sophie making fun of me for not understanding emoticons.'

'He's just some kid.' Anthony shrugged his shoulder. 'The cops take him aside, ask him what I said. He's not stupid. He talks at them until finally he tells a story they like, in the hopes that they cut him some slack.'

'So they've got like – nothing on you? Except circumstantial evidence and hearsay?'

'Not sure what else they'd need.'

'Oh. Right. What does your lawyer say?'

'I don't think she knows about Mrs B.'

'I'll call her. Mrs B refused to even meet her lawyer and . . .' Ocean blinked back sudden tears. 'I can't leave her in here, Anthony. I can't even *think* of her in here. She's a mother to me. My parents always had each other, but I always had Mrs B.'

He ran a meaty palm over his face. 'You know how many old ladies invite me to tea? Ask me to change the light bulbs in their bathroom?'

'Wait, she asked *you* to change the light bulbs? That's my job. She's so sexist.'

'You're like three feet tall.'

'On the outside, you might not've run across this, but there's this technology called "ladders."'

'I'll have to look into—' he started, when the bell shrilled on the wall.

Ocean wished she could give him a hug. 'We'll figure this out, okay? We're going to figure this out.'

'If we don't,' he said, 'I'm going to miss those whales.'

* * *

Ocean sat in her car in the hot parking lot, thinking about a community of barnacles hitching a ride on a migrating whale. Thinking about a community closer to home. Why would Mrs B confess to a crime she didn't commit?

To protect someone. Of course. To protect Anthony, in this case. Except . . . what if she wasn't protecting him? What if she was protecting someone else?

Ocean felt sick. Sick of keeping calm, sick of carrying on. Sick of imagining Mrs B in a jail cell. She wanted to scream. She hated feeling so helpless. So when she got home, she sat in the living room and swiped through pictures of herself with her ex-wife, Zoe. Trying to make herself feel even worse, apparently.

Worked, too.

Then Riley came home, grunted a greeting, and stomped toward her room.

'What is wrong with you?' Ocean demanded.

'What are you talking about?'

'Ever since the police were here, you've been even moodier than usual.'

Riley scowled. 'Screw you.'

'Did you see something that night? Did you *do* something?'

'Yes, Mother. I killed him.'

'I'm fucking serious,' Ocean snapped.

'No, I didn't do anything! I didn't do anything, okay? I didn't see anything, I didn't hear anything.'

'Then what is wrong with you?'

Riley threw her backpack onto the floor. 'You! You're what's wrong with me!'

'I know you're hiding something, Riley.' Ocean made

herself take a breath. 'I can't help you if you don't tell me what it is.'

'You can't help me anyway, okay?'

'Not okay,' Ocean said. 'What the hell happened?'

'Nothing happened.'

'Then what aren't you telling me?'

Riley clamped her jaw, then said, 'You weren't here.'

'I was on a date.'

'Yeah, right.'

Ocean didn't know what that meant. 'I mean . . . I *was*.'

'Would you shut up for one second so I can tell you?' Riley glared. 'You weren't here until later. So I left for a while, okay? And no, I didn't see anything, I didn't hear anything – I just left?'

'Where?'

'With Audrey, okay? For a smoke.'

'Weed? Vapes?'

'Vapes are for losers.'

'So weed?'

'No, not weed. Cigarettes.'

'Jesus, Riley. You're smoking cigarettes? What the hell is—' Ocean realized all at once, and the living room turned red with her anger. 'Miles was home alone? He was home alone when someone was getting murdered twenty feet from his bedroom door?'

'That's why I didn't want to tell you.'

'You left him *alone*?' Ocean said.

Riley burst into tears, ran into her bedroom, and slammed the door.

63

LILY-ANN

The internet connection froze twice while Hamilton was downloading the cop's video.

He griped about satellites in geostationary orbit but Lily-Ann didn't mind the delay. She used the time to finish assembling the Greek salad for lunch.

'Finally!' he called from his home office. 'It loaded. I'm starting it. Should I wait? I'm not waiting.'

In the kitchen, she sprinkled the seasoned chickpeas.

'Okay, I'm starting it,' he called. 'There's nothing on the screen yet. Just a weird angle of a walkway.'

She wiped the rims of the bowls.

'The one leading to Dedrick's front door. It's a doorbell camera. Wait! There's a shadow. Oh, no, that's just a bush.'

She poured two glasses of water and squeezed lemon in them, wondering if that might discourage Hamilton from offering less-standard beverages.

'Here! Movement! A figure. A man. Anthony. It's Anthony. And he's gone.'

Lily-Ann stepped into his office, precariously carrying salad bowls and glasses. 'Help.'

'It's only like six seconds,' he told her, standing to take the water glasses. 'I'll replay it.'

On his right-hand monitor, he rewound the video player, then played the footage at a quarter speed. Frames flickered past.

Lily-Ann saw a walkway. A blur of motion.

A man reached toward the camera.

Big man in dark clothing.

A baseball cap and a cloth mask obscured his face.

When he moved his arm, his tattoo appeared.

A crude drawing of an angel's wing on his throat. And when he turned his head, a single frame showed the feathers bursting in flames behind his ear.

'Anthony.' Hamilton froze the image before inspecting his glass. 'Is this water?'

'With a squeeze of lemon.'

'Huh. So we know Anthony broke into Dead Rick's house.'

Lily-Ann stabbed an olive with her fork. 'We don't know why.'

'For money,' Hamilton said. 'Which is, I believe, often the motivation for burglary.'

'A crime of opportunity, then.' She frowned at the screen. 'He didn't kill Dedrick, but he knew he was dead, so he took advantage of his empty house?'

'So he's a criminal, but not a murderer. Does that help Mrs B?'

'Only if—' She frowned suddenly. 'Wait. Back the video up a second.'

Hamilton pressed a key a few times, and the image jerkily rewound.

'There, stop.' She looked closer. 'That's not Anthony.'

'What do you mean it's not Anthony?'

'That's not his tattoo.'

'Feathers and flames, that's him.'

Lily-Ann shook her head. 'It's almost as horrible, but it's not *his*. There's an odd number of feathers, which gives some symmetry which Anthony's, with an even number, lacks.'

'How is odd more symmetrical than even?'

'Because the central—'

'Wait, no. That doesn't matter. I mean – are you sure? That's really not Anthony?'

'I am. It isn't.'

'Okay.' Hamilton thought for a moment. 'So either some other guy with a near-identical tattoo happened to break into Dead Rick's house, which is—'

'Vanishingly unlikely,' Lily-Ann said.

'I was going to say "zero."'

'Or?' she asked.

'Or . . .'

'Or someone faked those tattoos. They're drawn on. In order to implicate Anthony.'

'Who'd do that?'

'The murderer.'

Hamilton tabbed the video back a few frames. 'There's no clear image of his face. He looks pretty tall. You recognize him?'

'From a blur of skin? No.'

'So we have to tell the cops that this isn't Anthony.'

'Yeah,' she said.

'Except . . .' Hamilton swiveled his chair toward the left-most monitor, which showed a medieval-looking tavern in *Realm of Rangers*. 'Can we do that without exposing my friend? We're not supposed to have the video.'

'This is a job for Ocean. She's in touch with his lawyer.'

Hamilton pronged a few chickpeas. 'I'm not sure what any of it means.'

'Which parts?'

'Well, the tattoo proves that Anthony didn't break into Dedrick's house.'

'Unless he was there, too.'

'Talk about vanishingly unlikely. Someone's trying to frame him.' Hamilton rubbed his nose. 'Of course, Sophie said he slunk out that night. So he went *somewhere*. For all we know he's just out of frame.'

'True. We have no idea where he went.'

Hamilton spun toward Lily-Ann. 'I don't see how this helps Mrs B.'

'If we can get Anthony released, she'll retract her confession.'

'So then . . .' He wrinkled his nose at the lemon water. 'We don't need to follow through on your plan? Instead of telling the cops what we, uh, "saw" that night, we can tell them about this?'

'We should cover all our bases, Hamilton.'

'And then . . . then Mrs B will come back and everything will return to normal?'

'For a certain definition of "normal",' Lily-Ann told him.

64

SOPHIE

I'd never been inside a police station before.

On the level of set design, the lobby wasn't as intimidating as I'd expected. Less so than the local DMV. The floor was patterned tile and the receptionists' windows were behind glass, but surrounded by warm wood paneling. There was a wall of photos of cops getting awards and a mural of dolphins leaping in the ocean.

I took a breath and listened to my pulse. Then I crossed to the window and asked for Detective Sergeant Enible.

'I don't have an appointment,' I told the receptionist. 'I'm sorry. I just . . . if he's in, I need to talk to him. It's about the murder of— at the Marigold Cottages. I'm sorry, of James Dedrick. He's the victim.'

The receptionist asked me to wait, and I sat on the nearest bench. I was too shaky to get any comfort from my phone, so I just sat there. A few minutes later, a door opened in the wall with the award photos, and Detective Enible came into the lobby.

He looked bigger in the police station, bigger than I remembered him being in my cottage. He greeted me warmly, like we were friends, and brought me deeper into the building. It didn't look like a police department. It looked more like an insurance company, with quality construction and muted colors.

As I followed him to his desk, I practiced my monologue. I focused so hard on what I wanted to say that I started babbling before I sat down:

'After a trauma in college, which I will describe if necessary, though I'd prefer not to, I've had a tendency toward hypervigilance. I can submit a psychologist's statement if you need. Sorry! I just started talking. But, um, I don't want to forget anything. So anyway, I am sometimes hypervigilant. Which is why I stopped by here. To talk to you. Sorry that I didn't make an appointment.' The apologies weren't part of my monologue, of course; they were just a tic that I despised. 'What I wanted to tell you, which I didn't tell you before, though maybe I should have, is that on the night of the – on the night of James Dedrick's death, I was having an episode. Not an episode, sorry, I shouldn't call it an "episode". I had trouble sleeping, that's all. So I sat up. That night. All night. At the window. Sometimes it helps for me to, um, focus. So I focused on Mrs B's cottage and she didn't leave. I watched. She didn't leave all night. So she can't have killed Dedrick. There's no way. Because she didn't leave her house. I watched. And the blood is just . . . she rubbed her knobkerrie in the ground at the scene. I'll get you that statement. From the psychologist.'

He looked at me for a few heartbeats. Then he said, 'Sophie Gilman. I've been expecting you.'

65

VERNON

Vernon disliked eating at his desk, but with all the shit coming at him from the DA, he didn't have time for a leisurely meal. When Golda Bakofsky had confessed to the crime, she'd thrown a wrench into the gears. Exactly like she'd intended.

Of course she hadn't killed anyone. He knew who the killer was, and it wasn't a little old lady who couldn't perpetrate a jaywalking if you gave her a new pair of legs.

But prosecutors were like horses. Twitchy and nervous until you strapped blinders on them. Once you did? Then they charged forward, trampling anything in their path.

Except Vernon wasn't that far along, so Golda Bakofsky's

false confession had a real shot of screwing his case. Maybe it already had. That's why he'd come in early, eating breakfast at his desk, hustling the paperwork along. The easier he made this, the more likely it didn't get derailed.

That was his mindset when the first visitor arrived: Riley Mistral, a freshman in high school. Ocean's daughter.

'I thought your mother told you not to talk to the police,' he said.

'Yeah, 'cause she's not dumb. So, um, I know Mrs B didn't hurt anyone because I was watching her all that night.'

'And why were you doing that?'

"Deep breath, then take the plunge," she told him.

'I'm not familiar with the phrase.'

She scoffed. 'It's from *Kim Possible*?'

He liked her, this miniature spitfire. He couldn't help himself. And the more she groused at him the fonder he grew. Her arty, lesbian, cranberry-juice-sounding mother must've done something right. The girl was lying through her teeth, of course, but marching into the department to bullshit him to his face? Impressive.

'Weirdly, that still means nothing to me.'

'She's a kid who spies, okay? So I was *Kim-Possibling* Mrs B the night she says she killed the guy. Except she didn't, 'cause I was watching.'

'Well, that solves that,' he said.

'You should be writing this down.'

'Does your mother know you're here?'

She hesitated for the first time. 'Yes?'

'You're a terrible liar, Riley Mistral. And I mean that in both senses.'

271

'Huh?'

'I'll add your testimony to the file,' he lied. 'Now, should I have the truant officer deal with you, or send you to school in a patrol car?'

'Um, can I ride in back?' she asked.

So he sent her away, then finished breakfast and sat through a conference call during which he could physically feel the DA's office losing their nerve. The case against Anthony Lambert was slipping away.

He didn't explode at the prosecutors, though he was tempted. How many times had they pushed a bullshit case – for *their* career, for *their* legacy – and he'd played along? Still, he kept his cool.

Then he got a nervous call from Lawrence Hamilton, claiming that he'd been awake the night of the murder, watching the stars through his new telescope with Lily-Ann Novak, and they hadn't noticed anything suspicious, which included Mrs B leaving her house at any time.

Vernon was tempted to ask if they'd noticed Riley with her *Kim Possible* spy gear.

And finally, later in the afternoon, he got an earful from Sophie Gilman, who sat across from him and talked about 'hypervigilance' like the words meant more than 'hyper' and 'vigilance.' When she finished babbling, he said, 'I've been expecting you.'

'Oh!' she said. 'Um, really?'

'Are you aware that lying to the police is a crime?'

'No?' she said.

'On the night of the murder, you had an episode, Lawrence Hamilton and Lily-Ann Novak were awake with a telescope, and Riley Mistral was, and I quote,

'*Kim-Possibling*' Mrs Bakofsky. That's all from this morning. I've never met anyone so well-alibied.'

'Hamilton's first name is *Lawrence*?' Sophie Gilman flushed, then started to speak, then stopped and flushed some more. 'Sorry.'

'The odd thing is, not one of you noticed the murderer. You all saw Mrs B *not* kill anyone, but none of you saw who did.'

'Sorry,' she whispered.

He leaned toward her. 'Two things. First, don't lie to the police. That's a crime. You want to join Golda Bakofsky in lockup?'

Sophie Gilman trembled.

'And second,' Vernon continued, 'I know she didn't kill anyone. Because I know who did. You want to share testimony that helps *her*? Then stop protecting *him*. Instead of all this shit, admit that you saw Anthony Lambert commit the murder.'

66

OCEAN

The vivid stripes and delicate floral patterns in the background of the painting worked to obscure the central figure, exactly as Ocean intended. She wanted to present the woman as a negative space, almost. One that drew the eye via absence, or exclusion. Part of her Hostile Architecture series.

Except she couldn't concentrate on her art.

She kept trying to force herself, but no luck. With a

growl of frustration, she left her studio – a.k.a. the canvas tent on their patio – and found herself in Mrs B's kitchen.

For no reason.

She'd already unearthed the list of instructions – like a dog-sitter's to-do list for extremely neurotic Italian greyhounds – and entered half the tasks into her calendar. So she didn't need to be there. She just missed Mrs B, that was all. She worried about her. Every time she took a breath of fresh air, she remembered that Mrs B couldn't.

So she made herself a cup of terrible instant coffee with condensed milk, then sat in Mrs B's chair with the cheetah-print pillow, her legs crossed, one ankle twitching anxiously.

The house sounded empty. The hum of the fridge, the ticking of a clock. It still smelled like Mrs B, though, like the yahrzeit candles she lit for her dead relatives and the incense she lit for what she liked to call her 'Mrs BMs'.

The only way to bring Mrs B home was to figure out who killed Dead Rick. Had Anthony actually robbed the guy's house? Where was the *real* murder weapon? What did all the little secrets and twists mean, with Sophie's stalker, Ybarra's pressure, Nicholas's attitude, and Lily-Ann's husband?

Ocean took one awful sip of coffee before emptying the cup in the sink.

'C'mon,' she said, to get herself moving. Maybe she'd find the answer to at least one of those questions in the house somewhere.

She went into Mrs B's bedroom, pulled the sewing basket from the closet, and dumped the whole thing onto the bed. She found a key among the spools of thread and silk pincushions, and unlocked the writing desk drawer for copies of Mrs B's legal documents. She ignored most of them: lease agreements, Mrs B's marriage license, her husband's death certificate.

In the very bottom, she found Mrs B's will.

She'd never looked at it before. She'd never wanted to – and, uncharacteristically, Mrs B hadn't asked her to. Usually, Mrs B showed Ocean everything, but she hadn't shared that.

Ocean flipped through a list of bequests . . . then paused when she recognized her own name. She shouldn't look; that's not what she wanted to know, but she couldn't help herself. She scanned the page and saw that Mrs B had set aside a trust for each of the kids. More money than Ocean made in ten years, enough to cover tuitions at good colleges.

Ocean felt tears well in her eyes, then she read what Mrs B had left *her*: her collection of international keepsakes, her jewelry, and all her love.

'Old bat,' she muttered, wiping her tears away.

She kept flipping through papers until she came to the big item. The property. The Marigold Cottages. She scanned the legalese, flipped the page, then swore in surprise.

'Nicholas?' she said, not quite believing her eyes.

Yep. *Nicholas Perez*. Right there in black and white.

What the hell?

That meant he was closer to Mrs B than just some family friend's child. He couldn't be Mrs B's son, could he? Probably not after all the miscarriages. Still, there were other ways. Except surely they would've been closer if they'd been mother and son? Instead of him avoiding her at all costs. Or did that have something to do with *why* he ignored her?

Yet he'd inherit the Cottages upon Mrs B's death.

Ocean didn't know how that related to the murder, but she couldn't imagine it didn't. A guy who'd wanted to invest in the Cottages had been bludgeoned to death, and the secret heir lived a stone's throw away.

67

LILY-ANN

The driveway of Lily-Ann's former house on the Riviera rose at a gentle angle between purple flowering bushes and a curving adobe wall. She'd missed the view over downtown, with East Beach and Stearns Wharf in the distance. The gray-blue of the winter sky was starting to warm into the vibrant blue of summer, like a cathedral ceiling over the city. Who needed to travel when you already lived in paradise?

The house itself was two stories, and still painted a surprisingly cheerful pale yellow. Surprising because Piotr preferred sleek to cheerful. South-facing French doors led onto the deck from the great room and kitchen, and two guest bedrooms were tucked away in the wings.

The primary bedroom was upstairs, past the overspilling vases of hydrangea, rose, and protea silk flowers that Piotr only allowed because they'd cost five hundred dollars apiece.

Through the open double doors, Lily-Ann lay in the warmth of Piotr's king bed, tracing her fingertips along his smooth, unmarked neck. No tattoos. No feather or flames. Just the lingering scent of grapefruit and nutmeg – Alpha Eau de Parfum, which Piotr largely wore because of the name.

She frowned, though she wasn't sure what was upsetting her. Sleeping with Piotr again? Or the fact that she hadn't yet told Ocean, or anyone else at the Marigold Cottages, that the tattoo captured by the doorbell camera didn't match Anthony's? Which felt like a betrayal, particularly since she'd told Hamilton to keep quiet, too.

She wasn't sure how the information would affect Mrs B's situation, though. She thought she should wait until Mrs B was released – *if* she was released – before introducing a new element to the investigation.

Maybe that's what was upsetting her: having to choose between Anthony and Mrs B. She didn't want to undermine the case against Anthony, if it would leave Mrs B locked up. She enjoyed Anthony's company. She liked his solidity and his silence. Still, she felt more responsible for Mrs B. So, for the moment, she'd keep that information between her and Hamilton, and not even tell Ocean. She and Hamilton understood each other – both of them desperate to impose order upon the chaos – but Ocean was too comfortable in the world, too attached to her principles.

Piotr caught her frown and said, 'You look worried.'

'A little.'

'There's nothing to worry about as long as he's behind bars.'

She didn't respond. No matter how many times she told him, Piotr wouldn't believe that she wasn't afraid of Anthony.

'The world's a scary place.' Piotr rolled toward her. 'Especially for a woman living alone. That was a close call.'

She traced his cheekbone where Anthony had a tattoo.

'I can't believe you had a murderer living across from you.' Piotr looked into her eyes. 'Move back in, Lily-Ann.'

'With you?'

'Of course with me,' he said. 'It's not like you're seeing anyone else. Let's start again. Start fresh.'

'Why?'

'To wipe the slate clean.' He showed her his most boyish smile. 'To give ourselves another chance. We can . . . we can be partners again.'

She stood from his bed and went into his bathroom. She'd missed the Bianco Carrara marble. Not to mention the deep, luxuriant tub and the vanity that held extra towels and all her cosmetics. Still, she'd come here for the last time. The Marigold Cottages was home now, while the house on the hill was merely Piotr's.

Though perhaps Lily-Ann would remodel her bathroom in the cottage. Add a proper soaking tub. Mrs B wouldn't mind . . . well, once she was freed from jail.

At the mirror, Lily-Ann wiped the flaked mascara from under her eyes and smoothed her hair with Piotr's gel. And she realized that *both* things were bothering her: sleeping with Piotr and withholding the information about the tattoo.

She went back into the bedroom and found her black knit dress on the chair next to the bed. She slipped it over her head and stepped into her shoes and said:

'It's time to get a divorce.'

'What? Bullshit. You're joking.'

'No.'

'Don't be stupid, Lily-Ann! I mean, did you even hear me? We're starting again.'

'No,' she said. 'It's time.'

68

SOPHIE

I'd left the police station on Friday in a bit of a panic, and texted the group chat for an emergency meeting of the Marigold Cottages Murder Collective. The detective's words still rang in my ears: '*That's a crime. Do you want to join Mrs B in lock-up?*'

We needed to coordinate better.

We needed to communicate better.

We needed to plan.

We got together yesterday, and I was finally reviewing my notes. I hadn't looked at them earlier, because I didn't want to think about what happened.

End of Act II, maybe?

SCENE 3-ISH

HAMILTON'S living room isn't looking
quite so pristine anymore: a visual echo of
how everything feels like it's falling apart.
HAMILTON'S ever-changing poster is a
Rorschach blot.

SOPHIE
We need to coordinate better. We need to communicate
better.

NICHOLAS
Wait, back up. No way. That's not . . . you all did <u>what</u>?
All of you?

SOPHIE
We gave Mrs B alibis. Yes, apparently all of us. I told
the detective that I'd been awake all night, which
happens sometimes, so it's not . . . but also, Lily-Ann
and Hamilton said they'd been stargazing.

HAMILTON
Quasar-gazing, actually, though we weren't. But if we
had been gazing, that's what we'd have gazed upon. A
quasar is a galactic nucleus powered by a supermassive
black hole.

NICHOLAS
So you all lied to the cops? That sounds dumb.

HAMILTON
Yes! Thank you. I'm terrified. I'm scared. Now that you
mention it, I'm terrified. It was Lily-Ann's idea.

SOPHIE
Also, Riley said she was watching Mrs B as part of a
TikTok challenge or something—

OCEAN
Riley called him? <u>My</u> Riley?

280

SOPHIE
Uh, no. She visited. In person.

OCEAN
At the police department? My daughter?

SOPHIE
Sorry. Sorry.

HAMILTON
What's the cop going to do? What kind of fine are we looking at? Is it a <u>criminal</u> charge?

OCEAN
Goddamnit, Riley. She skipped school to visit the cops?

SOPHIE
I don't think the detective's going to do anything, this time.

HAMILTON
But he can. He could. If he wants to.

SOPHIE
He said if we really want to help Mrs B, we should admit we saw Anthony behaving suspiciously. Like, I think he meant we should make things up to blame Anthony instead of making things up to cover for Mrs B. Like he wanted us to <u>lie</u>.

OCEAN
My parents are right. There's no trusting cops.

NICHOLAS
How much more evidence do they need? They've got
that prison statement and a video of him in Altadena.

LILY-ANN
Anthony didn't break into Dedrick's house.

OCEAN
Based on what? How clean he keeps his kitchen?

HAMILTON
We reviewed the video. Well, we traded it for an enchanted
bane weapon.

LILY-ANN
The tattoo isn't Anthony's. It's almost identical, but not
quite. He didn't do it.

OCEAN
Are you sure?

LILY-ANN
Would I mistake one tattoo for another?

OCEAN
If it's not his, whose is it? You think someone just drew
it on? Otherwise . . . oh. It could belong to a friend of his.
With similar prison tats . . .

NICHOLAS
Just because Anthony didn't rob Dedrick doesn't mean
he didn't kill him. I cannot believe you all went and lied
to the cops.

HAMILTON

(Leaving the room)

I think we need refreshments.

SOPHIE
You can't believe it because you don't care about her!
You don't care about anyone.

NICHOLAS
Right, that's why I'm here. Because I <u>don't</u> care.

OCEAN
Why didn't you tell me about the tattoo?

LILY-ANN
Because you would've gone straight to Anthony's lawyer
with it and I didn't know how that was going to affect
Mrs B.

OCEAN
So you thought you couldn't trust me.

LILY-ANN
Yes.

NICHOLAS
So the cop took your statements. You signed your
statement? He can press charges any time he wants?

LILY-ANN
If he can prove we're lying, which he cannot.

HAMILTON

> (trying to cool rising tempers, enters with an
> armful of Ensure bottles)

Drinks, anyone? There's chocolate and vanilla. I didn't get
original because that's not a flavor. It's an adjective, so—

NICHOLAS
Is that Ensure?

HAMILTON
I thought, we're all under stress, so if anyone's not eating
properly, a meal replacement drink might come in handy.

OCEAN
I can't deal with you right now.

NICHOLAS
Not the time, Hamilton.

HAMILTON
What do you care? All you ever do for Mrs B is hide from
her!

> (SOPHIE rises to NICHOLAS'S defense for stupid
> reasons that she didn't want to think about.)

SOPHIE
Well, you only care because she doesn't mind that you're
a shut-in.

LILY-ANN

> (to NICHOLAS)

Does Mrs B subsidize your rent? Do you pay less than the going rate?

NICHOLAS
How is thát your business?

LILY-ANN
I know Ocean pays substantially less than Mrs B could charge.

OCEAN
We didn't all marry rich, Lily-Ann. Don't you have a prenup with Piotr?

LILY-ANN
Yes.

NICHOLAS
Is that why you put off divorcing him? You get more money every year you stay married?

HAMILTON
What does that have to do with anything?

NICHOLAS
It's ice-cold, if the person you love most in the world is a legal contract.

SOPHIE
It's true that Lily-Ann could kill some L.A. asshole without blinking.

HAMILTON

(thrusting Ensure at OCEAN)

Blinking is a semi-autonomic action.

OCEAN
Fucking hell, Hamilton. Get that out of my face!

SOPHIE
You don't need to be mean to him.

OCEAN
Is your daughter cutting school to visit the cops? Is the woman who raised you rotting in a cell? No, but you're still always the victim, Sophie. But hey, maybe you're drunk right now and won't remember any of this in the morning.

NICHOLAS
Whoa, whoa. There's no reason to yell at each other when—

EVERYONE
'You shut up.' 'Nobody asked you.' 'Like you care!' 'Why are you even here?'

OCEAN
For his inheritance.

HAMILTON
The average person blinks over four million times a year.

EVERYONE
Shut up, Hamilton!

NICHOLAS

(to OCEAN)

How often do you even pay rent?

SOPHIE
What does she mean, your inheritance?

NICHOLAS
The paint fumes are rotting her brain. She plays artist
while Mrs Bakofsky pays for her whole life.

SOPHIE
But Mrs B is having trouble paying her bills. I'm not sure
if that means—

OCEAN
No, she's not.

SOPHIE
I heard her say it! 'I'm having trouble paying the bills.'

OCEAN
Because she doesn't know how to use fucking Zelle,
Sophie.

SOPHIE
Oh. Sorry. Sorry.

287

EVERYONE
'Sorry, sorry, sorry. It's all you say.' 'Stop apologizing all the time!' 'You don't need to say sorry every other word.'

LILY-ANN
I believe the conversation has strayed somewhat from the central point.

(HAMILTON slams the door open.)

HAMILTON
I want you all to leave.

It was the kind of scene that worked better in a movie, with the camera rotating in a circle, faster and faster, highlighting the group's angry faces as the score rose in the background, until Hamilton slammed the door open, the *bang!* too loud for a quiet theatre.

I'd like to say that I invented it all for my play. That in real life we calmly discussed how to save Mrs B and Anthony – and how to keep the rest of us out of jail for lying to the cops.

But no. That scene was basically transcribed.

Including the part where I realized that Mrs B 'having trouble paying her bills' just meant she didn't know how to use Zelle.

So . . . yeah, when Mrs B and Anthony needed us most, we fell apart.

69

NICHOLAS

So *that* went well.

For years, Nicholas had wanted to make his mark without knowing how. Sure, he'd done some good work at the planning office yet mostly he'd just drifted along. He wanted to invest himself in something, but damn: those people were *too* invested, specifically in each other's lives.

And the way Sophie's face had crumpled when Ocean said she always played the victim. Standing in his kitchen the next evening, after starting a potato baking, Nicholas couldn't stop seeing her expression.

'Screw it,' he said, and turned off the oven.

He went outside and through the courtyard to knock at Sophie's cottage. A shape moved behind the glass, then she opened the door. Her eyes were swollen and her hair was down. He'd never seen her hair down before.

'Hi,' he said.

'Yes?' she asked.

'I just wanted to check you're okay.'

'Oh.'

That didn't give him a lot to work with, in terms of continuing the conversation. So he just stood there like an idiot for a few seconds. 'So. Are you?'

'Yes. No. I don't know.'

'That's my default answer, too.'

She pulled her hair into a bun. 'That's such a lie. You're *always* okay. You're offensively okay.'

'I'm not. I'm a harmless mess.'

'Ha. You're just . . .' Sophie blinked back sudden tears. 'Well, um, thanks for stopping by.'

'Ocean didn't mean it,' Nicholas told her. 'She's just scared for her kids and for her, uh, adoptive mother. She lashed out.'

'I know.'

'And it's not true. You're actually quite brave.'

Sophie let out a laugh. 'I'm so not. I'm a little trembling . . . ha! I can't think of a metaphor, that's how bad I am. I'm a little trembling—'

'Snow leopard.'

She squinted. 'Huh?'

'Snow leopard.'

'Okay, sure. Um . . .' She stepped back from the door. 'You can come in.'

He followed her inside, then stopped before he stepped on the index cards scattered across her living room floor.

'Is this for your play?'

'Yeah,' she said from the kitchen. 'Tequila or goat milk?'

'Do you really have goat milk?'

She peeked her head out of the kitchen and her smile transformed her face. 'No, I gave it to Hamilton, so he wouldn't be sad.'

He felt himself smiling in return. 'In that case, tequila sounds good.'

She disappeared again and he looked around her living room. A few pictures with her family, a few more with herself and some girlfriends. A whole bookshelf of plays. Everything from Aeschylus to playwrights he'd never heard of. Which made him want to flip through them, but he was more curious about the notes on the floor.

So he stood there looking down until Sophie brought him a lowball of tequila on ice and said, 'What did Ocean mean about your inheritance?'

'Is that why you invited me in?' he asked.

'A little.'

'And you're not even going to apologize for it?' he teased.

'Stop trying to change the subject,' she said, curling onto her sofa. Her slim body seemed to disappear under the black fuzzy top and pants she wore. 'What did she mean?'

'Okay, well . . .' He sat at the other end of the couch. 'Okay.'

'Take your time.'

'Uh,' he said.

'But hurry up and tell me already.'

'Okay,' he said, taking a sip of tequila. 'She's right. Ocean's right. I'm in Mrs B's will.'

'Because you're Mrs B's illegitimate son?'

'No, it's nothing like that.'

'Then what is it?'

'I'm *Mr* B's illegitimate son.'

'No. Really? No way. Wow.' She squinted at him. 'Yeah, that's absolutely *nothing* like being her son, I was so wrong. So . . . what happened? Why are you so mean to her?'

'I'm not mean to her. I just avoid her.'

'Meanly.'

'Not meanly! I . . . I've never talked about this.' He

291

looked past her, toward the shelves of plays. 'What happened is, her husband had a one-night stand with my mother. Or I guess a one-week stand. I never wanted to hear the details. Growing up, I saw my father once every month or two. He was, like, grandfather-aged, but he paid child support and, you know . . . loved me. So when he died, in his will, he asked his wife, Mrs Bakofsky, to take care of me in *her* will.'

'Oh,' she said. 'That's a lot.'

'Yeah. She thinks I'm the grandson of his childhood friend, like he promised to take care of me for old times' sake.' He took a fortifying slug of tequila. 'I don't know. I've always felt weird, my father asking his wife to leave me so much after he had an affair. He betrayed her. I'm the other woman's son. Asking Mr B to make me her heir is just weird.'

'So you avoid her . . .'

'Partly from embarrassment. Partly because I don't want her to think she owes me anything.' He shrugged. 'She doesn't. My father asked her to do this, but it's her choice. So if I stay away from her, y'know . . . I figure that lets her choose.'

'Oh,' she said. 'I see. I get it now.'

'You do?'

'Yeah,' she said. 'You're an idiot.'

'Hey! I just confessed my deepest, darkest secret.'

'Well, first, that's a terrible deep, dark secret. It's not like you killed someone.' She grimaced. 'Err, I hope. But do you really think Mrs B doesn't know exactly who you are?'

'Yes?'

'She's not dumb.'

'No, but—'

'Do you look like him?'

'Maybe a little.' He didn't want to think about that, so he changed the subject. 'And I have way better deep, dark secrets.'

'Sure you do,' she said, sipping tequila like she was trying to make it last. 'Like what?'

'No way. It's your turn. You tell me a secret.'

'Everyone knows my secret. I was stalked in college. The guy never touched me or anything, but I had a stupid breakdown and I'm still a mess.' She set her glass down on the coffee table. 'Way to kill the vibe, Nicholas. Now tell me about you.'

'Fine. My father took care of us, right? I mean, financially. Which made things easy. So I feel like I just . . . skate along. On the surface of things. You know? I stay in the shallow end.'

'Yeah,' she said.

'You know why you remind me of a snow leopard?' Nicholas asked.

'My polka-dotted fur?'

'They're good at hiding in the open. But when you finally see them, you can't believe you ever missed something so striking.'

Sophie picked up her glass, then put it back down. She looked at him, then looked away. Then she looked at him again, and a loose strand of hair fell across her face.

He gestured to the floor. 'Can I help you work on your play?'

'Yes. Please. Let's work on the play.'

293

70

OCEAN

The entire drive to Ventura, Ocean kept telling herself that this was a stupid idea. First, because it was hopeless. And second, because she didn't even know why she cared.

Was she trying to impress her absent parents? Sure, they'd retired to Texas to spend more time with the country's top polluters at protest marches, instead of seeing their grandkids, but maybe *this* would prove she was a good person.

Ocean almost turned back when the traffic slowed, but she kept driving. This whole idiotic expedition was based on two sentences that Anthony had let slip in casual conversation: how his best friend inside had dreamed of spending every day of his freedom on the Ventura Pier, and how they got tattooed at the same time. He shared so little that she found herself putting a lot of weight on what he did say.

Maybe too much.

Anyway, the traffic helped her clear her head, after losing her temper yesterday at Hamilton's house. God, what she'd said to Sophie. Way to lash out at an abuse survivor, Ocean. She'd contacted the local domestic violence hotline last week, to put Kelly Hesse – and her husband – on their radar, then she'd followed through by snapping at poor Sophie.

Well, she'd apologize this evening. But first, she needed to take a short walk on a long pier.

She didn't see any dolphins before she reached Ventura.

She always considered a dolphin sighting along the stretch of ocean next to the highway a good omen but she continued on anyway. She parked at the beach and grabbed doughnuts from Treehouse Bakery, which the kids loved – and where they validated her parking. So, at least the trip wouldn't be a complete loss.

Then she headed out onto the Ventura Pier. She almost missed Hamilton giving her facts about the place to make it more interesting. She should probably apologize to him, too.

People strolled along the pier, holding hands and taking in the view while families ate at the picnic tables outside the fish restaurants. Ocean focused on the fishermen. That's what Anthony had told her, that his friend TG spent every spare minute on the Ventura Pier. He'd dreamed of fishing on the pier; he'd vowed to devote his life to the fishing and lazing. Yeah, it was a long shot – and she still didn't know why she cared – but at least the *aak-aak* of seagulls and the dinosaur gazes of the pelicans soothed her. They didn't give a shit about anything.

The air was brisk as she walked farther along, and the tide simmered through the wooden columns beneath her. In the next five minutes, she asked three fishermen if they'd caught anything before she spotted him.

A tall man, but skinnier than Anthony. Sprawled on a plastic beach chair, holding his fishing rod casually in one hand, like he didn't care about fishing, he was just enjoying the day. He wore a stained white T-shirt and beige Dickies. In the small cooler beside him, she saw what looked like hard seltzer.

Also crude tattoos covered his forearms and his throat.

Ocean ambled closer, and yeah: a tattooed wing wrapped around his neck and turned into flames behind his ear.

Lily-Ann had been half-wrong about the tattoo on the doorbell camera outside James Dedrick's house. It wasn't a fake, meant to incriminate Anthony. It was part of a pair of near-matching tattoos that a couple of buddies got in prison.

She crouched down to the man's level, facing him. She'd expected him to look like Anthony. And, sure, there was some overlap, both of them being tattooed white men in their late thirties who looked like a long stretch of hard road. But this guy's face was more mobile, more expressive, returning her inspection with equal interest.

'Doughnut?' she said, offering the box. 'There's maple bacon and chai cream.'

'Maple bacon?' he said, like he couldn't believe it.

'It's good.'

He took one and thanked her and made a performance out of his enjoyment.

'Are you TG?' she asked.

He eyed her for a moment, then swallowed another bite. 'Inside I was. Here, I'm just Perch.'

'I'm a friend of Anthony Lambert.'

'Fuck off!' His face brightened with delight. 'He told you to visit? He's got such a stick up his ass. He won't let me violate parole, made me promise to stay away.'

'That makes him a good friend.'

'He's the worst,' he said, fondly, before turning serious. 'Wait, shit. I heard he's in trouble.'

She tilted her head. 'How'd you hear that?'

'Online. What happened, my little nephew knew that I wanted to hang with, uh, my known associates, right? At least stay in touch. I told him, what if Anthony dies? Right? I wouldn't even know. So my nephew sets an alert on my phone for his name. Just being a brat, you understand? Showing off that it could be done. But the other day, up pops Anthony Lambert. Involved in some shit.'

Ocean watched TG polish off the maple bacon, then explained what chai was, and then she said, 'Listen. I'm Anthony's friend. So I don't care, but after you saw the news, you broke into the dead guy's house in Altadena.'

TG went still and tense.

'You knew James Dedrick's house was empty,' she told him. 'Because the news said he was dead, with no close family.'

'Uh,' he said.

'You were caught on video, breaking in. Not your face, just your tattoo. They think it's Anthony's.'

'Shit,' he said.

'Yeah.'

'*Shit.*'

'So I'm going tell the cops that the tattoo isn't his,' Ocean told him. 'It's close, but not quite. You got them at the same time, huh? Yeah. Well, if they start looking for similar tats, how long before they find your name?'

'Shit,' he said again.

'And you're on parole,' she said.

'And I'm on parole,' he agreed.

'You're a friend of Anthony's,' she said. 'So I wanted to give you a heads-up. I'll tell the cops when I get back to town. Late this afternoon. So if you think it's time to . . . I don't know. Take a trip, or change the tat? I don't know.'

'You wanted to give me a heads-up,' he said, repeating her words.

'Yeah.'

'I see why you're friends,' he said. 'You and Anthony.'

'You do?'

'A badass busybody who thinks you know what's best for everyone?' He toasted her with his half-eaten chai doughnut. 'You're just like him.'

71

LILY-ANN

The deliverables chart looked good, but Lily-Ann wasn't ready to add her approval. Something felt unpolished. So when the phone rang, she answered on speakerphone, her gaze still on the laptop screen.

'This is Lily-Ann.'

'It's Debra,' her divorce lawyer said. 'I already heard back from Piotr.'

'That was fast.'

'Well, we already worked together on the prenup. Which, I'm happy to say, he's not going to contest. So everything should move quickly and smoothly. Emphasis on should.'

'Good,' Lily-Ann said, making a note on her chart.

As Debra discussed debts and alimony, Ocean knocked on the front door, then poked her head inside.

Lily-Ann stood from her desk and waved for her to come into the living room, and the two of them listened to Debra on speakerphone for a minute before she ended the call.

'You're divorcing Piotr?' Ocean asked.

'Finally.'

'Why now?'

Lily-Ann plopped herself on her usual side of the couch and motioned for Ocean to join her. 'Because I can't think of a reason not to. No, that's not right. Because . . .' She paused, feeling uncharacteristically embarrassed. 'Piotr doesn't love me.'

'Oh,' Ocean said. 'I'm sorry. That doesn't feel good.'

'It's fine. He never did. That doesn't bother me.'

'It's *not* fine, Lily-Ann.'

'Mmm. But I've come to realize that he doesn't even *like* me.'

Ocean gave her an indecipherable look. 'Anthony does.'

'Does he?'

'And I do. Hamilton does, Mrs B does. We all do. Even after . . .' She scrubbed her short hair. 'I need to apologize to Sophie.'

Lily-Ann rarely apologized; she couldn't see the point. So she said, 'Did you find Anthony's friend?'

'Yeah.'

'Did you ask him about the night of the murder?'

'Yeah. He had no idea where he was or what he was doing. He didn't strike me as the kind of guy who's great with schedules. So I asked about enemies. Like if anyone from prison would come for Anthony.'

'Or want to frame him,' Lily-Ann added.

'I didn't get that far, because he mocked me for the question. I don't know. I guess once you're out, you don't carry your grudges anymore? I don't get it, but he said the same thing Anthony said. This didn't have anything to do with prison.'

'That's a pity,' Lily-Ann said.

'Yeah, it'd be pretty convenient.'

'I didn't want to tell you about the tattoo not matching Anthony's.'

Ocean nodded. 'Because you worried about Mrs B. You didn't want to say anything that would keep her in jail.'

'Yes,' Lily-Ann said. 'I'm still not sure I should've said anything.'

'You know what you are?'

Lily-Ann straightened the pillow she was leaning against. 'I have some ideas.'

'Lovable, Lily-Ann. That's what you are.'

'Stop,' she said.

Ocean didn't lose one iota of her earnestness. 'Don't let anyone tell you different.'

'Yeah, yeah.' Lily-Ann stood and grabbed her laptop from the desk, then returned to the couch. 'So what's our next step?'

'For helping Mrs B? I don't know.' Ocean gazed out the window. 'We could agree amongst ourselves about a single alibi, and then offer that to the detective?'

'I think we're past him believing an alibi from any of us.'

'Oh, true,' Ocean said. 'But he knows she's not guilty.'

'I suppose as long as an alibi is on the record, it should undermine any prosecution, whether or not they believe it.'

'Yeah.'

'If he keeps her locked up,' Lily-Ann said, 'it's only to pressure us to accuse Anthony.'

'If that asshole keeps Golda behind bars as a hostage, to force us to tell lies about Anthony, I swear by all that's holy . . .' Ocean took a breath. 'That's such a cop move. Who cares about the lives ruined, people destroyed, as long as you close the case? I try not to agree when Riley gets all "ACAB" because yeah the institution is broken but individuals in a flawed system are—'

'I'm not familiar with the acronym.'

'ACAB. All Cops Are Bastards. Which is painting with maybe too broad a—' When her phone rang, she glanced at the screen. 'Huh. Speaking of ACAB.'

'It's the detective?'

Ocean nodded, then answered and said a few words.

Lily-Ann considered the chart on her laptop.

Ocean said a few more words. Then listened. Then she hung up and said, 'Well, add the cop to my apology list.'

Lily-Ann looked up from her work.

'They're releasing Mrs B this evening. The cop's arranging with me to pick her up, to make the transition as easy as possible.'

Though she was still concerned for Anthony, Lily-Ann felt an unclenching in her heart. She didn't think of herself as a highly emotional person, because she wasn't, yet the relief warmed her. She *liked* not being a highly emotional person, but Mrs B had never done anything other than accept and embrace her; the thought of Mrs B suffering discomforts, much less deprivations, angered her a frightening amount.

'That's wonderful news,' she said.

'We should call the Murder Collective back in session for the day after. To clear the air . . . and to welcome her home.'

'I'll bring the beverages,' Lily-Ann said, then paused for a moment. 'When this is all over, I want to paint this room. Will you help me pick a color?'

'Sure.' Ocean eyed the furniture. 'What're you thinking, beige?'

'Closer to eggplant or chartreuse. Do think Mrs B would mind?'

'I think she'll be delighted.'

72

NICHOLAS

Well, shit.

Of course Nicholas wanted to achieve something, to make his mark in life. And sure, he wasn't satisfied drifting along the surface. Still, that didn't mean he wanted to sink in over his head, to get mired in the weeds and muck.

But now?

He heard the crack of wood against James Dedrick's skull. He could almost feel the impact in his hand as he saw the body fall. Slowly. So much more slowly than he'd imagined, almost like Dedrick was simply lying down for a nap in the hawthorn hedge.

Sitting in his office, ignoring his work, Nicholas thought about that crack of wood – and shuddered. Okay. Look forward, not back.

He couldn't change the past, but the future was anyone's game.

He needed to fix this. Untangle himself from the weeds and make it go away, whatever the cost.

73

SOPHIE

I wasn't surprised when Ocean knocked on my door and apologized for what she'd said at Hamilton's house. I was a little surprised by how sorry she *looked*, though. She really hated hurting people.

'Apology accepted,' I immediately told her. 'How's Mrs B? You brought her home last night?'

'Yeah, she's . . .' When she smiled, Ocean transformed into a mischievous Peter Pan. 'She's the same. You'll see.'

'No tattoos?'

'Not yet. I'll see you at the meeting tonight?'

'Of course. Who else would take notes?'

'What are you doing with those? Have you solved the crime yet?'

'"Course not. What am I, Sherlock Holmes?'

'Sophie Holmes,' she said. 'Have you shown them to Lily-Ann or Hamilton? Maybe they can piece something together.'

'Uh, not yet. I'm a note taker, not a note sharer.' I conveniently ignored the fact that I'd shared everything with Nicholas, including my ideas for scenes and staging. 'Sorry.'

Ocean gave me a dubious look, possibly because I'd relapsed into apologizing for no good reason.

'Got to get to work,' I said, ushering her out. 'See you tonight!'

* * *

Act??

SCENE???

HAMILTON'S living room is bedecked in streamers
and there's a big WELCOME HOME sign, except
each letter is a chemical element or particle:
tungsten (W), electron (E), lepton (L).

(I missed the rest, but I remember Molybdenum was
backwards to make 'oM.')

At the door, LILY-ANN hands out drinks with little
umbrellas.

SOPHIE

(to HAMILTON)

I'm sorry, too. I shouldn't have said that. I just . . . I wish
the cops would stick to fighting dragons online.

HAMILTON
Oh, there aren't dragons in Realm of Rangers. Not
dragons plural. There's only a single dragon, the Elder
Castellan.

SOPHIE

(faking interest)

Oh, yeah? What's he like, then? Breathes fires and all
that?

HAMILTON
Lightning! And her eyes glow blue.

MILES

(not faking interest)

Have you seen her? Whoa. Have you traded with her?
Are you in a guild?

HAMILTON
I'm a guild leader. Well, a co-leader. Of the Netherwood
Poets. Do you want to join?

MILES
The Poets! That's the best guild in the game!

(Across the room, LILY-ANN speaks to OCEAN.)

LILY-ANN
I know it's time, but I'm a little nervous about being so
alone.

OCEAN
One thing you're not is alone. We've got you. Some cranky
bitch might yell at you for marrying rich, but that doesn't
mean anything.

LILY-ANN
Oh, I did worse than marry rich. I was born rich. Piotr
married rich.

SOPHIE
Really? Ha! Way to screw with my sexist assumptions.

OCEAN

(consulting phone)

Wait, wait, she's coming.

HAMILTON
Oh! Should we hide? Turn the lights off? Turn the lights off and hide?

OCEAN
You yell surprise, you'll give the old woman a heart attack. Just gather 'round. You, too, Nicholas.

(Nicholas stays in the back of the room as the door opens and Riley escorts Mrs B inside.)

HAMILTON

(à la 'surprise!')

Don't be alarmed!

MRS. B
Look at you all! Everyone's here. And a bigger pack of liars I have never seen. Ocean told me what you did. Giving false alibis to the police! You should be ashamed, you lovely, lovely people.

SOPHIE
How are you? How was . . . You look good. You look great.

MRS. B
I slept for twelve hours last night. At my age, any longer

than that and they recommend checking for a pulse. And Ocean's been feeding me and I'm so pleased to be home.

LILY-ANN

(escorting MRS B to a chair)

Lemon water? A glass of wine?

MRS. B
I don't suppose you have any Ensure.

HAMILTON

(running off to get it)

Ha! Ha-ha!

LILY-ANN
Was jail terrible?

MRS. B
Well, yes and no. The facilities are disgraceful. More like a kennel than anywhere people should live. Or even dogs, for that matter. However! You'll never guess who I met there.

OCEAN
How could we guess? Of course we'll never guess.

MRS. B
That's why I said that, Ocean. I met a lovely young woman named Brittany. She and her friends are prostitutes. I

mean, I suppose this town is big enough for that sort of thing.

SOPHIE
We did have a murder, after all.

MRS. B
Very true! She didn't use the word 'prostitute,' though. We really ought to bring back the old terms. Wouldn't it be better to call yourself a 'ladybird' or a 'dolly-mop'?

(NICHOLAS starts edging toward the exit.)

RILEY
You're making that up. Dolly-mop? No way.

OCEAN
Maybe we could not talk about sex workers in front of the kids?

MRS. B
"Sex workers"! That's what they said, Brittany and her friends. The term is a little clinical, isn't it? I'll recommend 'wagtail' when they come for dinner. Such sweet girls. They took care of me, at meals and making sure my bed was comfortable. If only I had another cottage to rent. I don't like to judge, but I do wonder if they're as happy as they could be, in their work.

LILY-ANN
Perhaps we should focus on one problem at a time. Are you no longer a suspect?

MRS. B
Apparently I never truly was. Which is insulting, if you think about it. Claiming I was incapable of doing such a thing. I told them and told them, but they refused to believe me.

OCEAN
So ageist. We should start a petition to get you back in jail.

MRS. B
At least, on the bright side, according to Anthony's public defender, I muddied the waters. The prosecution is afraid of how a jury might react to my star turn in the witness box, explaining that he's innocent.

HAMILTON

(presenting Ensure)

Also, they have no evidence except hearsay.

MRS. B
So tell me, my dears: How exactly are we going to free Anthony?

(The door slams behind NICHOLAS after he leaves. The lights switch off, darkness falls on the stage.)

End of Act?? Maybe.

Also: What the hell was wrong with him?

74

LILY-ANN

Lily-Ann agreed to meet Gregory Ybarra for a meal. Largely to learn more about him, because if she didn't, her inquiry would feel incomplete. Especially after Ocean told her that Ybarra had been pressuring Mrs B to sell the Marigold Cottages. But also because he'd offered to buy her lunch at her favorite vegan restaurant. She hadn't eaten there since they got a Michelin star and doubled their prices.

She could afford them, of course, but overpaying always made her feel, ironically, cheap. Still, she'd happily listen to Ybarra for the twenty-seven-dollar umami burger and the twenty-four-dollar grilled salad.

'I'll also have the herbal coffee,' she told the server. Another twelve dollars.

'I like a healthy eater,' Ybarra said.

'I like a clean-shaven chin,' she told him.

'Ah,' he said, rubbing his white beard. 'Well! I think I'll have a coffee, too.'

He talked about various coffees he'd enjoyed until the meal came, then between bites explained why he'd invited her. 'I understand you're a woman of means.'

'You mean I'm wealthy?'

'That's exactly what I mean,' he said. 'Your family is from Palo Alto, no?'

'Los Gatos.'

'Then I should fire my assistant. She assured me it was Palo Alto.' He laughed at his own joke. 'So! The reason I asked you to lunch, other than to enjoy your company, of course, is to present you with an investment opportunity.'

'Because James Dedrick is dead?'

He choked on his jackfruit taco. 'Well, I must admit he was my first choice.'

'You invited him to inspect the property. Did you know he'd be at the Marigold Cottages that Friday night?'

'To be honest, I'd expected we'd look the place over in the daylight on Saturday. I'm a traditionalist that way. But young people – well, real estate is the new California gold rush. You've got to get out there with your pickax and your mule, even if it's the dead of night. Truth is, I figure he just wanted to take a peek without me around.'

'You've, uh, prospected with Dedrick before?' she asked, proud of herself for expanding the metaphor.

Ybarra shook his head. 'We tried a few times, but nothing ever came together.'

'And now you're looking for someone to invest in your purchase of the Marigold Cottages?'

'No, no. That's handled. I'll handle the purchase. What I'm looking for is someone to invest in *developing* the Cottages, in light of the new zoning.'

Lily-Ann focused on her grilled salad for a few bites. 'Is Mrs B selling?'

'Not as such. Not as yet. But I'm worried for her. I'm concerned. I've known her for years and she's . . . declining. And considering her recent behavior? Getting involved with the police? Confessing to a murder? That is not a good sign. Quite the contrary. I'm worried she'll soon be declared incompetent.'

'That would make the purchase more difficult, no?'

He waved away her concern and started telling her about his vision for the *new* Marigold Cottages. Twenty-eight units, modern Spanish architecture. Mixed floor plans, rooftop terrace, while more modestly retaining the courtyard . . .

He mentioned several times that he was pleased Lily-Ann didn't have a 'morbid emotional attachment' to the current Marigold Cottages. At first, she thought he was praising her professionalism, but she soon realized that he thought she was slumming, renting there. That was the only reason he could imagine that she wouldn't live in a larger house, one that she owned and in which she gained equity.

All of which made perfect sense, and was absolutely wrong; so apparently *she* didn't make perfect sense. She liked her tiny cottage. She liked her eccentric, interfering neighbors. Perhaps she wasn't as unfeeling as he expected. Perhaps she wasn't as unfeeling as *she* expected.

When she smiled at that thought, Ybarra's eyes sparkled. He thought she was smiling at him and started throwing figures around. Mostly how much profit she could expect to shake down from what he was tentatively calling 'the Marigold Property.'

So she smiled even wider, thanked him for the lovely meal, and left.

75

OCEAN

When Anthony's friend had called her a *'badass busybody who thinks she knows best,'* his tone had turned the words into a compliment. Well, 'badass' turned any criticism into praise. Plus, Ocean had been intrigued to hear that description applied to Anthony. How much of a busybody could you be when you barely said anything?

On the other hand, she knew – mostly because Riley kept telling her – that sticking your nose into other people's business wasn't universally admired.

She did have to admit, though, that asking Sophie to meet her and Lily-Ann for drinks at Capriccio on Friday night was a tiny bit interfering. Still, she really did want to compare notes about the murder.

Lily-Ann and Ocean walked from the Cottages together and met Sophie there on her way home from work. Even early, the restaurant was crowded with locals who loved big plates of pasta and the bocce court on the patio. Lily-Ann made the host seat them in the best booth in the farthest corner, then ordered a plate of fried artichokes and a bottle of expensive Chianti the minute they sat down.

Ocean enjoyed the appetizer as she told the story of her trip to the Ventura Pier.

'So, wait,' Sophie said, nursing her first glass of wine. 'You just walked up and introduced yourself to him?'

'Anthony told me his friend spends every waking hour fishing at the pier,' Ocean explained, settling more comfortably in the upholstered booth. 'And I knew he had a distinctive tattoo, one that matched Anthony's. I figured he was the man who broke into Dead Rick's house. He knew it was empty, an easy score.'

'I guess it wasn't so vanishingly unlikely,' Lily-Ann murmured.

Sophie shook her head. 'I don't mean how did you

recognize him, Ocean. I mean . . . an ex-con, a violent felon, and you just introduced yourself?'

'Oh. Well, we were in a public place. And, y'know, he's a friend of Anthony's.'

'I'm not sure I trust *Anthony* that much.'

Lily-Ann looked up from the menu and frowned at Sophie. 'There's something that no one told you.'

'Oh, god, what?'

'It's about Anthony,' Lily-Ann said.

Ocean began to protest. 'Lily-Ann, I'm not sure this is—'

'Anthony?' Sophie tilted her head. 'Why would anyone not tell me something about Anthony?'

'They think you're fragile,' Lily-Ann explained.

Ocean lifted her glass to her nose instead of saying, *Because she* is. She inhaled, trying to detect the notes of cherry and chalk the server promised, but she mostly just smelled red wine.

'They're protecting you from an upsetting episode,' Lily-Ann continued. 'For fear, I suppose, of intrusive thoughts. Still, I think you should know.'

Sophie swallowed. 'What upsetting episode?'

'One night, when Anthony worked as a bouncer, he found you passed out drunk in the street. He carried you home to keep you safe. That's why Mrs B trusts him.'

Sophie set her glass down a little too quickly. 'You mean, like, he picked me up and . . . really?'

'Yes.'

She squeezed her eyes closed. *'Really?'*

Ocean drained her own glass. 'Yeah. Mrs B asked me not to say anything.'

'Why not? I can't believe everyone knew but me!

What the absolute fuck? He carried me home? Like, from downtown?'

'Yes,' Lily-Ann said.

'Why didn't she tell me?' Sophie repeated.

'Because she's a busybody who thinks she knows what's best for everyone,' Ocean said as the server approached. 'Where do you think I got it from?'

They all ordered pasta, then Lily-Ann told Sophie, 'Mrs B thinks you're recovering from a terrible shock. Also, that you're thriving. She worried that telling you would set you back.'

Sophie frowned. 'I can't decide if that's kind or creepy.'

'It's both,' Ocean said. 'I'm sorry. Lily-Ann is right. We should've told you. But Mrs B needs to be needed. She's always been that way, and you—you're good for her. She perked up when you moved in.'

'She did?'

'Yes,' Lily-Ann said.

Sophie gave a tremulous smile. 'She thinks I'm *thriving*?'

'Well, other than being carried home blackout drunk by ex-cons,' Lily-Ann said.

'Lily-Ann has news, too,' Ocean said, to move the conversation along.

'Do I?' Lily-Ann thought for a moment. 'Oh, yes, of course. I'm divorcing Piotr.'

Sophie gave a delicate snort of laughter, then apologized. 'I'm sorry! I shouldn't laugh.'

'Yes, you should,' Lily-Ann told her.

'It's only, my dad? He thinks Piotr is the perfect catch. Hell, even Nicholas has his eye on him. He told me he saw him at, uh, the Bathhouse?'

'There's a bathhouse in town?' Ocean asked, feeling once again that she was getting old. 'How'd I miss an entire bathhouse?'

Sophie smiled. 'It's an oyster bar. Superexpensive. I looked it up.'

'No.' Lily-Ann's brows drew together over her sharp blue eyes. 'It can't have been him.'

'Why's that?' Sophie asked.

'He's allergic to shellfish, and extremely aware of it. He'll change tables if anyone nearby orders lobster.'

Ocean sipped her wine. 'Hamilton's Clamato juice would've killed him.'

'He didn't speak to me for three days after I tried a bite of escargot,' Lily-Ann said, while Sophie fiddled with her phone. 'He was furious.'

'Over a single bite?' Ocean asked.

'Well, mostly because it took me two days to realize he was giving me the silent treatment.'

Ocean huffed a laugh. 'Is escargot even shellfish?'

'They're mollusks,' Lily-Ann said.

A silence fell when the server brought the pastas. Ravioli for Sophie, arrabiata for Lily-Ann, and puttanesca for Ocean. 'In honor of Mrs B and her ladybirds.'

'We're going to need a bowl of Parmesan,' Lily-Ann said.

While they waited for the cheese, Sophie showed them her phone. 'Nicholas sent a picture. That's definitely Piotr.'

Ocean couldn't make out much more than a blur, at first. Then she saw two leathery, wealthy-looking men sitting at a table with two blonde, hungry-looking women, along with a dead ringer for Piotr.

Lily-Ann frowned at the screen. 'You're right. That is him.

'With a couple Russian guys,' Sophie said, reading a text from Nicholas. 'He says, uh, "two oligarch-looking guys and their terrifyingly blonde wives."'

'Not Russian. They're from Florida,' Lily-Ann told her. 'I recognize the one on the left; he's a big-time investor. He was huge into NFTs and I don't know what else.'

'He looks sleazy,' Sophie said, as the server came back with the cheese. 'Ooh, if he's the mafia, that'd be a great addition to the plot!'

'He's not mafia,' Lily-Ann said, 'just greedy and extortionate.'

'What plot?' Ocean asked.

'Oh, uh . . .'

'Does it involve the notes you still haven't shown anyone?' Ocean bit into her pasta, then added more Parmesan.

'I showed Nicholas.'

'Oh *really*?' Lily-Ann asked, with more teasing in her voice than Ocean had ever heard from her. 'And now you're texting him about oysters.'

'Don't you start!' Sophie said. 'I think Mrs B is trying to set us up.'

'She really does adore you,' Ocean said.

'Because she wants me to get with the guy who doesn't like her?'

'Because,' Ocean told them. 'Nicholas is her heir.'

317

76

SOPHIE

I didn't know what to think about Anthony carrying me home. I didn't know what to think about *myself*. Yeah, I drank too much sometimes, but not in a bad way. Not in a harmful way. Just in a fun, partying way. And sure, sometimes I missed a few hours, but . . .

Anyway.

I didn't know what to think about that, so instead I thought about Nicholas inheriting the Marigold Cottages. I mean, he'd told me he was inheriting something, but the entire *property?*

Did he know? I doubted it. I guess there were lots of secrets at the Cottages, and that was only one of them. Should I pretend I didn't know, the way no one had told me that I'd passed out on the street in my smallest skirt?

Did I owe Anthony for carrying me home? Did you owe people for *not* being horrible?

Who was I kidding? He'd been a lot better than non-horrible to me; he'd been positively decent. So yeah, I owed him decency in return. Yet so far, I'd only shown him suspicion and chilly politeness. If he ever got out of jail, I'd work on that.

I'd work on *me*.

Maybe I'd even thrive.

The idea of thriving, like Mrs B had said, gave me a warm feeling . . . which only lasted until I thought about myself passed out on the street. Unconscious, vulnerable. With gangs of drunk men walking past. The perfect victim.

And I won't lie: after Lily-Ann and Ocean told me about that, I'd handled the revelation really well . . . until I started crying halfway through my jog this morning.

Running along Olive Street, bawling.

So maybe I wasn't thriving quite yet. Though, on the other hand, why couldn't I cry and thrive at the same time? That sounded like my kind of flourishing: the weepy kind.

I didn't want to need protection. I didn't want to feel weak, but I damn sure didn't feel strong. I felt brittle and tenuous. Still, maybe part of that, part of being strong, was letting people take care of you. Accepting help from people who you cared about, and who cared about you in turn.

Deep thoughts for an early morning, so I pulled my hair into a high ponytail and went to knock on Nicholas's door. To tell him about his inheritance. If I didn't like people keeping secrets about me, I shouldn't keep secrets about them.

He opened the door, looking sleepy and mussed, and I realized it wasn't even 7 a.m. yet. He wore a T-shirt and boxer briefs, and I almost apologized and told him I'd come back, but then I noticed the waffle in his hand.

And by in his hand, I meant in his actual hand. He was standing there holding a frozen waffle.

'Waffle,' I said.

'Huh?' He looked at his hand in surprise. 'Oh. Huh.'

Then he turned and shuffled back inside.

I followed him into his kitchen, where he put the waffle on a plate and said, 'Coffee.'

'Yes, please,' I said. 'No, I mean—' He gestured to his coffee cup. 'I meant to pick up the coffee, not the waffle, I-I just woke up.'

'So you're *not* going to make me coffee?'

'Oh! No, of course.' He looked blearily at his coffeemaker. 'Um, so . . .'

'I'll get my own coffee. You put pants on.'

He frowned at his bare legs. 'You're wearing less,' he said, which wasn't true because I was wearing leggings. Then he muttered under his breath and left the kitchen.

I poured myself coffee, then poked around in Nicholas's kitchen. Channeling Lily-Ann. Checking his fridge. Checking his cabinets. There was something intimate about it. And let's be honest, I liked him. I liked his passion for theatre and I liked his face and I liked that he tried to protect Mrs B from feeling any obligation to him.

I just liked him, okay? It was okay to like someone. It was definitely okay to like someone while sober. And Nicholas was the someone I liked.

I sipped my coffee and sat at his kitchen table.

His cottage was the largest on the property, and his kitchen was quite nice. It had the same original wooden cabinets as the rest of us, but his had been painted a pretty steel blue. The tile countertops had been replaced with light granite and the appliances looked new. I wondered if Mrs B had customized it for him.

As I waited for him to reappear, I fiddled with the papers on the table – and caught a glimpse of the signature page of a legal document.

So I listened for his footsteps, then pulled that page closer. *Nicholas Perez.*

Gregory Ybarra.

I frowned and flipped to the first page. The legal document was brief, but the text mentioned 'the intention to be legally bound,' which sounded serious. And I knew that I should just look away. No decent person found a legal document in someone else's house and read it.

But yeah, I read the agreement. Then I reread it, my heart sinking and pounding at the same time. *What the hell? What the absolute hell, Nicholas? I like you. I like you but—*

'Sorry about that,' he said, coming in from the hallway. 'Takes me awhile to get going in the morning.'

I stood and shook the page at him. 'What is *this*?'

'Uh,' he said.

'Inheriting some money? That's what you told me. But you're inheriting the whole fucking property! I came to tell you, because Ocean and Lily-Ann told me and it didn't seem right that we should keep it a secret from you, but I guess you knew already.'

'I didn't know until the other day. I—'

I shook the papers again. 'What the fuck is this?'

'It's a . . . you read it?'

'It's a betrayal, that's what it is.'

'Yeah, Sophie. Like coming into my house and digging around in my stuff for—'

'You shut up! It's not like that! This is Mrs B! The Marigold Cottages are her love and her legacy. This is her home! And you're going to sign the whole thing over to fucking Gregory Ybarra?'

'That's not . . . Would you listen? That's not what I'm doing, Sophie!'

'Then explain,' I demanded, because I wanted to believe him so badly. 'Explain how this isn't you signing the property over to Ybarra.'

'Well, it is. I mean, instead of me inheriting, he'll inherit but-but Mrs Bakofsky will already be gone when that happens, so it's not a betrayal.'

'Why?' I asked. 'Why would you do this?'

Nicholas clenched his jaw. 'I work for the city, Sophie. We need more rental units. In town. More affordable housing inventory. More density in walkable neighborhoods like this one, where—'

'She'd hate this!' I slammed the document on the table. 'You know she would. She wants you to own the property, not Ybarra. She wants you to own Marigold and she wants Marigold to stay Marigold!'

He took a shaky breath. 'Why do you care so much?'

'Why do you care so *little*? You know she'd hate this! Tell me she wouldn't.'

He lowered his head. 'I know she'd hate it.'

'Then why are you—' And I started crying. 'Why are you doing it, Nicholas? If you need money, she'll help. If you need to sell, let's get everyone together; we'll figure something out.'

'I don't—'

'Why *do* this to her? To us? To me?'

His lifted his head and said, 'Because I want to.'

77

VERNON

Everyone knew that the old lady had confessed to the crime because she was trying to undercut the case against Anthony Lambert. She'd even brought a fake murder weapon to the station.

She got away with it, too. She'd startled the DA's office, and now Vernon needed to release Anthony from custody. At least, for the moment. Until more evidence emerged.

Well, fair enough. You couldn't simply ignore the confession of a neighbor with a blood-smeared club. You just couldn't. And Vernon was a law-abiding man. Still, part of him wished he could just make Mrs Golda Bakofsky and her anarchic bullshit disappear.

He was a good cop and a good mentor. And that mattered to him. Yet a decade after his last promotion, he still hadn't made the kind of mark that secured his future – or his reputation. That mattered, too. He wanted to be an inspiration, to leave a legacy.

And now Anthony Lambert was going free.

Vernon swiveled in his chair and looked through his office window. The day was too sunny. Like nobody had committed murder and then walked away without paying the price.

78

SOPHIE

This was not a scene for the play. This was not for art. This was for me.

I was supposed to work that weekend, but I left early. I was too upset to chat with the graphic designer about the new posters. I wasn't just upset, I was seething.

'*Because I want to*,' Nicholas had said.

The perfect summation of selfishness.

I liked him. I didn't know why, but I liked Nicholas. Sometimes I met people who clicked with me. At least,

I used to. People who I had more in common with than drinking and partying. And when I got to know Nicholas a little, I'd thought, *Here's someone who gets me.*

Then he'd looked me in the eye and said, '*Because I want to.*'

So I went home from the New Vic Theatre early and almost crawled into bed. But I didn't. I was too pissed. Instead, I paced my living room.

Then I stopped pacing and scowled at the tequila bottle on the windowsill. Just a few fingers left. I wanted to polish it off and start on the bottle of wine I'd bought for too much money, thinking I might impress Nicholas the next time he came over. I unscrewed the tequila bottle . . . then flashed to a picture of myself sprawled on a sidewalk.

I was so tired of feeling weak. So tired of feeling helpless.

I didn't use to be this way. I used to stride through the world without checking over my shoulder. When I ran track in high school, I was the girl the other girls relied on when things got too stressful or rough. And they'd been there for me. Living at the Marigold Cottages brought back those feelings, of being protected *and* protective.

Losing that part of me for so long infuriated me.

I'd tell people, '*Hesse didn't really do anything. He didn't touch me.*'

As if because he'd only terrorized me, he wasn't that bad. He'd only invaded my privacy, my safety, my life. He'd only played cruel games and poisoned me against myself . . . *because he wanted to.*

'How about what *I* want?' I asked the empty room.

Then I slammed from the cottage and into my car and screeched away to pay a visit to Neal Hesse.

Yes, I'd known he lived in town. Of course I'd known. I knew where he worked, where he lived, I knew his hobbies and his face.

That's what they didn't tell you. I was so frightened that *I'd* started stalking *him*. That's what they didn't tell you. What they did was, they made themselves the most important person in your life.

I didn't fucking sleep for three weeks after I'd discovered he lived in town. I'd been so scared, blindly scared – but now I was blind with anger.

I couldn't remember the drive. I couldn't remember the free-way or the stop signs through his neighborhood. I remembered pulling into his driveway, though. I remembered slamming on the brakes. I remembered that my breath fogged the windshield and sounded like panting.

I sat there trembling. With fear or with fury? I didn't know at the time, and I still don't. Then for a moment, I faltered. What was I doing here? What was I doing? Well, I was crying again.

Maybe I'd never stopped.

But my tears gave me strength.

I left my car and pounded on his front door with the heel of my hand. I never wondered if he'd be home on a late Saturday morning. The thought never occurred to me.

I pounded until my hand ached – and the door opened. A woman stood there, holding a baby.

'Where is he?' I demanded.

She glanced aside nervously, and I pushed past her to find Neal Hesse standing in the living room, where the wall-mounted television played a football game. He was wearing sweatpants and a black polo, but his arms were both royal purple. The same shade. And his elbows were bent at right angles and . . . they were casts.

He was wearing casts. *Two* casts. How the hell had he broken both his arms?

I laughed.

Behind me, the woman said, 'D-do you know her?'

I laughed again. 'That's a good question. That's a great question, Neal. *Do* you know me, Neal?'

'No, I-I don't . . .'

'You've been in my room, Neal. You were in my underwear drawer. Do you know me?'

'What are you doing here? I have a wife— I have a family!'

'You waited for me after class. You sent me messages, didn't you? You left me little gifts.' I took another step forward. 'Do you think you fucking know me?'

'G-get out,' he said. 'Get out of my house.'

'Oh, you don't like me up in your space?' I asked, moving closer.

'Just leave us alone!'

'You watched me sleep,' I snarled, and kneed him in the balls.

When he bent over, I shoved him so hard that he stumbled against the coffee table and fell to the floor.

'You watched me sleep,' I repeated, looming over him. 'But you don't know me.'

79

NICHOLAS

The circuit breaker usually popped if he used the toaster oven and blender at the same time. Though not always, which surprised Nicholas. Either the circuit could handle the load or not; what was with the variation?

Today, though, he'd been melting butter in the microwave, too. So the power died and he went outside, squeezed behind the bushes, and flipped the breaker.

And that's when he saw Anthony walking quietly across the courtyard to his apartment.

From what Lily-Ann had told him, Nicholas owed Anthony. They all did. Anthony had taken care of Sophie. Nicholas still didn't exactly enjoy living in a fishbowl, but he paid his debts. Well, maybe not to Mrs B. Well, at least he tried not to accrue more.

So he squeezed out from behind the bushes. Wiped himself off and thought for a minute. Then he followed Anthony to his apartment.

When he got there, the front door was open and he heard noises from inside. Heavy breathing? A sort of gasp? He listened until he understood what he was hearing, then he tapped his knuckles on the open door and looked inside.

There was a *Welcome Home!!!* poster on the wall. Bright and sloppy, drawn with Magic Markers. In the corner, below pictures of gray whales, Nicholas saw a big looping signature: *MILES!*

And Anthony was standing at the table holding a bouquet of wildflowers. Well, maybe not a bouquet.

It looked like Miles had picked a sprig of every single flowering weed that was in bloom within a three-block radius.

Anthony stood there with the bouquet in his big hands, his shoulders shaking as he wept. Tears running down that mean-looking face. He didn't even try to hide them when he spotted Nicholas at the door.

For a second, Nicholas thought about getting Ocean from next door, because she'd know how to handle this. But screw it. Sometimes you needed a man to awkwardly thump your back.

So he stepped into the apartment and said, 'It must've been hard. Going back inside. It must've been so rough.'

Anthony tried to speak, but squeezed his eyes closed instead.

'But you're here now.' Nicholas put his hand on Anthony's arm. 'You're home now.'

Anthony took a shuddering breath.

'Bring it in, man,' Nicholas said, and gave him a hug.

He even thumped his back. And after tensing for a second, Anthony relaxed. He exhaled, then took a deeper breath.

Then he said, 'Nobody ever gave me flowers before.'

80

OCEAN

When Ocean thought about childhood dinners, she thought about lasagna paired with a basic green salad and a steaming loaf of overly buttered garlic bread. Super old-school, super delicious. Pure comfort.

She decided to replicate the feeling that evening, and was checking the lasagna, when Mrs B walked through the front door with Anthony.

'You're out!' Miles screamed, hurling himself at Anthony. 'Oma said today or tomorrow – I kept bringing fresh flowers! Did you get my flowers?'

'I did,' Anthony said, spinning Miles in a circle.

'Did you like them?'

'Loved 'em,' Anthony said, plopping Miles onto the couch.

'I made you cupcakes, too, but we ate them all.'

'I like flowers better,' Anthony said.

'You do not,' Riley said, raising her Sharpie-inked face from her phone.

Anthony frowned at her. 'Are you stealing my look?'

'No,' she told him. 'I'm *improving* your look.'

'Except you're going to stop now that Anthony's back,' Ocean announced from the kitchen, wiping her hands on a dish towel.

Riley shot her a dangerous look, but before she snapped, Anthony said, 'I'm saving up to get mine removed.'

'I hope not all of them, dear!' Mrs B said, from where she was inspecting the lasagna. 'I quite like the ones on your chest.'

'Nah, just my face.'

Ocean narrowed her eyes at Mrs B. 'When did you see his chest?'

'I'm quite spry for my age,' Mrs B announced. 'You'd be surprised the things I see.'

'Oh, here we go,' Ocean said.

Mrs B tittered. 'I *asked* to see them, of course.'

'Ooh, will you show me?' Riley said.

'No,' Anthony said.

Riley made a face at him, then said, 'Come sit next to me, Mrs B. This is the gardening game I wanted to show you. I'm planting petunias, like, outside.'

'There can never be too many flowers,' Mrs B announced. 'Hamilton tells me that there's a species of petunia which are exclusively pollinated by hummingbirds.'

'Hamilton is cool,' Miles said. 'He got a whole box of wasabi soda delivered.'

'Gross,' Riley said.

'Can I help with anything?' Anthony asked Ocean.

'You want to mince garlic?'

'Sure.'

So she brought him into the kitchen and gestured at the cutting board and knife and the bulb of garlic.

'The whole thing?' he asked.

'Seven or eight cloves,' she said, and turned back to the living room.

'Ocean?' he said.

She stopped. 'Mmm?'

'Thanks.'

'For what?'

His smile actually moved his mouth that time. 'Don't make me start a list.'

'I wouldn't dare,' she said, with a smile of her own.

Back in the living room, she watched Riley show Mrs B her game while Miles hung over the back of the couch, thrilled that his sister was including him. It was such a mundane, forgettable moment, yet those were the times that mattered most. The brief, lovely moments that comprised a lifetime, each one a tiny dab of color in a Pointillist painting.

'Hello,' Lily-Ann said, stepping inside without knocking.

'Lily-Ann,' Mrs B said, with a wrinkle-eyed smile. 'I didn't know you were invited.'

'I brought some polish for Riley,' Lily-Ann said.

'That's good,' Ocean said, not bothering to say she hadn't invited Lily-Ann. 'She's so unpolished.'

'*Nail* polish, Mother.' Riley shoved her phone at Miles and hopped up from the couch. 'Ooh, these are Chanel!'

'The colors don't suit me.'

'Oh, my god, I'm obsessed!' Riley babbled for a minute about the pearl and pink-shaded polishes. 'I can do the best ombre effect with these.'

'Just don't show me,' Lily-Ann said.

'But it'll be gorgeous.'

'Please. My hairdresser once gave me ombre hair and I almost had an aneurism.'

'What is ombre hair?' Anthony asked from the kitchen doorway, his gaze intent upon Lily-Ann.

She was wearing a purple wrap dress and wedge mules. Her red hair fell in a strictly defined bob and her peach lipstick looked freshly applied. She was as beautiful as ever but softer, somehow.

'Ombre is a wash of one color into another,' Ocean told him. 'It's a gorgeous blending effect, but irregular, like sunsets.'

'Extremely irregular,' Lily-Ann said.

'You don't like sunsets?' Anthony asked her.

'No.' She considered. 'However, sunrises are acceptable.'

Anthony watched her gravely. 'I'll keep that in mind.'

Ocean glanced at Mrs B, who looked offensively smug. In an effort to keep her from saying anything about the sexual tension in the room, Ocean told Miles, 'Set another plate for Lily-Ann.'

'Thank you,' Lily-Ann said, not bothering with a pro forma refusal.

Which Ocean appreciated. She'd never had much patience for all that *Oh, I couldn't* and *Well, if you insist* stuff. Instead, they just sat down and ate.

81

LILY-ANN

Lily-Ann enjoyed the lasagna and the company, but wondered why Ocean hadn't offered real dessert after such a good meal. A bowl of early tangerines didn't qualify.

On the other hand, she'd liked how Anthony had peeled one for her, his thick fingers surprisingly delicate as he pulled the wedges apart.

She felt his gaze on her. She enjoyed his admiration, which told her what she'd wanted to know. She sometimes struggled with identifying her feelings, so she'd developed a sort of short-cut. If a man's scrutiny left her cold, that meant she wasn't drawn to him. However, if the exact same scrutiny struck a spark of warmth in her? That was a very different thing.

And when she stood from the table to say goodbye

after dinner, Anthony followed her outside. She enjoyed letting him walk her across the courtyard to her cottage. She enjoyed the shape of him beside her – and she wanted to address an issue in private, too.

She paused at her front door. 'I spoke with Sophie earlier.'

Anthony watched her.

'She confronted Neal Hesse. The man who stalked her. She told me that both of his arms are broken.'

When Anthony shifted, shadows fell across the tattooed half of his face. 'Good.'

'She thinks he had a bicycle accident. But he didn't, did he?'

'No.'

'That's where you were, the night of the burglary?'

'Ocean showed me where he lived,' Anthony said.

'And you took that as an invitation?'

'Yeah.'

'Well, it wasn't one,' Lily-Ann told him. 'Ocean wouldn't ask for that kind of thing.'

'Ah.'

'But *I* would. Except if I asked, I'd *ask*. You don't have to guess with me.'

He looked down at her, his body close and his eyes hungry. He wanted to touch her.

She saw his desire and she said, 'You can't go around breaking people's elbows, Anthony. You understand that? Even if it's for a good reason, even if they deserve it. That is not a thing you can do.'

'You think I was wrong?'

'Almost certainly,' she said. 'Though I'm glad you did it.'

He shifted closer, wordlessly asking permission to touch her.

She wasn't ready, so she unlocked her front door. 'Good night, Anthony.'

'Good night, Lily-Ann.'

She liked how he said her name.

82

OCEAN

After Lily-Ann and Anthony left, the kids retreated to their bedrooms and Mrs B talked Ocean into a game of Gin Gin. They used to play gin, but once Ocean turned twenty – which was the legal drinking age in Mrs B's mind – they'd agreed that the occasional game of Gin Gin was more fun.

So while Mrs B dealt the cards at the dining room table, Ocean mixed gin and seltzer with lemon and a hint of maple syrup. She liked how the syrup swirled and dissolved. She brought the glasses into the dining room, thinking that she needed to tell Mrs B she'd found her will. Well, that she'd *searched* for the will. She was only a little ashamed, because she still thought she had good reason, but that didn't make an apology any less necessary.

Still, she wasn't sure how to broach the subject. At least not until after they'd each won a hand, Mrs B discarded, and said, 'There's something I need to tell you about Nicholas.'

'There's something I need to tell you, too,' Ocean said.

'Oh! About Nicholas?'

'Sort of.'

'Well, I'll go first.' Mrs B picked up a queen and set her cards down in a triumphant fan. 'He's my heir, Ocean. When I go, he'll inherit the Marigold Cottages.'

'Oh,' Ocean said. 'Yeah.'

'Honestly!' Mrs B huffed. 'That was the least-satisfying revelation of my entire life!'

'Why him?'

'Well! Thank you for doing the absolute bare minimum and asking a single boring question.'

'I'm sorry,' Ocean said, 'but I already knew.'

'What? How?'

'That's what I needed to tell you. Uh, while you were in jail, I snooped around and found your will.'

'Ocean!'

'Yeah. Sorry. I shouldn't have invaded your privacy like that.'

'Privacy shmivacy, you ruined my surprise!'

Ocean laughed. 'So I'm sorry for that, instead. I thought I might find a clue about who killed Dead Rick. Or, y'know, why you'd turned yourself in. To prison. And gave me a heart attack.'

'Hmph.' Mrs B sipped her cocktail. 'Are you disappointed I'm not leaving the property to you?'

'Yeah, I'm shocked. You always said you wouldn't, and now you're not.' Ocean set her cards down. 'What disappoints me is that you didn't tell me about the money for the kids.'

'Oh, you saw that?'

'You weren't going let me *thank* you? That's huge for them. For us. Huge. And you weren't going to say a word.'

Mrs B took Ocean's hand. 'You're the closest thing I

have to a daughter. I'd leave it all to you, but . . . Nicholas is my husband's son.'

'No!' Ocean stared at her. 'Really? Leonard? What, he had an affair?'

'He did.'

'What a schmuck! I did wonder about that but . . . no. Really?'

'Finally, a satisfying response. Nicholas doesn't know that I know. I don't want him to feel awkward or guilty. He's more sensitive than he lets on.'

'It doesn't bother you, your husband had a child with another woman?'

'I loved Leonard despite all his faults, and he loved me despite all mine. I won't pretend he's the only one who caused ripples in our marriage. Can you even imagine the sort of person who never makes mistakes?' Mrs B shuddered. 'What a horror.'

'You didn't consider divorce?'

'No. I only wish that I could've been, could *still* be, a stepmother to Nicholas. His mother passed away, too. She was so young. The Marigold Cottages were Leonard's signal success and leaving it to Nicholas would please him so much. And I see Leonard in Nicholas, sometimes, when he doesn't know I'm looking.'

'Are you sure that's a good thing?'

Mrs B swatted her arm. 'It's a *very* good thing. I love who I love, despite their faults. Speaking of which, next time at least *pretend* to be more surprised when I reveal a lifelong secret.'

'Sorry,' Ocean said through a smile. 'If things continue like this, the Cottages will have no secrets left.'

83

LILY-ANN

As Lily-Ann removed her jewelry in her bedroom, she wondered about the tattoos hidden beneath Anthony's clothing. Maybe she could impose a pattern upon the chaos. The thought appealed to her, and she smiled at herself in the mirror.

Then she heard a scratching behind her, and wrinkled her nose in irritation: a twig from the hedge outside had somehow fallen against her bedroom window. Snapped from a branch and tossed by the wind. And now, in the top-right corner of the window, a few leaves pressed against the glass.

Lily-Ann sighed. There was no good reason to fix it at this time of night, except that she wouldn't be able to fall asleep knowing it was half asleep there.

Cursing her own rigidity, she threw on a cashmere robe and shoved her feet back into her wedge mules. She went outside through the front door. Sure enough, a brisk wind was moving the trees around. She headed to the rear of her cottage on the gravel patch between her place and Sophie's, picking her way through the darkness in her unsuitable shoes, careful not to turn an ankle.

The crunch of her feet in the gravel sounded loud in the quiet night.

She winced when a pebble got stuck in her mule, then squinted at her window. Ah! There was the offending branch. It was shorter than she'd expected. It had clearly broken off a larger branch that lay on the ground, then jammed itself between her cottage and the hedge, in the worst possible spot, the only place she'd notice from inside.

She raised onto her tiptoes but couldn't reach the twig.

So she bent down for the larger branch, planning to use that to poke the twig loose, and a shadow broke free of the hedge. A dark shape, taller than she was, falling toward her, swinging a—

A hammer.

A hammer whipped through the air over her head. Exactly where she'd been standing a second earlier, before bending for the branch.

She didn't understand. Nothing made sense.

Her first thought was that a hammer was the worst tool to use to free a twig caught in a window frame.

Her second thought didn't form before a weight crashed into her shoulder and threw her forward.

She shrieked in surprise. The crown of her head slammed the wall of the house, then she found herself on the ground, gaping upward in incomprehension, as a man in a ski mask loomed toward her, his breath a terrified rasp. Almost a sob. Like he was the one being attacked instead of—

Instead of attacking *her*.

Her mind snapped into focus. Right. Yes. That's what was happening. A man hiding in the bushes was attacking her. Had he been peeping in Sophie's window? Crouching in the bushes like the killer had been?

Oh! What if this *was* the killer? Of course it was.

Yes.

And now he was striking again.

The man stood there with a hammer in his gloved fist, panting down at her.

'You tried to kill me,' she said.

Apparently that was the wrong thing to say, because he grunted and leaned toward her, raising his hammer again.

She kicked at him and missed by three feet but her mule whipped off her foot toward his face. He recoiled and she started crabbing backward on the ground, trying to get away from him.

He grabbed her ankle and she twisted and kicked again so he shoved her leg away and took two steps toward her face, toward her head, and she couldn't even try to stand up. If she tried to stand, he'd have all the time in the world to swing again, to punch the flat of the hammer through her skull. So she crawled and twisted, then threw a handful of gravel at him but he didn't even flinch.

The hammer came down and she jerked her head to the side. She heard the hammerhead's impact an inch beside her temple. Gravel spat against her face, then the man lifted the hammer again, and the sharp edge of the claw end tore her skin.

84

SOPHIE

I was half asleep in bed when I heard a shriek. A single shriek and then nothing.

Probably a catfight, or the fragment of a dream.

One thing I knew it *wasn't*? Neal Hesse. That much I knew. That much was guaranteed. It wasn't fucking Neal

Hesse. I almost wished it was. I didn't care about a catfight or a dream. But if it was Hesse, I'd push him over again, and this time I'd break his knees.

After my confrontation with Hesse, I hadn't known how to feel. Triumphant? Possibly. Gleeful? A little. Even more scared than usual, waiting for the other shoe to drop? Sure, for a moment.

But mostly I'd felt free. Like I'd finally walked away from What Happened Before. Like What Happened Before would never happen again.

Except then I'd called my mother. And as always, she clarified one thing: I couldn't talk to her without making everything worse. So I'd gone to Lily-Ann instead, which helped me settle into a happy thrum of satisfaction. Lily-Ann didn't know how to dig deep into emotions, but she asked these brutal, unfeeling questions that I really appreciated.

Anyway, by the time I went to bed, I felt more like myself than I had in years. Who knew that violence actually *was* the answer?

So after I heard the noise, I just lay there calmly beneath the blanket.

I wasn't going to check the window.

I wasn't hypervigilant.

I was free.

85

OCEAN

Sixteen years earlier, when Ocean and Zoe had decided to have kids, everyone had made the obvious comments.

Of course Zoe, with her wide hips and nurturing softness, would make a natural mother. And Ocean, with her scrawny build, angular features, and uncompromising need to break into the L.A. art scene?

Well, she'd make a mother, too.

Instead, what Zoe had done with her hips and softness was fall in love with another woman two months after Miles turned four.

By that point, the obvious comments had fallen away. Because, though Zoe had been the one to give birth, it was Ocean who'd woken up when the kids cried at night, who'd comforted them, encouraged them, scolded them, and argued with them. Who'd taken sole custody when Zoe moved to Europe with her new girlfriend.

Ocean was still an artist to her core. That would never change. And she resented when people told her she was a natural mother. She wasn't. It wasn't natural; it was a fuckton of work. But god, did those kids make it worth it. Even Riley, with her grumbling and her drawn-on face tattoo, made Ocean almost painfully proud.

She snorted at the thought as she lay in bed, awoken by a baby's cry in the night. After all these years, she still couldn't sleep through that sound. Despite knowing that there *was* no baby. Little Miles, who she semi-accidentally called 'the baby' sometimes, would be taller than she was in like twenty minutes.

Ah, well. What could you do? She wondered if a coyote's yip in the night would always sound like a baby's cry to her, then rolled over to get back to sleep.

86

LILY-ANN

The pain from the hammer scraping her temple made Lily-Ann cry out. Or maybe whimper, she couldn't tell.

Her vision blurred.

The gravel jabbed her elbows as she tried to move, but her arms didn't work. Shock and fear pressed on her with a suffocating weight.

The man made a noise in his throat. Behind his ski mask, he seemed to stare at the blood on her face.

And in that moment, she recognized his eyes. Then she recognized his build. Hell, she even recognized how he swung a hammer, though she'd never seen him swing one before.

Her mind dulled, her thoughts slowed. She didn't understand why he'd killed James Dedrick. Even now, she resented that loose thread, that unresolved cell on the spreadsheet in her mind.

He crouched over her. One gloved hand in the gravel, the other holding the hammer above her head. For a heartbeat, nothing moved. A deadly tableau. Then she saw his eyes change and his shoulders tighten for the final blow.

And she realized who'd killed James Dedrick.

The final puzzle piece snapped into place. Everything made perfect sense. The unanswered questions, the bizarre behavior. Well, everything made *some* sense. Nobody's behavior made perfect sense, in the end.

Like now. Why did he feel the need to kill her?

The hammer moved – and a sound cut through the night.

An alarm? Shrieking tires?

No, a scream. A high-pitched scream, getting louder. Getting closer.

The man spun toward the noise. Toward Sophie Gilman, in nothing but an oversized T-shirt, her mouth open, her hair whipping, a bottle of tequila in her right hand, gripped by the neck.

Sophie swung the bottle at the man, still screaming. She missed by a mile but he staggered sideways to get away from her, and she swung and swung. She kept missing, but it didn't matter. She drove him farther and farther from Lily-Ann.

Then Ocean shouted from across the courtyard – and Lily-Ann heard the man flee across the gravel through the courtyard.

Lily-Ann lost a few seconds, the world spun, then she found Sophie and Ocean kneeling beside her, pressing a cloth against the cut on her temple.

'—looks scratched,' Ocean was telling Sophie. 'Only a little blood. She's fine, she's going to be fine.'

'Thanks to you,' Lily-Ann whispered to Sophie.

Sophie wiped the tears from her face.

'You saved my life,' Lily-Ann said.

'Turns out,' Sophie said, 'I'm still pretty fucking vigilant.'

'You're not going to say "sorry"?' Lily-Ann asked.

'No, you jerk,' Sophie said, with a tremulous half smile. 'How's your head?'

'Not too bad. Ocean's right. I'll be—' She saw Ocean raise her phone. 'No! Don't call the cops.'

'What? What're you talking about?'

'Don't call them. Don't call the police.'

'That's not—'

'Ocean, listen!' Lily-Ann snapped. 'Don't let anyone call them.'

Sophie chewed her lower lip. 'Don't you need an ambulance?'

'No,' Lily-Ann said. 'Just get me to bed. I-I can't seem to stand.'

'Because you *do* need an ambulance,' Ocean said.

'Trust me,' Lily-Ann told her, as possibilities unfurled in her mind. 'For the Marigold Cottages. For Mrs B. Don't call them.'

'Are you sure?' Sophie said.

'Just help me up,' Lily-Ann said.

'Okay,' Ocean said.

But it was Anthony who knelt beside her. One of his arms snaked beneath her knees, the other braced her back. She put an arm around his neck and he lifted her smoothly. He carried her into her cottage and through her living room, then settled her onto her bed.

'Oh,' Lily-Ann said. 'Oh, my.'

87

OCEAN

There weren't many people she'd trust with a decision not to call the cops after being attacked by a man with a goddamn hammer, but Lily-Ann was one. Maybe the only one. Despite being – justifiably – in shock, Ocean could see her mind working. And when she'd said, '*Trust me . . . For Mrs B,*' Ocean had trusted her.

So instead of calling 911, she opened the front door for Anthony while he carried Lily-Ann inside.

'Do you want me to stay with you?' Ocean asked.

'No,' Lily-Ann said.

Anthony laid her gently on the bed, then straightened. 'I'll be on your patio. Shout if you need anything.'

'You're going to spend the night outside my front door?'

'Yes.'

'That's silly.' Lily-Ann tilted her head like she was listening to a distant voice. 'And I . . . I'd like it. Though first, you see that twig in the window?'

He followed her gaze. 'No problem,' he said, and went outside.

'Is *that* what you were doing out there?' Ocean asked. 'Getting rid of a twig?'

'Yes, I . . .' She paused. 'Yes.'

Ocean didn't understand that pause, or the sudden heaviness in the room. Then an inkling occurred to her. 'Wait. Listen. Shit. Someone *baited* you out there with that? Holy shit, Lily-Ann. We need to call the cops.'

'No. Not yet. Let me think first.'

A scraping sounded at the window, and the twig vanished. Ocean disinfected and bandaged Lily-Ann's cut, then Anthony returned to loom in the doorway.

'You need anything else?' he asked Lily-Ann.

'Stay inside,' she told him. 'Stay on my couch.'

Ocean found blankets in the hall closet for Anthony, then went outside and breathed in the night air. Cold and fresh. An attacker, in the Marigold Cottages, trying to smash Lily-Ann's head with a hammer? That felt worse than the corpse had. More frightening, more personal. The attacker knew that a misplaced twig would lure Lily-Ann outside. Which crossed strangers off the list. The killer knew her.

Why had they targeted her? Did she know the identity of the murderer?

Ocean was no fan of the cops, but they couldn't let this slide. Well, she'd talk with Lily-Ann first thing in the morning. She was safe enough tonight, with Anthony watching over her like a mother hen. A big, bald, tattooed hen.

A car drove past on the street, and a half-moon shone low in the cloudless California sky. For a moment, Ocean felt apart from the world. Standing alone in the night. But 'apart' was the last thing she was. Not only because of the kids, but because Mrs B forged connections. That's what she did; that's how she lived. And maybe Ocean took after her, a little.

She glanced toward Sophie's house, feeling a spark of pride. Frightened Sophie Gilman, bursting from her house with a bottle of booze like a vengeful maenad. Imagine that. Though she was probably shaking now. Well, Ocean would check on her if the message she'd sent didn't rouse Nicholas.

Huh. She really *was* taking after Mrs B more and more, sending texts like that. Better than turning into her real mother, she supposed.

She heard rustling, then Nicholas trotted past without seeing her. He knocked on Sophie's door. So Ocean could stop worrying about that, at least.

She watched him for a moment before her phone rang.

'Are you okay?' Hamilton asked.

'Yeah. Just shaken up a bit.'

'How's Lily-Ann?' Hamilton made a noise in his throat. 'A hammer? Do you think it's the same weapon that killed Dead Rick?'

Ocean hadn't even considered that. 'I don't know.'

'Should . . . should I come sit with her?'

For a moment, Ocean didn't answer. 'No, that's okay. Anthony's staying on her couch.'

'Oh, good,' Hamilton told her. 'She won't let you call the cops?'

'No. And I don't understand why. I'll talk to her tomorrow.'

'Okay. This is a bit much, Ocean. I mean, after Dead Rick. That happens once, fine. But twice? I don't know . . . Sophie really charged the guy?'

'Like an angry bull.'

'Wow. Wow. She's my hero.'

Ocean thought about him offering to leave his house to comfort Lily-Ann and said, 'Yeah. Heroes can surprise you.'

88

SOPHIE

I paced in my living room, twitchy with nerves. My throat hurt from screaming. I kept glancing at the tequila bottle I'd swung at the man. I kept remembering him crouching over Lily-Ann, a hammer in his upraised hand.

My mind refused to slow down. I needed to take a deep breath but I kept panting. Then a knock sounded. *Finally.*

A distraction. Company. I opened the door expecting to see Ocean, but instead found myself looking at Nicholas.

'You *asshole*!' I snarled, still jumpy from adrenaline.

'I'm sorry,' he said, raising his hands in surrender. 'I'm sorry, Sophie. I heard about what happened and I didn't want you to be alone.'

'Because that's all that matters, what *you* want,' I said, and slammed the door in his face.

'I didn't want to sign the place over to Ybarra, okay?' he said, from outside. 'I didn't want to, Sophie. I still don't want to.'

I opened the door a crack. 'Then why did you?'

'Because I didn't have a choice.'

'Why not?'

'I can't tell you,' he said.

I slammed the door a crack. 'Bullshit!'

'It's not my secret to tell.'

'I'm so sick of bullshit!'

Then I stormed away and threw myself on the couch and didn't cry. Because screw him, I was done crying over assholes.

A minute later, he spoke from outside my open living room window. 'There's video. There's video of the murder. That's why I signed.'

I sat up. 'Wh-what are you talking about?'

'There's video. It's . . . bad. After I watched it, I saw it every time I closed my eyes. Hell, I could *feel* the blow.' He took a breath. 'So I guess the reason this happened now begins with a zoning change that rewards denser development in the area. More units means more money. But also more housing inventory, which—'

'Nicholas,' I said, to get him back on track.

'Right, uh, but that's why Ybarra invited Dedrick here in the first place. Why he made this new push for the Marigold Cottages . . .'

He kept explaining, telling me about murder and blackmail. He didn't tell me everything, though. He kept some parts to himself. His explanation was missing sections. There were plot elements he was afraid to share with me.

So I said, 'Come inside. I've had enough of men hiding in bushes.'

When I opened the front door, I got a better look at Nicholas. Good enough to realize he was wearing nothing but black boxer briefs and a purple fleece hoodie.

I glanced at his bare legs. 'Really?'

'I was in a rush. Are you okay? God, Soph, you chased off an attacker with a bottle of tequila?'

'I also kicked my stalker in the balls yesterday.'

'Badass.'

'Yeah, so don't fuck with me.' I led him to the couch, then hugged myself under the throw blanket. 'Okay, so who killed Dead Rick?'

'I . . . that's not the point. That doesn't matter, not for all *this*.'

'It matters to me.'

'Why?'

And instead of apologizing, I confronted him. 'Because you're not telling me. That's why. You don't trust me enough to tell me.'

'Okay. Yeah. That's fair. But I . . . do you trust me enough to take my word for it? That you don't have to know?'

'No,' I said.

'Then I'll tell you,' he said, and exhaled.

89

VERNON

That morning, twelve hours before the second murder at the Marigold Cottages, the husband called again. Piotr Novak. What a name. He didn't have an accent, so Vernon chalked the spelling of 'Piotr' up to pretension. Which matched the rest of the guy. A little too slick. Like the victim, Dedrick.

Still, Vernon appreciated him as a potential resource, even if he hadn't figured how to best utilize the guy.

'My wife lives not twenty yards from this ex-con,' Piotr Novak told him. 'And it's not just Lily-Ann. The landlady is a hundred years old. There's a little Asian girl, a couple of young kids. He's a danger to them all. He already killed one person. What happens if he snaps? He's surrounded by potential victims like a smorgasbord.'

'I sympathize, Mr Novak,' Vernon said. 'And I don't disagree.'

'So why can't you *do* anything? At least put a police car there. I'm coming back from a weekend in Big Bear or I'd be driving by every ten minutes myself. I just . . . I don't know what to do.'

'If you want my advice—'

'Please,' Piotr Novak interrupted, without waiting for it. 'Yes, please.'

'Talk to your wife, and the other tenants,' Vernon

continued. 'If she – if any of them remembers anything from the night of the murder, believe me, I'll handle Anthony Lambert. Make sure they dig deep, that's what you can do. Give me a handle on Lambert. All I need is testimony, you understand?'

'I do, Detective. Thank you. I just worry about Lily-Ann. She's not always entirely, uh, competent.'

'If she were my wife?' Vernon said, 'I'd tell her to move away until we get him.'

'Lily-Ann's not great at listening to people who know better. She's just as likely to dig in her heels.'

Vernon considered for a moment. 'Then you might talk to Sophie Gilman about your concerns. I suspect she's more persuadable.'

'I'll do that,' Piotr Novak said. 'Thanks for listening. Again. I, uh, I'm on the way back from Big Bear. I'll talk to her then.'

90

LILY-ANN

The corner of the window glowed with morning light. A nice clean edge, with no obstructions, no . . . twig?

Oh! When memory returned, Lily-Ann took a sharp breath. She exhaled more slowly. She was safe now. Her head ached, but not badly. The dull throb was almost comforting. She smelled toast and coffee.

'Anthony?' she called.

His bulk appeared in the bedroom doorway. 'Coffee?'

'Yes, please.'

'Cream, sugar?'

'Neither.'

He vanished, and she heard him rustling in the kitchen. She propped herself higher on a pillow, and that's when her head started pounding. Not so comforting anymore.

Anthony reappeared with a novelty mug that said 'CDO' and one of her white plates. The plate was fine but he must've rummaged deep into her cabinets for the mug, which had been a gift from Piotr. 'CDO' because someone with OCD would prefer the letters in alphabetical order.

The plate contained two slices of toast – cut diagonally – a heap of scrambled eggs, and a chunk of butter.

'I don't know how you like your eggs,' Anthony said.

'So you guessed scrambled?'

'They're the only kind I can make.'

'Hard-boiled,' she told him.

'I'll try that next time,' he said.

Which was pretty forward of him, so she said, 'Good.'

'How's your head?' he asked.

'Throbbing. There's Advil in my medicine cabinet.'

'One or two?'

'Two,' she said.

He went into her bathroom and brought her two Advil and a glass of water. Just like that. No nonsense. She made her need clear; he took care of it. Like the previous night, moving the twig.

So when he turned to leave, she said, 'Stay here.'

He looked at the spindly-legged chair beside her bed but didn't sit. He said, 'Are you sure about not calling the cops? Ocean's pretty eager.'

'I'm sure.'

'You're worried they'll blame me?'

'No,' she said.

He looked at her. 'Because . . . you know who it was?'

'Yes.'

He looked at her.

'My husband,' she said.

His unpretty face grew harder.

'Last week, Nicholas saw him with an investor I recognized. In an oyster bar. Which made no sense. Piotr is deadly allergic to shellfish; he wouldn't meet anyone there if he weren't desperate.' She took a sip of coffee. 'And remember his lucky tie? He's in serious trouble. That's why he wanted to get back together with me, but instead I asked for a divorce.'

'The money is yours,' Anthony said.

'Yes.'

'That's what he meant, talking about how much you're worth?'

'You didn't know?'

'No.' He rubbed his bald head. 'So he tried to kill you before you divorced him, so he'd get the money?'

'Right.'

'Why aren't we calling the cops?'

'Piotr's smart enough to have an alibi. For last night, at least. It's my word against his, and gaslighting is his superpower.'

Anthony grunted.

'So instead of focusing on that attack, we need to focus on the previous one.' She set her CDO mug down. 'We need to give the cops evidence that he killed Dedrick.'

91

SOPHIE

I was still reeling from the murder of James Dedrick and the attack on Lily-Ann. And from the revelation that Anthony had carried me home one night, the confrontation with Neal Hesse, and of course – mostly – the latest shock, the secret that Nicholas had shared with me.

And today was my morning off. I had too much time on my hands, so I'd cope by distracting myself. By taking notes and editing the scene I'd roughed out at Hamilton's house . . .

Act III

SCENE??

HAMILTON is alone in his living room, fussing with a table of beverages at the door. Sodas, juices, milk: he's got everything. The visual aid – the poster he's printed – is of Thor's hammer.

OCEAN

(offstage)

—because you were almost murdered, Lily-Ann! He was seconds away from bashing your head in. That's why we need to call the police. He tried to beat you to death with a hammer!

(HAMILTON frantically rips down the picture of Thor's hammer a moment before OCEAN, LILY-ANN, and ANTHONY enter.)

LILY-ANN

I told you, he's not stupid, he'll have an alibi. If I say I recognized him, he'll make it look like I'm crazy. He'll have planned for that. Oh! Lemonade! How lovely, Hamilton.

HAMILTON

Life gave me lemons. Um. Can I interest anyone in a wasabi soda for breakfast?

ANTHONY

Yes.

OCEAN

(to LILY-ANN)

Why do I feel like you're keeping something from us? Such as, for example, the identity of the person who killed Dead Rick.

LILY-ANN

Piotr killed him. His attack on me last night proves that. He's that kind of man; he'd stick to exactly the same MO.

OCEAN

Okay, so you recognized him, fine. We know it was your husband. But why? Why would he want to kill you?

LILY-ANN

For my money.

ANTHONY

She's rich.

OCEAN

I thought . . . huh. Okay, but how are you so sure Piotr
will have an alibi for last night?

LILY-ANN

(pulling out her phone)

Because I know him. And because he does. Look at his
Instagram. Pictures showing him at Big Bear.

OCEAN

But listen. We don't have any evidence about Dead Rick's
murder. Shouldn't we just tell the cops that Piotr did it,
and hope they find some proof?

LILY-ANN

You know it's not that simple.

(NICHOLAS enters, escorting SOPHIE and a
beaming MRS B.)

NICHOLAS

Speaking of things that aren't simple, I, uh, have a secret
I'd like to share.

MRS. B

A secret we'd like to share. Is that Ensure? I've never
seen that flavor. Cherry cheesecake? Pour me a glass,
won't you, Hamilton?

OCEAN

Can we please focus on, y'know, the murderous attack
on Lily-Ann that happened like ten hours ago? Can I get

a little help here, convincing her to call the goddamn police?

SOPHIE
Definitely. After Nicholas reveals his secret.

MRS. B
It's not just <u>his</u> secret, dear.

SOPHIE
I'm sorry, it's both your secret. Which I don't want to spoil, but it's this: Nicholas is Mrs B's late husband's son!

EVERYONE
'What?' 'You're his stepmother?' 'No way.' 'You're related?' 'How long've you known?' 'Did you know?'

NICHOLAS
I always knew – I thought Mrs B didn't. I didn't want to impose, like I have some kind of claim on her.

HAMILTON
So he's your dead husband's son?

MRS. B
Born, as they say, out of wedlock.

NICHOLAS

(smiles teasingly at MRS B)

Thanks for clarifying.

MRS. B

Oh, dear! I wasn't thinking. Pardon me. What a thing to say!

HAMILTON

(to NICHOLAS)

Cherry cheesecake?

NICHOLAS

I'll stick with water, thanks. So my father asked Mrs B to leave the Cottages to me in her will. That's the other half of the secret. I keep telling her, she has absolutely no obligation.

MRS. B

I never feel obligation. Only inclination.

OCEAN

Great! Now that that's cleared up, can we talk about—

HAMILTON

My theory is, the first time Piotr tried to kill Lily-Ann, Dead Rick noticed him hiding. Waiting to attack her. So Piotr – when he was spotted, he bashed Dead Rick on the head. The cops blamed Anthony, because he looks so much like a . . . an Anthony.

SOPHIE

We know Piotr attacked Lily-Ann but that doesn't mean—

LILY-ANN
That we have any evidence. <u>Exactly</u>. We can't tie him to
the Dedrick murder. That's the problem.

NICHOLAS

(definitely hiding something)

Right. No evidence, Sophie.

SOPHIE
Oh. Yes, of course.

OCEAN
Why do I feel like you're hiding something?

LILY-ANN
Sometimes a lie is tidier than a truth.

HAMILTON
Take your seats, everyone. The Marigold Cottages Murder
Collective is now in session.

MRS. B
Oh, what's on the vendetta today?

HAMILTON
One item: How do we find enough evidence to put Piotr
away for good? Think back to the day of the murder.
Did you see anything? Did you miss anything? Can you
remember anything that you forgot?

End of scene.

92

OCEAN

Ocean felt strange, returning to her art studio after a Murder Collective session. How could she spend the morning chatting about murder and assault, then spend the afternoon working with oil and enamel?

At the meeting, she'd cast her mind back to the night of the murder. She'd been out late that night – well, late for her – on a date that was clearly doomed from the start. She didn't remember seeing anything suspicious, though. Nobody did.

At least not yet.

Yet now, surrounded by the comforting scents of linseed oil and oxidizing paint, her mind kept slipping to the murder. So she stopped work early, and was taking out the trash when she heard Anthony's door open. She hoped he was sneaking off to Lily-Ann's for an afternoon rendezvous, but instead he headed for the street.

'Anthony?' she called.

He turned and raised a hand in greeting.

'Off to work?' she asked.

'Sure.'

She felt her lips thin. She knew his schedule; he wasn't going to work. Which meant that, evidence or not, he planned to serve a little justice on Piotr Novak.

'You should give me a heads-up before you assault anyone,' she told him. 'So when the cops come around I'll know what to say.'

'You're going to alibi me?'

'Do you need an alibi?'

'No,' he said.

'Bullshit, Anthony. Don't do anything stupid. Mrs B's attached to you. Sophie's grateful and determined to show it. Hell, even Hamilton thinks you're the hummingbird whisperer.'

'All I did was put up two feeders.'

'And Lily-Ann, she's definitely attached to you. Even worse, my kids are in love with you. So *you* might not care, but none of us want to see you back in jail. What's the plan? You going to break Piotr's elbows, too?'

'Lily-Ann told you what happened to Sophie's stalker?'

She eyed him. 'Neal Hesse. Yes. Speaking of which, what's going to stop him from pressing charges?'

'He never saw my face.'

'Would he need to? You're kind of distinctive.'

'Plus, he knows I know where he lives – and if I need, you'll give me an alibi.'

'You're not going to fix this by assaulting Piotr,' she told him. 'That cop is looking for any excuse to lock you up. Don't break Miles's heart.'

'Okay,' he said.

'Okay, what?'

'I was just going for a beer.' He looked embarrassed, and maybe even truthful. 'It's too early, so I didn't want to tell you.'

'You're shitting me. Really? Because of my mom glare?'

He shrugged, and she noticed a hint of humor in his stony face. 'I won't go near Piotr. I promise. There's been a lot happening. I just need to think.'

'That's not what you need,' she told him.

'It isn't?'

She gazed meaningfully across the courtyard. 'You know what you need.'

'Yeah,' he said. 'Courage.'

'Ha. Go on, Anthony. You've got this.'

'Drinking would've been easier,' he said, but he headed for Lily-Ann's cottage.

93

LILY-ANN

The bandage covered her temple in a nice sterile white, but a purple-yellow bruise appeared a few inches below Lily-Ann's left ear. She didn't even remember hitting her neck. Maybe when she'd fallen?

She covered the bruise with Huda Beauty concealer. Which she adored. Swab on a layer as thick as asphalt and your skin still looked like skin.

She wondered if it would cover tattoos. Maybe she'd buy a tube for Anthony. His facial tattoos still bothered her. Because they were horrible. She didn't think she'd mind the ink on his chest or back as much. She wasn't sure why.

She looked at herself in the mirror. She didn't often feel in thrall to her emotions, but memories of the attack kept surfacing without warning, giving her chills. Well, her husband had tried to murder her. Perhaps a little emotion was justified.

She'd refused to tell the police about Piotr's attack for

one simple reason: she wanted to hang the murder on him instead. She'd lose in any 'he said, she said' scenario against him. She knew that. So if she wanted him punished for trying to cave her skull in with a hammer – which she very much did – she needed to prove he'd killed James Dedrick.

Except she wasn't sure how. Not yet. She had access to his digital footprint, as well as to his house and office. To everything he owned, outside of a few safe-deposit boxes. So there must be some way. She simply needed to puzzle out the right approach.

Now that her neck looked okay, she'd get a little work done. Let the real problem simmer on the back burner while she adjusted proposals.

Except the thought of back burners led her to the stove instead of the laptop. She was upset. Cooking would calm her, so she started making a risotto, which was her go-to comfort recipe. Not her favorite comfort *food*, but all the stirring soothed her, for some reason.

She'd barely started when the bell rang. She wiped her hands on a kitchen towel, then opened the front door and found Anthony standing there. He didn't say anything for a few seconds, though he looked like he wanted to.

She lost interest in waiting and said, 'Come in,' then returned to the kitchen.

'I was going for a drink,' Anthony said, when he entered behind her. 'But, uh . . . I wanted to check on you.'

'I'm good.'

'Good.'

'Do you still want a drink?' she asked.

'Yes.'

So she poured him a glass of the Pinot Grigio she'd uncorked to make the rice. It was from a local vintner and cost too much to cook with, but she didn't care. Then she poured herself a glass. She felt him watching her stir the risotto. Add stock, stir, add stock, stir. The scent of the onions and mushrooms filled the kitchen and steam touched her face.

He told her she was beautiful.

She switched off the heat and thought for a second. Then she took his hand and led him to the bedroom. She stopped at the end of the bed and faced him. She liked the solid size of him. She put her hand on the back of his smooth scalp and brought his mouth down to hers.

He made a hungry noise in his throat.

She broke the kiss and inspected his face. She liked his big hands and his broad shoulders and his wounded eyes but she said, 'Your tattoos are horrible.'

'Your voice is wonderful.'

She frowned at the word on his cheekbone. JEWELS. She said, 'Don't move an inch. Can you do that? Can you not move?'

'Yes,' he said.

So she closed her eyes and felt his face. His brow felt symmetrical. His cheekbones felt symmetrical. His ears nearly matched as did his collarbones. The muscles of his shoulders and arms, hard bulges beneath her fingers, were mirror images.

With her eyes closed, she unbuttoned his shirt.

He made the noise again.

His pecs felt symmetrical. His ribs were the same on both sides. When she pressed against his naked chest to reach around him, to feel his shoulder blades, they matched, too.

She said, 'You're beautiful, too.'

He started unbuttoning her shirt, and she felt his hands trembling.

'Has it been that long?' she asked, smiling into the darkness behind her eyelids.

'Since it mattered,' he told her.

'Lift me onto the bed,' she said, and he did.

94

SOPHIE

Nicholas picked me up after work and we stopped at the harbor on the way home.

We walked out on the breakwater, under the row of flags snapping in the wind. We watched a portly seal heft itself onto a green metal buoy, and a bald man fall off his paddleboard. We didn't quite hold hands. On the way back, Nicholas bought fresh fish like a man who knew how to buy fresh fish, which I found pretty sexy.

He cooked me dinner at his house. Broiled vermilion rock-fish with broccoli and rice. Nothing was fancy, but everything was just right. Which impressed me. I wasn't a great cook. I made an outstanding shortbread, but that was the extent of my culinary skills.

We knew we needed to do something about what he'd told me. We didn't know what, specifically, but *something*.

Still, we'd decided to enjoy an ordinary dinner first. So we chatted and chopped in his big kitchen. He didn't offer me wine. Was he concerned about my drinking? That was sweet and annoying at the same time.

Mostly annoying, so I said, 'Is there any wine?'

'White in the fridge,' he told me. 'Red in the cabinet.'

'Are you having?'

'Nah, but help yourself.'

'Oh. That's okay.'

We talked about his family over dinner, by which I meant I interrogated him. His history with Mrs B was so bizarre and fascinating and dramatic. Then I reciprocated by telling him about my family, which was boring and petulant.

When we ran out of things to say, he asked about my play. So I told him about my ideas for structure and theme, and how I planned to streamline the story. And he listened. Like, really listened. And occasionally he even asked insightful questions.

When I mentioned I was struggling to come up with the right ending, he said, 'What's more important for the spine of the story? Finding out who killed James Dedrick? Or finding out what happens to all the weird characters you're writing?'

'The weirdos are more important,' I told him. 'I love those weirdos.'

'I'm getting pretty fond of them myself.'

So yeah, I was definitely going to sleep with him. I'd never been great at giving those signals, though. At least not while sober. So when he told me he didn't have anything for dessert, I insisted he come to mine for shortbread.

Despite the warm night, goose bumps rose on my arms as we crossed the courtyard. The sky was a deep blue, shifting toward black, and faint strains of the song

'Twerkulator' seeped from Riley's window – clearly chosen to drive Ocean nuts.

When I smiled at the thought, Nicholas smiled along with me. At his own thoughts, I guess. I brought him into my kitchen and started preheating the oven like a boss. We discussed the pros and cons of flavoring versus simplicity, then added chai spices to the recipe.

As the shortbread baked, I told him some behind-the-scenes tales of the New Vic Theatre and he reciprocated with city planning stories. We argued happily about who dealt with bigger divas, then we took plates into the living room. We sat on the couch, and I shifted closer and closer to him . . . until a tapping sounded at the window.

A visitor, bringing news.

So much for an ordinary night.

95

LILY-ANN

'Let me try,' she told Anthony, grabbing her Huda Beauty concealer. 'As an experiment.'

He touched his cheek tattoo. 'Okay.'

'I'm curious if this works,' she said.

Anthony let her apply one coat, then said, 'When I slept on your couch?'

'You should've joined me.'

'I heard Nicholas talking to Sophie.'

'You . . . how?'

'He was outside her window. Telling her about a video. Of the murder.'

Lily-Ann tilted his head roughly to the side to examine her work. 'And you're just mentioning this *now*?'

'Yes,' he said. 'Nicholas told her that Ybarra was here the night of the murder. He foll—'

'Here at the Cottages?'

Anthony grunted. 'Ybarra followed Dedrick onto the property. He recorded the murder on his phone.'

'He has video but didn't show the cops?' Lily-Ann raised her hand before he could answer. 'Which means what? He's using the video for leverage?'

'For blackmail,' Anthony said.

'To get the property?' Lily-Ann nodded slowly, putting the pieces together. 'That's how Nicholas knows about this. Ybarra was pressuring him.'

'Yeah,' Anthony said, then told her the rest of it.

'Let me think.' She almost started a second coat of concealer, then stopped herself. 'Okay, go get Mrs B. Quietly. I need to talk to her. Bring her here.'

He left without another word.

Lily-Ann stripped the Frette sheets from her bed. Still classic white, still nondescript and wrinkle-free and fancy. Which made them the opposite of Anthony, who was distinctive, weathered, and humble. She liked how he treated her; she liked how he made her feel.

After she remade the bed, she meditatively scoured the tile kitchen counter with grout cleaner. Planning what she'd say to Mrs B, and what *everyone* would say to the police.

She needed to keep Piotr from hurting her again. She needed to punish him for trying to kill her – and she needed to protect the people she cared about. She understood the puzzle now, but she no longer simply wanted to fit the pieces together. Now she wanted to arrange them to achieve her goals.

She thought about Ybarra recording the murder, then using the video for blackmail. The thought hadn't occurred to her before, but of *course* evidence of a crime wasn't only leverage against the perpetrator, but against anyone who loved them.

Which confused matters, as it gave so many people a motive. Lily-Ann would've preferred a murder committed among people who didn't care about each other. Well, no such luck. So how should she frame everything that had happened?

And why on earth hadn't Anthony returned with Mrs B yet?

Lily-Ann dried her hands, then crossed the room and opened her front door. She looked outside for Anthony but only saw the cool, dark, quiet courtyard. So what was the problem? Piotr had an alibi for her attempted murder. A fake one, but still. And what was the solution? He *didn't* have an alibi for the attack on Dedrick.

As her gaze picked among the shadows, she felt a shiver of fear. After a moment, she realized why: the evening courtyard reminded her of the attack. Of Piotr looming from the darkness with a claw hammer.

Lily-Ann had never been afraid of the dark. In fact, she usually found brightness harsh and agitating, while gloom felt more soothing than threatening. Yet now, suddenly, the darkness frightened her?

No.

She wasn't going to let Piotr ruin that for her. She wasn't going to indulge in fear. She wasn't going to give him that much power. She inhaled deeply, then exhaled slowly—

And she heard a noise.

A scuffle? A gasp? A thud?

No. No, her mind was playing tricks on her. Her *fear* was playing tricks on her, even though she'd just decided not to feel any. She exhaled again. She'd always resented the unwanted intrusion of messy emotions, and Piotr's involvement only made it worse.

Enough of that. She needed to focus on more important things. She needed to construct a narrative for the cops, to paint a compelling picture . . . but Sophie was the storyteller and Ocean was the artist. Well, Lily-Ann would think of this as a cipher, then. She was best at solving those. She just needed to assemble the correct elements in the correct order.

Which she started doing, until Anthony murmured her name in the darkness.

A moment later, he appeared, looking un-characteristically flustered. His breath came fast and one of his hands was shaking.

'What happened?' she asked.

He told her that when he'd arrived at Mrs B's cottage, he'd heard voices. Or one voice, really. Not angry so much as gleeful.

'I listened in,' he said.

'What'd you hear?'

'Ybarra was there. He was inside with Mrs B. And he told her . . .' Anthony took a breath. 'He said he was on the way to the police, with his phone. With the evidence.'

'Shit,' she said.

'And then I saw him leave.' Anthony swallowed. 'And then—'

'What? What happened?'

'Another murder.'

For a moment, he couldn't say more. Then he managed to tell her, and she needed to think through everything all over again, from the start. She needed to solve a new cipher, an urgent one. Her mind drew connections faster than ever, ticking items off a list, making progress toward a specific, achievable goal.

'Do you remember the total unique words in *Infinite Jest*?' she asked.

'The code to Piotr's office,' he said. 'No.'

'2-0-5-8-4,' she told him. 'You don't have a license but you know *how* to drive, right?'

'Yes,' he said.

'Take my car.' She reached for the keys. 'And do exactly as I say. I need to stay here and make sure nothing gets worse.'

Ten minutes later, she was tapping on Sophie's window.

96

OCEAN

Ocean and Miles shared a late-night bowl of popcorn across the table. While he memorized state capitals for his quiz, she surreptitiously checked her dating site.

Three messages, all of them boring. She backtracked and inspected her profile photo. At first, she'd used a picture of herself looking paint-dabbed and scruffy in front of a half-finished canvas. Aiming for arty charm or something. When that hadn't worked, she'd switched to a picture of herself looking like a normal human being.

Except that wasn't working, either.

As she started composing a reply, texts popped on to her screen. She ignored the first few, trying to focus on resurrecting her love life, but then they grabbed her attention.

Sophie
There's a body. Outside Mrs B's house

Sophie
Another body

Hamilton
Dead or alive?

Sophie
A corpse. Dead. A dead corpse

'What the fuck?' Ocean murmured.
'Oma,' Miles scolded.

Lily-Ann
Have you been drinking?

Lily-Ann
You're serious?

Nicholas
I'm with her

Nicholas
She's sober as a judge.

Hamilton
A judge in Alabama gave a Black woman 496 days in jail for unpaid traffic tickets, which is more than the sentence for negligent homicide.

Ocean
On my way

Ocean stood from the table. 'Lock the door behind me.'
'Huh? Why?'
'Just— listen, it's nothing, just lock the door.' She looked toward the hallway. 'Riley!'
No response.
'Riley!' Ocean shouted over the booty music. 'Come sit out here with Miles.'
Then she shoved her feet into her shoes and rushed outside.

Lily-Ann
We are, too.

Nicholas
Who is we?

Lily-Ann
Anthony is with me.

Hamilton
In Indiana, three drunk judges shot up a White Castle and kept their jobs.

When Ocean turned the corner, she saw Lily-Ann holding Anthony's arm as if for support – but also guiding him in a long curving path around Mrs B's cottage. First toward the street, then scuffing along the hedge.

Trying to stay away from the body? Ocean sympathized, but she was pretty sure they were trampling the crime scene. She almost told Lily-Ann that she'd chosen the wrong time to make a mess, but instead paused to calm herself. Another death. Another corpse. She needed to keep her shit together.

Anthony and Lily-Ann stopped near Sophie and Nicholas, who were standing together. Almost touching. No, *actually* touching. Giving brief, noncommittal brushes of reassurance and support, borrowing strength from each other.

Despite her fright, Ocean felt a pang of jealousy. Two couples, plus her. She crossed toward the hedge and spotted the body. Skinny legs poking from under the leaves, ending in a pair of orthopedic oxfords.

'Pull him out,' Lily-Ann told Anthony. 'Check if he's breathing.'

Anthony brushed the hedge aside, disturbing the scene further. Still, they needed to know if the guy was alive. Though he looked pretty dead, especially considering the blood splatter, from which Anthony didn't even flinch.

He just took hold of the skinny calves and pulled the body into view.

Sophie and Nicholas recoiled from the sight of the corpse. Leaves and dirt adhered to the sticky blood thickening on the man's once-white beard.

'That's Ybarra,' Ocean heard herself say. 'Gregory Ybarra.'

'He's dead,' Anthony said.

Mrs B made an inarticulate noise, coming down her front steps, one hand to her throat.

'What was he doing here?' Sophie said, as Ocean moved to comfort Mrs B.

'Getting beaten to death with his golf club,' Anthony told her, nodding toward a putter caught in the hedge.

Ocean put an arm around a trembling Mrs B. 'It's okay. Okay, shhh.'

A truck rumbled past on the street.

A dog barked somewhere.

'This is worse,' Nicholas said, shining his phone's flashlight. 'Worse than the video. I-I could *feel* the impact just from watching, from hearing the sound. I could . . .' He took a shaky breath. 'There's blood on the . . .'

His light caught a smear of blood on the shiny blue metal head of the putter.

Mrs B gasped and Ocean squeezed her tighter as a bitter taste rose in her mouth.

'That's not Ybarra's club,' Lily-Ann said. 'That's not the club he carries.'

Everyone looked at her.

'That's a Mizuno blue putter,' she explained. 'Piotr uses the same brand.'

Ocean took a shaky breath. 'So whose club is it?'

'That's the big question,' Lily-Ann said. 'And I have a big answer.'

'Okay,' Ocean said. 'Okay.'

'The first thing to consider,' Lily-Ann said, her calm gaze moving from one person to the next, 'is that Piotr tried to murder me with a claw hammer. But how does he fit into the death of James Dedrick? How does he fit into *this*?'

'Do-do you know how?' Ocean asked her.

'We need to call the police,' Mrs B said.

'We'll call the police in a moment,' Lily-Ann said. 'And this is what we'll tell them.'

97

VERNON

Somebody was blowing smoke up his ass. Vernon recognized the sensation. There were lies being told. That wasn't surprising. Even innocent people lied to the cops. Hell, in Vernon's experience, innocent people lied the most. They didn't know which truths to avoid, so they scrambled to conceal anything embarrassing or even faintly illegal, which was pretty much everything.

He didn't mind the lies. They didn't bother him. What bothered him was, he couldn't tell what was behind them.

Still, he kept asking the obvious questions, like: 'Who knew that Gregory Ybarra walked with his golf club?'

'Every single person who ever passed him on the sidewalk,' Ocean Mistral told him, with a note of disdain. 'And if not for his bushy white beard, there would've been complaints.'

'You weren't a fan?'

She frowned toward the crime scene. 'I shouldn't speak ill of the dead.'

'Are you kidding? That's the foundation of every homicide investigation.'

'Well, I barely knew him, but he bugged me. I don't know why. He seemed fake.'

Vernon pursued that, but didn't learn anything. So he asked if she'd noticed anything unusual, never quite naming Anthony Lambert but keeping his ears pricked for anything that might implicate him.

Ocean Mistral didn't give him the slightest dog whistle. She said she'd talked with Anthony Lambert in the courtyard at around three or four o'clock. 'He was going out for a drink.'

'Yeah?' Vernon said, feeling a spark of hope.

'I, uh, might've scolded him a little. Too early in the day, you know?'

'You *scolded* him?'

'Maybe a little.'

He tapped his notebook with his pen. 'Most women, they'd cross the street not to talk to a man like him.'

'You're the expert on what most women would do?' She gave Vernon a few seconds to not know how to respond, then said, 'After we spoke, Anthony turned around and went to Lily-Ann's.'

'What, right then?'

'Yup. There's a romance brewing. I think he, uh, set his sights higher than a drink. I'm pretty sure he's been with her ever since.'

'Mmm,' Vernon said, then excused himself to speak with Mrs Golda Bakofsky.

'I'll come along,' Ocean told him.

He thought about that, then nodded as if he had a choice, and she led him into the old lady's cottage without knocking.

'Well, hello again, officer!' Mrs Golda Bakofsky said, appearing from the living room. 'I'm not supposed to speak with you. Anthony was clear about that.'

'Was he?' Vernon asked.

'Oh, extremely. He said that we jailbirds should know better. Never talk without a lawyer present, that's what he said.'

'It's good advice,' Vernon admitted. 'But just in terms of background, did you know Gregory Ybarra?'

'Oh, yes! I've known him for years and years. He owns three buildings in the neighborhood; he bought the first one back in . . . well, I don't quite recall.'

She spent ten minutes giving him a muddled rundown of Ybarra's real estate history, then explained that she hadn't seen or heard anything unusual that evening. Finally, she offered him an herbal tea and her heartfelt apologies for not answering any of his questions.

So he headed across the courtyard to talk to Lily-Ann Novak. He rang the bell and looked toward the crime scene. Two bodies. Thirty feet apart. Same MO. Damn.

Heavy footsteps approached from inside the cottage. He expected the woman, but Anthony Lambert opened the door. Vernon politely asked him to fuck off to his studio, then greeted Lily-Ann Novak without much more deference.

'Gregory Ybarra's skull was caved in with his own golf club,' Vernon told her, hoping the brutality would shake her up a little.

'No, it wasn't,' she told him.

'Huh?'

'That's not his club. He didn't use a three-hundred-dollar Mizuno putter to scare away dogs.'

'A what now?'

'A Mizuno blue ion putter.'

He eyed her. 'You don't look like a golfer.'

'My husband golfs,' she told him. 'And he prefers Mizunos.'

'Is that right?'

'Yes. He has a putter exactly like that one.'

So Vernon made a note of that; of course he made a note. But then he moved on to talk about the murder. 'According to what you told the uniformed officer, you were with Anthony Lambert most of the day?'

'Since late afternoon.'

'Where?'

'Here.'

'Doing what?'

'Eating risotto and fucking,' she told him. 'And we didn't eat any risotto.'

He coughed into his fist, then asked a few more questions before leaving. She didn't give him any worthwhile answers. A Mizuno blue putter. Hmm. Well, he'd look into that, but Anthony Lambert remained his primary suspect. Vernon put no weight into Lily-Ann's alibi for him. Women always alibied the men they slept with. That was a given.

He decided against talking to Anthony Lambert just yet. Better to make him wait. He spoke with Sophie Gilman instead, figuring she'd respond to a little firm guidance. She might even tell him that nothing was happening between Lily-Ann Novak and Anthony Lambert, or that she'd seen the big man on his own during the day, maybe outside her cottage . . .

Except she didn't.

No matter how he clarified his questions, no matter how hard he pressed, she didn't bend. Instead, she told him that yes, her neighbor was 'hooking up' with Anthony Lambert, who she hadn't seen alone on the property in days.

She struck Vernon as uncharacteristically unapologetic, which made her far less useful than he'd hoped.

'Nicholas picked me up from work,' she told him, 'and we spent the evening together, first at his house, then back here to make shortbread. We didn't see anything, though. At least *I* didn't, and Nicholas didn't say anything about . . . oh!'

'Yes?' Vernon asked.

'Well, I'm sure it's nothing. But I remember catching sight of someone on the street by the mailboxes. For a second, I thought it was Piotr. Lily-Ann's husband.'

So Vernon spoke to Nicholas Perez, who recounted the evening almost too-identically. Buying vermilion rockfish, whatever that was, making dinner for Sophie Gilman at his house, then walking to hers to bake cookies. He was pretty sure he remembered Sophie mentioning Piotr Novak, and definitely recalled hearing an engine and thinking 'sweet ride.'

'A Beemer,' Nicholas said. 'That's Lily-Ann's husband's car, isn't it?'

Vernon said, 'Is it?'

'Oh, I don't know,' Nicholas said, looking alarmed at being put on the spot. 'I'm not saying it was his car, just a BMW, and he drives one, that's all.'

Vernon wrote that down, too, thinking about Piotr Novak calling him, saying that he wanted to drive around the block to keep his wife safe.

And finally, he crossed the courtyard and spoke with Anthony Lambert. Well, finally he spoke *at* Anthony Lambert.

'A second body,' he said, settling in at the kitchen table in the little studio. 'Found thirty feet from the first. They're related, that's not in doubt.'

Anthony Lambert opened his refrigerator. 'Glass of milk?'

'The wife's got me on nonfat,' Vernon said, with a sigh of regret. 'You killed the first guy, we both know that. The ME said the blow landed badly, or it might not've finished him. I figured you gave him a smack, you didn't mean to kill him. Does that sound right?'

Anthony Lambert poured himself a glass of milk.

'So I've got some sympathy about the first guy,' Vernon said. 'But this one? This was no accident. This one you were *trying* to kill.'

Anthony Lambert returned the carton to the fridge.

'Except your lady friend tells me you've been with her all day,' Vernon continued. 'Which is extremely convenient.'

Anthony Lambert took the seat opposite and drank his milk.

'Well, that's not what she said. You want to hear the quote?' He flipped through his notebook but didn't bother reading the words. 'She said you spent the day eating risotto and fucking, and you didn't eat any risotto.'

And Anthony Lambert smiled. Actually smiled.

'Holy shit,' Vernon said. 'You're really with her?'

'I hope so,' Anthony Lambert told him, with almost painful earnestness. 'God as my witness, I hope so.'

And that, at least, was no lie. That was not the smoke

being blown up his ass. That was true. In fact, that looked to Vernon like the best thing that ever happened to Anthony Lambert. Which unsettled him, in a way.

Though not as much as what greeted him a few minutes later, when he left the studio apartment.

First, a yawning Ocean Mistral looked up from her phone and didn't say anything, because she was yawning.

'Are you waiting for me?' he asked.

'Yeah. We've got something to, uh, share with you.'

'Who's we?'

She twirled a finger in the air. 'The residents. I'll show you.'

'Lead on,' he said.

She brought Vernon to Lawrence Hamilton's cottage, where he refused another glass of milk – odd – before entering a living room to find most of the residents sitting on couches and chairs. All of them except Anthony Lambert, Golda Bakofsky, and the Mistral children. They were quiet, facing him. Which was a little unsettling, except that Ocean Mistral must've texted them that he was on the way.

Standing at the far end of the room, Lily-Ann Novak said, 'Thank you for coming.'

'I never miss a séance,' he said.

Sophie and Nicholas laughed, and Hamilton said, 'Alexander Graham Bell believed it was possible to contact the dead.'

'Oh, Hamilton,' Ocean Mistral muttered.

'Everyone, hush!' Sophie said. 'Listen to Lily-Ann.'

'Thank you, Sophie.' Lily-Ann turned her cold gaze upon Vernon. 'Detective Sergeant Enible. We believe we know who killed James Dedrick and Gregory Ybarra.'

These people. What the hell was this, some kind of neighborhood mystery club? Well, maybe they'd finally pass him a clue he could use. 'I'm all ears.'

'The inciting incident was Anthony moving to the Marigold Cottages.'

Vernon spread his hands. 'I'm with you so far.'

'What you don't know,' Lily-Ann continued, 'is that my husband is in serious financial trouble.'

'That's Piotr, P-I-O-T-R Novak?'

'Correct. He is facing a financial reckoning. Too many bad gambles are coming due at the same time. He's desperate.'

'And you know this how?'

'He's my husband,' she said. 'And he's been looking for his lucky tie.'

'Uh-huh,' Vernon said. 'But you're not eating risotto with *him*.'

'The tax-harvesting management documents don't lie, Detective Sergeant.' She gave him a solemn look. 'I have access to many of his financials.'

Vernon nodded. Easy to check. 'So he's got money trouble?'

'While I do not,' Lily-Ann told him. 'I am wealthy.'

'Is that so?'

'My husband is my heir,' Lily-Ann continued. 'He was set to inherit the whole of my estate upon my death. However, we've been separated for four years and I recently spoke with him about divorce. Not long before the first murder. Then Anthony moved in.'

'Now this is getting interesting.'

'Anthony is not only a convicted felon,' Lily-Ann said, 'he *looks* like a convicted felon. What did you call him, Sophie?'

'Um. A gentle giant?'

'Before you knew him.'

'Oh. Yeah . . . um, Serbian Thug Number Two?'

'Precisely. And not long after he moved in, I mentioned his arrival to Piotr. At around the same time that I mentioned my decision to divorce. An unfortunate combination of facts. That is when Piotr decided to kill me.'

'For your money.'

'For my money.'

Vernon tapped his notepad again. 'Well, he didn't do a good job of it. I mean, thank the lord and all his rosy cherubs, but how does that explain the murders that actually occurred?'

'The earliest cherubs had four faces and cloven hooves,' Hamilton said. 'And the heads of different animals . . . er, but Lily-Ann was talking. I didn't mean to interrupt.'

Lily-Ann gave him a little smile. 'Thank you, Hamilton. It explains the murders, Detective Sergeant, because my husband decided that Anthony would make the perfect, ah . . . what's the word?'

'Fall guy,' Ocean said. 'Patsy?'

'I was thinking scapegoat, but yes. Fall guy.'

'Do not,' Sophie told Hamilton, raising a finger mock sternly, 'tell us the origin of the word "scapegoat"!'

Hamilton gave a shamefaced smile and Lily-Ann continued. 'Piotr knew that Anthony was the perfect scapegoat. The police would naturally suspect the violent criminal of committing the violent crime.'

'Naturally,' Vernon agreed.

'However, much to Piotr's misfortune – and my fortune – James Dedrick came late one night, on a whim, after a few drinks, to inspect the property. Or perhaps not on a whim. Perhaps he arranged to meet Gregory Ybarra. In any case, he surprised my husband in the bushes where he – my husband – was lying in wait to attack me.'

Vernon scratched his jaw thoughtfully. 'Okay, I see where you're going. James Dedrick spotted your husband in the bushes, ready to pounce. Piotr panicked and killed him, and that explains that.'

'Precisely.'

'Except then the same exact thing happened with Gregory Ybarra?' Vernon asked, letting disbelief show on his face. 'Your husband returned weeks later for another shot at you, and that time *Ybarra* caught him?'

'We're not sure,' Ocean Mistral told him. 'My personal theory is that Ybarra witnessed the first murder. Dead Rick said he'd stop by that night to look at the Marigold Cottages, so Ybarra was there to meet him. Instead, he saw Piotr bash his head in. So he tried to blackmail Piotr. He needed money for his real estate stuff, right? And his investor was suddenly dead.'

'Ah,' Vernon said. 'Then Piotr came again last night and killed Ybarra to keep everything quiet?'

Sophie Gilman perked up. 'Or maybe Ybarra *did* accidentally spot Piotr getting ready to attack Lily-Ann, just like Dead Rick had.' She gave a wicked little smile. 'I like that better. It's messier. More like real life.'

'Either way,' Lily-Ann Novak told Vernon, 'we know that Sophie very probably saw Piotr on the street yesterday.

385

We know Nicholas very probably heard his car. I definitely took the first step toward getting the divorce last week, as my attorney can attest. And the murder weapon very probably belongs to Piotr.'

Vernon rubbed the back of his neck. 'So he killed the guy with his *own* golf club?'

'Yes.'

'Then what happened to Ybarra's?'

'We wondered about that,' Lily-Ann said, 'and decided that Sophie's right.'

'As always,' Sophie chimed in.

'Life is messy,' Ocean explained to Vernon. 'Piotr brought his own club to commit the murder because he didn't want to wrestle Ybarra for his. He wanted to hit him from behind, then run away.'

'Yeah,' Sophie said with a nod. 'Except something happened. It turned messy. So he panicked and grabbed the wrong club before he took off.'

'Not bad.' Vernon frowned in thought. 'I mean, it all depends on how his financials look. And maybe his putter is still in his golf bag; this is a different one. Or he could have an alibi.' He considered Lily-Ann Novak. 'Maybe his alibi is even better than Anthony Lambert's. Still, it's not bad.'

He wasn't lying, either. He continued to feel the smoke blown up his ass, but he saw the benefits of this scenario. Well, a benefit and a drawback.

The benefit: the theory explained not one but both homicides. And closing two murder files at the same time would be his career-capping triumph, his crowning success.

The drawback: Anthony Lambert would walk free, after he'd definitely killed the first guy.

So Vernon wouldn't make any sudden moves, not yet. He noted the testimony, he documented the possibility, but he didn't pursue anything.

Not until days later, when he started seeing results.

First, Piotr Novak had spent the evening in question alone, after his return from Big Bear the previous night.

Second, Piotr Novak really was staring down the barrel of financial ruin.

Third, if Lily-Ann Novak had died in a tragic choking accident, the vast majority of her money went to Piotr Novak.

Fourth, damn that was a lot of money.

And fifth, glorious fifth? The beautifully tied bow on top of this gift?

Fifth was Piotr Novak's fingerprints on the murder weapon. Praise the stupidity of criminals, his fucking fingerprints were on the golf club.

Smoke or no smoke, Anthony Lambert or no Anthony Lambert: if you *could* take the win, you *did* take the win. And if that became Vernon's legacy, all the better.

98

OCEAN

When she opened the door of Hamilton's cottage, Ocean heard the sound of happy chatter and smelled the scent of baked cheese.

She went inside, and Hamilton handed her a flute of champagne – so she laughed.

'What?' he asked.

'Champagne.' She lifted the glass to toast him. 'You nailed it this time.'

'Oh, it's not champagne,' he told her. 'It's sparkling wine. That is, it's from Santa Ynez, so it's not *officially* champagne. Except it really is champagne, unofficially.'

'Well, it's exactly what I wanted, Hamilton. Thank you.'

He blushed the same color as his hibiscus-print shirt, then gave the kids glasses of sparkling cider.

Ocean smiled and glanced at Mrs B sitting on the couch with Nicholas, telling him tales of her dissipated youth. She'd already told him tales of his father's dissipated youth; Ocean figured she didn't want to feel left out.

Sophie stepped inside next, holding a plate of shortbread cookies. She reached for a glass of champagne, and Nicholas watched keenly over Mrs B's shoulder.

'Oh, give me a break,' Sophie said. 'I never drink much if I'm not out with friends.'

Still, she took a glass of the cider instead, then turned with Ocean to watch Lily-Ann set yet another dish onto the dining room table. A full Mediterranean spread was laid out already, with dolmas, Halloumi, chicken skewers, roasted potatoes, yogurt, and a chopped salad. After everyone sat, Lily-Ann added spanakopita and moussaka while Anthony brought a heaping tray of steaming pitas.

'They're fresh-baked,' Lily-Ann said. 'Anthony made them. He's trying sourdough next.'

'I'm pretty good with baguettes,' he said.

Which was not a sentence that Ocean ever expected to hear from Anthony. Of course, she also wouldn't have expected him to take Miles on a whale-watching tour with him and Lily-Ann. Twice.

'My theory is that the existence of sourdough starter proves the simulation hypothesis,' Hamilton announced. 'It's the culinary equivalent of punching trees in *Minecraft*.'

Which meant nothing to Ocean, but Miles started chattering with Hamilton about *Minecraft* – and the simulation hypothesis – as everyone dug into the meal.

Well, Mrs B didn't dig, she pecked. And she took the opportunity to tell the story of her honeymoon in Greece, during which she'd gone to a concert in a lovely public garden with her husband, except they'd read the map wrong and ended up in someone's private lawn. She'd been so sure it was the right place that she'd convinced a dozen other tourists to join her, and eventually the homeowners brought out bottles of ouzo while demanding that their uninvited guests sing for them.

She looked happy.

She looked complete.

And seeing her there, surrounded by people who loved her, a knot loosened in Ocean's heart. She didn't need to worry about Mrs B. This ragtag family, this collective of misfits, would look after her, just like she'd looked after them.

99

SOPHIE

At long last, I fell silent, letting the final words of the play linger in the air.

Then I turned to the audience and said, 'The end.'

The audience leapt from the couch, clapping wildly

until I gave him a little sweatpants-wearing curtsy.

'It's so good, Soph,' Nicholas said.

'Still a little rough.'

He took me in his arms and kissed me. 'So, *so* good.'

Act Unseen

SCENE UNHEARD

A view of the empty, nighttime courtyard, with three doors to either side. From the street, SOPHIE staggers drunk into the Marigold Cottages.

LILY-ANN

(downstage right, in a spotlight)

And this is what we'll tell them. Well, most of us know much of what happened, but I'll explain the rest. The story starts when James Dedrick came to check out the Marigold Cottages. He saw Sophie stumbling home . . .

(An extremely drunk SOPHIE fumbles in her bag for her keys. JAMES DEDRICK enters from the wings. He watches SOPHIE pass out at her door, her keys spilling from her hand. And behind him, a Shadowy Figure observes from the street.)

JAMES DEDRICK

Location, location, location . . . and a drunk bitch inviting me inside for a good time?

(Ad-lib graphic threats as he grabs an
unresponsive SOPHIE and starts dragging her
inside . . . MRS B strides forward and clubs him
with a knobkerrie. DEDRICK cries out, then
stumbles toward the exit.)

LILY-ANN
Mrs B killed him. She's the killer. She heard what he was
saying to Sophie, what he was planning. She just wanted
to scare him off, but . . .

(MRS B, shocked by her own actions, retreats as
DEDRICK takes another few steps, then falls dead
at the hedge.)

She didn't even know he'd died until the next morning.
She didn't want to tell Sophie what happened. She didn't
want to subject her to that kind of shock. The only
problem . . .

(She gestures to the Shadowy Figure, who steps
forward to reveal he's GREGORY YBARRA.
Recording with his phone, his golf club under one
arm.)

Gregory Ybarra blackmailed Mrs B with the video he
took. Well, he tried blackmailing her. He forced her to
show him her will, so he knew Nicholas would inherit.
But she wouldn't sign over the property. That's what he
wanted. The Marigold Cottages.

(Lights flash red and blue across the stage.)

Then Anthony was arrested. So Mrs B confessed. To help Anthony, but also to prove to Ybarra that she'd go to jail before she'd give him the Cottages. As Ocean says, she's a tough old bat.

GREGORY YBARRA

Nobody believed she killed him, but I showed Nicholas the video. I told him she'd die in prison if he didn't sign on the dotted line. She'd suffer, she'd weaken, and she'd die. So he signed. I promised I'd wait till she passed away to seize the property, so she'd never know, but I didn't need to wait. So I didn't.

(YBARRA displays the contract and phone.)

I visited Golda on my way to the cops and showed her the contract. The Marigold Cottages were mine. I had the property and all she had was a prison cell.

(The clang of a prison cell door.)

LILY-ANN

I sent Anthony to fetch Mrs B. We needed to talk. He overheard Ybarra telling her that she'd die in prison, after spending her final years in a concrete box. Ybarra was going straight to the cops, so Anthony waited and . . .

(YBARRA strolls toward the exit, swinging his un-blue-tipped golf club. ANTHONY grabs his club and kills him. YBARRA falls.)

No one will be shocked to hear that Anthony doesn't count foresight among his many virtues. His plan, at that point, was to destroy the evidence of Mrs B's guilt and hope he didn't get caught.

ANTHONY

      (riffling through YBARRA'S pockets for the
            contract and phone)

You're the reason I didn't get caught.

LILY-ANN

He told me what happened. So we switched Ybarra's golf club with my husband's and rubbed it against the flecks of blood on the leaves of the hedge, left over from Dedrick's murder. Piotr deserves jail. He tried to murder me. And now we all have to choose. Will you tell the police you saw Piotr lurking outside the Cottages? Will you not tell them the truth? Hamilton says that eight thousand homicides go unsolved every year in the US. What's two more? Anthony and Mrs B belong here. We all do.

      (Blackout. Curtain. End of play.)

'Strong ending,' Nicholas told me.
'Yeah,' I said. 'It's a shame that I can't use it.'

ACKNOWLEDGMENTS

Many thanks to Caitlin Blasdell, Pete Wolverton, Claire Cheek, Kelley Ragland, Catherine Richards, David Rotstein, Alisa Trager, Sara Eslami, Ken Silver, Kayla Janas, Meryl Levavi, and Ally Demeter.

AUTHOR'S NOTE

Thank you, Santa Barbara.

We'd never mistake Castillo, Carrillo, and Cabrillo streets in real life, but we have taken a few liberties in this book. We can only apologize – and promise that all 'mistakes' are intentional. Also, while you might think you spot a few local businesses in the following pages, any resemblance to actual commercial enterprises we adore is completely coincidental. They're definitely not real. You're imagining things.

Jo Nichols is the pseudonym for husband-and-wife team Joel Ross and Lee Nichols. They published over thirty books in five genres and wrote an animated series for Netflix before they sat down to write *The Marigold Cottages Murder Collective*, their first mystery.